ALL
ROADS
END
HERE

ALSO BY DAVID MOODY

ALL ROADS END HERE

DAVID MOODY

ST. MARTIN'S GRIFFIN NEW YORK

ALL ROADS END HERE. Copyright © 2019 by David Moody. All rights reserved. Printed in the United States of America. For information, address St. Martin's Press, 175 Fifth Avenue, New York, N.Y. 10010.

www.stmartins.com

The Library of Congress Cataloging-in-Publication Data is available upon request.

ISBN 978-1-250-20627-5 (trade paperback)
ISBN 978-1-250-10844-9 (ebook)

Our books may be purchased in bulk for promotional, educational, or business use. Please contact your local bookseller or the Macmillan Corporate and Premium Sales Department at 1-800-221-7945, extension 5442, or by email at MacmillanSpecialMarkets@macmillan.com.

First Edition: February 2019

10 9 8 7 6 5 4 3 2 1

A few years ago I fell out of love with writing. The ideas stopped coming and the words stopped flowing. I rejoined the real world and ended up working with the best bunch of people, doing a frighteningly similar job to Danny McCoyne in *Hater*. This book is dedicated to my Charging and Enforcement colleagues, past and present—you've kept me sane, kept me grounded, and given me an endless stream of stuff to write about!

ALL
ROADS
END
HERE

1

They call it the battle-bus. It was a standard double-decker once—nothing special, one of hundreds that drove up and down the city's commuter routes, packed with people—until the Civil Defense Force fighters repurposed it into a weapon of war. Long gone are the days when this thing carried students, shoppers, and workers. It might only have been a couple of months ago, but the battle-bus is as much a deterrent now as the all-terrain trucks, armored jeeps, and tactical support vehicles it rides alongside.

On one side of the bus there's a painted-over advert for a film no one saw. On the other, an equally obscured ad for shampoo. *Remember when all that stuff mattered? Remember when we watched films? Remember when we washed our hair and gave a damn about how we looked?* Today all that's important is staying alive.

Metal grilles have been welded over the windows of the bus, slits cut out for the barrels of rifles or the brutal blades of knives or the sharpened points of spears or whatever else the fighters can find to keep those foul Hater bastards at bay. It's their fault, all of this. Those evil fuckers deserve everything that's coming to them.

The bottom deck of the bus is packed full of people. Militia fighters pressed up tight against each other, looking combat-ready, feeling anything but. Because unlike the enemy they're about to face, this is alien to them. You have to match their aggression and speed, that's the key. They'll kill you quick if you spend too long thinking about it.

The guy at the front of the line with a Beretta used to be a teacher, but his classroom's now empty. The woman immediately behind was a stay-at-home mum, but there's nothing left for her to stay at home for, and anyway, her home's just a shell, an empty box leaking memories. Now she's out here day after day, seeking revenge for the slaughter of her family. She'll tell you she's just doing her bit to help keep the wheels turning, but that's crap. Coming out here is vengeance and therapy rolled into one. She realized that when she felt the cathartic rush the first time she skewered one of those vile Hater creatures on the meter-long length of sharpened metal railing she carries with her at all times.

The top deck of the bus is empty, for now. The plan today is simple—same as yesterday and no doubt the same as tomorrow. Find anyone human who's left alive out here and get them safely within the city's makeshift walls.

There are more than thirty people in this ragtag convoy of military and civilian vehicles, heading toward one of the largest groups they've found in a long time. A scout spotted a pocket of survivors sheltering in a clinic on one of the main routes into town. No one knows who these people are, where they came from, or how long they've been here, but they're still alive and they're like us and, right now, that's all that matters.

Damn Haters are everywhere, though. They come from all angles at once and never give up. The way they focus on the clinic is proof positive there are people worth saving in there.

The Haters' approach is scattershot—many individual attacks

combining to become a continuous yet largely uncoordinated blitzkrieg. By contrast there are preplanned strategies and agreed tactics behind the response of the quasi-military Unchanged forces. They approach the battle zone bunched up tight like a rolling road block and then, as they near the clinic, CDF fighters lay down suppressing fire, picking off the Haters now swarming toward them from either side.

Despite their lack of cohesion, however, the Haters are no less effective. Some of them are armed but, for the most part, *they* are the weapons. Their advantage is both in their numbers and their sheer aggression. Right now, this battle is their only focus. Nothing else matters. They exist for the kill.

The drivers in the CDF convoy keep their speed up, because a vehicle traveling at speed is a weapon of its own volition and a vehicle moving at anything less than full-pelt out here becomes a target. The guy behind the wheel of the bus is still struggling to adapt to what his life has become. He's been driving buses around the city center and surrounding suburbs for almost twenty years. All he used to worry about was kids doing drugs on the top deck and the stream of drink-fueled verbal abuse he'd be subjected to most Friday and Saturday nights. Today, his bus is a weapon.

Almost there.

Right on cue, two bikers break ranks and accelerate toward the clinic, weaving through the carnage and swerving to avoid random Hater attacks. These are the brave ones, the bus driver thinks as he watches them race away. The men and women on bikes are the ones who risk everything to clear the way for those who follow behind. It's a vital job they do, because after two and a half months of fighting, there are few roads left passable out here. Upturned and burned-out vehicles, rubble from buildings, and other less identifiable rubbish covers the ground. Grass verges and weeds have been left to grow wild and there always seems to be at least one corpse in view. If not a whole body then a limb or two or, at the very least, telltale crimson stain reminders that the summer rains haven't yet washed away.

A man appears up on the edge of the flat roof of the clinic, gesticulating wildly, pointing out a route through the debris the survivors left to make things more difficult for their attackers (though even the most optimistic refugee knows it'll take more than a few car wrecks to stop those blood-crazed bastards getting through). This haphazard obstacle course has at least slowed down the Hater assault, giving the refugees a chance to either fight back or run like hell.

There's a battered red Vauxhall Astra parked across the clinic door. Another survivor climbs out through a ground-floor window and jumps into the driver's seat, releasing the handbrake and letting the car roll back enough so it clears the door. He's given an unexpected shunt by a vicious Hater who hurls herself at the front of the Astra with scant regard for her own safety. The guy behind the wheel scrambles over into the backseat as the filthy, half-naked woman repeatedly smashes first her fists and then her head against the cracked windshield. He's seen too many Haters like this before. They are the very worst of the worst. The only thing that matters to them is the kill. She punches the glass again and breaks through, slashing her skin. She doesn't even notice, totally focused on the terrified man she has cornered. She rips the broken windscreen away with shredded fingers, only stopping when an ex–bank clerk shoots her in the back at point-blank range from the relative safety of the battle-bus.

Fifteen minutes ago this place was silent as the grave, but there are Haters everywhere now. They're still swarming out of the shadows like insects, converging on the convoy with an unquestionable, unspoken collective aim: to kill everyone not like them, to wipe out every last one of the Unchanged.

A number of particularly agile attackers focus on the bus instead of the clinic, hanging off the metal grilles and trying to climb up onto the roof. Most are dislodged by the rudimentary yet effective weapons brandished by the resistance fighters; speared, stabbed, and slashed. One makes it as high as the top deck before being shot in the chest through a window by a fighter who's just raced up the stairs.

More Haters are streaming through the gap that's opened up in front of the clinic now that the Astra has shifted. The guy still stranded in the car crouches out of sight in the footwell, waves of Hate flowing along either side like he's caught in a flash flood. The bikers try to draw them away, buzzing around like flies. It works to a point, but luck has just run out for one of them. He's brought down by a pack of feral Hater kids who take him out in a pincer movement, then fight with each other to be the one who strikes the killer blow. One of the kids is shot, the force of the blast blowing the scrawny child off her feet, but the others don't even notice, don't even look up.

Another vehicle joins the fray. It was tucked out of sight behind the battle-bus until it was needed. It's a Ford Ranger—an ugly, angular pickup with bull bars at the front. The driver uses it as a battering ram, punching a hole through the attacking hordes, mowing scores of them down with a remorseless, almost Hater-like brutality.

Inside the clinic, the twenty or so people who've been sheltering here have realized this is a full-on rescue attempt, not just an attack. It was impossible to be sure when everything kicked off, but now there's a desperate scramble to gather up supplies and belongings and whatever else they can before the battle-bus reaches them. There's no time to plot or plan or explain—just wait for the nod then run. The nervousness is toxic. Standing on this side of the door it's impossible to know exactly what's happening out there. The air is filled with screams of pain, shouted orders, straining engines, constant collisions, and gunfire. It's a cacophony of noise which washes and swirls, confusing and directionless, filled with anger and hate coming from both opposing sides.

The lookout returns from the clinic roof and pushes through the mass of people waiting to leave. He barks a one-word order to the person at the front. "Go!"

The woman nearest the door is in her mid-thirties. She's brandishing a gun she's not sure how to use, but when she shoves the door open and the first Hater appears, she shoots. The recoil nearly wrenches her shoulder from its socket. The people behind push her forward and though she manages to take out another Hater with something of a lucky shot, two more drag her down and kill her before she's even realized she's been caught.

The killing of the woman leaves a gap that's wide enough for most of the refugees to pour through. It's less than a twenty-meter dash from the front of the building to the waiting battle-bus, and though twenty meters is nothing, today it feels like a marathon. The exodus from the clinic is a chaotic mass sprint for the line. People who've worked with each other for weeks to stay alive now compete to survive, and several of the slowest are isolated and picked off with ease by the Haters. One guy—late teens, maybe early twenties, all full of swagger and talk until he got out here—is traumatized. He stops running and just stands there in the midst of the madness, numb. He's swallowed up in the blink of an eye. Dead in seconds.

It's utter chaos out here now, people everywhere. The only distinction between the two opposing sides is the level of aggression on display, the ferocity of the fighting. To the casual observer it looks like a mass brawl that's growing exponentially. The Haters are incensed by the close proximity of their Unchanged prey, intoxicated by the insatiable bloodlust which consumes them, more and more of them running straight at the bus and straight to their deaths. Bodies pile up—it looks like there are more people dead than left fighting now—and then everything changes.

Job done, the driver of the battle-bus blasts the horn, and the purpose of his signal is clear: *We've got as many as we're going to get. Time to get out of here.*

A volley of grenades is launched in the general direction of the now abandoned clinic. Are the munitions thrown by a Hater trying to flush out any remaining Unchanged, or by an Unchanged fighter wanting to wipe out the scores of kill-hungry Haters now crowding into the building? Whoever is responsible, the result is the same. The right wing of the clinic explodes outward, belching blossoming flame then acrid black smoke. The detonation causes a momentary distraction which allows the Unchanged convoy space to change direction. Bikes and jeeps weave in and around the butchery, doing what they can to protect the battle-bus as it turns a slow and clumsy arc in the debris-strewn road. Inside, its passengers cling on for dear life. Those refugees who've made it to the top deck crouch and hide below the seats. Of the twenty or so people who left the clinic just now, only seven have survived.

The convoy accelerates back down the road, only to be met by another wall of Hate coming the other way. What's left of this world is rarely quiet and the concentrated din coming from this particular trouble spot has attracted Haters from miles around. They're coming here in droves now. The driver of the Ford Ranger accelerates into the crowds again, swerving and skidding to bring down as many of the enemy as possible, but his dogged resistance comes to an abrupt end as he's rammed from the side by a flat-bed truck carrying more Haters. The entangled vehicles collide with a bus shelter. One Hater finishes off the driver of the Ford, the others race toward the battle-bus.

There's a lone figure lying on top of the shelter who steadies himself as it shakes and groans with the violent impact. He's sep-arated from the street-level madness by the narrowest of mar-gins, little more than a couple of precarious meters of dead space. This is the last place he'd be if he had any choice, but it's been his best option today. He found the survivors in the clinic sev-eral days back and he's been in the vicinity ever since, biding his time and waiting for someone to come mount a rescue operation. He knows that everything comes down to what happens in the next few minutes. He's not as scared as he thinks he maybe should be. He's been in tighter spots than this before and he'll no doubt be in tighter spots again. Assuming he survives, that is.

Matthew Dunne exists on the periphery of everything, living on the fringes and moving through the shadows. It's how he's managed to stay alive in the days and weeks he's been on the run. How much of it is down to luck he's not sure, but one thing's for certain—no matter how long he's managed to last so far, he only gets to fuck up once. Is today the day his luck finally runs out?

Matt's been up here for almost a day and a half, watching the drone activity overhead, knowing it could all kick off at any sec-ond. This was a decent-sized group, large enough to warrant a full-scale rescue attempt. The waiting's over and he knows that any second now he's going to have to make his move. He just hopes his body won't let him down. He's been flexing his legs as best he can all day, but lying still like this, he's worried he'll have cramped up. He won't know for sure until he has to run.

All he carries with him is a rucksack half-full of scraps and a rock climber's ice axe he found when he spent time hiding in a sports store week before last. So far he's only used it as a tool, not a weapon, but it's good to have the option. This is everything he owns. Everything he hasn't yet reclaimed, that is. He's hoping the rest of his life is where he left it in the middle of the city just a few miles from here. That's assuming there's anything left of his hometown, of course, but the signs are good. The increased air activity indicates there's something still worth fighting for around here. He just won't know what it is until he gets there.

Fingertips outstretched, Matt pulls himself nearer to the edge of the shelter roof to see what's happening. Jesus Christ—the carnage is worse than he'd imagined. Endless chaos in every direction, pitched battles still raging, bodies everywhere. He always feels a pang of guilt: *I could have done something . . . I could have helped . . .* but he also knows that if he had, he'd likely be dead, too. Keeping his distance like this is the only reason he's lasted so long out here.

Just ahead, the driver of the bus slams on the brakes as a Hater on a motorbike cuts across in front of him. The size difference between the two machines is vast, but it's still instinctive for the bus driver to hold back and not use his vehicle as a battering ram. An Unchanged soldier behind the wheel of a jeep, however, has no such qualms. He hits the Hater in the saddle side-on with full force, sending both the killer and the bike skidding across the street and leaving an unexpected swath of clear space.

This is it. Time to move.

Matt slides off the bus shelter roof, drops down, and starts to run. There's plenty of stiffness in his legs and his speed is a fraction of what it needs to be. He accelerates through the pain, half-sprinting, half-limping toward the convoy, dividing his attention between where he's trying to get to and everything in between. This is the part he couldn't plan for: once he's reached the convoy, how does he get their attention and get onto one of the vehicles without being shot at, impaled, crushed by Haters, or all three?

There is another option. There's a footbridge up ahead, spanning the width of the wide road. He was hoping it wouldn't come to this, but he always knew it probably would. Same end result but with a hundred times the risk.

His pace increases with each step as the stiffness in his bones subsides. Thankfully, it looks like his usual trick is paying dividends—the madness continuing to unfold all around the stop-start convoy is enough of a distraction to enable him to race along the fringes of the battle unnoticed. The less fuss and noise he makes, the better his chances.

The convoy's still moving, but it's like driving through treacle. They've probably got enough muscle and firepower to get through, Matt thinks. Just about. He overtakes then runs ahead. Almost at the footbridge.

Matt swerves around the back of a Hater woman as she attacks a lone Unchanged soldier who's crashed his jeep and is running for his life. The soldier scrambles for his rifle but the woman's speed and ferocity is too much. He makes eye contact with Matt for the briefest of moments, eyes wide and desperate for help, but Matt just keeps running because the longer he's out in the open, the greater the chance this'll be the day it all goes wrong and he ends up like the poor fucker he's just ignored.

There are still more Haters coming, wave after wave of them pouring into the street like a pitch invasion at the end of a football final, desperate to spill Unchanged blood.

Matt makes himself stick to his plan (for what it's worth) and ignore the panic that's rising in his throat like bile. There's a nagging voice in his head screaming *you're fucked . . . you should have stayed where you were, you idiot*. But Matt's had enough of waiting. He's been taking baby steps home for weeks and now that he's almost made it back, the temptation to sprint for the line is impossible to ignore. He was always going to have to make a move like this sooner or later. He's starting to think later might have been a better option.

He's a couple of meters short of the footbridge, and about fifty meters ahead of the slowly advancing battle-bus. In front of him is a mob of between twenty and thirty Haters, all of whom have him in their sights. Matt runs straight at them.

Going up.

He takes them by surprise when he darts left and pounds up the spiral slope onto the footbridge; a long, wheelchair-friendly, corkscrew climb upward. Looking down through the railings, he sees waves of them coming after him. The pursuing pack splits, racing toward the opposing ends of the bridge, cutting off his escape. They've got him trapped and they know it. All exits reduced to zero.

Or so they think.

Matt's one step ahead of the game. Always has been. Can't afford not to be. These days a split-second advantage is all that separates the living from the dead.

He's halfway along the length of the narrow bridge, exposed and in full view. And as the resistance convoy finally picks up some speed, the enemy's focus shifts to the lone idiot up high. Matt stops. He just stands there and waits as Haters come at him from both directions. The fastest are terrifyingly close. He can almost feel their breath on him, can smell their doglike stench.

Timing is everything.

Just one second longer . . .

As the nearest Hater lunges for him, Matt climbs up onto the safety railing and jumps off the bridge. He lands hard on top of the battle-bus as it passes underneath and he hammers the serrated pick of the ice axe down through the metal skin of its roof, giving him a solid anchor. He wraps the nylon strap around his wrist again and again and holds on for all he's worth, the strap so tight that if he was to be thrown from the bus, he'd likely leave a severed hand behind. He flattens himself down and spreads his weight, maximizing his surface area to reduce the risk of being thrown off, at the same time hoping the street-level fighting will continue to be more of a distraction than him being up here. He has visions of bayonets and gunshots coming up from the top deck to try and force him off.

What have I become?

Sometimes Matt's unrecognizable to himself. The journey home has changed him. He looks back at the seething crowds he's left behind on the bridge, baying for his blood, and thinks *I'm not like you.* The Haters are dangerous as hell, but they're increasingly predictable. He's trained himself to think like them and anticipate their next move, then do the exact opposite. And then he thinks about the people in the battle-bus. *I'm not like you, either.*

Facedown. Breathing hard. Relieved but nervous. (Relatively) safe for now. It's only now that Matt allows himself to believe he might finally have done it. Next stop, home. Nine weeks, three days, eight hours since he was last there. Back to Jen. Christ, he's missed her. The thought of seeing her again takes the faintest edge off the painful emptiness he's felt for weeks.

2

Matt used to know this area well, though it's taken him a while to work out precisely where he is. Watching the world from this height is disorientating. There's a tenuous familiarity, but everything's changed; torn apart and turned upside down and left looking nothing like it used to. It makes him wonder what kind of condition home will be in when he finally gets there. The journey back has taken so damn long, slow shuffles and baby steps all the way. Endless diversions. Countless nervous hours spent sitting still, waiting for danger to pass. It's been the slowest crawl. Less than two hundred miles has taken almost eighty days. But he was always going to come back, even if it took ten times as long. How could he not?

Matt thinks back to the last time he traveled by bus, the last time he was in a vehicle of any description, come to think of it. He'd had company then. Sometimes he regrets leaving Paul O'Keefe to die, but he knows Paul wouldn't have given him a second thought if their positions had been reversed. Matt often thinks about how Paul murdered their friend Natalie so he could secure his own seat on the boat home. At the time Matt had been appalled but now, in retrospect, he wonders if some of the things he's done to survive have been any worse. *I did what I had to do,* is what he tells himself. It's funny, he has memories of Paul saying something similar.

Matt learned fast that even though the world is an infinitely more violent place now, it still takes brains more than muscle to stay alive. He's always been a realist who erred on the side of caution (it's the ex-accountant in him) and though people used to see that as a negative trait, his ability to sidestep trouble is actually what's kept him alive. In a war as one-sided as this, you risk everything if you try going toe-to-toe with your enemy. Only trouble is, when you duck a punch in the face out here, someone else usually takes the hit instead. He's lost track of how many people he's left behind with bloodied noses (or considerably worse).

It's hot up here on the roof of the bus. The early-summer sun burns down, heating up the metal surface he's lying on, frying him like an egg, but the discomfort's a small price to pay for the separation from danger. The bus lurches as the road turns right and the militia fighters downstairs release a volley of gunfire, driving back a frenzied Hater attack before it can properly get started. One of the military vehicles behind follows up with a heavier artillery strike, pounding the enemy into submission with a howitzer. The weaponry at their disposal is reassuring.

Matt wonders if there's a single square meter of the country left where people aren't killing each other? From what he's gathered on his slow-motion travels these last nine weeks, the largest cities which haven't yet fallen to the Haters have become refugee camps. Tactically and logistically it makes perfect sense to isolate *us* from *them*, but the prospect of mixing with any other people again makes him feel uneasy. He's done what he can to avoid everyone else since nearly getting his fingers burned early on. He spent a couple of days in the company of a girl called Sarah. She'd been following a similar strategy to him: keep quiet, keep out of the way, let everyone else panic and draw away the Haters. He should have seen it coming, though. When push came to shove, she didn't hesitate to throw him under the bus. The pair of them had been backed into a corner and had split to stay alive, agreeing to rendezvous later a little further down the road. But Sarah never had any intention of meeting up again. Matt had been her stooge. From the moment they'd separated she'd been intent on sending the attacking Haters after him. She'd have done for him too if he hadn't been one step ahead of her game. Suspecting trouble, he'd already doubled back and sent the Hater hordes flocking in her direction instead.

He's not sure if Sarah survived. He hopes she did. She wasn't stupid like Paul, she was just . . . just too much like Matt. The two of them were never going to get along. They'd have been constantly risking each other's necks to save themselves.

The bus is powering along again now. Matt peers down over the side as they drive through the remains of a fairly typical residential street. Seeing the place reminds him of a stranded family he came across, early days. Just thinking about them makes his heart sink, even now. In more than two months of frequent low points, that day was the lowest of all. He grips the ice axe handle tight and buries his face. He does his best to forget but whenever he starts to remember the family's faces, it's always hard to stop.

He'd stumbled on them by chance while investigating signs of recent occupation: mum, dad, and three kids hiding in an attic bedroom. They'd knocked through to the loft space of an adjacent house and that had thrown him off the scent for a while but, once he'd found them, they'd panicked in unison, figuring he was a Hater. He'd tried to explain, tried to convince them they were all on the same side, but his pleas had fallen on collective deaf ears and by the time Mother had accepted that if he had been there to kill them he'd have done it already, it was too late. Their panic and noise had attracted the first few Hater scouts, and when the family had refused to shut the fuck up, Matt had no choice but to abandon them or go down with them. He climbed out of a Velux window and took shelter on the roof, clinging on to a crumbling chimney stack where, precarious and exposed, he'd heard every last scream of each of the five deaths. Their hunger temporarily sated and assuming the place had been cleared of Unchanged, the Hater pack soon slunk off in search of more kills, oblivious to the fact he remained so close. Matt had stayed up on the roof for more than a day until he was certain they'd gone.

He'd taken what was left of the family's food, looting from around their bodies. Maybe he could have helped them, but it had been easier to sacrifice five lives and use their deaths as cover. It was him or them. By making themselves the target, they'd allowed him to survive.

There's a bump in the road that nearly sends him flying off the bus and he grabs the handle of the ice axe again with both hands. The wrenching pain in his wrists helps him focus on the here and now and forget about the *then and there*. But it's not all cut-and-dried, good and bad, right or wrong. Between black and white he's found there are a thousand shades of gray.

Ten days ago Matt took the mother of all wrong turns and ended up walking into the middle of a Hater encampment. Unable to get away for fear of being seen, he'd spent hours lying curled up in the mud just meters away from a huge mob of them, listening to their noise. War's a big deal for both sides, that much is a given, but Matt had been surprised how the psychological impact of the fighting appeared to be taking its toll on many of the Haters, too. Listening to them talk, he found himself beginning to identify with their plight, sympathizing almost. He heard them talking about how their lives had been chewed up and spat out by the conflict, same as his. It was the first time he'd heard the word *Unchanged* used to describe people like him, and the way they'd used the term sounded derogatory, as if people like Matt had failed to evolve. He, on the other hand, took it as a compliment that he'd not been corrupted by the scourge of the Hate.

The stench there had been vile and the close proximity of the Haters had kept him permanently on edge, but Matt's exhaustion had eventually got the better of him. He'd slept fitfully in the deep mud, camouflaged by the mire. Uncomfortable at first, as the hours had worn on it had clung to his body like a blanket, insulating him from the cold, the malleable ground molding to his shape like a memory foam mattress, holding him like a hand.

The Haters left hurriedly during the night, called away to battle. When, after several more hours, they'd failed to return, Matt risked getting up and moving on. He'd even had the nerve to stop and steal a little food from the dying campfire; a subtle *fuck you* to the enemy. Buoyed up by his insignificant little victory, he'd walked a couple of miles farther before making a discovery which, for the second time in less than twenty-four hours, made him question which side were the true architects of hate. He found a place so heinous that it had made him want to stop and give up there and then. He'd not just felt his heart sink, but also his soul.

Bodies, Matt had long since realized, could be useful. They're a source of clothing and supplies, as well as camouflage. He'd found playing dead to avoid attack was immeasurably easier when those people around him actually *were* dead.

On the run again after leaving the camp, Matt thought he'd

lucked out when he came across a stack of twenty or so cadavers in a clearing in a wood. But relief had turned to disgust and then to terror when he discovered he hadn't found twenty bodies, he'd found hundreds. There may even have been thousands. And the mounds of agitated earth and long, freshly dug-over scars in the ground nearby intimated there may have been many, many more besides, hastily dumped in anonymous mass graves. It was a death camp. Knowing the Haters rarely bothered to dispose of their kills, after exploring the site in the rapidly deteriorating daylight Matt reached the inevitable conclusion that this wholesale, mass-produced massacre had been Unchanged in origin. Finding what was left of the Haters from the campfire had been proof positive.

Still, he remembered thinking at the time, *needs must*.

The memories make the time melt. Another jolt in the road and he's back on the roof of the bus again, almost home.

3

Here we go again. Another abrupt change of direction and speed. The sounds of another skirmish growing louder by the second. Yet more Haters are attacking the convoy.

Matt lifts his head and risks looking around, focusing on distant features and landmarks as a distraction from the swell of violence immediately below. A distinctive clump of years-old trees on top of a dome-shaped hill just outside the city boundary— The Beeches, he thinks they're called—confirms he's on the right track at last. Turning to the east he catches a glimpse of an instantly recognizable industrial skyline, and the sudden familiarity makes him catch his breath. There's a building or two missing like knocked-out front teeth, as if the city itself has come off second-best in a schoolyard scrap, but there's no mistaking home. There's a haze of oily smoke hanging in the air that he can smell from all the way out here and the place looks disappointingly decrepit. *Jen's in there somewhere,* he thinks, and his pulse starts to race faster. Christ, he's missed her. He can't wait to see her and hold her and know that she's safe.

The road curves in the opposite direction now and Matt

adjusts his position, able at last to get a better view of home. There's much activity in the shadows of the city. It's been dry for the last week or so and great clouds of dust are being thrown up by vehicles which race around the outside of the encampment. Drones and helicopters are carpet bombing a region outside the city to the east, keeping more Haters at bay. That's a good sign, he thinks. If the Haters are being pushed back, then by default that must mean the population of the city is relatively safe. Lifting himself up onto his elbows, Matt orients himself. He sees the motorway and other arterial routes, but he has to hunt for them because they're not as immediately visible as they used to be. They're quiet. Cauterized. It makes sense because if you control the access routes, you control the flow of people. This is the only place he knows that still matters. It matters to the refugees who want to stay alive, and equally to the Haters who want them dead. In the immediate area at least, this place is pivotal. All roads end here.

But by far the best way to control the movement of people, Matt realizes, is to build a bloody big wall with a bloody strong gate. From his elevated vantage point he sees what he assumes is the main entrance into the city. There's a stream of people trying to get in. Protected by heavy weaponry and by persistent drones which hang motionless in the shimmering summer heat-haze, people are being funneled toward the mother of all checkpoints.

The noise level increases dramatically, and Matt looks up and sees that one of the helicopters has drifted out from the city to meet their convoy. He knows he has to get off the roof and get among the masses. Everyone looks the same from a distance, he thinks, Hater and Unchanged alike. They'll assume he's a stowaway Hater and try to take him out. He consoles himself temporarily with the thought that they wouldn't risk dropping a bomb on a bus full of survivors just to get rid of one potential Hater, would they? Then again, maybe they would. Imagine the damage a single Hater could do inside the camp. It doesn't bear thinking about.

The helicopter banks away to the right. Matt cranes his neck and watches it climb away, then buries his face again when the aircraft unleashes a screaming missile which roars toward him, filling the air with noise and heat and choking fumes. It hits the ground a couple of hundred meters beyond the bus and when the explosion dies down he sees that the target was yet another surge of Haters. Most of them have been killed outright, but a few stragglers remain and are taken out by more potshots from the battle-bus and the gunners on the back of other vehicles. One of the surviving killers—a huge, lumbering, blood-soaked bulk of a man—scrambles over a pile of rubble and runs toward the convoy, deceptively agile in spite of his size and his injuries. Killing means more to him than living. Fucker looks like he's been driven out of his mind by the Hate. He's hit by bullet after bullet until he finally drops.

And here comes another one.

A shot is fired from the front of the bus, hitting this next Hater in the shoulder. He's slowed but not stopped. The impact barely even registers, barely even causes him to misstep. He's hit in the belly by another bullet, but still he keeps coming. Breaking ranks, a biker soldier loops around the back of the bus and comes at the Hater like a medieval gladiator, carrying a length of metal pole like he's jousting. Even though the Hater's been blown up and shot twice, he's still got enough about him to sidestep the end of the pole and grab hold of it. He hoists the biker clean off his machine and the bike freewheels through the glass door of a long-dead branch of McDonald's.

The leather-clad soldier is up in seconds, but the Hater's

already coming for him. The soldier snatches a pistol from a holster and fires again and again and again, and it's only when the Hater's taken five more bullets (the last one right between the eyes) that he finally goes down. He hits the deck but his momentum keeps him moving forward, skidding through the dust and coming to an undignified halt just short of the soldier's booted feet.

Left behind by the convoy, the soldier sprints toward the ruined fast food joint to retrieve his bike, but he's not alone in his race for the building. Several Haters are gaining on him. His lungs are burning and his pistol's now empty, but all that's academic because before any of them can get anywhere near, another missile is launched from the circling helicopter, flattening what was left of the McDonald's and killing everyone in a ten-meter radius.

This is No Man's Land.

It's only when the effects of this most recent blast die down that Matt begins to truly appreciate the scale of the devastation here. A wide swath of land has been cleared around the city, all buildings destroyed. It explains why he was able to see so much from so far out. The purpose of No Man's Land is obvious: no buildings means there's nowhere to hide.

Matt pulls his ice axe free and starts sliding farther down the roof of the bus toward the back, figuring he'll stand a better chance if he can climb off here and join the crowds around the checkpoint. For the moment there are no vehicles behind. He leans over the edge and manages to wedge the tip of the axe in the corner of one of the metal window grilles, and he uses it to lower himself down. Taking advantage of the lack of weapon holes on the corner of the bus, and also its pedestrian speed, he starts to descend. *A few months ago I hesitated climbing down a rock face on Skek with a safety harness,* he thinks, *now look at me. I'm a new man.*

From his new vantage point he can better see the makeshift wall encircling the city. The gaps between most buildings have been filled in with cars and trucks, creating a vast blockade. Has this kind of improvised construction been repeated around the entire city? If it has, then he's impressed. A perimeter barrier like this, he decides, serves two purposes: it makes the people inside feel safe (even if they're not), and it also lets the Haters know this place will be no pushover. He knows his life might depend on these haphazard fortifications, but he can't help thinking the oversized gates they're now approaching remind him of King Kong's island in the movies. No, the entrance to Jurassic Park, that's it.

It's no laughing matter. He needs to get out of sight.

The lack of speed allows him to shimmy down the back of the bus unnoticed. Now he's ready to drop down and run but he waits because he knows it's all about fitting in here, not standing out. He hangs his head out to look down the side of the lumbering vehicle and sees they're almost at the gate, joining the end of a queue of other vehicles waiting to gain access. Heavily armed guards, watched by equally heavily armed colleagues, search each approaching vehicle for Haters. There's also a line of people here waiting to get in. Hauling bags and boxes of possessions with them, they're being funneled along a narrow path, fenced in by tall wire-mesh barriers on either side, topped with razor wire. It looks reasonably impenetrable and the refugees are treated with suspicion when they reach the border proper. There's plenty of manhandling from the military, followed by the expected neck-jab Hater-testing ritual he himself has been subjected to previously. The precautions are only to be expected. Letting just one

Hater into the camp could mean the death of thousands of people.

A helicopter thunders overhead, providing an unexpected distraction with its noise and blocking the sun momentarily, and Matt makes his move. He disentangles his ice axe then drops down and runs over to the wire mesh, trying to find a way in. The people already in the line recoil, not knowing who or what he is. "How d'you get in?" he asks, looking hopefully into faces which immediately look away. "Where's the entrance?"

He works his way along the fence away from the gates, knowing that the end's got to be here somewhere, a rippling wave of panic traveling with him as he moves. He finds the way in soon enough. And he finds the guards protecting it, too.

"Don't move a fucking muscle," a masked militiaman screams at him.

"It's okay," Matt says, "I'm not a Hater," and he raises his hands in submission as he walks toward the guard. He realizes there are other soldiers behind him.

"I said don't fucking move," the militiaman warns him again.

"I just—"

A thump from the butt of a rifle to the back of his skull and Matt's out cold.

4

When Matt comes around the first thing he feels is relief because he's still alive. The next thing he feels is absolute panic because he's strung up and naked, freezing cold. There are metal cuffs around his wrists attached to heavy chains which are slung through a steel loop affixed to the low ceiling. He loses his footing on the floor and slips, almost wrenching his arms from their sockets. His body fills with pain. He manages to regain his balance, but only for a second before a wave of nausea sends him reeling again. Bright lights blind him, increasing his anxiety.

"Not a Hater," he manages to say, voice little more than a pathetic last gasp.

"Remind me why we didn't just put this prick out of his misery," a gruff voice asks from the shadows behind the arc lights.

There's a woman standing next to Matt, a doctor in a grubby white coat, shielding her eyes. She looks pissed off. "Do we have to go through this every bloody time? If he was one of them he'd be trying to kill me."

"So why didn't he just queue up nicely like everyone else? You know the rules. We have to be certain."

The doctor moves out of the way. "Yeah, I know the rules. *Your* rules."

"Not a Hater," Matt says again.

If there's a response from his captors this time, he doesn't hear it. He's hit from out of nowhere by a fire-hose blast of ice-cold water, hard like nails and so strong it knocks him clean off his feet.

Arms wrenched. Searing agony. Nerves screaming. Muscles burning.

Matt's feet slip and slide on the water-soaked concrete until he manages to grip with his toes and steady himself again. Finally there's quiet; absolute silence save for trickling water.

The doctor angrily turns one of the lights around and illuminates a soldier with a brutal crew cut who has a look of utter contempt for everyone and everything on his face. "The test came back clear, you know it did," she says. "He looks okay, Sergeant."

"We can't take any chances. You heard what happened in Portsmouth last week."

"The test is almost completely accurate. The way he's reacting indicates that he's docile."

"Almost isn't good enough," the sergeant grunts.

"You're just doing this for kicks."

"Whatever." He gestures at the member of his squad who's operating the hose. "Do it. Douse the fucker."

Matt tenses himself up but it doesn't make any difference. The water hits him for a second time. He tries to protect his face by turning to one side, but in doing so he exposes his bollocks and it's like being kicked by a horse. The burning pain in his groin's so bad that it makes the icy water feel almost comfortable by comparison.

This time when the high-force deluge stops, the sergeant allows the doctor to get a little closer again. Matt just about manages to stay upright, desperate to make eye contact with her, desperate for help. She looks straight through him. She leans in, faces almost touching, then turns back to face the sergeant. "For the last time, there's no aggression reaction with this one. He's no Hater."

I tried to tell you that . . . Matt thinks but can't bring himself to say.

Now the officer gets up and walks over. Both he and the doctor look their prisoner up and down. His cross-country ordeal has left Matt in fairly reasonable shape, all things considered. He is bony and lithe, nothing left but muscle and sinew. His skin is tanned and weathered. He hasn't shaved for weeks and, until now, he hasn't so much as wiped himself down for the best part of two months. It's no surprise they think he might be one of those foul, animallike bastards marauding on the other side of the city wall.

Matt knows they're not looking at him, they're watching his reactions. The soldier leans in closer still, sneering face full of mock aggression, and Matt almost loses his balance again. "Pathetic," the soldier snarls.

"What's your story?" the doctor asks Matt directly. He looks from face to face, not sure if speaking will earn him another blast from the hose. "You came in *on* the bus, not in it. Why?"

"I hitched a ride," Matt says, confidence returning.

"But the whole point of the bus was to bring people in."

"Too dangerous . . . I stay away from numbers . . ."

"So why break into the camp?" the sergeant demands. He jabs a finger at Matt. "That's textbook Hater behavior right there."

"What do you mean you stay away from numbers?" the doctor asks. "Exactly how long have you been out there?"

"Since the start."

"On your own?"

"Yep."

The soldier's not buying it. "I'm supposed to believe you survived all this time on your own out there? Come on."

"It's true."

He grabs Matt by the neck and squeezes. Matt doesn't know how to react. By now he thought he'd be on his way back to Jen, not strung up and physically and verbally abused by the military. Christ, he'd have had better treatment at the hands of the Haters. At least it would have been over quickly with them. When Matt doesn't retaliate the soldier releases his grip and wipes his hand on the back of his grubby fatigues, then retreats. "Blast some more of that grime off him," he orders.

"Come on," the doctor protests as she quickly gets out of the way of the water. "You're as bad as they are. Hasn't he been through enough?"

"Do it," the officer says, unconcerned.

Matt's hosed down a third time. It's like being sandblasted. There's a momentary pause. He stands up straight but the hose operator has just been toying with him and knocks him down again with yet another torrent.

"That's enough," the doctor yells, her voice just about audible over the noise. The sergeant gives the order to stop.

Matt's barely conscious. His legs threaten to buckle, but the pain in his shoulders, arms, and wrists keep him upright. Another gesture from the sergeant and the chains are slackened. Matt drops to his knees in a wet heap, breathing hard. The doctor crouches down in front of him.

"What's your name?"

Matt looks up, checking for the whereabouts of the soldier with the hose before he answers. "Matthew Dunne."

"So where've you really been all this time, Matthew?"

"Been trying to get home."

"And where exactly is home?"

"Here."

The sergeant is standing right behind the doctor, looking down. "I'm still not sure about this fucker," he says. The doctor massages her temples, frustrated.

"He passed the test and he's not reacting adversely to us. He may well be lying about where he's been, but who gives a damn?"

"I do. If we let just one of those bastards in here then—"

"—then we're all at risk. I know, Sergeant, you've told me a thousand times."

"And I'll keep telling you because—"

"—because one is all it takes," she interrupts. "I get it. I know the score. But look at this guy."

"I watched a Hater kid half his size take out five of my men by itself."

"I know. Again, you told me. Look, I'm vouching for this one. I'll get him processed myself and I'll do the locked room test. If he really has been out there all this time, I want to hear what he's got to say."

The soldier walks away, unimpressed. "Waste of fucking time."

The doctor fetches a towel and wraps it around Matt's shoulders. "Thanks," Matt mumbles, shivering so hard it looks like he's convulsing.

"Don't mention it. I'll find someone to get those chains off you."

🕊

Her name is Gillian Montgomery, and she works—*worked*—in mental health, dealing with schizophrenics and people with bipolar disorder and all manner of other problems which have been reduced to trivial nuisances now given the tsunami of psychopathy that's swept the country. "I've seen all kinds of shit in my time, but I never came across anything quite like the Hate before," she tells him. It's just the two of them now. Matt's back in his own (filthy and stinking) clothes, sitting across a desk from the doctor. The locked room test is as straightforward as it sounds: you sit in a small, locked room with someone you're not one hundred percent convinced about, and if you're both still alive in an hour, chances are neither of you are Haters.

"Anyone know what caused it? What the trigger was?" Matt asks. "I've been out of the loop for a while."

"There is no loop anymore," she says, concentrating on her laptop more than she is on him. "And no, no one knows and no one cares. What's the point? What difference will it make? We are where we are."

"Fair enough."

Matt sits back on his chair and massages his aching neck and shoulders. He's less on edge now, less worried that he's about to be strung up and hosed down again. They fed him and let him use the toilet before locking him in here with the doctor. Strange, he thinks, how necessities feel like luxuries these days.

They had him fill out a paper form with all his details that he could remember. The doctor's just finished entering them onto the computer. "Can you still get online?" he asks.

"After a fashion. They call this the Central System. Just a database of who's where and who's what really. To be honest it's pretty unreliable."

"What's it tell you?" he asks, immediately thinking about Jen.

"If someone's been tested, they'll have a record. So if they came in through one of the checkpoints since the wall went up, we'll probably know they're here. But if you want to know where Aunty Alice is and how many people she's killed, you're out of luck. It's all academic, anyway. You don't need the internet to tell you everything's fucked."

And it occurs to Matt that as the last couple of hours haven't exactly gone to plan, and because he's been focused on toeing the line and staying alive, that he hasn't yet asked the most basic of questions. "So exactly just how fucked is everything?"

Dr. Montgomery stops what she's doing and pushes the laptop away. "Hard to say. It's all so . . . fractured. Fragmented."

"What do you mean?"

"It's the nature of the beast, isn't it? Society has been split down the middle—or not quite down the middle, depending on who you talk to—and it feels like making that split as wide as possible is the key to staying alive."

"And that's what's happening here?"

"That's exactly what's happening. We're isolating what's left of the normal population from the Haters and putting as big a gap as possible between us and them. You saw all the flattened buildings on your way in?"

"Yeah."

"No Man's Land. Makes it harder for them to hide and harder for them to get to us. They're all but invisible until they attack, so separation is our best defense."

"That test you do . . ." he starts to ask, rubbing a sore patch of skin on the side of his neck. "Does it work?"

"It's not conclusive, but it gives a pretty good indication. We look for elevated adrenaline and endorphin levels, and couple those measures with behavioral traits and other observations."

"Behavioral traits?"

"If someone starts trying to gouge your eyes out while the test's being administered, chances are they're a Hater. You were pretty lucky the way you came in here just now. I've seen people less likely to be a Hater who've been killed just in case."

"So why am I still here?"

"You must have caught the sergeant in a good mood."

"That was a good mood?"

"You're still alive, so yes."

Matt looks around, trying to take it all in. "So what you're saying is, no one really has a clue what's going on?"

"I'm not saying that at all. They're trying to kill us, and we're trying not to be killed, that's what's going on. It's pretty relentless. They don't give up, those bastards. They just keep coming."

"They're not getting in, though. This place must be pretty well organized."

"There's some kind of structure and a basic plan, if that's what you mean. This is a hell of a thing that's happening here. There's never been a war like this before. They're calling it the final war. Everything's broken down to an individual level, and that makes it all so much more complicated."

"But there are still people in charge, right? Someone's still calling the shots?"

"Taking shots, yes. I'm not so sure about calling them. The Civil Defense Force are in control now, primarily because they have all the guns. They're more militia than military, but they get the job done. I've been hearing stories about active Hater-controlled military units, and that prospect scares the shit out of me."

Matt rocks back on his chair and lets that sink in for a second.

The doctor gets up and helps herself to a bottle of water from a table at the back of the room. This is as much a cell as anything: four walls, one door, no windows. The only illumination comes from a desk lamp and the laptop screen. There's a ceiling-mounted camera but it doesn't seem to be working. Matt reckons the authorities (what's left of them) have better things to do than watch what he's up to and, anyway, he's stuck here until they say otherwise. "So what happens next? What happens to me now?"

She leans against the back wall. Shrugs. "They let you go, I guess."

"And that's it?"

"What were you expecting? Some kind of civic ceremony in Millenium Square because you made it back in one piece?"

"Don't mock me."

"Sorry. Sarcasm's about the only emotion that's still functioning. I've been on shift a long time. I'm tired."

"How long?"

"Two weeks. I gave up going back to my billet. The floor of the office is just as comfortable as the floor of someone else's house and it's safer here, too. You're okay, though, aren't you? You're from around here. You can just go back home."

"It's been a long time," Matt says. He feels disproportionately nervous at the prospect of going home. Anything could have happened in the months he's been away.

The doctor sits down again and checks her watch. "They'll be here to let you out in a few minutes."

"Okay."

She studies his face. He looks away, uncomfortable under examination. "So did you really survive on your own out there?"

"Yep."

"Just by tiptoeing around and keeping your distance?"

"Pretty much."

"There's a lesson there for the rest of us, I think."

"I wouldn't recommend it."

"You must have really got into their heads."

"Who, the Haters?"

"Haters, other survivors . . . everyone I guess. You must have known where the trouble was to be able to avoid it."

"There's trouble everywhere out there."

"Any survival tips you'd like to share in case it all goes to hell in here? I could do with a few pointers."

Matt likes this woman's humor. She makes him smile. It's been so long it makes his face feel weird. "As far as the Haters go, just make sure there's someone else nearby who'll distract them for you, some other poor sod who'll make more noise or scream louder than you and keep them occupied."

"And how d'you make sure you're not someone else's distraction?"

"That part's easy. You watch what everyone else is doing and you make sure you do the opposite."

MIDLANDS REGIONAL PROTECTION ZONE
INFORMATION FOR RESIDENTS

Welcome to the Midlands Regional Protection Zone
— You're safe here —

Welcome to the Midlands Regional Protection Zone. This is a difficult time for all of us, and we want to reassure you we're doing everything in our power to maintain order and keep you and your loved ones safe. Please take a few minutes to familiarize yourself with the information contained in this leaflet. By following these simple guidelines we can ensure our camp remains secure while our troops work to restore order to the rest of the country.

Jenna Holbrook
ACTING CAMP COMMISSIONER

OBEY ORDERS

The Civil Defense Force (CDF) are here to help and protect you. You must do as they tell you. Civil disobedience will NOT be tolerated under any circumstances. If you act like the enemy, you will be treated like the enemy.

MISSING PERSONS

We understand you might be worried about family members, friends, and other loved ones who may be missing. We will do everything we can to help you find them, but information is limited. These are unprecedented times and there have been huge numbers of casualties and defections. We're doing our best to keep a record of everyone in the Midlands Regional Protection Zone, but we can't be held responsible for any inaccuracies. There are information points at the City Arena and in Millennium Square, but be prepared to wait to be seen. You are only permitted to request one Central System inquiry per week. Unauthorized access of the Central System is forbidden.

FOOD AND WATER

Ration packs are available from the City Arena, Horsfall Road, and Gannow Park. Take only what you need. Do not stockpile food. Remember—if you take more than your allotted supply today, there may be less available for you tomorrow. Drinking water is provided from the standpipes found at most major interchanges. Please note, it may be necessary to restrict the availability of the water supply to ensure demand can be met throughout the camp.

HEALTH AND SANITATION

Report to the Royal Midlands Hospital if you or a member of your group is unwell. At peak times it may take our

staff a while to see you. Be patient. Aggressive behavior will not be tolerated—again, if you act like the enemy, you will be treated like the enemy. Please see our additional leaflets SANITATION IN THE HOME, WHAT TO DO IF SOMEONE DIES, and AVOIDING THE SPREAD OF DISEASE, for information on waste removal and general hygiene matters.

MOVEMENT IN AND OUT OF THE CAMP

Is not permitted under any circumstances without an official permit and a military escort. If you leave the camp without the necessary authorization, you will not be readmitted.

ACCOMODATION

If you are not a local resident, report to the housing team within the administrative section based at the City Arena who will arrange accommodation for you. If you are a local resident, you will be required to take in as many additional people as we deem necessary. Refusal to accept houseguests will result in your property being compulsorily seized. You may also be removed from your property if you do not cooperate. We realize this may be a difficult option for you, and we apologize in advance.

Refuse Collections
Please leave all rubbish in designated areas and it will be collected and disposed of in due course.

Volunteering for Work
If you have medical experience you are hereby compulsorily required to attend the Royal Midlands Hospital.

If you have experience of working in security, including the armed forces, the police, the prison officer service, private security firms, or any role involving crowd

management, then you are hereby compulsorily required to report to the Department of Works based at the University School near the City Arena.

You can earn extra food credits by volunteering to help keep our camp running smoothly. We have vacancies in public sanitation and food distribution.

Vehicles
Only official vehicles which carry a valid permit may be used.

Civil Disobedience
WILL NOT BE TOLERATED UNDER ANY CIRCUMSTANCES

The CDF have absolute authority to deal with any offenses under the terms of the recently enacted Emergency Measures Bill.

5

Matt slips the leaflet into the back pocket of his trousers. Things haven't felt normal for a long time, but today is increasingly surreal. In the space of a couple of hours he's gone from being Public Enemy Number One to no one, and if that wasn't enough, he's now faced with this. He remembers watching the news on TV and seeing footage of refugee camps in different countries following endless wars and natural disasters. He was always thankful it wasn't here and it wasn't him. Well now it is.

There are people everywhere. It's impossible to stand still and he's carried along with a human tide of new arrivals being absorbed into the masses. Matt's emerged from the checkpoint-cum-prison-cum-processing-center close to the City Arena. He came here a couple of times with Jen. Overpriced, oversized, and overhyped, people paid a fortune to come here and watch bands playing live in the distance. Today, though, there's free access. All the doors are open and winding queues of people snake in through every available entrance. He looks inside as he walks past and sees the vast, bowl-like building is nothing but lines. Queues to join queues. Armed guards and loudspeaker announcements.

The longest lines by far are for food. Should he queue up? He thinks he maybe should, but he hasn't been around this many people in a long, long time and he's reluctant. He's spent weeks avoiding everyone else. It'll take time to get used to being shoulder to shoulder again. He's already missing the space.

Beyond the arena queues it's every man, woman, and child for themselves. Nothing but movement. Faces come at him from all directions like a fairground horror ride. Matt moves toward the side of the road and sticks to the shadows. He reassures himself by remembering this is a Hater-free zone. He might not want to engage with his fellow refugees, but at least he doesn't have to worry about them trying to rip his fucking throat out. Not yet, anyway.

When Matt catches a glimpse of his reflection in the dusty window of a long-shut shop, he does a double take. He feels suddenly self-conscious. Despite having been hosed down, he's still a fucking mess. Long, shaggy hair. Odd shoes. Holes and tears. For a fraction of a second it almost matters, but he knows nobody here gives a damn what he looks like. Fact is, everyone and everything looks a fucking state. Staying alive is the only thing that's fashionable these days.

Wait . . . I know where I am . . .

It's taken a while, but he's just worked it out. Everything looks so different to how he remembers. Empty spaces have been filled, tents and other makeshift shelters occupying grass verges and strips of parkland. Because there's no traffic, the once obvious lines of the roads have become blurred, the curbs obscured by mountains of garbage stacked up like dirty drifts. The warm air stinks. When Matt looks up instead of down, though, there's more familiarity. Save for the missing top third of a once distinctive communications tower that's been decapitated, the view above street level is largely unspoiled. The illusion is shattered when a pair of ugly Chinooks crawl across the otherwise empty blue sky. Noise echoes off the buildings on either side of the street, briefly muting the monotonous hum of the crowds.

This place is an auditory and visual overload, but it's not volumes and numbers that have caught Matt out, it's the sheer difference; the stark contrast with the empty silence of the rest of the world. Everything familiar is now unfamiliar. He's only been inside the camp proper for a matter of minutes, but it's long enough to know that nothing here's like it was anymore. Look at that electrical store over there, for example. It used to be full of TVs and computers and vacuums and washing machines and microwaves. All those things are still present, but it's full of people too; living, eating, and sleeping in the store. Matt watches an extended family re-arranging their makeshift home-space. Two men lay a fridge-freezer on its side on top of a couple of washer-driers, building a wall between them and everyone else.

Is it going to be like this everywhere?

He turns a corner and stops dead in his tracks in front of a filling station. The retail kiosk is empty-shelved and shuttered, the fuel pumps dried up and useless, but the forecourt itself has been repurposed by a bunch of kids playing football. *Playing games,* for Christ's sake! There are nine of them of various shapes and sizes, kicking at a goal formed from the stretched-out hoses of two pumps tied together to form a sagging, black rubber crossbar. Their ball has seen better days, but for all these kids care they could be playing the FA Cup final on the pitch at Wembley. That makes Matt feel surprisingly morose. He's never been much of a sports fan, but it says something about the state of what's left of the world that a staple of the British sporting calendar like the FA Cup final won't be played this year. Or any other year for that matter. That's how it feels to-day, anyway.

But it's not the game that's got Matt's attention, it's the kids themselves. They're the closest thing to normal children he's seen in months. It's not what they're doing that matters, it's what they're not doing. They're the first people he's seen for a long time. Who aren't thinking about how to survive. They're not thinking about food or shelter or staying safe and quiet and alive, they're just lost in their game. It gives him a little hope. Just a little, mind.

Engine noise. Coming from behind him. Gaining fast.

Matt presses himself back against a wall as a military vehicle trundles into view. Some kind of tactical support machine, it looks like. An ugly, angular-looking beast with crushing tires, surrounded by a phalanx of marching soldiers with even more of them riding on the back. They move slowly and methodically along the street, expressions hidden behind visors, weapons primed and held clearly visible. People move out of the way with-out complaint, either out of respect or fear or a combination of both. Matt tries to melt into the shadows, feeling disproportion-ally conspicuous even though he knows he's just another face in the crowd. It's a relief when they pass by, but he waits a while longer before moving, just to be sure.

It must be late afternoon by now. Four o'clock? Maybe as late as five? Matt's days have long lost any structure. The nine-to-five and the comforting rigidity of the working week have gone. Now the days are interchangeable and he does things when he has to, no consideration for the earliness of the hour or the lateness of the day. He's got used to this fluidity, so why now is he wishing he had a watch to check? He's wondering whether he's got time to try and make it back to the house tonight, or if he should wait till morning. There's no logical reason to delay, but every fiber of his body seems intent on imploring him to slow down. It's as if he doesn't want to go back. It's just nerves, he knows it is, but he's having trouble keeping them in check. All the effort of the last nine weeks has been building up to this.

What if she's gone?

What if she doesn't recognize me?

What if she doesn't want me?

For all its size, the city feels small tonight. The jets and helicopters and drones which frequently crisscross overhead compound the illusion of being in a bubble. It's like something out of a Stephen King novel, Matt thinks. Or *The Simpsons Movie.* Remember that? He wonders how long pop culture references will stay valid in this increasingly dystopian-feeling world. Books and films already feel a lifetime ago.

The light's starting to fade and the buildings have become shadows. The grid's down. Streetlamps stay dark, usurped by occasional freestanding, generator-powered lighting towers, the kind that used to be used to illuminate construction sites and road works. There are standpipes on the corners of the widest roads. Queues of people stretch out behind them, arms loaded with bottles and jars and whatever else they can find to carry water.

It's not just the power supply that's failed, Matt's starting to realize, it's the whole infrastructure of the city. It's no surprise, really, because right now all that matters here is keeping the outside out. Nothing in this place is what it used to be. There's no one swimming in the swimming pools, no books being read in the libraries. Schools are lesson-free. Pretty much every build-

ing he's so far seen, irrespective of its intended purpose or design, is just another shelter now.

He's getting close to home.

The Co-op supermarket he and Jen shopped at is desolate. He
remembers stocking up here the day they moved into the house,
giddy with excitement, filling their basket with things they didn't
need, determined to make something special of their first night
in their new home. The shop looks alien now with its sign unlit,
its shelves empty, and its automatic doors wedged permanently
open like a gaping maw. It's been stripped of its plastic retail soul
and stocked with people instead.

Matt walks down Galton Road, a long, straight street which
runs alongside a park which itself backs onto a golf course. At
this time of day he wouldn't have expected to see anyone here,
but every available scrap of grassland has been filled. A shanty-
town of tents and makeshift plastic shelters has sprung up, illuminated by torches and campfires. There's a deep, mumbling
soundtrack to the place: generally subdued low frequencies save
for the occasional high-pitched interruption. Raised voices. More
kids. Dunkirk spirit, his gran used to call it. Folks pulling together to overcome adversity. But he still feels out on a limb. *All
these people, and I haven't spoken to anyone.*

At the corner of Galton Road and West Boulevard are more
soldiers manning a temporary base with a watchtower. There's
no shortage of firepower. The CDF troops are impervious, eyes
hidden as they scan the crowds. But there's no dissent here, no
trouble at all. An eerie, almost unnatural calm lies heavy over
the place. The reason, Matt decides, is obvious. It was spelled out in
the leaflet in his pocket—*if you act like the enemy, you will be treated
like the enemy.* Having a bad day? Feeling pissed off? Someone
angered you? Be careful what you say and how you say it: they'll
call you a Hater. He knows all it would take is a suspicion.

West Boulevard is a long downward slope of a road with a wide central reservation between the two carriageways (now another campsite). A key route between the suburbs and the center of town, it's a mass of teeming movement. Folks spill out onto the silent roadway as they go about their business, though other than fetching food and water, Matt can't understand what kind of business that might be now that the gears of society have temporarily ground to a halt. He's in no mood to ask because he has other things on his mind.

Home.

He's almost reached East Kent Road now, and his heart's pounding. He's spent weeks trying to get back here, living on a knife-edge, snatching moments of sleep whenever he's been able, foraging scraps of food. It's only now he's made it that he finally feels it in his bones. Every muscle aches. Everything hurts. The effort of all those hours and all those miles is catching up with him, yet part of him wants to make one more trip around the block. He's looking for delaying tactics because he knows that everything hinges on what happens next. All that he's been through will have counted for nothing if she's not here.

Old Matt would have found an excuse to put things off, but he's a changed man. Whether he's changed for the better or worse is subject to debate, but he now marches toward the house with a newfound burst of energy and an unexpected swagger, a curious sense of pride. He's risked everything for Jen. *There's not one person here who's been through as much as I have to get home,* he thinks.

East Kent Road is one of the quieter side streets, but there are plenty of people here. Most houses appear to be occupied except for one of the larger, more expensive homes, which has been ravaged by fire, no doubt something to do with the flame-licked wreck of a van that's come to an undignified halt half-in and half-

out of a downstairs bay window. It looks like the house is trying
to spit it out.

What happened in that house?

Were there Haters here?

Were some of my neighbors Haters?

Stupid question: he didn't even know his neighbors. Anyway,
he'll have all the answers in a minute, because he can finally see
home now. The initial outward signs are positive. There are signs
of life, with flickering lamplight visible in one of the windows.
His car's still on the drive where he left it. Feels like a lifetime
ago since that morning when his now deceased colleague Gavin
picked him up and drove him to the station to meet up with the
rest of the office team and catch the train north to the port to
take the ferry to Skek. Hard to believe he's the only one who
made it back . . .

He instinctively checks his pockets for his door key but it's
long gone. He rings the bell but there's no power and no noise
so he knocks instead, rapping his knuckles hard on the wood.

Nothing.

He knocks again. And again. And once more for luck.

Still nothing.

He steps back, looking for signs of movement; twitching curtains . . . anything.

Then something.

There's definitely someone inside. He can see them moving behind the frosted glass, leaning forward and looking through the
spyhole. Jesus, he can't wait to see her. He runs his fingers through
his unkempt hair, trying to comb his long, greasy locks into some
semblance of order.

The door opens on the security chain. A face appears, but it's
not one he recognizes. Younger than him. Male. Mixed-race.

Clean-shaved. Dark, piercing eyes. The two of them regard each other in silence for a few dragging seconds; a mutual *who the fuck are you?* moment. Then the lad in his house speaks. "What?"

Matt's answer is simple and to the point. He resists the temptation to lose his temper. Whatever happens, he knows that wouldn't end well. "I live here."

"Bullshit."

"Not bullshit. My name's Matthew Dunne. I live here with Jen. Who are you, and what are you doing in my house?"

The door slams shut in Matt's face. He goes to knock again but stops himself because he can hear voices on the other side. What's going on? Has this kid moved his mates in here, and are they hatching a plan to sort Matt out? There are at least three people in the hallway now, taking turns at the spyhole. His mind starts racing, trying to work out what they've done to Jen and what he's going to do about it.

He looks for another way in. He checks for the spare key they always kept under the plant pot out front, but it's gone. He thinks he could climb over the side gate and try and get in through the back, or maybe just put a brick through the bay windows and break in that way? He discounts that idea immediately, figuring that to attract attention like that would be the absolute worst thing he could do. He's risked so much for so long to get here and he can't afford to throw it all away now. The movement and the muttering inside continue. Then, after what feels like an eternity, the chain slides across and the door opens inward.

There she is.

"Hi, Jen."

"Matt? Matt, is that really you?"

"Yeah, it's me."

6

"Where have you been?" she asks once she's sure it's really him.

"Trying to get home."

"But it's been months."

"Tell me about it."

They're at opposite ends of the hallway. So much distance covered, but he can't take the final few steps. Matt's aware of other people in the house, but he's not interested in them because he's completely focused on Jen. He's struggling to believe he's made it and she's still here and still human. He's half-expecting this to be some fucked-up, fear-fueled hallucination. Any minute now he'll wake up lying in the mud outside a camp full of Haters. Or worse.

The bloke who answered the door forces his way into the conversation, literally positioning himself between the two of them, watching Matt like a hawk. "You okay, Jen?"

"Yeah, I'm okay."

Matt sees there are more faces watching from the door into the lounge. A middle-aged woman with two kids; a painfully thin girl, and a younger lad. She tries to surreptitiously herd them back into the shadows as they crowd forward, inquisitive.

It's an uncomfortable standoff which Jen ends when she moves past the man in the middle of the hall. "It's okay, Jason," she says quietly.

Now it's just the two of them facing each other again.

"Sorry I took so long."

"I didn't think you were ever coming home. I thought . . ." She's in floods of tears before she gets anywhere near the end of her sentence. Matt reaches out for her and the two of them melt into each other's arms.

The kitchen is filled with clutter and shadows. Matt and Jen sit at the table, a dull, battery-powered lamp lighting the space between them. The conversation is sporadic. Matt looks around the room for reassurance, some familiarity to cling on to, but it all looks so different to how he remembers. There are piles of other people's belongings where his things used to be. Dirty clothes and used crockery. Even though they rented, Jen was always so house-proud. It doesn't feel right to be sitting here in the squalor and gloom. A flash of light from a passing CDF patrol lumbering down the street outside illuminates both of their faces momentarily. Jen's staring at him. Won't take her eyes off him.

"I missed you," he says, taking her hand in his.

"I thought I'd lost you," she replies.

"You're kidding. It'd take a lot more than the end of the world to split us up."

She smiles, but it doesn't last long. "I should have so much to say to you, but I don't know where to start."

"We've got plenty of time. You don't have to say anything."

The house feels different because there are other people here. Matt has a hundred questions on the tip of his tongue, but he figures Jen has thousands more so he keeps quiet and waits for her to speak. He's not left waiting long. "Why did it take you so long to get back?"

"You've seen what it's like out there, haven't you?"

She shrugs. "Heard more than seen. There's no TV and I—"

"Take everything you've heard and multiply it by a thousand," he says, cutting across her. "I'm not sure how I managed to do it. I did it all on foot. I swear, a lot of the time I was covering less than a mile a day. First sign of trouble and I had to hide and wait for the Haters to disappear."

"I thought you were dead."

"I'm sorry," he says, though he doesn't know what he's apologizing for. "I'd have got a message to you if I could. The phones are dead, email's dead, there's no post . . . there was nothing I could do."

"You were only supposed to be going away for the weekend . . ."

He shuffles his chair closer and puts his arm around her, a little uncertain at first. "Missed you," he whispers, his mouth close to her ear. This moment is all Matt's thought about since he left for Skek that morning. Getting back to this place and this woman means everything. He revels in her warmth, her touch . . . even her smell. "The whole bloody world has gone to hell. Everything's changed. You're the only thing that's stayed the same."

She rests her head on his shoulder. "Are things really that bad?"

How much does he tell her? He could go into detail about the things he's witnessed and the things he's done, but what would it achieve? He wants to protect her, not terrify her. "Yeah," he says, unconvincing, "things are pretty shit." *Understatement of the century,* he thinks. A quick change of subject is called for. "So who are our houseguests?"

"I didn't have any choice," she says, pushing away, immediately defensive. "The soldiers came looking for spare rooms. There was nothing I could do. They made me take them in. They did it to everyone. There's about twenty people in that big house on the corner."

"It's okay. I understand. It's good that you've had company. I'm glad you weren't on your own."

"I told the army you were coming back, but they weren't having any of it."

"I get it, Jen, it's fine. So who are they?"

"Mrs. Walker and her kids are living in the lounge. She's really nice. She helps me out loads. Her husband was . . . one of *them*. She only just got out of her house in one piece. They come from right over on the other side of town. Her father-in-law was in hospital at the Royal Midlands. He died a month or so back. Cancer. Couldn't get the drugs anymore."

Matt thinks it's strange to think people can still die of relatively natural causes these days. "Sad to hear," he says, instinctively.

"Yeah, they couldn't finish his chemo. Really sad, it was. And Sophie, one of her kids, she's diabetic. It's been a real struggle getting insulin for her."

"What about the other guy? The flash-looking bugger who let me in. What's his story?"

"That's Jason. He's been really lovely, too."

"And he's on his own?"

"There was another lad with him for a while, but he went out to get food one day and didn't come back. Don't know what happened to him. Jason had a really nice place. Lovely flat. He showed me pictures on his phone."

"And you've been okay with all these people in the house? You never used to like it when we had people to stay."

"I didn't have any choice, I told you. The army said they had to come here and you weren't around so I just had to deal with it. I'm just lucky I didn't get anyone difficult. Don't know what I would have done without Jason. He's the one who goes out and gets food for us, and little Sophie's medicine. Me and Mrs. Walker share the cooking."

Right on cue, Mrs. Walker enters the kitchen. She stops in the doorway but Matt acknowledges and gestures for her to come in. The poor light doesn't do anyone any favors, but he thinks she looks particularly haggard and he's struggling to work out her age. She's probably in her thirties judging by the age of her children, but she looks much older. Her straw-colored hair is scraped back from her tired-looking face. "Sorry to interrupt," she says, sounding uncertain. "Just need to get some water for the kids."

"You're not interrupting," Matt says, and he gets up to move out of the way when she tries to squeeze past him. The kitchen feels like it's shrunken in size. The whole house does, actually. Mrs. Walker reaches for a half-full water carrier. He picks it up and helps her fill a jug. "Nice to meet you, by the way. Thanks for everything you've done for Jen."

She acknowledges him and she's polite enough, but there's no warmth there. She rests a hand on Jen's shoulder, then nods and slips past to get back to what's left of her family.

When she's gone, the conversation doesn't immediately re-start. Matt craves all the old nothings they used to talk about: *Did you have a good day? What's on TV tonight? What are we having for dinner?*

Jen's equally uncertain. "So what happens now?" she asks, and she wipes away an unexpected tear.

"I don't know. To be honest, I'd only planned things this far. Didn't dare think about anything else."

"Do we just pick up where we left off? Pretend the last three months didn't happen?"

"Yes, please." His answer comes quickly, instinctively. He's not sure where this is going. One thing he does know is that her ominous questions are making him feel more nervous than at any point when he was out alone in the wilderness. "Is that okay?" he adds hopefully. "I haven't changed, Jen," he says, though that's just for her benefit. Truth is, the meek accountant who disappeared off to Skek that morning is long gone.

"You have. Look at you. Your hair, your beard . . . It's not a good look."

"I'll shave. Give myself a buzz cut."

"You smell different."

"I know. I'm not kidding, Jen, what I've seen in the city since I've been back is luxury compared to what's going on outside."

"You *sound* different. You talk different."

"What am I supposed to say to that? I've hardly spoken a word for months. I couldn't say anything to anyone out there. Did my best to stay away from everyone, actually. You've got to believe me, Jen, I'm still me."

"I still don't understand why it took you so long. It's been *months*."

Matt struggles to think of a way he can fully convey the scale of what he's been through without terrifying Jen completely. His head's filled with an endless procession of grotesque images he's been doing his best to block out. He can't tell her about the death camp he stumbled across, or the family who died while he survived, or the scores of refugees he watched being killed earlier today as he hitched a ride on the roof of the bus into town. "Not yet," he says instead. "I need time to get my head together."

Now she's crying freely. "And all I've had is time. You don't know what it's been like sitting here waiting for you day after day. I thought you were dead. I thought you were never coming home."

"Everything all right in here?"

It's Jason.

"We're fine," Matt tells him.

"I'm really tired, I'm going to bed," Jen says and she picks up a lamp and goes to leave.

"You sure you're okay?" Jason asks as she passes him.

"I'm okay," she says as she goes upstairs.

Jason waits until she's out of earshot. "Must be a lot for her to take in, you turning up like this."

"Were you listening to our conversation just now?"

"Nope."

"Good."

"But I was sitting at the bottom of the stairs."

"Why?"

"Because I wanted to be sure Jen was all right."

"What's it to you?"

Jason holds up his hands in mock surrender. "Absolutely nothing, but she's been good enough to give me a roof over my head, and I don't know where I'd be without her. A lot of folks would give everything they have to trade places with me."

"Most folks don't have anything left to trade."

"I know that, too. Look, I've clearly not seen anywhere near as much of the fighting as you have, but I get it."

"Good."

Matt goes to follow Jen, but Jason blocks his way. "She talked about you all the time," he says. "She's really struggled with all of this."

"I think I know my girlfriend pretty well, thanks very much. I don't need you to tell me how she's feeling."

"I'm just saying . . ."

"What?"

"I'm just saying you might need to give her some space. Go easy on her. Don't force it. Let her get used to the idea of having you around again."

"Thanks for the advice," Matt says, and he follows Jen up, leaving Jason on his own in the kitchen.

He uses a lamp and two mirrors to fill the small bathroom with light, then starts hacking at his hair with a pair of scissors he finds in the cabinet. When he's finished, he trims as much of his beard away as he can. The bin's full by the time he's finished. Enough hair to stuff a pillow.

He tries cleaning his teeth, but the toothpaste tastes too strong. He fills the basin with tepid water from a jug and uses a flannel to wipe away the remaining grime that the soldiers' hose didn't blast off. A little deodorant—a long-forgotten scent—then he's done.

When he looks in the mirror he sees himself for the first time in what feels like forever.

He gently opens the bedroom door, wincing when the hinges creak. He can just about make out Jen's shape lying in bed in the dark, facing the wall. She's already asleep, and he doesn't want to disturb her. He curls up on the floor under the window and covers himself with a spare duvet. The boards are hard and he'll ache in the morning, but despite the discomfort and the constant noise coming from the streets and skies outside, he knows he'll sleep better tonight than he has in weeks.

7

His sleep is fitful and uneven, but long and overdue. Several times during the night and morning he wakes with a start, sweat-soaked and breathing hard, disoriented and filled with a vile, nauseous fear that he's vulnerable because he's dropped his guard. Instinctively he reaches for his rucksack and the hilt of the ice axe, then panics when he can't find either. He fights with the covers like he's trapped in a captor's net, kicking and flinching.

Then he remembers. There are no Haters here.

But even though he's physically exhausted, his conscience conspires to keep him awake. He's still on alert, refusing to let go. This doesn't yet feel right. When the world is so fucked-up and dangerous outside, how can it now be that he's lying in his bedroom at home in relative comfort?

An entire day disappears with barely any interaction with Jen or any of the other people in the house. They keep away—*she* keeps away—and he wonders what she's thinking. He's worried she's frightened of him, of what he's become. And she doesn't even know the half of it. He can't tell her anything. Not yet.

It's late again now. The hours have evaporated. There's some semblance of a basic routine left here, that much is clear, but he's way out of sync with the rest of the household. Jet-lagged without having been abroad.

The door creaks open, startling him. Jen brings him some water and a little food, which he devours hungrily. She stands and watches.

"Your hair looks worse," she says.

"Thanks."

"I'll sort it out for you later."

"Just cut it all off."

"I'll cut it properly. You've left enough for me to style."

"Just cut it all off," he says again, sounding more aggressive than he intends. "No one has their hair done nice these days. It'll make me stand out."

"I cut Jason's hair for him."

"Lucky Jason."

"Why did you sleep on the floor?"

"I didn't want to keep you awake."

"You think I slept at all last night? Having you back here's been a bit of a shock."

"I know. You used to it yet?"

"Getting there, I think. You?"

"Like you said, getting there."

She sits down on the floor next to him. Shuffles up against him. He finishes the last scraps of food and looks up, feeling her eyes on him. He's eating like an animal. He puts down the bowl he's been licking, embarrassed. She fishes in her pocket and hands him a Snickers bar. He looks at it like it's made of gold. "I kept this hidden away. I know they're your favorite."

"Jeez, Jen . . ."

"I kept it on top of the kitchen cupboard where no one else

would find it. I told myself the only person who was ever going to eat it was you. I was keeping it for when you came home."

He opens the chocolate and wolfs it down. "I bloody love you," he says, mouth half-full. He leans across and tries to kiss her but she recoils and pushes him away.

"You still stink," she tells him with her customary lack of tact. "There are places you can go. Couple of streets down near Camomile Way there are some showers, Jason said. Open-air things. Like car washes, he said they were."

"Cool, thanks."

"Opposite that takeaway you used to like."

"I know the one." Even though he's just eaten, Matt's stomach rumbles at the thought of takeaway food. "Think it'll still be open?" he asks, semiserious.

"What, the takeaway? I doubt it."

"I'm kidding," he says, and she nudges against him, unamused. Then she laughs. "What's so funny?" he asks.

"Just thinking about that time you went to get us a curry and—"

"—and the bag split. Yes, I remember. Very funny."

"Oh, but it was, though. You left a trail of chicken korma all the way down the road. How you didn't realize the bag was getting lighter is beyond me!"

"I know, I know . . . I'll never live that down."

"It's the way you handed me this dripping, half-empty bag!"

"We still had a good night, though, didn't we?"

"Only because we went to bed early. You took full advantage of me drinking the best part of a bottle of wine on an empty stomach."

"Yeah . . . a good night," he says, daydreaming about all the things they did together that night, in this room, in that bed.

If it wasn't for the thunderous chopping of helicopter rotor blades overhead and the bright, sweeping searchlight which spills across the bedroom, this might almost feel like it used to. Almost. *We should ban talking about the past,* Matt thinks. *It hurts too much when you have to come back to the present.* For Jen's sake he says nothing. He lets the conversation continue to drift along its gentle, old-world trajectory.

"Remember when we were looking to rent this place and we viewed those flats over on Eastside?"

"I remember. We couldn't have afforded to stay a week in that place."

"Beautiful, though."

"Anyway, what of it?"

"That's where Jason's place was."

"Was?"

"Yeah. It's on the wrong side of the wall now. He can't get anywhere near."

"So this place is a bit of a comedown."

"He's just grateful to have a roof. We all are."

"You'll get no argument from me. Can't tell you how good it is to be home."

She gets up and goes over to the wardrobe. "Remember the size of the bedroom in that flat?"

"The kitchen was as big as the whole of our downstairs. It was too big for just the two of us. And too expensive. Way too expensive."

Jen throws some clean nightclothes over to him. "Get changed, Matt. Chuck out those old things, they're ruined."

He catches a T-shirt and holds it to his face, sucking in its washing powder smell. He peels off his sweat-soaked rags, uses them to wipe himself down, then drops them in the bin. "Thanks. That's better."

"I gave some of your things to Jason. He ran out of stuff and I didn't know if you were coming back."

"Thought his T-shirt looked familiar last night," Matt says, managing a wry grin. "I was thinking how stylish he looked."

She shakes her head. "You may be many things, Matthew Dunne, but stylish has never been one of them."

"What are you doing now?" he asks, watching her every move.

"Going to bed. I'm tired. You?"

"Same, I guess."

"You sleeping on the floor again tonight?"

He shuffles awkwardly. "That's up to you."

"It's our bed," she says. "Tell you the truth, I've had enough of sleeping on my own recently."

With her back to him she undresses then pulls a long, shapeless nightshirt over her head. She climbs into bed, folding back the corner of the duvet on his side and inviting him in. He's hesitant, bizarrely nervous. He lies down next to her and the mattress feels so soft, so comfortable, that he thinks he'll never stop sinking into it. There's no physical contact between them, but maybe that's a step too far for tonight. Jen's lying on her side now, watching him, her bright eyes glistening in the glow of the searchlights outside.

"It's good to be home," Matt says, and his voice cracks, almost overcome.

"Jason said he'd show you the camp tomorrow. Show you the ropes."

"Sounds good."

"He knows his way around. I'm really glad he's been here. I don't know what I'd have done without him."

"It should have been me. I'm sorry I wasn't here for you."

"It wasn't your fault. I get it, Matt. I understand."

It's impossible to contain his emotions now. Two and a half months' worth of pent-up fear and frustration and uncertainty comes flooding out. "I just wanted to be here with you. I'm sorry, Jen. I should never have gone away."

"You're home now. Stop apologizing. Really glad you're here."

She puts her arm around him and holds him until they both fall asleep.

8

Matt and Jason walk away from the house together in search of supplies. It's a gloriously sunny day, relentlessly bright. Hot for the time of year. Too hot. The kind of weather where you want to do nothing but lounge around and soak up the heat, definitely not the kind of weather to be under this kind of pressure and up to your neck in this many people. They can hardly move. It's impossible to walk in a straight line without swerving around someone coming the other way or tripping over someone who's set up camp on the pavement. Sources of shadow are craved. In a ransacked superstore car park filled with abandoned cars (many of which appear to have become makeshift homes), a crowd has formed under the branches of a solitary yew tree in the middle of a traffic roundabout. Other people are lying in the shade of ticket payment booths, bus shelters, hedges, and anything else they can find.

Matt's still not used to being able to make noise without fear of retribution. Jason, on the other hand, finds it equally difficult to shut up. "There's two ways to get food these days," he explains. "You work or you queue."

"And what's the difference?"

"Well, one's a shit-load harder than the other."

"No, you idiot. I know the difference between working and queuing. What's the difference in terms of what you get?"

"I wouldn't know. Depends on the kind of work you do, I guess. I'm sure workers get more, if that's what you mean. We don't have to put ourselves out, though. We've got these." He holds up a bunch of papers.

"What are they?"

"Mrs. Walker and the kids get a bit extra on account of the girl being sick. No, mate, the only kind of work here is hard work or even harder work. There's a problem with sanitation and garbage, in case you hadn't noticed the stink—"

"I had."

"—so you can either get involved in that and literally be up to your neck in shit, or you can sign up to join the CDF."

"Don't know which sounds worse."

"Exactly."

"So you don't do either?"

"No point. It's about getting a balance, isn't it? Until you got back I was the only one providing for your missus and the Walkers. That's been a full-time job in itself."

"I appreciate what you've done for Jen. You're off the hook now, though. Pressure's off."

"I can't see the pressure being off around here for a long, long time."

There's a standpipe across the way with an endless queue of sun-baked people behind it. The water flow has been interrupted. One soldier's on the ground trying to sort the plumbing out, while another leans over him, telling him what to do. Three more keep the queuing civilians in check, marching up and down the line in full uniform, weapons clearly visible. If there is any dissent, it's kept well hidden. "This place is a frigging powder keg," Matt says, thinking out loud.

"Damn right it is. And that's why you don't want to go and get yourself conscripted. They get more food than the rest of us, I'm sure, and I wouldn't say no to getting my hands on one of their rifles and some ammo, but those fuckers are first in line. When the shit hits the fan, whatever direction it comes from, they'll get it full-force."

"You don't think the shit has already hit the fan?"

"Well and truly, but you can't tell me that's the end of it. Even when we've got rid of the Haters, there's gonna be a real fucking mess left to sort out. A real fucking mess."

They cut through a road between two buildings which is so tightly packed with shadow-grabbers it's an effort to get through. Matt's confused. "I thought we were going to the arena for food?"

"Queues are longer there. There's another place."

"There were a few distribution points listed in that leaflet they gave me."

"Yeah, one was closer to the house but it dried up a couple of weeks back. Just the two left now."

"Where's the food come from?"

"Outside. Apparently the CDF's working to extend No Man's Land. They go out, they kill, they loot, then they come back. That's what I've been told. Fucking mad if you ask me. See, that's another reason why you don't want to volunteer. You end up risking your neck for other people's dinner."

"But it's okay for other people to risk their necks for you?"

"Yeah, I know . . . Hands up, mate, I'm a hypocrite, but I'd rather be a hypocrite with a pulse than a do-gooder who gets their brains blown out while they're looting to keep the neighbors fed, don't you think?"

"I don't know what I think anymore."

They take a shortcut across the park at Galton Road. A series of gray tarmac walkways crisscrosses the overcrowded grassland, allowing them to move a little quicker through the encamped masses. In the distance there are soccer fields being used as helicopter landing pads. A children's play area has become a heavily guarded military stockpile. Behind a tall wooden fence that looks to have been recently erected, a fire burns. Matt wonders what it is the soldiers are incinerating.

"So what was it like?" Jason randomly asks.

"What was what like?"

"Being out there?"

"Fucking terrifying," Matt admits. "I was living on my nerves. Couldn't switch off. Couldn't drop my guard."

"It was pretty shitty here, too," Jason says, and it's clear he only asked his initial question so he could tell Matt about his own ordeal. "The military were going house to house to start with, flushing out the Haters. Frigging frightening, it was. You couldn't react when they came to the door. I had a friend who had a friend who got himself executed 'cause they thought he was one of *them*. There's a test they do, you know."

"I know," Matt says. "I had it done. Think I'd be here if I hadn't?"

"Yeah. Suppose not."

Matt considers telling Jason about the different times he's been tested, or the torturous follow-up to the test he endured at the hands of the military, but he doesn't. Jason's not listening. He's too busy talking.

"Once the lines had been fully drawn and we knew who was who, that's when the city went into lockdown. Me and my friend Amit got involved in building the wall. You've seen the wall, right?"

"Parts of it."

"It's not really a wall as such, but that's what they call it. Just lots of little barricades, really. Almost goes all the way around the whole camp, though. You block a street with vehicles, then fill in the gaps with whatever else you can find . . . you get the picture."

"So what happened to your friend? Jen said there was two of you when you arrived at the house."

"Amit had been staying with me at my flat. My place was the dog's bollocks. Plenty of space, five floors up, nice and safe. But then they built the wall, and I was on the wrong side. Got up one morning and I had about half an hour to get out before the CDF sealed the place off. Right back at the beginning, that was. I'm glad I got here when I did, though. Wasn't long after that space started running out. New arrivals these days end up camped out in places like this." He spreads his arms and gestures at the thousands of people living in the park.

"You still haven't told me what happened to Amit."

"Dunno. God's honest truth. Told me and Jen he was going for water one morning, and I never seen him again. Anything could have happened."

"And you've not tried to find him?"

"What's the point? I know that sounds harsh, but like I say, anything could have happened. Probably found himself something better, knowing Amit. It's every man for himself these days. You should know that better than anyone."

The gates on the far side of the park are a struggle to get through. More people and more soldiers. There are hawkers here too, trying to trade possessions for food. "I don't have anything," Matt tells a persistent kid who's trying to palm off an expensive-looking bracelet. Jason grabs Matt's sleeve and pulls him away.

"Don't lose your temper. You've gotta let them know who's boss without showing too much emotion, else they'll think you're a Hater."

"Have any of these people even seen a Hater fight?"

"Probably."

"Have you?"

"'Course I have. Thing is, all you need these days is a suspicion. Innocent until proven guilty? Forget that shit. You're guilty till proven innocent now."

"Yeah, I know," Matt says, recalling how he was chained up and hosed down.

Up ahead is the Royal Midlands Hospital. Matt remembers it being opened, a few years before the war. It's an unusually shaped metal and glass structure which always looked completely at odds with its otherwise bland urban surroundings. Gleaming, futuristic, and new, it's now anything but. Yet it still stands in stark contrast to the regularity and engrained dirt of inner-city living. From a distance it always reminded him of the hulls of three huge boats, part-buried side by side with their bows sticking up out of the ground. Today the hospital looks as worn-down and beaten as everything else. A battle-damaged shell on the very edge of the city exclusion zone. A fire looks to have broken out there recently. Parts of the left outer tower are skeletal and black, skin and cladding scorched away like a burn victim.

They must be nearing the food distribution point. "We're getting close, aren't we?" Matt says. There are more people here, and for the most part they're not going anywhere. Matt's hesitant, but though he tries not to let Jason see, he's not as good at keeping his feelings hidden as he thinks he is.

"Problem?" Jason asks.

"I'll be okay. Just get freaked out by the crowds. It's too soon."

"This place is nothing but crowds. The rate they're coming in you won't have any choice soon."

"How close are we to the wall?"

"Couple of minutes' walk," he replies, nodding over to their left. "Why?"

"I want to check it out. Think I'll be happier once I know how well protected we are."

Jason obliges. They take a detour and are soon at the very edge of the city-camp. The street they're now walking along has been abruptly truncated about fifty meters ahead, cut off midway along its length. There are cars upon cars upon cars in front of them, stacked up and layered across the road, stretching from the wall of one building to the wall of the building directly opposite. There are scores of people taking shelter in the shadows of the brutal, abstract-looking blockade. "Happy now?" Jason asks. "No fucker's getting through that."

9

Matt's arms are burning. He's wishing he'd left his hair long, too, because there's no respite from the sun out here. They've been queuing for food for a couple of hours now and he doesn't know how much more of this red-hot inertia he can take. "I can't stand this," he tells Jason.

"You get used to it. You don't have any choice."

The queue for food has been shuffling forward at a miserable speed, and the lack of progress makes Matt's guts churn. It's the fact he doesn't have any control here, the fact he has no option but to keeping move at the slothful speed of everyone else that bothers him. It makes him feel exposed. "And we're just supposed to stand here and wait?"

"You got a better idea? There's worse ways to earn a living if you ask me. No pressure, you don't have to think . . . just stand your ground and top up your tan."

I've been risking my life every day for the last two and a half months, and now you're telling me I should be topping up my tan? Matt thinks but doesn't say.

From where they're standing the snaking line of people ahead looks much shorter than it is. It's an optical illusion, because what they haven't seen until now is that the queue turns sharp left down another truncated road, then right a short distance farther and back onto the road they've been following. It makes Matt's heart sink. "Jesus, that's going to add another couple of hours onto this at least."

"And? You got somewhere better to go?"

Matt thinks pretty much anywhere would be better but, much as it pains him to admit, he also knows Jason's right.

Another half hour and they find themselves nestled up against the improvised border wall. At least there's a little shade here, though everyone wants to get under cover so it means even more people bunched together in an even tighter space. A group of CDF soldiers are handing out cups of water about a hundred meters from here, well away from the queues, but neither Matt nor Jason dare risk leaving the line to fetch any. "Bastards do it on purpose, I'm sure they do," Jason says under his breath, less than impressed. "Wouldn't hurt them to walk down the line with drinks once in a while."

It's getting increasingly difficult to stay still here. Matt's being jostled from either side by other people, yet he knows he can't risk letting his frustrations show. *If you act like the enemy, you will be treated like the enemy.* But there's only so much he can take, and when a group of people behind become agitated and start pushing him forward, he loses his temper. He angrily spins around, ready to take out his frustrations on the idiot that's just shoved into him, but he doesn't.

"What the hell?"

At the bottom of this part of the improvised wall is the wreck of a coach. The space under its chassis has been filled with rubble, and other ruined vehicles have been piled up at either end of it to block the way. More rubble dropped on top of the coach has caused its roof to buckle in the middle, but for the most part it's still in one piece and its windows are largely intact. And that, Matt thinks, might not be a good thing.

More people are leaving their places in the queue. Some drop back, reversing away from the coach blockade, while others clamor farther forward. Many of them, he notices, now have their faces pressed against the coach's dusty windows and are looking through and out the other side into No Man's Land. Matt does the same, and his worst fears are immediately realized.

Haters.

There's a mass of them coming toward the camp, maybe as many as a hundred. This is a coordinated attack, that much is immediately clear. Most of them are on foot, but the farthest forward are driving battered old cars and trucks. One vehicle in particular catches Matt's eye. It's a huge supermarket lorry, being driven at what he suspects is its maximum speed, straight at the city wall.

Jason's right behind him, pushing to get a better view, preventing Matt from moving. Matt turns and grabs him by the collar, then pushes him away. "Move!"

Jason trips as he starts to run and Matt picks him up off the floor, all thoughts of getting food and water forgotten because he knows what's coming next. Other people realize too, but most remain oblivious. The British cliché of folks standing in queues and refusing to give up the spaces they've rightfully earned has never been truer or more risky. Matt retreats a safe distance away, and the whole world becomes silent like a vacuum as he waits and watches.

The Hater-controlled truck has been well aimed. Its driver steers into the back end of the coach rather than hitting it square on, and physics takes care of the rest. The rear of the coach is punched out of line, and its sudden, violent displacement has two immediate effects. First, much of the precariously balanced ballast on top of the coach comes crashing down. Second, a breach opens up in the barrier that's just wide enough for the enemy to start piling through.

Sheer fucking panic.

The fastest Haters are through and onto the slowest Unchanged in seconds, killing them with such savage ferocity that other people are stupefied and unable to react. Like many others, Jason just stands still and watches as the enemy pour into the camp in serious numbers.

Matt, however, does not.

While most people who aren't numb with shock have now turned tail and are sprinting deeper into the camp, Matt instead drags Jason sideways across the narrow road. Jason tries to protest and run with the others. "Got to get out of here. Fucking hell, man, we've got to—"

Matt's not having any of it. "You run if you like, but if you go either backward or forward right now, you're a dead man."

Jason's still struggling. "Let me go . . . got to get away from the wall . . ."

Matt almost loses his grip on the other man, but then rugby-tackles him, wrapping his arms around his waist and moving at such a pace that the pair of them don't stop until they hit the wall opposite. Jason's still fighting with him, but Matt's not reacting. Instead he rolls them both along until they reach a door, then he kicks it open and they fall inside a skeletal shell of a once proud office building.

"What the hell are you doing?" Jason screams. "You'll get us both killed, you fucking—"

His words are silenced by gunfire. Standing to one side of a broken window, the two men look out onto a horrific scene outside. "Did you not see them coming?" Matt asks, shouting over the noise.

"The Haters?"

"No, the CDF."

Truth is, Jason was too preoccupied trying to get away from the Hater threat that he didn't see what Matt saw: a line of CDF fighters advancing toward the breach in the city wall, all guns blazing. Now the troops are standing in a ragged line which stretches the width of the street, hacking down the waves of furious Hater fighters who continue pouring through into the camp. The firing only started a few seconds ago, but the casualties from both sides are already massive in number.

"So what are we supposed to do now?" Jason demands.

"You do what you like, I'm getting out of here."

"And how do you think you're going to do that? We should have got out while we still had the chance. We take one step out that door now and they'll kill us. Shoot first, ask questions later."

"So we wait."

"You think that's going to work? Jesus, you don't have the first clue, do you?"

"I'm still alive, aren't I? My tactics worked for the last three months. Now shut up before someone hears you."

There's little chance of that, because the cacophony of noise outside is incredible. Matt risks looking out again and sees that the defensive CDF line is slowly advancing back toward the breach. A few seconds later and the volume increases still further. A jet roars over the city from out of nowhere and begins carpet bombing the Haters on the other side of the city wall.

"See?" Matt says. "We wait. We sit here until the fighting stops, then sneak away when no one's looking."

"And that was your survival strategy out there, was it?"

"Pretty much. Like I said, it worked."

Matt moves away from the window. The building they're in is a dilapidated ruin. Ransacked and stripped-out, this place has been abandoned. He thinks it's strange that it's been completely overlooked, though, when there are people living in just about every other building he's come across. Too close to the city boundary for safety, perhaps? When there are more muffled explosions nearby and the wall he's leaning against shakes wildly, he realizes it's more likely the building's unused because it's on the verge of collapse.

"We should go," he tells Jason.

"Were you not listening to me just now? We can't get out."

"Not through the front door, no. Just need to look for another exit. Need to bide our time."

"You do realize if any of those CDF bastards catch us they'll kill us."

"Then don't let them see you."

"Christ, you're infuriating. Do you have any idea how you—"

Jason stops talking. Matt's relieved, but the relief is short-lived. There's a new noise now. Not as loud as gunfire or bombers, but much more concerning. It's not the sound itself that worries him, it's where it's coming from.

He goes through a doorway without a door into a long, partially collapsed corridor, then uses a mound of rubble to climb. He jumps up and catches the edge of a first-floor floorboard with his fingertips and manages to haul himself up onto the next level. Jason's standing directly below and Matt grudgingly helps him up.

The noise is louder up here, because the outer walls of this building have collapsed in places, leaving it just an exposed frame. "What is it?" Jason asks.

"Did you notice the gunfire's mostly stopped?"

"So what are they doing?"

Matt's answer is simple. "Construction work."

They peer through an egg-shaped hole in the brickwork. Matt's right. Apart from a few guards stationed in key positions to pick off rogue Haters, the rest of the CDF troops are now working to rebuild the barrier. Vehicles are being maneuvered into position—some manhandled, others pushed into position by tanks. Crowds of people are fleeing the area, scurrying out of the way like a pack of rats, terrified of being trapped.

Trouble is, the barrier's moved. It's being rebuilt about fifty meters closer to the center of town.

"We're on the wrong side of the wall now. Christ, you picked the perfect building to hide in, idiot. Now we're really screwed," Jason yells.

Matt doesn't react. Instead he turns back and jumps the hole in the floor through which they just climbed. Jason follows, creeping around the edges of the chasm rather than risking jumping it.

"And now you're going the wrong way," he shouts.

"Up is the right way," Matt shouts back.

The entire building shakes as the construction continues on one side and the carpet bombing restarts on the other. Another wave of aerial bombardment obliterates the remaining Haters still foolish enough to be anywhere near the battle zone.

Matt finds another staircase and goes up, then ducks out through a gap in the rafters. He lies down on his belly on a flat section of roof near the eaves. He's out of sight but has a panoramic view of the frantic activity below. Jason stays a short distance behind him, remaining under cover. "What now?"

Matt glances up at him. "Now we wait."

They're up on the roof for several more hours. Matt changes position frequently, peering down onto the chaos below from different angles. Jason won't shut up. "What's your problem?" Matt asks. "You didn't have an issue queuing up for food for hours on end. This is even easier."

"We could have died."

"Yeah, but we didn't."

"We're not home yet, there's still time."

"Too soon. Just need to wait a little while longer."

"We're never going to get out of here."

"We are."

"We don't have any food. Jen and the Walkers will need food."

"I know. I'll deal with it."

"You're full of shit, you know that?"

Matt says nothing.

Another hour and it's time.

Matt makes his move. He doesn't wait for Jason or tell him he's going, but the other man's up and on his feet immediately and sticks to Matt like glue. "How are we going to—?" he starts to ask, before Matt silences him with a stare.

Cautiously working his way back down through the creaking, warrenlike building, Matt goes from room to room. This was once some kind of medical practice. Right at the opposite end to the door through which they originally entered during the gunfight is a fire exit. Matt carefully prizes it open, peers through, then waits.

"You been here before? Did you know this door was here?"

"No, but there's always another way out. Have you ever been in a building that only had one way in or out?"

"Suppose not."

"Tell me, Jason, when we were up on the roof just now, what were you thinking about?"

"What, apart from how we're going to get out of this mess?"

"Yes, apart from that."

"Nothing really."

"That's what I thought. You're going to have to do a lot better than that. You need to start paying attention. Focus."

"Who the fuck do you think you are, talking to me like that?" Jason's about to give him a mouthful of abuse, but Matt's already gone. Jason follows him outside, squeezing through the fire escape before it swings shut.

Out on the street, Matt has emerged behind a pile of corpses; Haters and friendlies alike, all dumped together, all the same now they're dead. The smell is appalling, but he doesn't react. Instead, he gets down on his hands and knees and crawls around the pile, then slides under a CDF truck full of guards looking the other way, before getting up and nonchalantly walking away, melting into the crowds like nothing's happened.

It's only when they're halfway home that Jason realizes Matt's carrying a bag full of food, ripped from the tight grip of a dead man's hand.

"How was it out there today?" Jen asks when they get back. The two men exchange glances.

"It was okay, actually," Matt says. "About what I expected. A lot easier now I'm on the right side of the city wall."

"That's good," she says, and she looks relieved. "I was worried. I don't like the idea of either of you being out there."

"Needs must," Jason says.

"We've got to eat," Matt adds, and there's so much else he could say, but he doesn't. He doesn't tell her about the fighting or the bodies or any of what they've been through. Right now, he thinks, she doesn't need to know. He thinks she's already been through enough.

10

They don't agree on much, but both men know they have to go back out again next morning. Jason needs food, Matt needs to recce the camp. It's shaping up to be another sweltering, cloudless day and as soon as they're awake and dressed, Jason and Matt are back out.

The roof of the City Arena comes into view a short distance ahead, looming over the other buildings, the curve of its roof glinting in the rapidly rising sun. Matt heads straight for it. He wants to see as much of the camp as he can today. "I got caught napping yesterday," he says, angry with himself.

There are people here in absolutely staggering numbers this morning, and still more are being herded into the camp. "It's always like this first thing. Most new arrivals come in overnight," Jason tells him.

Matt bites his tongue and doesn't react when a kid barges into him and almost knocks him flying. He looks for the little shit in the crowds but is distracted by the state of the fancy new swimming baths the council opened here a year or so ago. It's a trendy, modern-looking, angular glass and metal building with floor-to-ceiling windows at the front and a first-floor gym. There's no exercising going on in there today, though. There are people all over the cross-trainers and treadmills and spinning machines, but no one's using them to keep fit. They're just there for folks to sit on or lean against. There are dour-looking children with their faces pressed up against the glass, gazing out over the sun-baked masses with empty eyes.

"We've just got to remember that this is all temporary," Jason says when Matt catches up with him again. "Okay, so it's all a bit shitty right now, but the most important thing is keeping the outside out like we saw yesterday. We can put up with all this crap because it's short-term, know what I mean?"

Matt's not convinced, but there's no point arguing. They round the next corner, then stop. The approach to the City Arena is a single, endless, unmoving mass of people. "Fuck me. This is the queue?"

"No, mate, this is the queue for the queue. I told you, it's always like this first thing. The lines move faster than you think."

"Unless the Haters turn up."

"They won't, not here."

"And you can guarantee that, can you?"

Jason doesn't bother to reply.

Up ahead, an advertising billboard has been covered over white, with black paint used to display key messages. It looks disturbingly amateurish: the letters are smaller and cramped together toward the far side of the sign.

FOOD AVAILABLE
OPEN 24 HOURS—7 DAYS
ONE PACK PER PERSON PER DAY
NO TROUBLE—ARMED GUARDS

They join the end of the line and wait. Already there are many more people queuing behind them. Matt lasts less than twenty minutes. "I can't do this," he says.

"Can't do what?"

"Stand here like this. We're sitting ducks. You remember what happened yesterday, don't you?"

"Yeah, but it won't happen here. They'd have to get through the whole bloody CDF first."

Matt's unconvinced. He's hemmed in, and he knows the longer he's stuck here standing shoulder to shoulder, the more chance there is he'll crack. There are soldiers looking down from forklift lifting platform watchtowers, adding to the pressure.

"What's going on over there?" he asks Jason, keen for a way out.

"Where?"

He points way over to the right, over the heads of the crowds and out toward another complex which looks busy but far less congested than the grounds of the arena.

"It's where you sign up for work."

"I'm going to check it out."

"Don't be an idiot."

"I told you, I'm not going to stand here and wait for another attack."

"And I told you, it won't happen. It's different here."

"Yeah, right."

"We need food, Matt. We can't go home without food."

But Matt's not listening.

The building Matt's approaching is an odd-looking affair. He remembers it being built: some kind of trendy experimental school paid for by a local university, all the latest facilities and technologies for a select few kids. There are queues here too (there are queues everywhere), but the numbers heading into this place are considerably lower than around the arena. Times are changing, that much is true more than ever today, but some constants remain. The reason for the diminished crowds is obvious—a single four-letter word which has been splashed in thick black paint across the whitewashed front wall of the building, right above the main entrance: WORK.

Nothing to lose.

If Matt's objective this morning is to get to know the camp better, then this seems the logical way of doing it. He joins the back of the line and is inside the building in no time at all. The shade is a relief but the sudden change in brightness and the multidirectional movement indoors makes it difficult for him to see. A woman manning one of several barriers starts asking questions, and for a second Matt doesn't even realize it's him she's talking to. "I said what's your name? Come on, I haven't got all day."

I bet you have, he thinks but doesn't say. Instead he gives her his name and the frazzled-looking woman consults an ancient-looking laptop. She waits, taps a few more keys, scowls, waits a little longer, then looks up again.

"You physically fit?"

"In my prime," he says. He's being sarcastic, but it also happens to be true. He's in the best physical condition he's been in a long time as a result of his prolonged stay out in the wilderness.

"Whatever," she grunts, unimpressed. "Any military or security experience?"

"None."

"Any medical training?"

"Nope.

"Any problems with manual handling?"

"No, nothing."

She hands him a card with his name and the date and time written on. "Take this through there," she tells him, and he does as he's told. He's fascinated by the limited information on the card (*I didn't even know it was Thursday today. Who knew it was May already?*) and he allows himself to go with the flow.

The main part of the school building is a lofty atrium, three stories high. Large glass sections in the roof let the open space flood with natural light, and the size of the atrium makes the combined sound of hundreds of people dissipate to a bearable level.

There are numerous chunky tables and benches laid out in lines filling the center of the floor space, each of them manned by exhausted-looking administrators where previously there would have been kids eating, studying, and socializing. There are belt barriers like he remembers from banks and stores and airport security lines controlling the flow and funneling people. While he's waiting in line he tries to work out the lay of the land. There's an increased military presence here but no immediately visible threat, and the school's in close proximity to both the military hub and the main food distribution point. Soldiers block the wide staircases on either side, carefully controlling the access to the higher levels. Matt doesn't know what you need to have on your card to get you upstairs, but he's damn sure his basic credentials won't wash. He's connecting the dots when the guy behind him (who's clearly picked up on the fact that Matt's been gawping for some time now) confirms his suspicions. "I know, right?" he whispers. "Makes you sick, don't it?"

"Does it?"

"Top-floor fuckers. How the other half live, eh? Doesn't matter how shitty things get, there's always someone ready to cream off the rewards while ordinary folk like you and me suffer."

"Sorry, I've not been here long . . ."

"Give 'em a fucking badge and they think it makes them more important than you. The chiefs are up there, for all the frigging good they're doing. No mixing with the likes of us."

"Nothing changes, eh?" Matt says, trying to keep a lid on the other man's barely contained contempt.

"Frigging Jenna Holbrook. I've never even seen her. Wouldn't know what she even looks like, if she even exists."

"Who?"

"Boss lady," he says, pointing upstairs. Matt vaguely remembers the name from the leaflet he was given when he first arrived at the camp.

"Ah, right."

"Bet she don't have to get her hands dirty just to get fed."

Matt's relieved when someone else starts shouting at him. "Next. Come on, for Christ's sake, there are people waiting."

The bloke behind shoves Matt toward an official sitting at one of the tables. He hands Matt a paper form.

"What's this?"

"A disclaimer. Sign it." He gives Matt a pen.

It's a side and a half of fine print. "Can I read it first?"

"Let me paraphrase, save us all the bother. You want food. Work needs doing. You do the work, you get fed. If anything happens and you get hurt or worse, tough shit."

"And if I don't sign?"

"You don't work and you don't eat."

"Come on, man, get a bloody move on," the guy behind Matt says. "What's the worst that can happen? We're all fucked already!"

Matt signs and passes the form back. "Don't know why you're bothering. Not like I'm going to sue you or anything."

"Just a precaution," the man behind the desk says with an insincere grin. "You never know what's 'round the corner these days. Give me your card."

Matt hands his card over and the official stamps it and gestures over toward the far right corner of the massive room. The maze of belt barriers forces him to go in that direction. It's either that or back out to join the sunburned food queues.

The door leads outside to a fenced-off sloping path which, in turn, takes Matt toward a compound about half a mile from the school. The only people walking this route are those who are heading out to work. He realizes where he is when he gets near. This was a council depot—a waste disposal and household recycling site. As he approaches he becomes aware of engine noise. Garbage trucks. A whole bloody fleet of them. He relaxes, because a day collecting rubbish from the overcrowded streets doesn't sound too taxing. He thinks he might have stumbled on a decent enough way to earn a crust and see the sights.

A woman at a gate takes his card from him. "You get it back when you leave," she explains. "Exchange it for food at the arena."

"So I still have to queue up?"

"Yeah, but it's a special queue for workers," she says, and he can't tell if she's being sarcastic or sincere.

Matt's bunched up with twenty or so other people. They're counted out in fives and sixes. He's number three of five—four men and one woman—and his group is sent over to a rumbling old truck on the far side of the depot. There's a grimy-looking guy wearing a high-vis jacket hunched behind the wheel. "You're covering B29 this morning, Smithy," the driver's told. Smithy gestures for the nearest two volunteers to join him up in the cab. Matt and the others are told to climb up and hold on to the back.

Matt doesn't have a clue what he's supposed to be doing here and he watches the others for cues. The lone woman hangs on to the side of the truck next to him. She watches as he screws up his face at the stink and looks for handholds. "First time out?" she asks.

"It's that obvious?"

"Yep."

"I don't know what I'm supposed to be doing."

"Picking up shit. It's not difficult. You've seen the amount of rubbish around here, right? We just fill the truck and dump it. It's not rocket science."

"So where do we dump it?"

"Now that's where the fun starts."

The stench is awful. Some of this crap must have been lying here in the gutter since day one. Matt's learned very quickly that there's no point trying to stay clean. Another bag just split on him, and his trousers are soaked through with bin juice. The refuse has fermented and liquefied over time, and the unexpected heat of the last couple of days makes it a thousand times worse. There are flies and maggots everywhere.

There's a sizable fleet of these trucks operating around the city-camp. Other than the military they're the only vehicles left on the roads, but even these massive machines struggle to get anywhere near the heart of the camp, such is the congestion along the impassable streets. The garbage patrols tend to busy themselves around the outskirts. *Every pile of crap we shift is a pile less to worry about,* says driver and crew manager Smithy, but it's clear this is little more than a token gesture. They're barely scratching the surface.

It didn't take a genius to work out where the rubbish was going to be dumped, but by the time Matt realized, it was too late to bail out. Smithy drives them to a checkpoint on the recently redefined city boundary and waits for a signal. Still hanging on to the back of the truck, arms aching, Matt starts to think maybe Jason had the right idea after all.

There's relative silence out here on the border: far fewer people, and just the clattering rumble of the garbage truck's engine and the buzz of mostly autonomous air traffic disturbing the quiet. The only people Matt can see are CDF. There are spotters on the roofs of empty buildings, watching the wastelands. Another soldier is sitting in the back of a canvas-covered jeep, controlling the drone that's circling overhead like a supersized fly ready to gorge on the refuse they're about to dump. The drone flies one last high-speed loop, racing out beyond the city then hurtling back again, then the buzz and crackle of static from Smithy's radio signifies that they've been given the signal. He puts his foot down and drives at speed. Matt and the others hold on for dear life.

Matt initially assumed that the refugee camp had been based around the geographical center of the city, but that's not the case. Though its built-up urban heart is a definite part of the vast, walled-in space, the bulk of the camp covers an area largely to the southwest of town which was predominantly residential. The exit they're using is at a point near the southernmost tip of the encampment, and they have a military escort for this part of the journey. Another jeep takes the lead, flanked on either side by bikers, with two more jeeps bringing up the rear. They follow what used to be one of the major routes out of town, then take a sudden diversion. Smithy follows the military across a track carved diagonally through the center of a football pitch, then down an improvised slope leading into a tunnel Matt didn't know was here, a remnant of the city's industrial past when railways and waterways connected this place to everywhere else. He must have driven over the top of it a hundred times but never realized. It's suddenly pitch black, and the combined noise of six straining engines echoes and reverberates. A short climb and the convoy bursts back out into the light. The safety of the camp is long gone. Now they're right in the heart of No Man's Land.

What the fuck have I done?

After struggling for so long to get home, Matt can't believe he's already outside the city again. He knew this area reasonably well. Kings Oak. It was a pretty unremarkable place with street after street after street of council houses thrown up after the end of World War II. Now, decades later, the surroundings have been pounded by a second blitzkrieg, and the sights Matt sees are eerily reminiscent of those he remembers from the history books he read at school. There's not a single building left unscathed. There are the footprints of homes, and the occasional half-wall remains upright, but for the most part there's just rubble and ruination. The scale of this destruction is astonishing, and it's made all the more remarkable because he knows this is the result of friendly fire. The area has been intentionally leveled so that any Hater attack will be visible from a distance, and while that's of some reassurance, it also makes him feel remarkably prone hanging off the back of this truck. Collateral damage is par for the course these days.

He can't see any, but he senses there are Haters nearby. He keeps his hands clamped viselike on the truck, because he knows the enemy is never far away. If he was on foot they'd be swarming over him like vultures in no time. Fuckers would rip him to pieces.

Before he can ask how far out they're going, the answer appears on the horizon. A mountain of debris rears up out of nowhere; a frozen tsunami of shite. The lack of any other landmarks makes the scale of the improvised landfill site they're racing toward incalculable. Scavenging birds swoop and dive, feasting on the plentiful pickings with scant regard for any of the dangers which concern Matt and the others. There's a heat-haze distorting his view, and Matt can see that parts of the heap are smoldering. Some sections are burning unchecked. He doesn't suppose it matters. As they near, Matt realizes the gigantic mess isn't as high as he initially thought, but it's incredibly wide. Because there's no specialist equipment other than the garbage trucks, the man-made mountain is spreading out, not growing up.

The truck comes to a sudden, lurching halt in the grubby foothills. "You stay behind that wheel, Smithy," Matt hears one of his colleagues warn their driver. "Don't you move a fucking muscle."

Most of the rest of the crew have done this before, and Matt follows their lead. They disembark then stand back as Smithy reverses his cumbersome vehicle toward the landfill. And then, ponderously slowly, and with enough mechanical noise and hydraulic hissing to alert any Hater within a ten-mile radius, the machine starts to empty. In spite of the danger, Matt's transfixed. It's a bizarre sight, strangely hypnotic. The tailgate and lift bucket at the back of the truck rise up and the hydraulic tank is emptied. An enormous brick of refuse is pushed out, almost like the truck itself is evacuating its metal bowels. The amount of crap the crew managed to collect between them is astonishing. He wonders how many more times they'll have to go through this routine today.

All his earlier worries about the stink and about dirt and dis-ease are long forgotten, because being out here in the wilderness like this, dangerously exposed, is more of a concern than any germ. As the others start to shift the rubbish they've dumped deeper into the site—a token gesture really—Matt feels a ner-vous, prickling fear born from the days, weeks, and months he spent out here alone. Right now he's unprotected and distracted, and it feels wrong. This is a million miles removed from the mea-sured, quiet, and stealthy approach which kept him alive before.

The bottom falls out of a soggy cardboard box he's carrying as he tries to chuck it on the landfill. Fortunately most of the contents are nonperishable, but as it hits the deck he notices little things: kid's toys, ornaments, family photographs . . . how many hundreds of thousands of memories lie scattered here? It's sobering. For a moment it's almost overwhelming. "Keep mov-ing," one of the crew grunts and he barges Matt out of the way to get past. And though Matt does move, he sees something else that roots him to the spot with fear.

The first Haters are here.

The soldiers are aware. They form a protective perimeter around the civilians and Smithy revs the engine of the truck, making sure everyone's alerted to the approaching threat. For a second Matt's worried their driver is about to leave without them.

Matt sees two Haters coming directly at the group. He can't tell if the fastest of them is a man or a woman. Slim. Lithe. Mus-cular. Long hair whips wildly around its face. Arms and legs pump hard until a soldier's single well-aimed bullet brings the killer crashing down.

"Time to go, driver," another one of the CDF fighters yells.

"I'm going as fast as I can," Smithy yells back, but he's not go-ing anywhere just yet. He's waiting for the tailgate of the truck to drop back down into position before the crew can board and get the hell away from here. It's painfully slow.

A second Hater gets closer than the first managed. This one, a teenage boy, is close enough that Matt can see the fury in his eyes before he too is brought down with a hail of bullets.

Three more incoming.

The next group approaches from over the top of the landfill. The fastest of them thunders down toward the truck and its crew. The Hater's hunger for the kill is such that the closer he gets, the harder it is for him to coordinate his movements. Each heavy footstep causes mini-avalanches of rubbish to fall, threatening to turn into a single, grime-filled downward surge. Another round of automatic gunfire brings all three of the monsters crashing down the slope together. One of them rolls over and over, eventually coming to rest in a heap several meters in front of Smithy's truck. But she's not done for yet and despite the fact her legs are now useless, she reaches out and drags herself forward.

The truck's tailgate finally locks into place with the long-overdue clunk of metal on metal and a satisfying hydraulic hiss of relief. Matt starts toward the vehicle but another man puts an arm out and holds him back. "Wait," he warns, and Smithy slams the truck into gear and rolls it forward, crushing the pelvis of the Hater woman still writhing on the ground.

"Right, now move," the other man orders, and Matt jumps up onto the back of the vehicle. From his elevated position he can see even more Haters coming, racing across the wasteland. Most of them are still a fair distance away, but there are several dangerously close and more now approaching by car. A Hater woman is standing in front of the slow-moving garbage truck like she's playing chicken, shimmying left and right. Distracted, she fails to notice the army jeep which drives right across the face of the advancing truck, instantly wiping her out. The CDF fighter behind the wheel sticks his hand out the window and gives the signal. He turns his jeep around in a tight circle and leads the convoy back toward the camp.

As they disappear down into the tunnel again, Matt sees that there are more soldiers up top. Many more. He looks back over his shoulder as the pursuing Haters are attacked with heavy artillery, pounding them into oblivion. He almost wishes he could stop and watch.

The fear fades. The relief is a high; an intoxicating adrenaline buzz. Matt's under no illusion—this was just a simple garbage run, insignificant in the grand scheme of things—but for a moment just now he was out in the open, no longer hiding, fighting back against the Haters. He threw no punches himself, but it still felt like he was the one hitting out.

It's good to be home.

The second run of the day is a far more straightforward affair. Matt's told by Mark Coles, the man who stopped him walking into the path of the truck earlier, that the morning's massacre was the exception rather than the norm. Second time around there's no trouble and no Haters, and by mid-afternoon it's job done. There's been no letup in the baking heat, but Matt's getting used to the temperature and the noxious stink and, he has to admit, he's enjoying the work. The physicality is strangely therapeutic. Cathartic. Lots of effort and noise when for so long he's been used to micro-movements and enforced quiet. And not only that, witnessing the slaughter of Haters is always an unexpected bonus. It was a glorious thing seeing them being hacked down like that.

The garbage truck crew stop near a patch of scrubland to catch their breath and rinse off. It's relatively quiet out here on the very edge of the camp, like another world. There's a stream here and they strip to their underwear and wash themselves down. It's a relief to be free from the sweat and grime, and the icy water is refreshing. Apparently ready for anything, Smithy has a few spare T-shirts in his cab. He throws one across to Matt. "Bring a change of clothes if you're coming out with me again tomorrow," he says before adding under his breath, "frigging newbie."

There's no urgency to get back. Once they've cleaned up, the crew relax for a while. In this grubby little oasis they're almost able to convince themselves nothing's wrong and the world hasn't fallen apart. It's only the noise of frequent CDF excursions to hold back the Haters that shatters the illusion.

Smithy disappears back into the cab of his truck and emerges with a six-pack of beer and some half-hitched food.

"Fuck me, Smithy," someone says. "You little beauty!"

The drinks are handed around and Matt drains his quick. Too quick. It's weak, supermarket-brand lager but it's the first alcohol he's had in a long time and it goes straight to his head. It's a warm, nostalgic feeling that's as good as he remembers.

They doze and daydream for another hour or so before heading back to the depot. Smithy hands out work permits for tomorrow, then sends them off to collect their pay. As promised, the workers get their own queue. Matt feels like a conquering hero as he's handed a bag of tins and packets of food. "Keep it safe," he's told. "Plenty of fuckers in here who'll rip your arms off for that lot."

11

East Kent Road is more crowded than when he left this morning, and Matt clutches his provisions close to his chest. He can't wait to see Jen's face when she sees what he's brought home. He resists the temptation to look at his stash until he's back, but the second he's through the door he empties it out onto the kitchen table. "Look at this lot," he says. She screws up her face.

"What's that stink?"

"I've been shifting rubbish all day." He moves toward her but she backs away. "It's okay, I've had a wash."

"Well, you need another one. You're not coming anywhere near me smelling like that. Get those clothes off, Matt. You might as well throw them straight out."

"But these are my best jeans."

"You should have thought of that."

"I didn't know what I was going to be doing."

"Not my problem. Get cleaned up, love. You can be such a dick at times."

"That's why you love me."

"Is that right?"

The heat of the day is still strong. Matt stands at the door into the back garden and strips. "Anyway, did you see the stuff I got us? I left it on the table."

Jen's poking through the tins and boxes. She finds a packet of ginger nut biscuits. "Love these," she says excitedly. She screws her nose up when she finds a can of caffeine-heavy energy drink. "This stuff's bad for you. Rots your teeth and screws with your brain."

"They gave it to me in a bag. I didn't choose it."

"Horrible nasty stuff."

The floorboards in the spare room above the kitchen creak. Matt looks up. "Jason's back?"

"He's been back ages."

"Did he get a lot of stuff?"

"Just a bit less than you did. He said you'd volunteered for work. Is it really worth the extra effort, love? The extra risk?"

"I think so."

"Well, I don't. You've got responsibilities, Matt. We need to make sure everything's okay here before you start worrying about anything else."

"It doesn't work like that anymore, Jen."

"Well maybe it should."

Matt's half-naked in the doorway still when Mrs. Walker enters. She's embarrassed when she sees him and makes her excuses. "It's okay," he tells her. "My fault. I keep forgetting we've got company. I shouldn't be getting changed in the kitchen."

One of the children screams out from the lounge. Mrs. Walker grips the worktop and drops her head.

"Tough day with them?" Matt asks.

"Every day's a tough day. I know it's hard for all of us right now, but try explaining it to them." There's an awkward silence.

An almost silence. The sounds of the kids bickering echo through the house. "Sorry about the noise."

"It's okay," Jen reassures her.

"Wait, I got some food," Matt says, covering himself up with a towel and moving back toward the table. "Do they like Red Bull?"

"They're a bit young. I'll have it, though, if it's going spare."

"Help yourself," he says, and he hands her the drink then sorts through for more things the kids might like.

"Can you really spare all this? I didn't come in here to scrounge."

"It's fine," he answers quickly. "Honest, take it. Enjoy it."

"Thank you," she says. "This should keep them quiet for a few minutes at least."

Once she's left the room, Jen wraps her arms around Matt and kisses him on the cheek. "That was nice. You're a good man." Matt's head is filled with images of battles and bodies, of the people he's let die so that he could survive. He doesn't feel like a good man. "You'll still need a good hosing down before you even think about getting into bed, though," she adds.

He's about to say something when Jason appears. Matt's starting to think he won't get a second on his own with Jen tonight. He goes back outside to wash again and Jason follows. "So what did they have you doing then, boss?" he asks.

"Dumping rubbish."

He shakes his head. "Mug's game, mate."

"I quite enjoyed it, to be honest."

"Made a difference, did you? Are the streets sparkling clean in some corner of this magnificent city?"

"Don't take the piss. Someone's got to do it."

"Yeah, but like I said earlier, it doesn't have to be you. Let someone else take care of it."

"If we all had that attitude, then—"

"Then what? You going to start lecturing me about how things would fall apart and society would crumble etcetera etcetera? I've got news for you, sunshine, it's already gone and happened."

"I get that. I've seen a hell of a lot more of it than you have, remember?"

"So you keep telling me, but it don't make sense. I brought home almost as much stuff as you did today. If you know how shit it is out there, why d'you keep risking your neck?"

"Because I need to know what's happening. I don't want to get caught napping."

"Bull."

"It's not. I don't want to just stand in line, day after day. You don't know how it felt being out there today and actually doing something positive. To be honest, I can't wait to go back out again tomorrow. Yeah, so it's a little more dangerous the way I do things, but it's making a difference."

"Who to? The masses out there or the people in this house?"

"Both. I keep telling you, we need to stay one step ahead."

"And you reckon you can learn more about what's happening from the back of a garbage truck at the end of some street or other than I can waiting in the food lines, right in the center of the camp?"

"Yes."

"I don't buy it."

"I don't care."

"You need to consider where your priorities lie."

"I don't have to explain myself to you."

"No, but I'm the one who'll have to explain it to your missus when you get yourself killed."

And with that, he's gone.

12

Matt reports for work again next day just the same. He doesn't make it as far as Smithy's crew this time, instead he's diverted with about fifteen other volunteers to a line of three tatty flatbed trucks, a different kind of cleanup crew. Although not built for speed, they're more maneuverable than Smithy's garbage truck. Not that it matters, because he overhears someone saying they're not going outside the city walls. Instead, they're going to Catthorpe Park—a mile-square patch of green in an otherwise heavily built-up part of the city-camp, close to the eastern border.

The roads here are more congested than ever, and it's stopstart all the way until the truck reaches the park. The entrance has been blocked off with just one way in and out as far as Matt can see. It's being guarded by what appears to be a whole squadron of heavily armed CDF soldiers. There's a solid line of them, all impervious in black with their faces hidden. On the orders of their commanding officer they break ranks to allow the vehicles through.

There are even more of the military inside the park, although there's less uniformity about these fighters. As well as not being so well equipped, they also appear less physically fit. If there were minimum height, weight, and age restrictions for signing up before this war, then those rules have almost certainly been scrapped now because if this is a battalion, then it's the most poorly regimented unit Matt's ever seen. If it wasn't for their ill-fitting fatigues, he wouldn't have known they were soldiers at all. Jason said something about people volunteering to fight for food (or just for the hell of it)—these men and woman must be the new recruits. They put the *civilian* into the *Civilian Defense Force*. Untrained, part-time soldiers who've been drafted into a full-time war.

There's plenty of work for the garbage crews here, of that there's no doubt. Even from a distance Matt sees that there's barely any grass visible through a layer of debris . . . what the hell happened? It's like how he imagines the Glastonbury Festival farm used to look on the day after the music stopped playing: grass dead and churned, rubbish everywhere. Empty tents and shelters. Scattered sleeping bags and blankets. Discarded possessions. There's no sign of civilian life, though. Everyone's gone.

As the trucks queue to gain access, Matt overhears talk of another Hater attack on the border being successfully repelled, and he hears a group of CDF fighters enthusiastically and graphically recount last night's battle in bloody detail. Hundreds of Haters killed, by all accounts. *Hundreds*.

The fighting has clearly had a profound effect on some of the volunteer fighters. For every regular soldier sharing bragging stories about the action they saw and the kills they scored, there are many others who are staring into space like the walking dead: vacant and lost, exhausted or traumatized, or both.

But if this place was as full of refugees as everywhere else, where are they? The park is empty save for the troops.

The trucks drive into the heart of the park, pulling up next to more soldiers. The camp boundary cuts across the space about a hundred meters farther from where they stop. The garbage crews unload and are handed facemasks and paper-thin hazmat suits. Matt takes his and puts it on alongside everyone else. The officer in charge looks exhausted, old beyond his years. "This whole area needs to be cleared," he says. "Get everything dumped on the other side of the wall. We've got a couple of hours before this space is opened up to civilians again, so get moving." As an afterthought, he adds a less than sincere "please."

Simple, Matt thinks. He's almost looking forward to the challenge. All around him white-suited figures start clearing the ground.

But here are the dead.

Once seen, they can't be unseen. They're everywhere, mixed with the detritus left behind. There are scores of them, and the harder Matt looks, the more he finds. Many have been crushed and trodden into the ground. One poor fucker has a caterpillar track imprint across the small of his back. Nearby, buried under a collapsed shelter, a young woman's corpse is contorted, arms and legs everywhere like she's still trying to fight off a long-gone attacker, her face frozen in an expression of wide-eyed terror. Other corpses appear remarkably unscathed, almost as if they've slept right through the chaos and simply failed to wake up.

It's not the first time Matt's had to deal with dead bodies. He finds it grim yet disarmingly easy. You just have to think about them as anything but human, he tells himself. This guy here, he looked Somali, and he has a kid of similar ethnicity tucked up alongside him. Doesn't matter. Can't think about who they were and what they meant to each other, they're just meat to be moved. That dead lady there, she looks like Rachel Green, a girl he used to know from college. Can't think about that, either. An old couple, wrapped in each other's arms in a final embrace . . . they're just cold neighbors now, no longer any other ties between them. After piling up the first few cadavers on the back of one of the flatbed trucks it all starts to feel routine, and Matt becomes disrespectfully dismissive. He opts to shift the thin ones before tackling the fat ones, leaving the bulk for someone else to deal with, and he avoids those that are particularly messed-up.

"You two, with me," a soldier orders, pointing in Matt's general direction. Matt looks around, but there's no question it's him and another guy nearby that the officer is talking to. "Come on, for fuck's sake," the soldier yells. "Get on the back of this truck. Now!"

Matt climbs up and perches on the edge of the flatbed piled high with the dead. The soldier gets behind the wheel and drives out toward the city wall, then exits the camp through a gap Matt hadn't noticed until now. More rubbish-strewn parkland stretches out ahead of them, a space more than double the size of the area the volunteers are working to clear. On the far side of this second patch of land, another towering wall. The man sitting opposite Matt pulls down his facemask and shouts across to Matt. "I never knew there were two walls."

Matt's seen this before. "There aren't," he shouts back, and he gestures toward a ragged breach in the second barrier they're approaching. "The Haters must have broken through again."

"You think?"

"No question." He nods back in the direction from which they've just come. "That's a new wall. Those fuckers have taken another chunk out of the camp."

Out beyond the camp's original perimeter, the devastation continues for as far as they can see. A couple of rough tracks have been hewn through the chaos, but there's otherwise been no obvious attempt to reclaim the land. The trucks go back and forth, transporting the bodies and dumping them in a pit that looks like it's been blasted from the ground with munitions for this very purpose. Then they're torched. Smoke, flames, and heat-haze billow up over the wasteland.

By the end of this day, Matt's done. He's seen enough to know what's happening here. He's spent a long, sweat- and blood-soaked afternoon shifting corpses, and he's physically and emotionally beat. The guy he's working alongside, however, is inappropriately chipper now the day's work is done. "Earned our crust today, mate, eh?" he says as they strip out of their hazmat suits and burn them. They're at the gates to the park which have just been reopened. Already people are flooding in, desperate to find a little more space than they had previously.

"Yeah," Matt sighs, "but at what cost?"

"Hundreds of Haters must have been killed."

"Hundreds of our people were killed."

"Christ, you're a proper ray of sunshine, ain't you?"

Matt stops himself reacting. He walks away, then turns back, deciding the words sitting on the tip of his tongue can't be left unspoken. "Don't you see what's happening here?"

"Yeah, we're beating back the Haters again and again."

"No, they're taking chunk after chunk out of the camp, and they'll keep doing it until we can't move. Every last one of us will have our backs against the wall."

"You credit them with too much intelligence, pal."

"But they *are* intelligent. They're like us. They *are* us. You don't credit them with enough intelligence."

"Sympathizer, are you?" he sneers.

"No, a realist."

13

Each day there are more people in the camp, and more in East Kent Road and the surrounding streets. Matt uses their numbers as a tide mark, measuring the human flood levels. But what's unclear is whether there are still more people coming in, or if it's because the size of the camp is reducing? He knows what's happening near the border, so now he needs to understand what his options are closer to home. Reluctantly he decides the only way he'll be able to know for sure is by spending some time around the City Arena and he agrees to queue with Jason. Two birds, one stone. If nothing else, it'll get Jason off his back for a while and stop him asking questions.

But Christ, it's hard doing nothing.

Matt's going out of his mind here. Inactivity, he's discovered this morning, is worse than activity. He's finding this harder than being on the other side of the city walls. Sure, one misstep out in the wilderness could have been the end of him, but while the danger's nowhere near as immediate in here, there's no question this is a similarly fragile and fractious environment. "What's the matter with you?" Jason asks, picking up on Matt's obvious unease. "Fuck's sake, chill out."

Matt bites his tongue and tries to focus on something pointless and insignificant to clear his mind. But in focusing on nothing, he momentarily forgets about everything, and when the queue shuffles forward, he doesn't. A less than impressed guy behind gives him a gentle shove, and that causes him to trip into the back of the person standing in front.

"That's what I can't deal with," he admits to Jason. "There's no space. No escape."

"Get used to it," Jason tells him.

The view from here is familiar. They're close to the school building where Matt previously found work. He's tempted to head back over there now. There might be something he can do that's less physical, something that'll play to his prewar clerical skills. As dull as it sounds, that place is the administrative hub of the camp, and that'll make it as good a place as any for getting a handle on the scale of the problems they're facing here. He remembers when getting his tie caught in the confidential waste shredder was the biggest physical threat he faced, but he knows those days are gone now. He's no longer the quiet office-jockey he used to be.

"How long have we been here?" he asks.

"About three hours."

"And how long do you usually have to wait?"

"All day."

"And has it always been like this?"

"Pretty much."

"Have you seen where they bring the food in?"

"No."

"Do they drive it in, air drop it in . . . ?"

"How the hell am I supposed to know? Fuck's sake, what's with all the questions?"

"Just trying to understand."

"What's to understand? There's a war going on and food's in short supply. We take what we're given, and we have to wait in line for it."

"Yeah, but how long are the lines? How many lines are there? How much food's coming in and where's it going? How much ends up in that school over there for the top dogs and how much—"

"Do me a favor and shut the fuck up, Matt," Jason interrupts. "You're doing my head in."

"I just don't know how you can stand there and not ask all these questions."

"Who says I haven't been asking questions? Has it occurred to you we just might not be able to find the answers?"

"That's crap. You just need to—"

Matt stops talking. His sudden silence unnerves Jason. "What's the matter?"

"Shh . . ."

He hears it and feels it before he sees it. There's a change in the air, a sudden shift. He looks around but all he sees is people in every direction.

And then it begins. A swell of movement. It emanates from somewhere way behind them and ripples out through the crowd, reactions increasing in strength as more and more people become affected. Matt's pulse is racing. He knows that even if whatever what's happening proves to be relatively minor, the implications in this fractious, tinder-dry environment are potentially vast.

"We need to get out of here," he says to Jason.

"We can't. We'll lose our place in line."

"We might lose a lot more than that yet . . ."

Jason grabs his arm. "Pull yourself together. Shit like this happens all the time. Walk away now and you'll never get any food today."

Matt wrestles himself free and starts to cut across the queues, moving toward the school building. More people are beginning to realize that there's a disturbance and are reacting now, and a sudden shift in the crowd allows him to slip through a slender strip of space which opens up between one group of people and the next. This part of the crowd has gone from well-ordered to frantic and chaotic in a frighteningly short space of time. Matt reaches the low brick wall which separates the school grounds from everything else and he vaults over it into a car park, then immediately crouches down for cover. Huge numbers of CDF fighters are beginning to pour out of the building in response to the crowd disturbance and are pushing their way through the masses toward the back of the food queues.

People are panicking. Others are doing everything they can not to panic, standing their ground and refusing to give up their places in line. Matt, on the other hand, isn't yet ready to react. He doesn't know enough about what's happening. Instead he looks for a better vantage point and as more people begin running for cover in response to the soldiers' arrival, Matt uses the back of a CDF truck to climb up into the low-hanging branches of a large pine tree. What he sees is fucking terrifying. It's also completely fucking impossible.

There's a solitary Hater, on the fringes of the food queues but right in the heart of the Unchanged camp.

For a moment Matt thinks it might just be a regular person who's lost control, but the unbridled savagery of the man he's now watching leaves him in no doubt that he's one of the enemy. All around him people scatter and run for cover, tripping over one another to get away. The Hater grabs straggler after straggler, killing like his own life depends on it.

This makes no fucking sense. How could this Hater have made it so deep into Unchanged territory? Surely he wouldn't have been able to make it past even one refugee before striking out? The Hate which drives him and his kind is instinctive and guttural. Haters lose all control when they're near to the Unchanged . . . they can't stop themselves. Matt looks for the telltale trail of devastation marking the route he took here, but there's nothing there. It's like this bastard has been dropped into the refugee camp from nowhere.

The killer is of average build, but what he lacks in physical presence he more than compensates for in sheer ferocity. Matt watches helpless as he grabs a young woman by her hair and viciously beats her. It's a sign of the crowd's collective fear of the Hater that despite their massive numerical advantage, they keep their distance. There's an ever-growing bubble of blood-spattered space around him. People frantically back away but can only get so far before they're bunched up against others trying to escape. They jostle for position, each of them doing everything they can to ensure they're not the Hater's next kill at the expense of whoever's around them. Bizarrely oblivious to everything, the monster continues to fight like nothing else matters.

The soldiers and militia fighters are closing in now—an arrowhead of black and gray uniforms slicing through the masses, and then a tank—*a fucking tank!*—trundles out of the shadows from behind the school building.

The Hater keeps battling like his life depends on it. He lunges for a teenage kid who's fallen in the confusion, dragging him back across the ground by his left boot, then drops on him like a pro wrestler before forcing a shiv up into the nape of his neck.

Matt doesn't want to look away, doesn't want to let the vile creature below out of his sight for even a second, but he forces himself to do so because he knows he surely can't be working alone, can he? Matt fears this must inevitably be the beginning of a coordinated attack, something of a magnitude which will dwarf the recent border battles.

Before the CDF fighters are close enough to open fire, the Hater is brought down by a single shot to the back of the head. It comes from the opposite direction to the advancing militia. A sniper? Matt immediately switches focus, desperately searching for the source of the shot, but it's hard because there's pandemonium down at ground level now, people scattering as the soldiers surge with renewed speed.

He sees something. It's the kind of behavior that sticks out a mile when you've spent weeks living on your nerves out in Hater territory and you're as mistrusting as he now is. You learn to not follow the herd, and the man he's spotted is doing exactly that. He moves with a definite purpose and appears deceptively calm as he heads toward the dead Hater, not away from him. There's no panic as he weaves in and around the fleeing crowds. He's in uniform—definitely military but equally definitely not part of the CDF faction based here. Is he Special Forces (if such a thing still exists)? A lone-wolf vigilante? Matt has no doubt that he's the one who fired the killer shot. He reaches the dead man's corpse, checking his job's done and at the same time confirming Matt's suspicions, then turns tail. Now he pushes people out of the way with mix of arrogance and aggression.

If one Hater can find a way in, who's to say there aren't others close behind? Matt has to know what this assassin is planning next.

He jumps down from the tree and follows his target at a cautious distance: close enough to keep him in sight, yet far enough back not to arouse suspicion. The soldier's easy to follow, because his movements are at odds with everyone else's. To the untrained eye he's just another face in the crowd, but Matt sees straight through him. He's trying too hard to go unnoticed. Occasionally he stops and feigns interest in something, or goes to change direction, then doubles back and goes the other way. He's using all the tricks in Matt's self-taught guide to staying alive.

A garbage truck crosses the road immediately in front of Matt, halting his progress temporarily. He slips around the back of the vehicle then pushes his way through a throng of people coming the other way. When he's finally in open space again he sees that the solitary soldier has gone. He runs toward a pile of discarded scrap which he scales like a parkour champ. He jumps across onto the roof of a car which, judging from the state of its four flat tires, hasn't moved in months, and gets a torrent of shouted abuse from a grimy-looking old woman who'd been asleep on the backseat. He ignores her tirade and concentrates on trying to find the missing soldier but it's no use. Nothing. He's long gone.

Matt continues farther down the road. He hasn't passed any turnings, so the soldier must have gone this way. Matt knows this part of town, but it looks very different to how he remembers, as if someone's taken a picture of the old world and processed it through a particularly shitty filter. There's a row of shops that were boarded up even before the fighting started, and a children's playground and small park filled with the obligatory mass of tents and cardboard shelters.

The soldier steps out in front of Matt, grabs him by the collar, and drags him into a dark corner around the side of the vacant shops, out of sight of just about everyone and everything else. There are a couple of kids lurking in the shadows but they scuttle away like beetles when they're disturbed. Matt's furious with himself. If this fucker had been a Hater, Matt would be a dead man now.

The man's face is inches from Matt's. "Why are you following me?"

"I wasn't . . ."

"Bullshit. Don't treat me like an idiot."

"I don't know what you're talking about."

The soldier slams Matt back against the wall and his whole body rattles with pain.

"Cut the crap. I clocked you when you were up your fucking tree. You might think you're smart, but you're an amateur, mate. Fucking clueless."

"So what if I was following you?"

"Now we're getting somewhere. Why me?"

"Because you shot a Hater in the back of the head just now."

He laughs. "A Hater? Get a grip."

"The CDF were way back. You took that fucker out."

"Did you fall out of that tree and hit your head?"

"Fuck you. There was a Hater attack right outside the school just now, and I think you know something about it. Most people ran away, you moved toward it."

"What exactly are you saying? You think I keep a pet killer and it got off its leash and escaped into the middle of the camp?"

"You and I both know that unless it crawled up through the sewers or was parachuted in, that bastard could never have got so deep into town without help."

"I don't know what you're talking about."

"I think you do. I know what I saw."

The soldier's had enough. He tightens his grip on Matt's collar again and drags him back out into the open. Matt's at a massive physical disadvantage. He's skinny as a rake, but the militiaman is stocky and strong, clearly well-fed. He's in far better condition that the majority of the other refugees in the camp. The perks of position? Whatever the reason, Matt knows the odds are stacked against him. He'd shout for help if he wasn't being choked, but he doubts anyone would risk getting involved. His best option is to play ball. He stops fighting and is marched along the street toward a black metal gate in a long and high, redbrick wall.

The soldier kicks the bottom of the gate with his boot and shouts to be admitted. "It's Franklin. Let me in."

14

Matt's hauled into an enclosed compound and dropped to the ground. There's movement all around him and by the time he's picked himself up he's surrounded by three more armed CDF fighters. Matt looks back over his shoulder, thinking he might still have a chance if he makes a run for the gate, but all he can do is watch as another militiaman slides it shut. A fifth man is blocking his way through.

"Look, I'm sorry . . ." he starts to say, figuring that aggression's not an option and that to resort to meekness is probably his best bet. "I don't want any trouble. Just let me go and I'll disappear. You won't hear anything else from me."

"What's up with this runt, Franklin?" one of the other soldiers asks.

"Nosy fucker, this one."

Matt tries to look past the weapons pointing at him and assess his surroundings. It's become second nature to look for another way out, an instinct born from nine weeks spent trying to stay alive. But all he can see right now is rifles, soldiers, and brick walls. Apart from the locked gate there are no obvious exits. A plaque on a nearby wall proudly proclaims "Steply Territorial Army Center."

A door opens with a creak and clatter on the far side of the courtyard. A woman dressed in full fatigues appears and marches over. She doesn't look at Matt; instead, the focus of her ire is Franklin. "What the hell's going on?" she demands. Matt risks looking and sees that she's older than he thought. Mid-fifties, perhaps. Her soft features don't match the brusqueness of her voice. "How did it happen?"

"I told them this was going to happen sooner or later," Franklin answers. "You know what they're like. They don't listen."

"You get back up there as soon as we're done here and you tell them no more fuckups, got it? I'll put a stop to the whole damn program if I have to. Understand?"

"Yes, ma'am."

The female officer is breathing hard, clearly furious. She takes a single step back and pulls on the hem of her tunic to straighten it. Matt watches the ill-tempered conversation as a spectator until she turns to him. He immediately looks down, withering under her glare. "Who's this?"

"A complication, ma'am," Franklin explains. "Tried to follow me back from the site of the incident just now."

"So why's he here?"

"Didn't want him making a nuisance of himself and fucking things up, ma'am."

Matt clears his throat. "Look, I don't know who any of you people are, but—"

Matt's badly timed interruption is brutally truncated by another soldier who threatens him with the butt of his rifle. "Speak when you're spoken to, prick."

"Manners, Mr. Henderson," the officer says. She gestures and Henderson stands down. Matt faces the boss lady. She's a good few inches shorter than he is, yet she seems to tower over him. Her authority is unquestionable. "My name's Estelle Bisseker, and I'm in charge here," she says, fixing him with ice-gray eyes. She pauses, studying his face intently. "Now who exactly are you?"

"I'm nobody."

"I know that much. What's your name and why are you here?"

"I'm Matthew Dunne, and I'm here because there was a Hater attack in the middle of town just now, and I think your man Franklin was involved."

"And why should that concern you?"

"Which bit of what I just said did you not hear? There was a Hater attack in the middle of town."

"I know."

"And that's all you've got to say?"

"That's all I've got to say to you, yes."

Matt's temporarily forgotten about the mess he's in and the guns pointing at him, because he knows the potential threat from just one Hater far exceeds the combined threat of all the Unchanged soldiers here and more besides. "Listen, I understand enough about Hater behavior to know it should never have happened. That thing must have had help getting into the camp, and if you or your people are helping the Haters, then you should be rounded up and shot along with them."

"Is that right?"

"Not that it matters, because if you are helping them, you won't last long anyway."

Estelle laughs. "Helping the Haters! Are you out of your tiny mind?"

"Possibly," he says, disarming her momentarily. Her expression changes.

"I can assure you we're absolutely not helping them. Quite the opposite, actually."

"And you expect me to believe that?"

"I don't expect anything. You can believe whatever you want to believe, I'm not particularly interested either way."

"So let me go."

"What, and risk you going back out into the camp and causing all kinds of panic?"

"I'll only do that if I don't get any answers. So are you going to tell me why the Hater was here?"

She pauses again, enjoying playing with Matt and making him work. "Put your guns down, boys and girls," she eventually says to her troops. "It's really not good for us all to be pointing weapons at each other."

"The weapons were only pointing in one direction," Matt reminds her. "I'm unarmed."

"Whatever, Matthew. The point is, we both have better things to be aiming at."

"What, like crazed killers let loose in the middle of this camp?"

"Yes, exactly like that. So tell me, why are you so interested? The Hater was neutralized before he'd done too much damage. Isn't that all that's important?"

"No, it's not. Wherever there are Haters, death follows. I've seen what they're capable of firsthand. Why was that thing in the city in the first place and are there more of them? That's what important."

Estelle's expression changes slightly. It's subtle, but Matt's becoming increasingly astute at picking up on people's facial expressions and reading their body language. She knows more than she's letting on, he's sure of it. He also knows she's not going to give up her secrets without a fight.

"I'm interested in you, Matthew. What's your background?"

"Accounts," he says without thinking, and she laughs out loud.

"Well then, you've done extremely well to stay alive, my dear little accountant."

"Don't patronize me. I was off the mainland when all of this started. It took me months to get home."

"A born survivor, eh?"

"If you say so."

"And how did you get back?"

"Very slowly. I've only been here a week."

"Fair play to you, that must have taken some guts."

"You believe this shit?" Franklin interrupts. Estelle silences him with a look.

"I think, Mr. Accountant, that you're probably quite a smart cookie. The fact you've made it this far puts you ahead of roughly ninety-nine percent of the residual human population of this city."

"You really expect us to believe he survived on his own out there?" Franklin asks Estelle, still not convinced. He has a look of utter disbelief writ large on his face. *"Him?"*

"Well?" Estelle asks. "How d'you do it?"

"I kept my head down. I moved slowly and only when there were none of them around. I used other people fighting as cover. When everyone else was heading in one direction, I went the other way."

"Go on."

"What more do you want me to say? That's how I tracked him," he continues, nodding at Franklin. "He stuck out like a sore thumb. Everyone else was panicking and running away from the Hater, he was gravitating toward the trouble. He hung back just enough to still see what was going on, but far enough away not to get caught in the cross fire. As soon as it was all over and he was sure he'd done what he'd obviously been sent to do, he got out."

"Very clever," Estelle says. "There's one thing I don't understand, though. If you're so cautious and careful, why risk everything to get back to this cesspit, and why risk following Mr. Franklin just now?"

"I told you, I'm an accountant. Risk is manageable."

"Explain."

"Things will always go wrong, it's about reducing the chances of getting caught up in the shit-storm. I had to come home because my girlfriend's here. I managed to call her when I got back onto the mainland, so I knew she was here. What else was I going to do?"

"And they say true love's dead," Franklin grumbles cynically. "It's enough to make you vomit."

"And I followed you for the same reason," Matt continues, glancing over at him again. "I knew you were trouble, and all I'm bothered about these days is keeping Jen safe. I needed to know what you were up to and why the Hater was here, dead or otherwise. And you still haven't explained."

"Is she all right?" Estelle asks.

"Who?"

"Your girlfriend, who d'you think?"

"She's fine, all things considered."

"Glad to hear it."

"Is every conversation with you this awkward?"

"Awkward? How?"

"The redirections. You're doing everything you can to avoid telling me about the Hater."

"It was a mistake," she says, answering his question without telling him anything useful. She looks over at Franklin, giving the distinct impression that the soldier's in for a dressing-down later. Someone's really fucked up.

"So you admit there's a link between you and the Hater?"

"I'm not admitting anything."

"Let's just get shot of him, Estelle," Franklin suggests. "This little shit won't think twice about—"

Estelle raises her hand, and Franklin immediately shuts up. The authority she wields here is impressive. "We should show Matthew here a little more respect. We are where we are. You did let him follow you back here, after all." She's talking about Matt like he's not there now, and he knows these theatrics are entirely for his benefit. "All we can do is try and convince him that every-thing we're doing is being done with the absolute best of inten-tions so we can bring this war to a swift end."

"The only way you can convince me of that is by telling me what it is you're up to."

"One step at a time."

"He knows too much already," Franklin says.

"And what do you suggest we do with him, dear? Bump him off? Make him disappear? How very cloak-and-dagger of you."

"Don't take the piss."

"Then stop living in the past. Don't be so blinkered. We could do with more people like Matthew onside."

Now Matt's feeling really uncomfortable and he immediately lets her know. "For what it's worth, I think your man here might be right. Just let me go and you won't hear anything from me again. Like I said, all I'm interested in is looking after Jen and making sure we both get through this in one piece."

He starts to move, and several of the guards edge closer. Estelle gestures for them to stand down. "Let's cut the crap and level with each other, shall we? You strike me as a realist."

"I am."

"Then you must know that the odds are stacked against us, that we're all going to struggle to get through this in one piece. Okay, so we're in a relatively secure position at the moment, but nothing lasts forever, does it? You've had to think outside the box to get this far, Matthew, and that's what we're doing, too. We're a military unit, part of the Civil Defense Force, but while most of our colleagues are either dealing with crowd control or going on the offensive, we're fulfilling a different function."

"How so?"

"We're hunting."

"Sounds suicidal if you're hunting Haters."

"We're not looking for trouble, if that's what you're worried about. The precise opposite, actually." She thinks for a second. "Maybe you could help us?"

"You must not have been listening. I'm no fighter. My game plan involves keeping away from the Haters, not running toward them."

"Yes, but we're back to risk management again."

"Are we?"

"I think so. You see, most people make the assumption that the split between the Haters and people like us is as clear as black and white, yes and no."

"It pretty much is from what I've seen."

"And I'll bet you haven't seen as much as you think, no matter how long you spent out in the wilds. There are strong Haters and there are weak Haters, smart Haters and stupid ones, just like us. We're focusing on certain segments of the changed population. When you think about it, there's a world of difference between the vilest Hater and the meekest person like us, but when you get closer to the middle ground, the differences aren't so stark."

"The middle ground?"

"There's not a lot to choose between some of our strongest CDF fighters and those Haters who are less aggressive. If anything, my troops probably have the edge."

Matt's not convinced. "You think?"

"I *know*. Tell me, Matthew, do you enjoy the food queues? Or are you working? I take it you're not volunteering to fight with the CDF, so do you enjoy your time clearing rubbish and bodies?"

"I quit. Too dangerous."

"So what are you going to do now?"

"We've got enough supplies for a few days yet."

"And after that? We could be here for quite some time . . ." She waits for an answer she knows isn't going to come. "Come with me."

Matt follows Estelle across the courtyard to a large, garage-like lockup. Two soldiers open separate locks, then Franklin opens a third. "It's not just you we don't trust," he says. "It's each other, too."

"Serious point," Estelle says as she steps forward and swings the metal door open. "It needs three of us to open this up. It makes sure we all play by the rules."

And Matt can immediately see why. As daylight floods into the long, rectangular building, he sees that there are shelves and shelves of supplies. Tinned food. Bottled water. Guns. Enough weapons to defend the whole bloody camp. "Jesus Christ," he says.

"Quite."

"You steal all this?"

"Depends on your point of view. I prefer acquired, but then again, pretty much all the food in this camp is stolen, if you're going to be pedantic about it. The economy's screwed, but as an accountant you already know that. You can try trading and bartering, but supply is never going to keep up with demand these days. It's all about scavenging now."

"So how did you get such a stash?"

"Because, like I told you, we operate in the places no one else goes. It's a wonderfully helpful by-product of the work we do."

"Care to elaborate?"

"Not today. Come back tomorrow and I might."

"I don't know about this . . ."

"Completely your choice," she says, and she steps into the building and grabs a few items of food and drink. She shoves them into a bag and hands them to him.

"What's this for?"

"A down payment. A peace offering, if you like. I need people to help support my troops, but the choice is entirely yours. You can walk away from here with your food and forget about us and never come back, or you can help. I don't mind either way. For what it's worth, I don't think you'll be able to resist. I think you'll be back, if for no other reason than to make sure we're not going to do anything that'll put the lovely Jen in danger. Am I right?"

"I'll think about it," he says, noncommittal.

"I know you will, Matthew."

15

The food's going down well tonight. It's a welcome distraction from the outside world. Everyone's present for an extended family meal around the kitchen table: Matt, Jen, Jason, and Mrs. Walker and her children. For once Matt's the one trying to keep the conversation flowing, because the gaps between words let the noises from outside in. They can hear Haters being pounded on the other side of the border, mortars and munitions detonating in the distance like fast repeat thunderclaps. Never before have bomb blasts sounded so reassuring.

Mrs. Walker's two children, Sophie and Billy, rarely emerge from the lounge. Both have sunken eyes and hollow expressions and hardly speak when anyone else is about. Sophie barely picks at her meal. Her younger brother is marginally more communicative, occasionally tugging on his mum's sleeve and pulling her closer so he can whisper in her ear.

"Pasta's lovely, Jen," Matt says, and Jason and Mrs. Walker both mumble in agreement, mouths full.

"Thanks. It's just a packet mix sauce. Nothing special."

"A decent meal makes all the difference when you've been out all day," Jason says. Matt resists the temptation to say anything. *A hard day's queuing?* Right now, though, Matt's head is full of other thoughts. Too many of them, if he's honest. He's distracted thinking about the Hater strike near the arena, and by thoughts of Estelle Bisseker, Franklin, and the military compound. He has a million and one questions. No matter how much bullshit and spin they put on it, the fact remains those people are connected to the appearance of a Hater in the center of the camp today. He needs to know why. He needs to know what they're planning next. He knows he has to go back there tomorrow.

"So where did you disappear off to?" Jason asks.

"What?"

"You disappeared and left me to it, remember? Where did you go?"

Matt toys with his food. "You know where I went. I wanted to see what that trouble was."

"What trouble?" Jen asks.

Matt curses himself, wishing he hadn't said anything. "It was nothing. Just someone losing their cool in the crowds. The military had it under control soon enough." He returns his attention to his food, filling his mouth so he doesn't have to keep talking.

Jen glares at him in the candlelight. "I know you too well, Matt. You're not telling me everything."

"There's not a lot else to tell."

"There is. You can stop trying to protect us all the time. We know things are rough out there."

"Honestly, it was just some guy who lost his rag. It's harder than you think, queuing up. It's like a pressure cooker, isn't it?"

Jason looks up from his food. "Oh, yeah, absolutely." He eats another mouthful, then looks across at Matt again. "You still got your rations for the day, though. Pretty good haul, too. How d'you manage that?"

Matt struggles for a believable answer which isn't incriminating. "Right place right time, I guess. Once things calmed down I just found myself near the front of the queue. Didn't plan it, it just happened."

"Lucky."

"Yeah, it was."

Another pause, then another question, this time from Mrs. Walker. "Are we going to be all right here?"

"Of course we are," Jason immediately answers. But Mrs. Walker's looking at Matt.

"What, do you want an honest answer, or just some bullshit to make you feel better?"

"Mind your language, love," Jen says quietly, almost apologetically. "The children don't need to hear that kind of talk."

"It's okay," Mrs. Walker says. "I want you to be honest, Matthew."

Matt wishes that hearing the word *bullshit* was the worst thing these kids are going to have to deal with. He puts down his fork and drinks a little water while he tries to work out what he's going to tell them. "I don't know is the honest answer. A lot of it depends on what happens outside the city, and we've got no control over that."

"I've heard there's been a lot of action out there recently," Jason interrupts, "and I've seen our boys blasting Haters to kingdom come."

"That's true," Matt agrees.

"But . . . ?" Mrs. Walker presses.

"Jason's right, we've seen a lot of Haters killed, but those gains have come at a price. We've seen lots of civilians killed too, and territory has been lost. There are still people coming in through the front gates, so our numbers are increasing while our space reduces, and there's not as much food as there was."

"Sounds like it's a question of time."

"You're right. The Haters have to be wiped out before conditions here become unsustainable."

As if to underline his point, there's an explosion in the distance, violent enough to make the crockery on the table rattle.

"So I'll ask you again," Mrs. Walker says, pulling Sophie closer, "are we going to be all right?"

"Like I said, I don't know. It depends on things that are out of our hands."

Later, Matt takes the Walkers some water. The lounge in which the family have been living is cramped, the musty smell almost overpowering. There's barely room to move in here; the entire floor space is given over to inflatable mattresses and a tangle of sweaty duvets and pillows. It reminds Matt of Stuart and Ruth's overcrowded cottage back on Skek. He feels the same unease today too.

"You didn't have to," Mrs. Walker says, taking the drinks from him. "We're fine."

"You're not fine at all. None of us are."

The children hide behind their mother. "She adores you, you know," she says.

"What?"

"Jen. She thinks the world of you."

"What's she been saying?"

"Nothing. She doesn't have to. It's obvious."

Matt's embarrassed. Awkward. "The feeling's mutual."

"I can see that, too. The fact you're here is proof positive. You must love her very much to have made your way back here the way you did."

"I do."

"I can't imagine what you went through out there on your own."

"I try not to think about it now it's over."

She gently pulls the children out of the shadows but keeps them close. "It hurts when you can't look after the ones who matter most, doesn't it?"

"From what I've seen you're doing absolutely the best job you could do in the circumstances. No question."

"You're a good man, Matthew."

"That's debatable," he replies, his head full of memories.

An awkward pause. "Go back to Jen," she says, and she touches his arm lightly. "Thank you."

"Jason said he's worried about you."

"Jason's worried about *me*?"

"He says you've been under a massive amount of pressure, and that it's bound to have taken its toll."

"And what do you think?"

"You have been through a lot . . ."

"I'm still me, though. Still the same Matt."

She's quiet for a moment, and the hesitation unnerves him.

"You're not the same, though, are you? How could you be? You haven't told me half of what you went through to get home—"

"And I don't want to."

"—but that speaks volumes in itself. We used to share everything."

"I'll tell you if you want, but I don't want to upset you. I could tell you about the people I saw being killed, the times I nearly died, the places I had to go, and the things I had to do . . . but what difference would any of it make?"

Matt puts his arm around her and pulls her closer. Faces almost touching, safe and warm under the duvet. At first she's starchy and unwilling, almost reluctant. He doesn't let go, and after a while she softens.

"I'll keep you safe, Jen, same as I always have. Remember when you got food poisoning when we were in Tenerife? I kept you safe."

She laughs. "You mean you held the sick bowl then got me to the doctor. Great job."

"And when the car broke down when we drove up to Edinburgh?"

"It didn't break down, we ran out of fuel. That was your fault."

"Okay, when we ran out of fuel on the way up to Edinburgh, who kept you safe?"

"It was the middle of the afternoon, I didn't really need keeping safe."

"I know. I'm kidding. I'm just trying to make a point."

"What point?"

"The point that if I have changed, I've changed for the better. All that shit I went through out there, it's made me better equipped to deal with things in here. I'm stronger now. I'll look after you, Jen. No fucker's going to hurt you."

"You never used to swear."

"I know. I live on the edge now."

She laughs again, and he pulls her closer still.

"Seriously, making sure you're safe and getting us both through this in one piece is my sole focus. It's my reason for being. I hated every second of being away from you . . . and now I'm back I . . ."

"What?"

"Come on, Jen, I used to be an accountant. This stuff doesn't come naturally to me."

"Just say what you're thinking."

He clears his throat, feeling more nervous now than when he spent the night hiding on the edge of a Hater camp. "Being apart from you and having to fight to get back here has made me realize you mean even more to me than before. You're everything, Jen. You're my world."

She kisses him. "See, told you you'd changed. You never used to be romantic."

And for the first time in months, with the world outside their door falling apart, they make love.

16

He's hardly slept. This morning what's left of the city is as gray as Matt's mood. A light summer drizzle has been falling for the last half hour, barely noticeable but still heavy enough to soak everything it touches. The road outside the house is marginally quieter, most people doing what they can to stay under cover.

When they reach the end of East Kent Road, Jason goes one way and Matt goes the other. "Where do you think you're going?" Jason asks.

"None of your business. Keep walking. Get into your queue, get your food, and don't say anything to anyone."

"I need to know what you're up to."

"No, you don't."

"This is bullshit. I'll go back in there and tell Jen you're—"

"You'll tell her nothing," Matt says. The calmness of his voice stops Jason in his tracks. "Do what you need to do, and I'll explain later."

"But—"

"Just do it," he orders, and he turns his back on Jason and walks away.

Head down, Matt makes his way through the hordes of refugees, going against the flow. He knows he could be on a hiding to nothing here, that he might be about to risk everything, but he also knows it's a risk he has to take. He has to find out what Franklin and the others are up to. His life and, more importantly, Jen's might depend on what he finds out.

He barely has time to catch his breath before Franklin pushes him toward the back of a battered Transit van. Before he's sat down it races out of the Territorial Army compound at speed, following a snout-nosed military vehicle which aggressively pushes through the crowds.

In the van, introductions are brief and perfunctory.

Behind the wheel is a woman called Jayce. She reminds Matt of Natalie, the girl he knew briefly on Skek. She has the same uncomplicated athleticism and directness. She keeps her focus dead ahead, not making eye contact with him or anyone else.

There are another two men in the back with Matt and Franklin. Chris Greatrex is short and unassuming and constantly chews the ends of his fingers. Matt thinks he looks as unprepared for whatever's coming next as he himself feels. Graham Porter, on the other hand, is muscular and tooled up and seems as keen to face a Hater as Matt is not to.

The uncomfortable silence in the van is a clear signal to Matt that he should keep his mouth shut. Observe, don't ask. The grime on the windows makes it hard to see out, and what's left of the city has changed so much that Matt struggles to work out where they are and in which direction they're traveling. Being under military escort, they're ushered through checkpoints without delay and are soon motoring out through No Man's Land.

Two jeeps from the last checkpoint they passed join the back of the convoy.

Matt catches a glimpse of the stumplike remains of a partially collapsed tower block he recognizes. He knows roughly where he is now. He used to use this road regularly, but where there were buildings on either side, now there's only rubble. The tarmac is a relatively clear gray scar cutting through masonry mountain ranges. This used to be a thriving commuter route, today it's barely a route at all.

"Nervous?" Franklin asks.

Matt shrugs.

"You should be."

"It'd help if you told me what we're doing out here."

Franklin manages a wry grin, enjoying taunting him. "Okay, listen to me."

"You do know how dangerous it is out here?"

"I said listen, don't talk. And yes, I know exactly how dangerous this is. Interrupt me again and I'll kick you out of the van and leave you to walk home, got it?"

Matt thinks he's probably not bluffing. "Got it."

The convoy slows as they approach the outer edge of No Man's Land, the point where the deliberate ruination ends.

"There's a lot that people don't understand about Haters. The vast majority are complete fucking monsters, but it's like Estelle told you yesterday, some of them can't compete."

"You reckon?"

"I *know*. I've seen it, mate. It's fate that's pushed them over to one side and us to the other. For every Hater you see that's a full-on psycho, you can bet there are others who are completely fucking lost. They're all as dangerous as each other if they're cornered, but some of them are as out of their depth as most of the poor fuckers stuck in the camp back there."

"So where are they all?"

"Hiding."

"Hiding! Bullshit."

"Not bullshit. We've hunted out loads of them, hiding like cowards, just waiting for this all to blow over so they can pick up the pieces of what's left of their lives. Thing is, as soon as they see people like us, they're compelled to react, so all you'll ever see is a crazed fucking Hater coming at you and you never get their backstory. We found this old guy a few days back, for example. He was hiding in the house where he used to live with his wife till he did her in. When we turned up, before he realized we weren't like him, he was begging us to go. He was shouting at us to leave him 'cause he didn't want to have to kill anyone."

"So what happened?"

"We kicked his bloody door down and put him out of his misery, obviously. But you get what I'm saying, don't you? So we're mopping up. Getting rid of the stragglers. If we can keep the outskirts of the city clear, the CDF can start pushing outward again when things calm down. We're reclaiming everything they've taken from us."

"You make it sound so easy."

Franklin shakes his head. "It's anything but."

"So where do I come in?"

"We're low on numbers."

"No surprise."

"Don't get me wrong, having you along for the ride wasn't my idea. Estelle's thinking is that if you really did get back here on your own cross-country, then you probably understand more about Hater behaviors than most."

"They kill. What else is there to understand?"

Franklin ignores him. "She's got it into her head that you might be able to help track them down."

"You're saying you're using me as bait."

"That's one way of looking at it."

"And how big is this operation? What kind of backup do you have?"

Franklin laughs. "As if."

"Fuck. There must be others?"

"There used to be. Best not to ask."

"Fuck," Matt says again.

"Look, it's simple. Find us a Hater, then hand over to Chris here."

Chris Greatrex doesn't react in the slightest. He continues to look out of the virtually opaque window, impassive.

"No offense, but he looks about as ready to fight as I am."

"Chris is a runner. Best in the business. Not that there is a business, mind. You get the Hater's attention, then hand over to Chris. He'll draw them out into the open and we'll take care of everything else." The van begins to slow down. Franklin clears a patch of glass and presses his face up against the grubby window. "Right, we're almost there. You ready?"

Matt doesn't think he's ever felt less ready in his life.

He's not sure if he's been down this particular street before, but it feels eerily familiar. He could be anywhere: there were nondescript suburbs like this scattered all around the city. Matt's walking between two rows of Victorian-era terraced houses. Most of the homes in this particular area were used as low-cost, multi-room student housing for the nearby university and medical school, and there are extra windows and doors and poorly designed extensions everywhere which add to the claustrophobia. This place is like a maze. There are no landmarks other than occasional gaps where buildings used to be and crater marks in the tarmac. He'll use the damage as markers to find his way back to the van.

But Christ, it feels wrong to be walking through these uncharted regions of Haterville like he doesn't have a damn care in the world. He knows the others are watching, but that doesn't make him feel a whole lot better. The standard-issue uniform they've given him doesn't help. He's wearing grubby black fatigues with a facemask that smells like someone just peeled it off the corpse of its previous owner. At least the mask should give him a few seconds' head start if (when?) he comes face-to-face with a Hater. His body language will give him away, though. He'll be running like his fucking life depends on it, because his fucking life *will* depend on it.

What he's doing goes against virtually every rule in the Matthew Dunne survival handbook, yet it has to be done. He's putting his neck on the line, but it's crucial to keep one step ahead of the game. *Knowledge is power,* he tells himself.

It doesn't take long to find obvious signs of recent activity. It must be Haters, he thinks, because who in their right mind would risk being out here like this (apart from him)? There's a rain-soaked sofa dumped in a garden with what's left of a body sprawled alongside it. It looks like they jumped for the seat from an upstairs window and missed. In other circumstances it might be vaguely comical, but Matt's not laughing.

If Franklin is to be believed, the Haters they're looking for are deserters; conscripted fighters doing everything they can to avoid fighting. All they want is to be left alone to get on with what's left of their miserable and broken, Hate-filled lives.

Matt edges farther down the street, looking for further inconsistencies, more signs of recent life. There are a couple of houses on this long, straight road which show signs of having been recently occupied. If these Haters are smart—and despite everything, he can't risk assuming they're not—then they'll likely be in hiding from the rest of the world. And if they're planning on staying here long-term, then they'll have covered their tracks. What better way to camouflage a hidden entry than by making the entrance itself appear impassable.

Got it.

Matt's interest is piqued by a house with its downstairs windows blacked out. He hesitates, checking over his shoulder to make sure Franklin, Graham Porter, and Chris Greatrex are close. They're holding back and waiting for his signal. Matt knows stealth is doubly important here. A straightforward, full-on group attack on a suspect building could be disastrous. As well as tipping off any hiding Haters, it would also alert any others in the vicinity. It's a balancing act. Matt feels like he's walking through a minefield on skis.

Focus!

He doesn't want to commit to the house where he thinks there may be Haters hiding. Instead he reverses direction and slips through the open front door of another house a few doors down. He waits for a second before entering, smelling the staleness of the air and listening for any telltale noises first, making sure the building's empty.

Christ, no matter how many times it happens, things like this still catch him off guard. Apart from the damp and mold in the open hallway, the building he's just entered is otherwise pristine. It's like a museum piece—just as its owners left it and a million miles removed from the chaotic madness outside. He looks around the place and can't help piecing together the stories of the people who lived here and their eventual fates. The wave of nostalgia makes him feel melancholy. He longs for a return to this kind of innocent normality, but he knows it's gone forever.

Downstairs, the house is a picture of suburban ordinariness. He looks up the staircase and begins to formulate a hypothesis. There are bloody handprints on the floral print wallpaper at the foot of the stairs. Their color is stale brown, not fresh red. Smeared by frantic downward movements, he notes, no other visible stains. From the lack of obvious damage down here, he thinks this was a relatively controlled exit, that this was more likely to be a Hater fleeing than one of their victims. One of them probably lived here and turned on their friends or family or lover upstairs. He's tempted to go up to the bedrooms and see if he was right, but instead he keeps moving, reminding himself he's got a job to do.

Out through the narrow kitchen and into a long and once well-tended but now wildly overgrown garden which backs onto another row of houses behind. Matt catches his breath when something rushes through the knee-high grass, but it's just an animal. A fox, feral dog, or cat or maybe even an engorged rat. All he sees is a flash of mange and dirty fur.

The suspect house is three doors farther along. With no obvious shelter out here, he crawls on his hands and knees through the undergrowth and overgrowth, tucking in tight against the waist-high fence between this garden and the next. There's a small wooden shed at the far end of the lawn. He uses it for cover so he can look back at the house he's had his eye on.

Christ, I'm good . . .

Matt's instincts are bang-on. There's a lone Hater prowling the upstairs of the house, nervously moving from room to room, scanning the outside world through a pair of binoculars. The middle-aged man is so busy looking for the source of the engine noise and movement at the far end of the street that he fails to see Matt crouching right under his nose. Matt waits a while longer until he's sure as he can be the Hater is alone.

Job done, he retraces his steps and reports back to the others.

He peels off his facemask. "Number thirty-seven," he tells Franklin. "Just one bloke in there, as far as I can see."

"You ready?" Franklin asks Chris Greatrex.

"Yep," he answers, voice flat and monosyllabic. He neither looks nor sounds prepared.

Franklin turns back to Matt. "Do it."

"You're sure about this?"

"Go rile that bastard up. All you have to do is get him out into the open, then let us take care of the rest. Just make sure you don't get yourself killed."

"Easier said than done. You've got my back, right?"

"Just do it," Franklin orders, shoving him forward again.

Matt runs back toward the Hater's house with Chris close behind. *What the hell am I doing?* The door's locked, but that's not an issue because Graham Porter appears from out of nowhere, carrying a metal battering ram which he swings at the lock. The door flies open, hitting the inside wall and bouncing back again, shattering the silence. Matt takes a hesitant step into the house, waiting for the inevitable thunderous noise as the Hater comes pelting down the stairs toward him, screaming and salivating and all-consumed with bloodlust.

There's nothing. No reaction.

In for a penny, in for a pound.

He goes deeper into the house. Sounding far more composed than he feels, he clears his throat and shouts, taunting the hidden killer. "Show yourself, you pathetic bastard."

Still nothing.

Matt stops when he hears floorboards creaking upstairs. The Hater's on the move.

"Come on, for Christ's sake, what's the matter with you?"

Matt's pulse is racing. He's dicing with death here, risking everything.

He sees shadows moving at the very top of the stairs. A hand on the wall. "Leave me alone," the Hater pleads, his voice cracked and hoarse. "Just let me be."

It occurs to Matt that the Hater probably hasn't yet realized that the enemy is in his house. No Unchanged in their right mind would risk coming here like this, would they? It would be suicidal. Matt knows he's going to have to spell it out to him. "Come on, you fucker, come and get me. I'm one of *them*!"

The Hater sounds like he's sobbing. Matt can see him now. He has his hands over his face, trying not to look, trying to delay the inevitable. "Just go . . . I don't want this . . ."

He knows the Hater doesn't have any choice. His actions, once triggered, will be driven by an unstoppable instinct. There's a pool of light halfway up the stairs spilling through a first-floor window, and Matt steps into it so the Hater can clearly see.

Their eyes meet, and it's like a switch has been flicked.

The Hater can't stop himself. The desire to kill Matt is overwhelming, the internal conflict tearing him apart. He's not brave, not strong . . . until recently he was just an ordinary divorced father-of-three who worked on a production line by day and propped up bars by night. He never wanted this, never asked for any of this . . . but he has to do it. He roars with pained frustration and hurls himself down the stairs at Matt who half-runs, half-falls back down the hallway and out through the front door. He immediately presses himself back against the wall of the house as the Hater bursts out into the open. He instantly forgets about Matt because Chris Greatrex is standing in the middle of the street front and center, goading him.

Chris waits a second or two longer, just enough to be certain that the Hater is entirely focused on him and committed, then he turns and runs like hell. Matt wants to follow in his wake, to watch the soldiers who accompanied them on this trip give the

Hater the kind of vicious treatment he's due, but Graham stops him. "We need to move."

"What about Chris?"

"He'll be fine, but we need to go. More of them will come. They always do."

"But surely the more we get rid of now, the better."

"That's not how it works. Get back to the van."

"I just don't know why you'd—"

"*Move!*" Graham orders, and he grabs a pistol from a holster on his belt and aims it straight at Matt. Matt freezes, and Graham fires. The shot goes over Matt's shoulder, whistling past his left ear. Matt spins around and sees that another Hater has been felled. "If you really want to stay, be my guest. The rest of us are getting out of here."

The van and one of the jeeps have stopped outside an overlooked cash-and-carry nestled on the farthest edge of No Man's Land. Both engines are left running, and their respective drivers remain in position. A number of armed CDF militia fighters are covering the building's entrances and exits, allowing Matt, Franklin, Graham, and two more soldiers to scavenge inside. "Where else d'you think we get our shit?" Franklin asks, breathless, as he and Matt cross paths in an aisle, both pushing loaded trolleys. "There's stuff everywhere out here, but no one else has the balls or the foresight to come and get it."

17

Matt does his best to act casual when he arrives home, but it's not easy. He's spent months having to suppress his emotions, but the close encounter with the Hater this afternoon was another unexpected release of pent-up frustration. It was cathartic. Adrenaline-fueled. Fucking awesome. Better even than being out on the garbage truck run with Smithy.

Jason's beaten Matt back and is sitting in the kitchen, talking to Jen. Matt deposits his earnings in the middle of the table and watches their reactions. Jen's excited, because some of the things he's got hold of are hard to find. He slips a couple of chocolate bars to Mrs. Walker for the kids.

"Word to the wise, Matt," Jason tells him. "The economy's all fucked-up. Supply and demand is all over the place. We don't need luxuries. Focus on essentials. Try and get the basics, 'cause that's what we're going to need more than anything."

"You mean stuff like this?" Matt says, pointing out the tinned food, fruit juice, and rolls of toilet paper he also brought back with him tonight.

"You got pineapple!" Jen says, spotting a tin among the pile. "I *love* pineapple!"

"I know you do."

"I mean, it's only tinned, but it's *ages* since I had any."

"I know."

"I used to live on the stuff!"

"I know! I saw it and thought of you."

She hugs him tight, and he holds on to her, not wanting to let go.

It's late and dark. The temperature has increased steadily all afternoon and evening and even now, long after the sun's disappeared, it's still stifling and close. Matt's sitting out on the small patio with Jason. Jen was here too, but she made her excuses a short while ago and went up to bed. It's just before midnight and still the air is filled with noise. The steady hubbub of the overcrowded camp is a constant earworm, regularly punctuated by other interruptions: crowd control, helicopters and drones, attacks being launched over the border . . . *The city never sleeps* was always the old expression. Matt thinks that's because it's too afraid to close its eyes.

"There's still people coming in, you know," Jason says. He's staring into space, his features outlined in the moonlight. "Down at the gates, I mean. The queue I was in today got funneled close to the entrance and I had a decent view. You wouldn't think after all this time that there were still that many people left out there."

"Yeah, I know. Crazy, isn't it?"

"You've seen it too, have you?"

"Not today, but I have seen them."

"Right."

"I guess people have just been hiding and waiting to be picked up."

"Suppose. Don't know where they're all going to go, though. We're running out of room." He pauses, then adds, "Running out of everything, actually."

There's a lull in the conversation. A black helicopter hangs in the sky a mile or so north of the house, close to the main entrance to the camp according to Matt's estimations. It hovers for a while, perfectly still, bathing the ground with its searchlight, before a drone Matt didn't even realize was there unleashes hell on the enemy below. "Fuck me," he says under his breath as muffled, grumbling explosions fill the air, noise on noise on noise. The ground shakes with the cumulative vibrations.

The helicopter drifts away and the sound slowly fades. The relative quiet is equally uncomfortable. Matt senses that all is not well with his housemate. He can feel Jason's eyes burning into him. "So where do you see this all ending?"

It's a simple enough question. Trouble is, there's no easy answer Matt can give. "It's like you said earlier, the economics of this world don't work. We have to assume the CDF are out there in decent numbers dealing with the Haters."

"And do you think they are?"

"I don't know. Thing is, it's out of our hands. We have to hope they do their job, but we need to keep our options open here."

"Stockpile supplies, that kind of thing . . ."

"Exactly. But there's another problem."

"Go on."

"Like you said, there are still more people coming in. By all accounts the food stocks are struggling with the existing demand. Too many mouths, not enough food. More mouths coming."

Jason's contemplative silence indicates that he understands the gravity of their situation, but his silence doesn't last long. "I've got another concern."

"What's that?"

"Are you selling us short?"

"What? Are you serious?"

"Deadly. Who you working with? Where did you go today?"

"I told you this morning, it's none of your business."

"Where did that food come from, then?"

"Which part of 'none of your fucking business' don't you understand?"

"It is my business, though, isn't it? Whether you like it or not, we're all in this together. The kind of stuff you brought home tonight doesn't come cheap."

"Right place, right time."

"Bullshit. You expect me to believe that?"

"I don't expect you to believe anything. To be honest, I don't care."

"Well, you should. There hasn't been food like that available in the camp for weeks, not from anywhere I've been. Like I said, we're all in this together and—"

"What exactly are you saying, Jason?"

He pauses before answering. "Look, I'll level with you, you're making me nervous . . . I don't know if I can trust you."

"Of course you can trust me. As much as I can trust you, anyway."

"Then tell me where you really got that stash."

"I worked for it. I hit it lucky, obviously."

Jason gets up and starts to pace around the patio, hands deep in his pockets, trying to appear calm and in control, but failing miserably. Matt thinks he's acting like a parent working out why the kid who should have been in by ten didn't get home till gone midnight.

"We're in a really dodgy situation here, mate," Jason says.

"I agree, we are."

"I've done everything I can to keep the people in this house safe."

"I know you have. And I appreciate it."

"I'm not going to stop just because you've come home."

"No one's asking you to."

Jason thinks again, choosing his words carefully. "Thing is, we all need to be pulling in the same direction here."

"I thought we were? Jen and Mrs. Walker are here looking out for the kids and each other, you and I are putting food on the table."

"I'm not so sure . . ."

"So what exactly are you saying? Are you accusing me of stealing that food, Jason? You didn't seem to have a problem when you were shoveling it down your neck at dinner."

"I didn't say you were stealing the food, but I don't know where you got it from and the fact you're being so cagey about it just makes matters worse. Like I said, some of the stuff you brought back hasn't been seen around here for weeks."

Matt knows he's got to tell him something to shut him up. "It is what it is. Look, I was out there on my own for a long time. I learned how to forage."

"So you did steal it?"

"No, I worked for it with some people I met when I did that other job a couple of days back. They're responsible for resource management, boring shit like that."

Jason's not convinced. "I don't buy it."

"And I don't care. Look, what difference does it make?"

Jason continues to pace. Matt watches his every step, looking for a way out of the conversation. But to get up and walk away now would imply some kind of guilt, and Matt's got nothing to feel guilty about. He just wishes his unwanted houseguest would keep his fucking nose out.

But he's not about to do that anytime soon.

"I don't trust you, Matt. Haven't done from the start if I'm honest. I don't believe anyone could survive on their own out there for so long."

Matt holds his hands out to his sides. "Well, here I am."

"Yeah, but look at you . . . you're nothing special. No offense, but you're just a fucking accountant."

"True. I can't argue with that. I know what I'm doing, though. Shove us both out onto the other side of the wall and I reckon I know who'll last longest. We can try it if you like."

"Cut the crap. Whatever it is you're doing, you're playing with fire. The risks are greater than I think you realize. This is a different world now, you know. It's a different city to the one you walked out on."

"I'd noticed . . . And I didn't walk out on anything."

"Thing is, mate, I'll level with you. I don't give a shit about you, but I'm not going to let Jen get hurt."

"Jen's my responsibility."

"Yeah, well someone had to step up when you weren't around."

"And I've already thanked you for that. I'm back now, so you can butt out and fuck off."

For a second Jason looks like he's ready to hit Matt, but he doesn't. Both of them know that any physical aggression these days could be catastrophically misconstrued.

"Just watch your step," Jason says.

"Is that a threat?"

"It's a warning. There's a difference."

"Well here's one for you—stay away from Jen."

"She deserves better than—"

"I said stay away from her. You're just a kid, Jason, a jumped-up little kid."

"I care about Jen and I won't let you hurt her."

"No, you care about yourself and making sure you've got a roof over your head and food in your belly. I went through hell to get back to Jen, put my life on the line again and again. I'm not going to let you or anyone else fuck it up."

18

Matt spends half the night staring up at the ceiling and considering his options, unable to speak. He doesn't want to leave Jen alone with Jason, yet he has unfinished business with Franklin. He also knows Franklin is his best source of food right now, and he has to take advantage of that while he still can, because Jason's right about one thing—this is the dodgiest of situations.

Franklin barely acknowledges Matt when he turns up for work next morning. "You came back, then."

"You sound surprised."

"Must be desperate."

Matt doesn't bite.

It's largely the same routine as last time. They leave the compound in the same van escorted by the same CDF jeeps and personnel carrier, and drive out to the same few square miles of ghost town on the outer rim of No Man's Land. Jayce is driving and Chris Greatrex is also present. There's no Graham Porter, though. His place is taken today by a bearded, surly-looking man who introduces himself simply as Priest. He's an ex-police dog handler (ex- because the police have been absorbed into the

146

CDF, Priest explains). He may be ex-police, but he's still a dog handler. He has with him a huge and beautiful-looking German shepherd called Bandit. The hound's a little unkempt but is clearly in his prime, attentively watching his master's every move, awaiting orders. The dog makes Matt feel redundant. He thinks he could probably hunt out and bring down even the most vicious Hater more efficiently than the rest of this crew put together.

Today they're concentrating on an area a few streets down from where they were yesterday. Franklin explains they're combing the streets systematically, but Matt's not so sure. He thinks he's trying to make things seem more organized than they actually are. There's no point working sequentially when you're dealing with an enemy as random as the Haters.

Bandit and his master check one side of a nondescript cul-de-sac while Matt covers the other. There's a Hater here somewhere, Matt's sure of it. A number of houses in this street have been ransacked—fairly recently, by the looks of things—and all tracks lead to the same front door. Whoever's inside this house has either been particularly lax in covering their tracks or they're just arrogant, ready to take on anything or anyone. It could be a trap. Matt gestures for Priest to come over, and Priest in turn signals back to make Franklin aware they may be on to something.

"In there?" Priest whispers.

"Think so . . ."

"But?"

"But it's a risk. Doesn't look like they've been hiding. They were outside recently."

He points out muddy footprints on the path leading up to the house. They're still wet.

"We'll use the dog."

Priest opens a side gate. He gestures for Matt to go through first, then follows him into the back garden. Matt gags as he squeezes between the fence and an overfull wheelie bin filled with household waste that's been left rotting for months. The stench is vile.

He peers around the corner. The back of the house is a junk-yard, filled with all kinds of scavenged crap. The remains of a recent fire are still smoldering in a crude pit dug in the middle of the lawn.

"You're the bait, Matt," Priest whispers. He's struggling to hold on to Bandit's collar. The dog's straining to be let go.

"Fuck that," Matt says.

"I'm serious. Go get yourself seen. If there are any of them inside, they'll be so fixated on you that they won't notice the dog."

Matt edges into the garden. A Hater skulking in the shadows downstairs sees him immediately and throws himself at the patio doors, all spittle and snarls, scrambling at the lock to get the bloody thing open. Priest boots the back door open and lets the dog loose, but the maniac behind the glass is so fixated on the Unchanged lamb to the slaughter who's just wandered onto his patch that he doesn't even notice.

Bandit hurtles into the house but the Hater gets the sliding door open and is on top of Matt before the dog gets anywhere near. Matt's on his backside in the mud, squirming as the Hater swings punches at his head. Priest smacks the back of the Hater's skull with a length of metal pipe before he can do any real harm and the ragged man hits the deck out cold, blood oozing from a vicious-looking dent in the side of his skull.

"Thanks," Matt says, panting hard.

"Don't mention it. Excitable little fucker, was this one."

Bandit's still in the house, barking like crazy.

Priest helps Matt to his feet. There's a brief moment of calm outside, then utter chaos as more Haters flood out of the building. Fuck.

They've disturbed a nest.

Matt realizes what's happening fast. Another Hater comes flying through the open patio doors, the dog hanging off his leg. Priest knows there could be any number of them in there and he snatches his pistol from its holster and puts a bullet between the Hater's eyes. Both he and Matt know the sound of the shot—always a last resort out here—will alert Franklin and the others to the imminent threat. "Go!" Priest shouts to Matt.

Matt sprints back down the side of the house with Priest close behind. Behind them, four more Haters. Bandit weaves between them and leaps up and sinks his teeth into the arm of another Hater who appears from nowhere, trying to cut off their escape at the front of the house. Matt shimmies around him and races away.

Up ahead, Franklin gesticulates for them to get out of the way. He's armed and is about to shoot, regardless of who's in the line of fire. Chris Greatrex picks his moment then sprints off in the opposite direction, dividing the attacking pack. Matt dives over to his left and ducks behind a low garden wall as Franklin opens fire, filling the whole world with noise for the next twenty seconds.

"Clear," Franklin then shouts. Matt picks himself up, checking all around for more of the enemy. He knows there are other Haters nearby. Though he can't yet see them, he can sense them coming. He can already hear another brutal encounter kicking off in the next street down from here. "Get back to the van," Franklin orders.

Matt hears engine noise and runs toward it. He takes a sharp right then immediately flattens himself up against the nearest building when he sees it's the pug-nosed military vehicle, not the van. He starts toward it, then stops. More soldiers are dealing with another pack of Haters. He can't see if they're the same Haters they flushed out of the house—they all look the same when you're running for your life—but they're clearly outgunned and outnumbered and won't last long. Several of the enemy are on the deck already, black-clad militia fighters beating them with batons, while others are picked off by a rifle-wielding soldier shooting from the roof of the transport.

The van appears in the mouth of another road opposite. Jayce revs the engine impatiently. Chris Greatrex grabs Matt's arm and pulls him toward it. "Come on."

"Wait . . ." Matt says.

"No time. Now!"

Matt delays a second longer. Something's not right. "Why haven't they killed them?"

"What?"

"There are three of them on the ground over there. They're still alive. Why aren't they killing them?"

"They will. They know what they're doing."

"But they should have done it already. They've shot all the others—"

Jayce blasts the horn.

"Does it matter? Stay here any longer and it'll be you who's dead."

Chris turns and runs to the van and Matt follows. Franklin's not far behind.

They're delayed a minute longer waiting for Priest and the dog. Franklin watches for them, impatiently tapping the barrel of his rifle against the part-open window. A few seconds later and the dog, then Priest, arrive. The van's already moving before Priest's fully inside. The toes of his boots scrape the tarmac as they race away.

Matt presses his face against the rear window as they drive past the end of the road where the military were left mopping up the last Haters. Was this even the right street? He's not sure anymore, but this must be the right place because there are numerous blood-soaked Hater corpses littering the far end of the road.

But there's no sign of the CDF fighters he just saw here.

There's no sign of their vehicle other than tire marks on the tarmac.

There's no sign of the three Haters they were beating. Their bodies have gone.

19

Matt races quickly through the crowds to get home, fearful that someone will see the food he has crammed into the rucksack he's carrying. The crew made a frantic stop at another reasonably stocked supermarket on their way back into the camp. At this rate when everyone else has run out of food, Estelle Bisseker and her troops will still be feasting.

There's a tangible change in atmosphere at the house. Jen looks worried. "Jason's not back," she says before he's even unloaded his stash.

"Well, I don't know where he is," Matt replies without thinking.

"But you were together, weren't you? You left here together this morning, anyway."

"We got split up in the crowds," he answers, backpedaling. "It happens. I'm sure he's okay. He can look after himself."

"I've got a bad feeling."

"You've seen what it's like out there," Matt says. "Anything could have happened."

"Yeah, that's what I'm worried about."

"He'll be fine. He managed perfectly well before I came home, didn't he."

"You should have stuck together."

"I work better on my own."

"He's always back by now. Will you go out and look for him?"

"It'll be getting dark soon. I'll never find him out there."

"You never should have left him. Please go and look for him. Do it for me."

Matt knows he has no choice. He also knows that anything could have happened to Jason in this increasingly crowded and dangerous cesspit of a camp.

"Okay, okay, I'll go. Keep the door locked and I'll be back as soon as I can."

As soon as he's out on the streets again Matt realizes this could be more serious than he originally thought. The amount of air traffic this evening is a dead giveaway. The skies are teeming with movement, crisscrossing spotlights bearing down through the dusk gloom toward one part of town in particular. He knows straightaway where they're focused. It's the City Arena.

As usual, the streets are heavily congested around the approaches to the last remaining food distribution center. It's hard to make out anything through the swarming crowds and he knows he'll have little chance of spotting Jason at ground level. There's a tall office block over to his left, but there's a glut of people blocking the only visible entrance. Matt instead climbs a mountainous pile of waste which has accumulated against the side of the building like a filthy snowdrift. It's semisolid on the surface, with buried wheelie bins and the skeletal frame of an old outdoor smoking shelter providing some much needed rigidity beneath the mire. He scrambles up until he's as high as a broken first-floor window, then squeezes through the gap. The view's not much better from here. Sure, he can see over the heads of the crowds filling the streets, but he knows it's not good enough and he starts to climb.

He's entered the building near the bottom of an enclosed stairwell—a fire escape, he thinks—and though the light is murky and dim, he's aware of people all around. They protest as he clambers over them to get higher, but the same principle applies inside as out: keep moving and keep climbing and don't let the shit you're wading through drag you down.

He uses the handrail to pull himself upward, catching occasional clearly defined glimpses of the overcrowded world here inside the block when searchlights slink through the windows, slicing through the dark. On some levels there are lamps and lights and campfires which have been lit on landings. Campfires indoors! It wouldn't take much for this whole damn building to go up like a torch. The human cost of such a disaster would be literally incalculable because he doesn't believe anyone has any idea how many people are packed in here. This building is close to the main gates. It's probably been filling up with arrivals since day one. It reinforces Matt's belief that the chances of him finding Jason out here are minimal. He could be searching all night.

The muscles in his legs are starting to burn, but he keeps climbing until the staircase runs out. Fortunately many, many other refugees have made this journey before him and the maintenance door leading out onto the roof of the office block is propped open. He finds that the outside is as crowded as inside and he picks his way through a chaotic maze of improvised shelters to get closer to the edge.

The view from up here takes his breath away. It's remarkable. Down at street level the camp is a brutal, hellish place to live, but from this height it has an unexpected beauty, almost serene. The ground-level chaos dissipates into a fuzzy haze and all Matt can see is an ocean of black punctuated by countless pinprick lights. Not as many as there used to be, granted, but there are enough bonfires, candles, gas lamps, battery-powered flashlights, and generator-powered floodlights down there to combine to make a difference. It's a wholly different kind of illumination to the light pollution he remembers from streetlamps and houses: softer and more muted, somehow warmer yet unsettling and un-familiar because the lights are no longer rigidly regimented by street-lines and other boundaries. Other than the arena, the only landmark of any note he can make out is the Royal Midlands Hospital. The massive building itself remains largely unlit, its distinctive outline appearing as a shadow against the darkening sky. It's somewhat illuminated from below by a densely packed mass of individual lights. Matt imagines there are thousands of patients, medical staff, and others gathered there . . .

But it's the contrast between the camp and the rest of the world which surprises him most. The perimeter of the camp is clearly defined from up here, because beyond its border there's nothing but black. Endless. Smothering. All consuming. As his eyes become accustomed he's able to pick out some signs of move-ment way beyond No Man's Land, but it's fleeting: the occa-sional flashes of distant battles and the dancing light traces of vehicles racing across the wilderness. There are Haters out there. Thousands, probably hundreds of thousands of them. He thinks all that separates *us* from *them* tonight is a fragile strip of black void.

High overhead, the dancing lights in the sky are as hypnotiz-ing as what's happening below. Searchlights and taillights criss-cross as aircraft race across the black. A low-flying Chinook refocuses Matt as it passes overhead en route to the City Arena, so low he thinks he could reach up and touch its belly. He pushes through the packed crowds to follow its flight. The roof of the cavernous, amphitheater-like building is open, and the Chinook begins a rapid descent into its bowels. He's never been a military buff, never had anything more than a passing interest in that sort of thing, but he wonders why a huge, heavy helicopter like the Chinook is being used here? Surely there are lighter, faster aircraft? It's hard to make out exactly what's going on and when a couple of onlookers shift to one side, Matt seizes the opportunity to squeeze through and take their place. He then worms his way farther forward still, slipping between and around people until he's reached the front edge.

The first thing he notices is the space around the arena. The wide concourse which, until now, has always been packed with people standing in the endless food queues, is empty. Some distance from the entrance to the hangar-like building, barricades have been erected to keep the population at bay. There's a heavy military presence patrolling the area. Machine gunners man lookout posts on the top of the arena walls.

The arena's numerous outer doors are closed. No one's going in, and no one's getting out. This doesn't make sense, because as long as he's been back in the city, this place has always been the hub. Pretty much everything seems to emanate from here: the food, information . . . There's an older guy standing next to him, watching intently. "What's going on?" Matt asks.

"Where you been all afternoon?"

"Somewhere else. Why? What happened?"

"All dried-up, mate."

"What is?"

"The food. They've stopped dishing it out. I mean, we all knew it was coming, but how did they think people were gonna react? If you ask me, they should have stopped more folks coming into the city and just looked after those of us who were already here, but they didn't. Just kept letting them through the gate."

"But if there's no food, there's no food. What else can they do?"

"I never said there was no food, I said they've stopped giving it out to the likes of you, me, and everyone else. Rumor is they're keeping what's left for themselves. Reckon that's what the helicopter's for, to get their people and their supplies out of here. They've been in and out since nightfall."

It takes Matt twice as long to get back down. The crowds bubble with an improbable mix of nervous panic and lethargy—he's convinced almost everyone knows that something's imminent here, but most see no point trying to do anything about it. All he's focused on now is getting home. Jason can look after himself.

Once he's outside, he skirts around the edge of the vast crowd being held back from the City Arena. The masses seem infinitely more fractious, but are they genuinely riled, or is it just because he's down at ground level with them again? Whatever the reason, being here makes him feel increasingly uneasy. He keeps his head down and tries not to make eye contact with anyone, but he looks up frequently to make sure he's moving in the right direction. He halfheartedly looks for Jason, but it's a pointless exercise. Too many people, too many faces.

The lookouts have gone.

He notices the soldiers who'd been watching the crowds have stood down. The fact there are no longer armed guards here makes him keener than ever to get away but it feels like he's swimming against the tide.

The Chinook is still audible, its powerful engines and double-rotor-blade noise being amplified and distorted by the bowl-like shape of the arena behind him. Matt notices the sound begin to change and he risks looking back as the aircraft climbs quickly, then banks away and disappears into the night. It leaves behind it a dark and empty place, the few remaining arena lights having been extinguished.

The helicopter noise quickly dies away, leaving an uncomfortable numb silence in its place. The quiet seems to last for several minutes, but in reality it's only seconds. Long enough for the crowds to realize that the City Arena has been evacuated.

The first screams and shouts and howls of protest, derision, and anger start to come from the abandoned masses nearest to the arena. Those individual voices soon combine and, before long, the evening air is alive with noise. Matt keeps walking, fighting the urge to look back again until it's safe. The light's almost gone, but he sees enough to know what's happening. The riled crowds break through the barricades which have been holding them back, no longer fearing retaliation because they know the military guarding the place have fled. They grab the wire mesh and rock it backward and forward repeatedly until the whole thing comes down in a chain reaction—falling in both directions at once. Hundreds of people trample over the collapsed metal barrier, racing toward the deserted building. They pour in through its now unguarded doors, desperate for food that isn't there.

Against the odds, Matt finds Jason on the way home. The other man looks visibly shaken and is walking along the middle of the crowded street, zombielike, detached from his surroundings.

Matt stops him. "Christ, Jason, I've been looking all over the place for you."

Jason's numb, slow to react. Matt's directly in front of him now with his hands on his shoulders, preventing him from moving. Jason just stares at him.

"We need to get back to the house."

"I thought I was gonna die," Jason says, his mind still back at the arena. "We were queueing for hours, packed in tight, then they just shut the doors on us and forced us back . . . The crowd started to turn and I thought I was going to die . . ."

"Yeah, well you didn't. Now pull yourself together and let's get back home."

Matt tries to speed him along but it's like Jason's feet have been nailed to the ground. "But you weren't there . . . you didn't see what it was like. There were people begging for mercy and they weren't listening. They cleared the square and . . ."

"And what you saw today was nothing. Par for the course. Get used to it. That kind of shit's going to get a lot more regular."

"Nothing? How can you say it was nothing? You could hear them screaming. People fighting. Attacking each other just to get away. I fucking hid. I just kept my head down and hid . . ."

Jason's noise and mounting nervousness is making Matt feel uneasy. "We'll talk about it back at the house," he tells him. "Not here. Not now."

"But you didn't see how they—"

"Not now," Matt yells at him, loud enough to make a sizable chunk of the nearby population stop and look. He regrets his outburst and pulls Jason away, virtually dragging him down the street.

20

They're in the bathroom together, brushing their teeth. The water in the basin comes from a jug and the light is from a candle, not electric, yet it feels deceptively normal, even after the events of the day just ending. It's easy to slip back into routine. When it's just the two of them, it's easy to forget. Jen nudges up against Matt, and he nudges back against her. She grimaces in the mirror, and he crosses his eyes and pulls a face. They finish brushing, then rinse, then kiss, then kiss again. For a moment there's a shared feeling that this might develop into something more, one of those beautiful moments of spontaneous lovemaking which used to creep up and take them both by surprise at the least opportune moment.

The lovers stop when a helicopter thunders overhead, the noise so loud that it makes the bathroom mirror rattle in its frame. The intrusive glare of a sweeping searchlight flooding through the window seems almost to put the two of them on show like criminals caught in the act. In a world fueled by hate, their tenderness feels bizarrely taboo. They separate and climb into bed on their respective sides.

"Are we going to be okay?" she asks him after a while. Matt can't bring himself to tell Jen the truth, and so just gives her what she wants to hear.

"I told you. I'll make sure we're okay."

"But everything you and Jason said about what happened tonight . . ."

"Sure, things are shitty. Worse than I thought, if I'm honest, but we'll be all right."

"You're just saying that."

She's got him banged to rights, but what's the alternative? "No, love, I'm not. We're in a better position than most, remember. We've got a little space and some privacy here, and I know where to get food. Don't you believe me?"

"I want to . . . it's difficult, that's all. I haven't seen as much of it as you, remember."

"That's probably a good thing." Matt thinks about her words. There's a question he's avoided asking because he knows how much it upsets her. "How long has it been since you left the house, Jen?"

"I can't help it. You know I can't."

"I know, but I thought you were getting better."

"I was, but all this knocked me right back, and since Jason and Mrs. Walker got here I haven't needed to go out. I can't help it. It's my nerves, you know it is."

"I know, love, I know . . . I'm just trying to understand. So answer my question: how long has it been since you left the house?"

She's crying. Reluctant to answer.

"It was the day before you left to go to that island with work. When we went to that pub for dinner. Remember?"

Matt's mind floods with memories put on hold for months: a Thursday evening meal in a quiet pub not far from here. An evening tempered with unease because he knew he was leaving her next morning to travel to Skek. Nice food, subdued company. But moments later those thoughts are filed back under *no longer relevant, no longer me,* and he's back in his fucked-up reality again. "You've not left the house in all that time? Three months?"

"You know how hard I find it."

"But the therapist said—"

"The therapist's gone, Matt, and everything's changed. Todd didn't help me prepare for the end of the world."

"I know. I'm sorry, I didn't mean to upset you. It's just there's going to come a time when—"

"—when I don't have any choice and we have to leave here. I realize that. And I will do it when I have to. It's not so bad when I'm with you. I know you're there for me, Matt. I know you'll keep me safe. I know you won't let anything bad happen."

He keeps his mouth shut, wishing he could share her confidence.

21

Jason knows which side his bread's buttered on (not that there's either bread or butter at the moment). When Matt gets up to leave next morning, he doesn't react. "Keep things under control here while I'm gone," Matt tells him. "Keep the door locked and don't let anyone in but me, got it?"

"Got it."

The trouble at the arena last night has had a noticeable ripple effect throughout the camp, and walking the overcrowded, fractious streets today is almost as daunting as the prospect of heading out into the wilderness and hunting down Haters. Seven in the morning or seven at night, the levels of activity and uncertainty in the camp are constant now.

Got to stay one step ahead of the game. That's Matt's usual thinking, and it's more important than ever today. He needs to take advantage of the moment and get as much food secured as he can, but that's not the only reason he's heading back to the CDF compound this morning. Something doesn't ring true about what they're doing. He knows full well that Franklin's just using him, but he's not entirely sure why. He figures as long as he remembers the CDF consider him disposable, he'll be okay. *Get more food before it's all gone, and figure out what the hell the CDF are up to—one step ahead of the game.*

What little structure and order there was in the camp is almost completely gone as a result of what happened last night. He skirts around the City Arena, which is predictably overrun this morning, people everywhere. The sign which proudly proclaimed food was available 24/7 has been felled.

The nearby school—previously home to the camp's top brass—has also been ransacked, although not, it seems, by refugees. Whether it's militia or CDF or a combination of both, he can't be sure, but the gates of the school have been locked shut and there's a heavy military presence behind them. A coup? Have the privileged few who sheltered in relative comfort here been forced out? A fire has ripped through the top floor of the building and most windows are now just charred black holes, scars contrasting starkly against the dirty whitewash. Papers drift in the wind. Many of the tables from the atrium have been stacked in front of the building and set alight. What used to be a kids' playground is now a car park for tanks and trucks and heavy artillery. Matt almost turns back, but he keeps walking. He knows he has to see this through.

"You came back again? Jesus, you must be more desperate than I thought."

"Morning to you too, Franklin," Matt says as he enters the compound. "Were you not invited to the party in town last night? Looks like the rest of your military mates have taken over."

"They don't know we're here and we're doing our best to keep it that way," he answers. "We're doing our own thing here, have been from the start."

"No shit."

The convoy has been expanded today—two motorbikes riding alongside the usual vehicles—and in the van it's a full house: Matt, Franklin, Priest (and Bandit), Graham Porter, Chris Greatrex, and Jayce. Matt finds himself crouched in the back of the van directly behind their driver. Jayce seems quieter than usual, not that she's ever particularly vocal.

"Lots going on out there today," Franklin explains. "Lots of activity around the airport, not far from where we're heading."

"The airport's still operational?"

"To a point. It's a CDF base. It's where most of the military have decamped to, by all accounts."

"So isn't that a bad idea? Shouldn't we go somewhere else, somewhere quieter?"

"Nope. We've been using military activity as cover on most of our trips out, or hadn't you noticed? It's a distraction. Gives the other side something to focus on other than us."

It's a standard enough operation. Weird, Matt thinks, how quickly he's getting used to this new routine. *Adapt to survive,* he tells himself. Even when he was alone in the wastelands for all those weeks, day-to-day survival became second nature. Almost routine.

Somewhere nearby, the Hater hordes are taking a hell of a pounding, although from deep within this maze of crumbling suburban streets it's impossible to know who's doing the firing and who's being fired at. Regardless, the constant noise and the jets which scream overhead are something of a comfort, camouflaging the crew's ground-level movements. It's reassuring, but the longer they're out here, the more vulnerable Matt feels. There are no uniforms or flags in this war, just people. He hopes none of the CDF pilots flying overhead decide to take him and the others out, just in case.

Whatever it is that's happening at the airport, it's big. The shelling has been going on for as long as they've been on the wrong side of the border of No Man's Land. Matt's found plenty of signs of recent activity here, but there are no Haters, just the places they've been. Christ, a battle the magnitude of this one must be Christmas come early for those fucking freaks. It'll draw them out into the open, just leaving the kind of shysters Franklin's squad are looking for still scurried away.

But after searching for more than an hour, Matt finds nothing. This place is a ghost town, packed with clues and hints but nothing else. He thinks it's time to pack up and ship out, and Franklin agrees and gives the order.

There's a high-pitched whine followed by a rush of air and a presumably stray (or possibly well-aimed) missile hits a nearby house. It's several streets away but the impact's so violent it's like the house next door has been hit. Then the house next door *is* hit, and it's clear the pilots overhead reckon there's something here worth firing at. The shock wave knocks Matt off his feet and he's lying in the dirt, trying to work out what just happened before he's even realized he's down. Covered in grit, he picks himself back up and looks around, stunned. Franklin's also staggering back to his feet. Bandit is suddenly straining at his leash, barking furiously. "Fuck's sake, dog," Priest curses, struggling to keep him under control.

The air is filled with dust and smoke, flooding through the gaps where houses used to be and drifting like a gritty fog bank. Bandit continues to bark. "Shut that fucking mutt up," Franklin warns.

"He's on to something," Priest says, still wrestling with the dog.

Matt knows what's coming next before it happens. Like rats fleeing a sinking ship, those Haters who survived the blast are on the move.

There are only four of them at first, but that's four too many. Scrawny, straggly fuckers. They clamber through the rubble then stop, shell-shocked, because the very last thing they expected to stumble across all the way out here was a group of Unchanged. Priest lets his dog loose. Bandit races ahead in a blur of teeth and fur and spittle, then leaps up and latches on to the arm of the nearest Hater.

They are a foul-looking, ragtag bunch; uniformly disheveled and unkempt as if everything which once made them human has been abandoned. A woman comes running at Matt screaming like a crazed banshee. The noise she makes is godawful: part rallying war cry, part ominous warning. To his relief Graham Porter fires off a shot, hitting her between the eyes. Her velocity is such that she keeps moving and smacks into Matt, deadweight. He goes down with her on top, fighting with the corpse all the way like she's still a threat.

By the time he's out from underneath the dead woman, the situation has deteriorated markedly.

There are more of them coming through the drifting smoke. Another three . . . four . . . seven. Two are quickly mowed down by gunfire. Someone grabs Matt's arm and he turns around fast, ready to defend himself. It's Chris Greatrex. "Go," Chris says. "Run like fuck."

A pained yelp from Bandit makes Matt turn back. A Hater has got the better of the beast. He has the dog in a headlock. A sudden, sharp twist and the deed is done. The killer casually drops the animal's limp, lifeless body to the ground, neck broken. Priest cries out at the loss of his beloved animal and fires into the crowd. The noise he makes is enough to draw even more Haters this way.

Chris shoves Matt in the small of his back. "Fuck's sake, man, did you not hear me? Run!"

This time Matt does move, racing after Chris, who pounds the street at an astonishing speed he has no hope of matching. Matt looks back and sees Haters coming after them. He finds a new burst of pace he didn't know he had. He's just about keeping up with Chris now, but Chris has energy to spare. "Split and loop back to the van," he shouts over his shoulder.

Chris goes one way and Matt the other. There's a gap where a small corner supermarket used to stand, and through it Matt sees that there are even more Haters circling, coming from all angles. The majority of them are converging on the gunfight he's just fled. Matt slips into survival mode again, figuring he can use the fighting as cover to keep himself alive. It doesn't sit well—it never has—but he needs to put himself first. Jen's depending on him. He has to make it home.

Getting out of the firing line is his priority, then looking for an escape route.

Matt kicks a flimsy-looking front door open and bursts into an empty house. He runs straight through and out the back, sprints the length of the garden, then vaults the fence. He breaks into the property backing on to the first and this time goes up instead of out. An upstairs room gives him a clear but relatively well-protected view of the street below where Franklin and the others are still fighting. They're struggling to hold a flood of Haters back. Fortunately, all the aggression in the world is no match for the CDF firepower. Some of the enemy demonstrate a modicum of restraint and hold back, clinging to the shadows of the buildings which line this anonymous suburban street, waiting for gaps in the gunfire. Many more, though, run headlong into the carnage, desperate to kill despite the inevitable cost.

Priest and Graham Porter are dead. Franklin's still fighting alongside several other CDF soldiers from the convoy. This is in danger of becoming a full-scale disaster as many more Haters pour into the area, fleeing one battle and stumbling into another. There's a military motorbike on its side in the road, its rider lying dead alongside it. Matt thinks if he could reach the bike and get to the keys, he might have half a chance of using it to get away. As it stands, if he doesn't make a move in the next couple of minutes, he'll be stuck here for the duration.

One of the jeeps appears. It swerves around a corner and skids to a juddering halt in the mouth of the road, and a soldier on the back lobs a series of grenades over the heads of Franklin and the others and into the sea of advancing Haters. Matt turns away from the window and presses himself back against the wall as what's left of the street outside explodes. Glass is blown in and the building he's sheltering in shakes unsteadily like it's about to collapse. He waits a second, then looks back outside. At first his eyes are drawn to the carnage below: a blackened crater in the road, a geyser of water from a burst main, and enough scattered limbs to reassemble double the number of bodies he thought were out there. Dust and debris. Slow-moving Hater survivors. Groans and screams and guttural roars of anger, frustration, and pain.

But then Matt's attention is caught by something else. It's Franklin and the others. They're alive and they're retreating.

Some of them are piling onto the back of the jeep, others are scrambling to get to the van which has also now appeared. Franklin pauses to put a bullet in the brain of a wounded Hater who comes at him with a twitching stump where her left arm used to be, then scans the area one last time before disappearing.

Fuck.

Matt knows he has to move now, or he'll be stuck here forever.

He crashes back downstairs and out through the front door. He knows he's running straight into the vipers' nest, but what option does he have? He sprints across the street, leaping over what's left of the dead and swerving around those who are still somehow on their feet. Most of the Haters who are still alive are focused on the van and the jeep which are racing away, and they don't realize Matt's there until he's gone. Drifting smoke provides him with a little more welcome cover, but he knows he's going nowhere fast out here. When a couple of stragglers realize that he's Unchanged and not like them, he becomes the sole focus of their collective ire.

He runs into another house on the opposite side of the road, then slams the door behind him and blocks it with a piece of furniture. He's been ducking in and out of buildings like this all day but this time it's different because he knows they're on to him. He can hear them clamoring to get in, and over their noise he can also hear the engines of the van and the jeep fading into the distance.

Stop moving and you're dead.

There are no more houses behind this one. No more streets. Just trees, as far as he can see. He goes out through the back door as the first Haters break in through the front, then vaults the waist-high fence between this building and its left-side neighbor to try and throw them off the scent. He drops to his hands and knees and crawls along the overgrown garden. He can hear them searching for him in the undergrowth next door.

Just keep going. Don't stop. Don't fucking stop!

When he reaches the fence at the end of the garden, he scrambles up and over, using a plastic storage box to help him climb. He's on top of the fence—straddling it with one leg either side—when one of them spots him. "Unchanged!" the woman yells, and the Hater stampede immediately changes direction, all of them coming his way.

Matt drops over the fence and hits the deck hard. He immediately starts running again, not knowing where he is or where he's going. The increasingly distant engine noise is directionless and offers no clues. He's in open parkland—a sea of knee-high, straw-colored grass—and he breaks right toward home, hoping he might still have the slightest chance of cutting off the van and jeep before they're gone.

A frantic glance back. They're throwing themselves over the fence, racing after him like the undead hordes in those shitty zombie movies he used to love. Hundreds of them, it looks like.

Voices up ahead. More Haters?

Matt rounds a corner and sees the snub-nosed military vehicle that's accompanied them on every one of these hunting trips he's so far been out on. It's parked up on a patch of scrubland with Chris Greatrex and several CDF soldiers crowded behind it. Matt runs toward them with renewed vigor, and breathes a sigh of relief when one of the black-suited soldiers appears to have spotted him.

Except he hasn't.

There's another pack of Haters closing in from the opposite direction, and the soldier lets rip with a volley of automatic gunfire. Several of them go down, but the rest of the herd continue oblivious, jumping the bodies of their fallen comrades. Matt dives for cover in a thicket and flattens himself to the ground as more of the enemy thunder past. He lifts his head and watches Chris and the others intently through a gap in the weeds, waiting until it's safe for him to move again.

What the fuck?

They're loading two bodies into the back of the military truck. Hard to be completely certain from this distance, but they don't look uniformed. Are they Hater corpses? This makes no sense, and is Matt imagining things, or are those bodies bound? And is that one still kicking?

Matt gets up again and runs. He flinches and ducks left as a CDF soldier hurls a grenade into one of the mobs of Haters. When he levels up and looks again, he sees he was right. The body now being bundled into the back of the vehicle has its ankles and wrists bound and its head is in some kind of restraint, but it's still thrashing. The prisoner writhes and squirms until a vicious club to the side of the head knocks him out cold. He must be a Hater, but that's insane.

There are two massive waves of attackers now converging on the military vehicle from different directions, and Matt's trapped in the middle, running a line between the hordes. With their work done, Chris Greatrex and the remaining troops pile on board and speed away, and all Matt can do is watch them leave.

He's stranded. Isolated. Screwed.

Or he would be if he hadn't just spotted the other jeep abandoned over on the farthest edge of the parkland.

He runs as hard as he can on already tired legs, but before he gets anywhere near the vehicle, he knows he's been spotted again. It was only a matter of time. He doesn't have to look around to see, he can hear them changing direction and coming after him, can *feel* them almost. More than a hundred Haters, all of them desperate to be the one to kill the lone Unchanged idiot dumb enough to be caught out in the open.

The driver's door of the jeep is hanging open invitingly. Matt dives inside then reaches back and snatches the handle, pulling it shut behind him and doing everything he can to avoid looking into the waves of hate coming his way. He feels for the keys in the ignition—*thank Christ*—then starts the engine.

The fastest Haters are on him, swarming around his vehicle. Matt slams his foot down on the accelerator and drives, leaving the foul fuckers for dust. They scramble in the street after him, charging through exhaust fumes and falling over each other in his wake.

Which way now?

Yet another swarm of Haters spills out of the park like an oil slick, filling the road ahead. He swerves around them, clipping one and hitting another full-on, then mounts the curb. The jeep bounces up onto two wheels then crashes back down. The wheel is almost wrenched from his hands but he grips it tight and somehow manages to keep control.

Way up ahead Matt sees a cloud of dust being thrown up by tires. It can only be the others—no one else would be foolish enough to be out here. He keeps his foot down hard and throws the jeep around another corner, skidding out into the center of the long, straight road home.

He can see the taillights of the military transport into which the Haters were loaded. Matt races to catch up, not just because he wants to get out of here, but because he needs to know what the hell is going on. Franklin's stories about hunting and killing rogue Haters were lies. They're capturing Haters *alive*, for Christ's sake. Are these people traitors? Hater sympathizers? Whatever their motives, Matt knows there's something very wrong here. He feels it stronger than anything he's felt since this whole fucking nightmare began.

22

He's onto them.

The speed of the military transport vehicle has dropped now they've entered the camp proper. As ever the roads are heaving with refugees and it's impossible to drive much faster than walking speed. Matt drops back as he follows the CDF transport. They're probably not interested in him, probably not even aware he's behind them, but he's not taking any risks. The stakes have been raised high now. There are live Haters in the camp. These people are playing with fire.

Matt expects the transport to follow the well-worn route back to the compound they started out from this morning, but it doesn't. Instead the driver keeps going, slowing down to a crawl as the density of the crowds around them continues to increase. There are as many people in the road as there are on the litter-strewn pavements, maybe even more. Matt knows it's going to be like this everywhere from here on in and he abandons the jeep, pocketing the keys. He continues on foot, knowing it's a damn sight easier to stay hidden this way. He's just another face among thousands.

It's hard to keep moving, though. The hordes of refugees are fractious. There's no real purpose to their movements, little direction. Some drift one way, some the other. Some stand still or sit on the curb, blocking the way and slowing him down. It's infuriating, but it matters little as the CDF vehicle's progress is being equally impeded.

People protest when he tries to overtake, then complain when he doesn't and he holds them up. He frequently loses sight of the armored beast he's following, but if he can't see the vehicle itself, he can see the gap it's plowed through the reluctant crowds. Matt puts in a short burst of speed to catch up as the transport takes an unexpected sharp left turn. The driver stops in front of a metal gate in an otherwise featureless wall. There's a loud blast on the horn then the gate opens slowly inward.

I've come this far . . . can't stop now.

Matt runs up to the wall and presses himself flat against it. Still dressed in his standard-issue soldier-like garb, he times his move to perfection and slips in alongside the military transport, keeping low and crouching in its shadow. No one sees him. No one knows he's there. The gate closes and he ducks down behind a pile of spare tires, wedging himself into a narrow gap. Over on the far side of a cluttered courtyard space he can see Jayce and Franklin casually leaning against the familiar battered Transit van, watching the proceedings. They more than likely think he's dead, and that's probably a good thing. He knew it from the start, but the fact he was clearly expendable angers him. There was never any question of looking for him when it all went to shit out in the wasteland just now.

The back of the armored truck is opened and the two Haters are dragged out. A man and a woman. Matt can see the woman more clearly. She's out cold and all trussed up, hands and feet bound tight with a pole threaded under her shackles. Two CDF fighters carry her inside like the carcass of a hunted animal they're going to spit roast over the campfire. Maybe that's it? Maybe he's got himself mixed up with a pack of particularly fucked-up, thrill-seeking cannibals? Nothing feels beyond the realms of possibility anymore.

The flurry of activity is over quickly, and Matt's left alone in the courtyard. Good. He prefers it this way. It's easier to operate when he doesn't have to think about anyone else.

Where the hell am I?

It's not the military compound, that's the only thing of which he's sure. Matt's sense of direction is usually pretty good, but right now he's floundering. The garbage and refugees means that every street in the city-camp now looks much the same as the last and the next and he lost his bearings on the way in. He carries out a visual recce of his immediate surroundings from his hiding place, both to work out his next move and identify a potential escape route. He has no idea what this place is or was. It looks civilian by design, but with some of the trappings of a mini-prison: a succession of nondescript, high-walled, largely windowless buildings packed tight together behind an encircling wall. It looks intentionally anonymous. You could walk past its featureless walls a hundred times and not even realize it was there. Matt thinks he probably did.

He's been hiding behind the tires for several minutes and there's been no visible activity. He edges toward the largest building and enters through an unlocked side door. The perimeter wall looks more than strong enough to keep the outside out, but the lack of security is worrying. There are live Haters in here, for Christ's sake.

Whatever Matt expected to find inside the building, this isn't it. It's very simply decorated—barely decorated at all, in fact—and the air inside has a stale, musty tang. It has the air of a relic:

not preserved, merely forgotten. Trapped in time. Overlooked and irrelevant. Just what Estelle Bisseker and Franklin clearly wanted.

Matt's in a plain-looking lobby space with a wooden staircase which climbs up toward an uninviting, shadow-filled landing, then appears to climb again. When he looks up, the building's original purpose is revealed. It's some kind of religious hideout. A faded rune painted across one of the magnolia walls indicates this was a convent back in the day. The jury's still out as to what's actually going on here, but he doesn't think nuns are pulling the strings. He imagines a flock of wizened old busybodies inhabiting these buildings, paying penance because their book told them to, then locking themselves away in their cold, threadbare rooms and whispering prayers into the empty air. Are they still at it here? Is that what this place is all about, righting society's wrongs? *Bring us a few sinning Haters and with God's help we'll put 'em straight . . .*

Matt already wants out of here, but he knows he can't leave. Not yet. He needs to know what Estelle, Franklin, and their lackeys are up to because whatever it is, he doesn't want himself or Jen getting caught in the cross fire. There are Haters here, he reminds himself again. There *will* be cross fire.

He climbs up as high as the first landing then walks along a narrow, poorly lit corridor with creaking boards. There's another staircase at the far end. There are voices coming from one of the rooms on this level so he continues past then goes up as far as he can until he reaches an atticlike space with a single entrance door which is ajar. He listens—no one's up here—then slips through.

Fuck.

Now he's really concerned.

Whatever these people are, he can also add sadists to the list, because the evidence is plain to see. This dank room stinks of blood and piss. The bare floor is covered with unsavory-looking stains and blotches. Worst of all, there are shackles and chains attached to the far wall, and the wall itself is pockmarked and splattered.

Change of plan.

Matt's now thinking that if he doesn't get out of here fast, those shackles might soon be holding him captive.

He's at the top of the steps when he stops moving. More muffled voices. Shouting this time. Is it an argument or an attack? He edges as far forward as he dares and looks down, craning his neck over the wooden banister. There's a trickle of light spilling out from under one of the first-floor doors. The altercation sounds serious but one-sided. A man with a deep, heavily accented voice is doing most of the talking, with little more than frustrated screams and curses coming from the other party. Matt creeps down to try and hear better because the poor acoustics of this ugly, warren-like building make it difficult to make out anything other than the occasional word. He clings to the shadows and edges closer then ducks around a corner when the door opposite flies open. The man with the booming voice emerges, chuntering angrily to himself, then slams the door shut and disappears down the main staircase.

Matt only manages a fleeting glance into the room, but it's enough. What he sees in those few brief seconds changes everything.

One of the Haters, strapped to a bed.

She's one of the killers he unwittingly helped round up today. Even if he hadn't seen her, her behavior gives her allegiance away. She constantly strains at the binds anchoring her to the bed, writhing maniacally, filled with nothing but absolute hatred and a desperate desire to kill.

Stunned, Matt turns to get out of here and walks straight into the deep-voiced man coming the other way. He reacts immediately, shouting at the top of his voice and filling the entire building with his sonorous noise. "One of them is loose! Upstairs! Help!"

Matt tries to explain but his words are drowned out by a tsunami of noise suddenly coming from elsewhere: the thunder of booted footsteps charging up the wooden stairs in this direction. Within seconds he's surrounded with weapons pointing at him from every angle. He immediately holds up his hands in submission. "Wait . . . please. Don't . . . I'm not a Hater."

Deep-voice pushes his way forward again, panic fading and confidence returning. There's a moment of hesitation from both sides in this sudden standoff: everyone regarding everyone else and asking *are you like me, or are you one of* them? When there's no immediate attack from either direction, there's a collective realization they're likely on the same side. Or different sides of the same side, at least.

"Who are you?" the man asks Matt.

Matt's not having any of this shit, there's too much at stake. He points into the room. "Why is there a fucking Hater tied up in there?"

The man doesn't react. Completely calm now, he remains infuriatingly impassive. "I'll ask you again, who are you, and how did you get in here?"

"And I'll ask *you* again, what the fuck is going on?"

Still the other man doesn't react. He casually glances at the firepower concentrated on Matt. "Is it really a good idea to be sounding off like this in the circumstances, friend?"

"I'm no friend of yours."

"We should feed this asshole to one of your pets, Joseph," one of the soldiers says with a sneer.

The man shakes his head disapprovingly, then returns his full attention to Matt. "Okay, last time of asking, what are you do-ing here? In the circumstances I really think you need to an-swer me. We've got all your exits blocked. You're not going anywhere."

"Just shut him in there and let that Hater bitch deal with him," a female CDF fighter goads. "We only just brought her in from the wastelands. She'll rip your fucking head off."

"I know exactly where she came from," Matt says. "I was out there too, and that's why I'm here now. I want to know why you're keeping Haters locked up inside the camp, and why I've been risking my neck helping you."

There's a commotion on the staircase. Franklin pushes his way up through the throng. "You?" he says when he sees Matt. He looks as confused and surprised as everyone else. "Don't you take the hint? What the fuck are you doing here?"

"That's what we're trying to establish," the deep-voiced man says wearily. "You know him, I take it?"

"Yeah, I know him all right. I thought he was dead."

"Sorry to disappoint."

"Is he trustworthy?" the other man asks, ignoring Matt's sar-casm.

"Jury's out," Franklin answers.

"Is Estelle here?"

"Yeah, she's in the office."

"Then I suggest we let her decide what we do with him."

Matt is hauled into a bare-looking office. Franklin's on one side and deep-voice—Joseph—on the other. Estelle Bisseker is sitting on the other side of a desk on a swivel chair, idly swaying from side to side but not taking her eyes off him. "We've got to stop meeting like this," she says, but Matt's not interested in her flippant small talk. He again launches into Franklin.

"You left me out there to die, you fucker."

"It's every man for himself outside the walls, you know that better than anyone," Franklin replies, refusing to be goaded.

"Yeah, I do now."

"You knew you were there as bait, right? The mission had been accomplished. That was all that mattered."

"Clearly. And what kind of sick, fucked-up mission was I a part of anyway? There are Haters in this building, for fuck's sake. In the middle of a frigging refugee camp. That's fucking insane. What the hell is this place?"

Franklin looks across at Estelle, who acknowledges his concern. She clears her throat. "There are five of them here at the moment, actually, and numerous more have been through our doors over the last few weeks."

"Tell him nothing," Joseph says. "The program is too important, Estelle. We can't risk it."

"Come on, Joseph, don't you think he's seen enough already? Matthew here is clearly a smart man. Tenacious, from what I've seen."

"You can say that again," Franklin interrupts. "Little shit won't stay dead."

Estelle sighs. "If we don't give him answers I've no doubt he'll try and find them out for himself."

Matt's tired of them talking about him as if he's not there. "Look, whatever you're doing, whatever your kink is, I don't care as long as me or any of the people I'm with don't get hurt."

"Good to hear," Franklin says.

"I'm not convinced . . ." Joseph grumbles.

Estelle sighs again. "Can we stop the pointless bickering please, boys?"

Franklin shuffles from foot to foot, suitably admonished.

There's an overlong silence before Estelle speaks again. "So what happened out in the field today exactly? Why is it we're all at each other's throats all of a sudden and Matthew's here asking all kinds of awkward questions?"

"We were operating close to the airport as you ordered. There was a missile strike closer to our location than we expected. It was just bad luck. It sent frigging loads of them heading in our direction."

"But you still got away and you still managed to bring back a couple of them with you?"

"Yeah. Couple of casualties, though. We lost Graham Porter, and Priest and that dog of his."

"Damn shame," Estelle says. "We didn't lose Matthew, though."

"No thanks to you," Matt says. "I don't know which is worse, being attacked by Haters or being shot at by the bloody CDF."

"That wasn't us," Estelle's quick to point out.

"It was the military. Of course it was you."

"We're *a* military," she says, "not *the* military. We're not officially CDF any longer. Most of them have disappeared, in case you haven't noticed."

"There doesn't seem to be a lot of difference from where I'm standing."

"Oh, there most certainly is. Out here we're autonomous now. There might have been an overall command structure to begin with, but so many links have been knocked out of the chain that the country's defenses have ceased to operate collectively. From what I understand, apart from a contingent who've assumed control of the main command center by the arena, there's been something of an exodus of us military types from the camp. I'll level with you, Matthew, we're not quite at the *every man for himself* stage yet. Every squad for themselves, perhaps. Right now it's all very . . . fragmented."

"This just gets better and better. I thought they were providing cover for us out there, but they're just as likely to take us out as they are the Haters."

"We're wasting our time here," Joseph says.

"No, we're not," Estelle corrects him. "We have to believe that when the war's over, what's left of the country will pull itself back together again. All we can do for now is defend and strengthen our little part of the world and hope the people we have here will survive. For now it's about keeping us apart from the Haters, and you, Matthew, are the kind of person who can help us do that. You're smart. You think first, act later, and that's a rare quality these days. You've been left to fend for yourself in the wild more than anyone else I've come across, and every time you manage to come back reasonably unscathed."

"Physically, maybe," Matt corrects her, because right now he's not sure what his emotional state really is. "And anyway, you're talking crap. You say you want to keep us apart from the Haters, but you've brought them into the city. How does that work? Do you have any idea what'll happen when they get loose?"

"Of course we do," Joseph says. "But you're making assumptions. You don't know what we're doing here."

Matt's not listening. "Because they will get loose, you know. I saw one a few days back . . . that's how I found Franklin, remember?"

"We remember," Estelle says. "Damn shame, that was. We thought he was making such good progress."

Matt shakes his head in disbelief. "You're out of your minds, all of you."

"Tell him," Estelle says, looking directly at Joseph. "Give him the full spiel."

"Are you sure?"

"I'm sure."

Joseph clears his throat, as if subconsciously underlining the importance of whatever comes next. "I'll start at the beginning. My wife and child were killed by a Hater back when this all began, and I went out of my mind. You wouldn't think so looking at me, I know, but I hit back. I *fought* back. I thought that the only way I could avenge my family's deaths was by killing, but I couldn't have got it more wrong. More killing just causes more problems."

"Fuck me," Matt groans, his patience being stretched to the absolute limit, "you're not going to tell me this is a frigging hippie commune, are you? Make love, not war and all that shite?"

"There's no need to be patronizing. But you're actually not a million miles off the mark. Thing is, when you hit someone, their immediate response is either to hit you back harder or to run. Usually they hit. That's what I did, but I soon realized that the more I fought, the higher the stakes became. The risks were increasing, but the situation wasn't getting any better. Eventually I realized I needed to look for another option, a different solution. And that's when I found Estelle and her people."

He pauses. Matt says nothing initially, but he's intrigued. There's an unexpected sincerity about this man which has caught him off guard. He may well prove to be completely deluded, but there's little doubt he believes in what he's saying.

"Go on."

"What we have operating in this building, Matthew, is a Hater reeducation program of sorts."

Matt can't help laughing out loud. "You've got to be kidding me."

"I assure you I'm not. See, my thinking is this: If we keep

fighting, if we keep attacking each other, then sooner or later there'll be nothing left. Not everyone wants to fight, and that includes some of the Haters, too. There are many of them who are so consumed by the Hate that it's their only focus, but equally there are many more out there who are lost, who *have* lost. When that bastard killed my family, he was almost as distraught as I was. He didn't want to do it, I'm certain of that now. Here we believe that there are some Haters who exist on the borderline, who can be pulled back toward civility."

"Bollocks."

"Why do you think we've been risking our necks out there?" Estelle asks. "You've been helping us catch the reluctant few."

"Yeah, I thought it was because they were easy targets."

"Not quite."

"So you're going to train them to behave again, is that it? Teach them tricks like dogs?"

"We're trying to reconnect them with the people they used to be, not train them to fetch sticks," Joseph says.

"I've heard it all now. So say you're able to get them to behave, then what? Do you just set them free?"

"What do you think? We get them out of the city."

"And then? Do you expect them to go back out into the wild and spread your word like bloody church missionaries?"

"Who knows what will happen. It's very early days still."

Matt's really struggling to get his head around any of what he's been told. "I'm sorry, and please don't take offense, but I think you're a bunch of absolute fucking cranks."

"And I don't blame you in the slightest for thinking that," Estelle says. She stands up. In her military fatigues she cuts a diminutive yet imposing figure. "Why don't you work with us, Matthew? I think you understand more about Hater behavior than you probably think. I realized you had something about you by the way you tracked Franklin back to base when we first met. Mr. Franklin here speaks very highly of you."

"I wouldn't go that far. I said I couldn't get rid of him, that's all."

"Mr. Franklin left me for dead today," Matt reminds her.

"Since we last met you've been out into the battle zone on several occasions and each time you've made it back in one piece. Most people go out once and either never return or vow never to go back out again. You've bucked that trend. You've also managed to find this place and break in. No one else has done that, either."

"Just lucky, I guess."

"I don't think so. There's no such thing as luck. My father used to say you need two things to be successful in this world, courage and luck. And if you've got enough courage, you don't need any luck."

"Very inspirational," he grumbles, sarcastic.

She allows herself half a smile. "Help yourself to some food from the stores here, then go home and get some rest. Why don't you come back tomorrow and spend some time with Joseph? Let him try and convince you. Yes, it might seem futile trying to shape the behavior of a handful of Haters when there are hundreds of thousands still out there, baying for our blood, but we believe it's an important first step. When our forces have finished pounding them out in the wastelands, when the enemy is exhausted and broken and starving and weak, we'll be ready to take back control. The people we're working with here will be the bridge between us, you mark my words. Don't write us off until you've seen what we've achieved."

23

Matt remembers his first day working with Ronan, Paul, and the others, back before the old world died. He'd had his doubts about Ronan's company from the outset, but had taken an uncharacteristic risk and accepted the job. Jen gave him a pep talk on the way out the door. "You don't have to stay if you don't like it," she'd said. "Just go and see what it's like." Weird how her words are rattling around his head this morning. It's true, though. If Joseph and the others are as crazy as he believes they are, he can just walk away.

Joseph's slopping out when Matt arrives at the repurposed convent, and he's immediately press-ganged into helping out. Matt thinks his life has reached a new low now, clearing up Hater shit and emptying it out in the yard.

"Before we start today, I need you to do something for me," Joseph says ominously as they work. "You have to lose your preconceptions and drop your automatic defense mechanisms while you're here. Nothing's going to happen to you."

"What defense mechanisms?"

"I see it in your every reaction. Someone makes a suggestion, you start looking for reasons it'll fail, not reasons why it might succeed. We're drowning in a sea of negativity these days. You need to have a positive outlook."

"Easier said than done."

"Granted, but by all accounts you've spent a good deal of time out in the open, surviving on your wits. You can only have done that by having a positive approach. You've no doubt also survived by being guarded and putting up barriers. Now I'm asking you to pull them down. What we're all doing in this situation—you, me, the Haters—is demonstrating the exact same behaviors. It's completely understandable . . . we're all driven by instinct. Now there's the mother of all differences between our instincts and theirs—"

"You're not wrong."

"—but what I'm seeing in you is the exact same thing I'm trying to instill in the Haters I'm working with. I've been thinking about what Estelle said yesterday. You approach things from a different perspective than most, and it gets results. It's almost like you have a kind of filter in place. Franklin was amazed you made it back alive and that you managed to get into this place. It shows real foresight and planning. A calmness, almost. The Hate has stripped away that rationality from most of the enemy. They see one of us and all control is immediately lost because all they want is to kill. So what we're trying to do here is teach them to show the same kind of restraint you've proved yourself capable of, to think first and hold the hate rather than just lash out."

The two men are standing at the bottom of the staircase at the entrance to the convent.

"You're staring at me, Matthew, but you're not saying anything. What are you thinking? Trying to work out whether I'm crazy or have a death wish or both?"

"To be honest, I'm not sure what I'm thinking."

When a surly-looking woman approaches, Joseph catches her eye. "Morning, Selena. How's Angie today?"

"A little calmer," the woman replies, sounding tired. "I was up most of the night with her. She's taking food and water from me now. She's advancing pretty quickly, all things considered."

"Mind if we go up and see her?"

"Be my guest."

Joseph climbs the stairs into the bowels of the convent and Matt follows. "Between you and me, Matthew, I think Selena's the best we have here. She's far better than me. I mean, I can get results, but she's so quick and efficient. She seems to cut the crap and gets straight to their heads and their hearts. A woman's touch seems to really make a difference. Maybe you'll get to see her in action. She mothers them. She's very good."

Matt's heard Selena's name before. "Wait . . . The Hater who got loose a few days back, he was one of hers, wasn't he?"

"Indeed. But it wasn't her fault. It just shows you just how difficult and unpredictable this process can be."

Joseph stops outside the same room where Matt was cornered last night and pushes open the door. Matt suddenly feels unbearably nervous. He knows there's a Hater in here who'd kill both him and Joseph in a heartbeat. Him especially, he thinks, as he's directly responsible for her being held here in captivity. He's relieved when he sees that Angie is still strapped tightly to the bed. The room smells rank. Sweat and musk and Christ knows what else. It's inhuman to keep someone in these conditions, he thinks, but then again, inhuman is exactly what these bastards are.

Joseph goes inside and gestures for Matt to follow. Angie is asleep, but not for long. She seems to sense the two of them there and her eyes open wide, panic-filled. She goes to sit up but her body is restrained. She tries to lift her head, but it's bound to the bed with a strap across her forehead. She tries to scream, but she's gagged. Joseph stands his ground in full view at the foot of the bed. The Hater's ire is barely contained, restricted only by her binds. But then she slows. Calms. Relaxes. Or is it resignation?

"That's good, Angie, really good," Joseph says. "Do you remember me? I'm Joseph. We spent some time together when you first got here. Remember why we brought you to this place?"

The Hater woman's eyes are wild. Expressions are difficult to read with the gag and the strap across her forehead, but Matt's sure he detects a subtle change. Then there's a definite movement. Christ, is this animal communicating with him? Is she nodding?

"Good, Angie, good. You thirsty?"

Another reaction. It's not much, but it's far less venomous than anything Matt's seen from a Hater before. Joseph picks up a bottle of water and takes a few tentative steps closer. Angie writhes on the bed as he approaches, but then appears to remember herself and relaxes slightly. Joseph waits—making sure it's safe—then carefully removes her gag and holds the bottle up to her lips. She drinks several large gulps, then drops her head back to the pillow, exhausted. He replaces her gag then ushers Matt back out into the hallway.

"So what do you think? When she was brought here yesterday she'd have probably bitten my bloody hand off if I'd tried anything like that."

He looks at Matt hopefully, but Matt can't match his enthusiasm. "What do you want me to say, Joseph? Yeah, so she's now the most placid Hater I've ever seen, but so what? She'd still kill both of us if she wasn't tied down. Do you really think this is going to make any difference?"

Joseph sighs and leans back against the wall. "I think it just might. Makes me feel better trying to do something, though, you know?"

"I get that, but is this really the best use of your time? You know what this reminds me of? Those frigging stupid dancing horses you used to see on TV. Remember them? Dressage, wasn't it? They had them all moving around in unison, nodding their heads and tapping their hooves on the ground in time with the music. All very impressive if you like that kind of thing, but by the end of it you had to ask yourself, what's the fucking point of a dancing horse?"

"You're far too cynical. Don't you see what I've proved here? The change that turned them into killers, it could possibly be reversed. It's likely an emotional, not a physical change. We already know the Haters you and the others have been bringing back from out on the fringes aren't ready to give up everything of the people they used to be. I believe there's still some good in them somewhere."

"Are you for real? They killed your family, remember? Do you have any idea how clichéd this all sounds?"

Joseph smiles, shakes his head, then looks down at his feet. "Forgive me. Okay, maybe I'm being a little too elaborate with my explanation. What I mean is, there's still a chance of reversing the damage these people have done by appealing to what it was that made them human in the first place. They're the same people, they just got caught up on the wrong side of the wave of change that's washed over the entire planet."

"And what about the Hater who got loose and started killing people by the arena the other day?"

"That was damn unfortunate. But you need to keep things in perspective, Matthew. We've had many more successes than failures."

"I think you're the one who needs to keep things in perspective. You're one man. You have, what, five Haters here right now according to Estelle? There are millions of them out there.

Millions. Do you expect these few to cure the whole damn lot of them?"

"No, but those we do help will go on to help others. It'll be exponential. You're right, though, it's a massive undertaking and I have no idea if it'll be successful, but we have to try, don't we?"

"We're bit players in the most far-reaching war there's ever been. You're kidding yourself if you think what you're doing is going to make any difference."

24

Despite the fact that East Kent Road is so full of people he can hardly move tonight, Matt's home earlier than usual. He's empty-handed, and the others are immediately concerned. "What's wrong?" Jen asks.

"Nothing's wrong," he tells her, deliberately vague, and he goes upstairs to change. He takes his time going back down. He sits on the end of the bed, trying to make sense of everything that's happened over the last couple of days.

When he finally goes into the kitchen, they're all there waiting. Mrs. Walker, Jason, and Jen are sitting around the table with one seat left vacant. "What is this, some kind of inquisition? Am I head of the household or prime suspect?"

"Neither," Jen says, and she gestures for him to sit down.

Mrs. Walker's the next to speak. She clears her throat, sounding as unsure as Matt's feeling. "I've not known you for long, Matthew, but I've seen enough to know that you're a decent man. When decent men like you come home from being out in a place as bloody awful as this city and they tell the woman they love that nothing's wrong, then it's blatantly obvious that *everything's* wrong. We're all adults here, and I need you to be honest. Level with us."

He can't help but laugh. "Be honest? I don't think anyone here's been completely honest for a while now. If we were being honest, we'd have faced up to the fucking awful situation we're in by now."

"I've been honest," Jason says, and Matt laughs again.

"You? You're the very worst, mate. You talk like you're the big man, all full of noise, but you never follow any of it up with action. First sign of trouble and you fall apart. You demonstrated that perfectly the other night when the food ran out at the arena. Where's your backup plan? I don't know how you've managed to survive for so long. I reckon everything you've told me so far is crap. All that stuff about your fancy flat . . ."

"That's true," Jen says, jumping to Jason's defense. "Amit told me. He showed me photos on his phone before the power died."

"Your flat?" Mrs. Walker interrupts. "Amit told me you were staying with your parents . . ."

"You see," Matt says.

"I never said I owned the flat."

"Okay, maybe not, but we assumed and you let us believe it." Matt watches Jason, who stares dead ahead into the evening gloom, then he turns to look at Mrs. Walker. "And your kid's not diabetic, is she?"

There's a collective intake of breath. "Jesus, Matt, have you lost your mind?" Jen says.

"I'm not denying the girl's sick, but she's not diabetic."

"That's out of order," Jason protests, animated again now the heat's off him. "I've been getting her medication."

"I know, I've seen it stockpiled in the front room. I'm sure Sophie is sick but she's not diabetic, is she? Our diets are so poor I reckon she'd have had all kinds of problems by now."

Absolute silence. Mrs. Walker has tears rolling down her cheeks. She reluctantly nods. "Sophie's always suffered with her health, but it's anxiety as much as anything. We're all anxious, though, everyone is. If I hadn't said something like diabetes she'd have been forgotten. I'm sorry . . ."

"I'm not angry," Matt says quickly. "I don't blame you. You've deceived the rest of us, but I think you did it for the right reason. You're just looking out for your kids."

"And what about me?" Jen demands, sounding more angry than Matt thinks he's ever seen her before.

"I love you more than anything, Jen, honest I do, but you're just as bad as the others. You're agoraphobic, but you won't say it. You never used to let me tell anyone. I used to have to make excuses. The people at work thought you were a figment of my imagination because they'd never met you."

"Why would I want to go outside now?"

"You wouldn't, and right now I'm relieved you haven't. How would I ever have found you if you'd left this house?"

"So why are you attacking me?"

"I'm not. I just can't sit back and watch you all carrying on like everything's going to be all right here as long as we keep the front door shut. The world's falling apart out there, don't you get it?"

"And you're perfect, are you?" Jason says, the venom in his voice barely contained. "Some kind of fucking genius because you managed to get back home in one piece?"

Matt shakes his head. "Nope. I think I'm the worst of the lot, actually. I've not been honest. I've been dumb and naive and every time I think I've taken a step forward, I look around and I've taken ten steps back. I've dragged you all back with me in the process."

"I think you still have a better idea what's happening here than the rest of us," Mrs. Walker says. "You've seen more of what's left of the world, that's for sure."

"Yeah, but he won't tell us about it, will he?" Jason snaps.

Matt looks down at the table and, for the longest time, he doesn't speak. "I don't want to tell you, because there's nothing we can do about any of it," he eventually admits. "What good would telling you do?"

"But we're not trying to fix this," Jason says, "we're just trying to stay alive. Shit, man, if you managed to stay safe on your own out there with hundreds of Haters all 'round you like you claim, you must be able to get us through whatever this place can hurl at us."

"He's right," Jen says. "What do we need to do to stay safe and stay alive, Matt?"

Another reluctant pause.

"Right now I'm struggling to see a way out. From what I've seen, the military or the CDF or whatever they're calling them-selves has splintered, and it's every one of these camps for itself."

"That's not necessarily a bad thing, though, is it?" Jason says. "You said before, it's just a question of staying put until the Hat-ers outside the camp have been killed or starved or whatever."

"Yeah, but how long do you think that's going to take? Weeks? Months? Years? Because that's the variable in the equation that none of us can work out. How are we going to survive for any length of time when there's no space here and no food? No clean water, no sanitation . . . and the longer we wait, the worse it'll get."

"So can we leave?" Mrs. Walker asks.

"And go where?"

"I don't know . . . there must be somewhere?"

"There isn't. However bad it is in here, it's a hundred times worse on the other side of the city wall. Trust me, I know."

"But you can get food," Jen says.

"Not anymore. As of today my source has dried up."

"Where were you getting it from?" Mrs. Walker asks. "Come on, you've been quick enough to criticize everyone else for being dishonest. Exactly how have you been keeping us fed?"

How much does he tell them? How much would they believe? Is there any point sharing any of what's happened to him recently? Right now he doesn't think he has anything left to lose. "I was helping a CDF faction."

"Helping them do what?"

"Track down Haters hiding in No Man's Land."

Jen's appalled. "Jesus, Matt. You've been outside the camp again?"

"I did it for *us*," he tells her, "but I'm done. What they're doing is futile and misguided and it's dangerous as hell. I'm getting out while the going's reasonably good."

"But why take such a risk in the first place?"

"Knowledge is power. Have you heard that old cliché before? I figured we might have half a chance if I got involved with the people who were supposedly in charge and tried to work out what they're planning."

"I can't believe you risked going back out there," she says. "Promise me you won't do anything like that again."

"I told you, I'm finished. I'm not going back."

An ominous silence descends on the kitchen. For a while the only noises come from other places: the kids bickering in the room next door, voices outside on the packed street, air traffic, distant fighting beyond the border. Jason takes a deep breath and asks the question everyone's thinking. "So what do we do? Sounds like we're in a lose-lose situation here."

There's an equally long wait before Matt replies. He's still looking down, and when he finally looks up he sees it's all eyes on him. "What? Are you expecting some great speech?" he says, sounding as empty as he feels. "I'm sorry. I've got nothing."

Jen gets up and storms across the room. "So that's it, is it? You go through all that shit to get back here, and now you're just giving up?"

"If anyone else has any ideas, I'm all ears."

"Please, Matthew," says Mrs. Walker.

Jen crouches down next to him and takes his hands in hers. "This isn't like you, love."

He looks into her face and feels the weight of the combined expectations of everyone in the house. He knows he can't just roll over, because that's no longer in his nature. "Fuck it, you might be right. Things look shitty, but being here's better than when I got back from that island."

"So how did you get through that?" Mrs. Walker asks.

"The golden rule that kept me alive out there was to look at what everyone else was doing, then do the opposite. Maybe we just need to do the same?" He's thinking on his feet now. "If we're going to stand any chance at all then we need to be one step ahead, but at the same time make it look like we're ten steps behind."

"You've lost me," Jason says.

"We act dumb. Right now we really only need two things, and that's a decent supply of food and to be invisible. We need to hunker down."

"Where?" Jen asks.

"Here, I guess. It's as good a place as any. It's the only place, if I'm honest. Did you never watch a zombie movie and think to yourself, why don't you idiots just lock the bloody doors and wait for everyone else to get themselves killed? The more desperate the rest of the people in the city get, the more they should gravitate toward the same places. The gates, the old food distribu-

tion points, the places where they can still get water . . . This is
a nothing house on a nothing street full of nothing people. No
one will come looking around here."

"You're sure about that?" Mrs. Walker asks.

"As I can be."

"But what about supplies?" Jason asks. "You said your source
has dried up, and you know as well as I do there's nothing left
out there."

Matt's mind is suddenly racing. "I think you'd be surprised.
We just need to apply the same logic and look where no one else
is looking."

25

First light.

It's been pouring down with rain for hours, clattering against the windows, and this sudden, monsoon-like downpour shows little sign of abating anytime soon. The sky overhead is a turgid mess of rolling yellow-gray clouds which look too heavy to stay up there, like they're going to drop and smother everything at any moment. Regardless of the conditions, Matt's outside. He knows he could probably still get food from people at the convent, but at what cost? The ever-increasing risks make the gains barely worthwhile. Instead, this morning he's giving Jason a master class in going against the flow.

What's left of this city never slows and never speeds up. It's a constant collective insomnia, an endless malaise. With no structure, routine, or purpose to their lives now, the masses simply exist. And without the regimentation and familiarity of the lives which they've been torn away from, they're lost. No internet, no TV, no movies, no magazines, no jobs, no schools, no homes, no point.

"Don't look," Matt tells him, conscious that Jason's staring at a simmering altercation on a street corner.

"What?"

"Don't make eye contact. Seriously. The more people you make any kind of connection with out here, the more they'll be watching you. You should know that by now."

Jason tries to do as he's told, but it's hard. "I do, but it feels different now. There are so many people out here . . . It's impossible."

"No it isn't, you just need to focus. Don't look at them, look through them."

"It's not that easy."

"I never said it was. You start staring someone out now and all they'll be thinking is *what do they want from me?* Or *what can I get from them?* Don't engage. Don't trust anyone."

Jason's distracted again, this time by the gangs of children he sees scavenging in the foothills of a refuse slag heap. They're all ages, picking through the waste for food like the kids from war-strewn Third World countries he used to see on TV.

Neither of the men has spent much time in this part of the camp before today, not since the city was cordoned off from the rest of the world. They've reached the fire-damaged Royal Midlands Hospital. What's left of it, anyway.

Over the weeks a makeshift field hospital has sprung up in the Royal Midlands' shadow and has grown like a weed, wrapping its tendrils around the main building while also spreading farther and farther out into the camp. No doubt its numbers became massively swollen by a sudden influx of the injured and displaced after the fire. It's easy to get distracted imagining the panic which must have gripped patients and staff alike as flames tore through parts of the monolithic building. Matt tries to put it from his mind as he leads Jason through a mazelike mass of rain-soaked canvas.

Of all the sights they've so far seen in this increasingly

godforsaken place, the field hospital is by far the worst. The heavy rain this morning is compounding the grimness, leaving the narrow gaps between shelters and stationary vehicles churned up and muddy like something from the First World War. In a wall-less shelter—little more than a grubby fabric roof supported by poles in each corner and a sagging crossbeam—a number of patients sit together in a miserable huddle, bandaged-up but otherwise forgotten. The look in their eyes is haunting. They say so much without saying anything at all.

"What the fuck are we doing here?" Jason whispers with more than a hint of nerves in his voice. "Seriously, man, this is a bad idea. We could catch all kinds of shit here."

"Have you not been listening to anything I told you? We have to go where nobody else goes."

"Yeah, but there are thousands of people here. What makes you think we're going to find anything they've missed?" Now that they're deep in the midst of this improvised medical facility, it seems to go on forever. Nothing but sickness on all sides. Jason imagines the people here fighting over single crumbs of food. Every face he sees is hollow-looking. Starved.

"Not here," Matt says. *"There."* He points up at the main hospital building, which looms large over everything.

"Are you fucking kidding? It'll be a thousand times worse in there."

"You're right. Nobody in their right mind is going to go looking for food in that place."

"Nobody but you."

"Nobody but *us*."

From a distance the three sections of the hospital building appear separate and distinct. Close-up, though, and it's clear that this is a single building which separates into towers at a much higher level. The place stinks of death. Christ alone knows how many people must have been killed when fire ravaged the building. The area around the burned tower is markedly quieter than everywhere else. Is it reverence or fear which keeps the masses away? Matt has no time for either.

He points at the part of the hospital which is most badly damaged. The building's once-white skin is almost exclusively black higher up save for a small patch which has been spared near the roof. "Look," he says to Jason, "that part was cut off by the fire. It'll be practically untouched inside."

Jason follows Matt down to the main hospital entrance. Like everywhere else, it's rammed with people. They could be patients, refugees, or staff, it's impossible to tell. Matt thinks they're just here because there's nowhere else, that as grim and uninviting as this building is, it's (just about) better than nothing. In places they're so densely packed that the crowd appears like a single writhing mass; arms and legs and heads everywhere, like some grotesque conjoined creature carpeting the ground.

On Matt's advice they're both carrying rucksacks filled with junk to give the impression they're looking for a place to stay, not looting. Jason appreciates his foresight now, because everyone here has something they're desperately clinging on to. A bag, a box, a suitcase, a crate . . . frantically grabbed remnants of their old existences packed up in haste as they ran for their lives. It makes him and Matt look unremarkable.

Every inch of floor space is occupied. The light inside the building is low and it takes a long time to negotiate between and around the refugees. As soon as Matt sees a staircase and an opportunity to get up off ground level, he takes it.

It's easy to be sure they're heading toward the fire-ravaged area, because the number of people reduces as the severity of the damage to the building around them increases. It's testament to the designers of this massive structure that the fire was relatively contained. Matt checks each level as they climb. The last three floors have been progressively more damaged to the point where the level they've now reached is nothing but black. "It's only when you're away from them that you realize how loud the crowds are," Matt says, and he's right. Other than their labored breathing and heavy footsteps, the only noise comes from the wind whistling in through broken windows.

"You're sure this is going to be worth it?" Jason whispers, because he clearly isn't. The staircase itself is blackened and charred now and the light has reduced to virtually nothing, all windows covered over with soot. Matt feels his way a few steps higher and realizes the way through is blocked by fallen debris.

"I'm sure," he says. "No one's been here since it happened. You can feel it."

Jason doesn't doubt he's right. "There's good reason for that."

"And that gives us an ever better reason for pressing on. Can't go this way, though. The fire burned itself out before it reached the top levels. The undamaged section is right above us, assuming we can get to it. We'll find another way up. There must have been more than one way."

Matt leads Jason along a ruined corridor which stretches out into the darkness. There's a glimmer of light at either end, but the illumination barely reaches the middle. That's for the best, he thinks. There are blackened bones covering the floor. It's impossible to tell where the people end and the building begins. Matt edges along the dirty walls, feeling his way and dragging his feet when the amount of detritus is too uneven to risk taking proper steps. Jason literally hangs on his coattails, following the noise he makes as much as anything.

A lift shaft. One sliding door is wedged open but there's no lift visible. There's enough metalwork on the walls of the shaft to hold on to and Matt nonchalantly slips into the small rectangular space and begins to climb. "You've got to be fucking kidding me," Jason says under his breath. His whispered words are amplified by the shape of the apparently bottomless chute.

"No joke, just move."

A short climb—it might just be one level, it might be several—and Matt's able to rest his feet on a narrow ledge while he forces another door open. He expects to find more fire damage, but doesn't. It's weird, surreal almost. They're above the devastation now, and up here it's like nothing ever happened. This part of the hospital feels trapped in the prewar. Pickled in aspic.

Unlike the patients.

There must have been scores of them left up here, unable to escape. The bodies are piled up against doors they've tried to get through, corpses wearing patient's gowns lying alongside those in hospital scrubs. No one got out of here alive.

Jason drags himself out of the lift shaft on his hands and knees, then vomits when he sees (and smells) a mound of decaying flesh dead ahead. Matt keeps going. He's seen worse. "This is nothing compared to the shit outside the city, believe me."

"We should go back," Jason shouts to him across the echoing, sarcophagus-like space. "There's no point. If there was anything worth taking here, this lot would have already had it."

But Matt's not listening. He's still heading up.

There are scraps of food on every level, pretty much on every ward and side room. Enough, with the medicines they also collect from cupboards they smash open, to fill both of their rucksacks. It's grim work picking through the remains, emotionally and physically grueling, but they have to do it. Near the top of the hospital building, where they find labs and offices and other empty spaces, Jason suggests this would be a good place for them to sit out the rest of the apocalypse.

"Bad idea," Matt tells him. "We'd never get the others up here."

"Yeah, but it would be worth the effort. Once we're here—"

"Once we're here we'd be stuck for the duration. A hiding place without a decent escape route is a tomb."

"I just thought—"

"No, Jason, you didn't. You just reacted and said the first thing that came into your head. There's a difference, and that's the difference you have to be aware of if you want to get through this. You might be right, we might be safe up here from the people down there, but this place would leave us prone. There'd be no quick way out if things go shit-shaped, and they usually do in my experience."

"You'll disappear up your own ass one day."

"Mock me all you like, I know what I'm talking about. Why do you think there are so many dead bodies up here? They couldn't get down. *We* wouldn't get down, not at any speed, anyway."

Enough talking. Matt's still climbing, this time heading up a precarious-looking maintenance staircase and out onto the roof. The rain's still driving down and the wind is fearsome. Head down, hanging on to whatever he can find for support, he walks toward the edge of the building and surveys the camp below. In spite of the low cloud, the view from up here is astonishing.

"What do you see?" he asks Jason.

"Same old, same old. Too many people, not enough space."

"Look closer."

"What?"

"Don't just accept what you see, start trying to read it. See down there?" He points to an area closer to the center of the camp, away from the hospital grounds. "I reckon that's a likely flashpoint, a bottleneck. It's an intersection. If anything happened around there you'd likely have people converging from all different directions. And over there . . ."

"Where?"

Now Matt's pointing in the opposite direction, closer to home. "Right over there. Nearer to our place."

"What, that empty space?"

"Yes, the space. Why's it there? It wasn't there last week, I don't think. Has it just been cleared? Is it too dangerous to be around there? Has it been sealed off because the Haters have attacked the border again? You see what I'm getting at? Don't just look at what's happening now, try and work out what's already gone and what might come next."

"What's that place?" Jason asks. Now he's the one doing the pointing, but Matt knows immediately what it is he's spotted. The high-walled military compound from which he first ventured out into the wilderness with Franklin and the others is surprisingly conspicuous from up high. The crowds are dense around its clearly defined perimeter.

"That place," he warns him, "is bad news. We stay away from there at all costs."

"Why? That where the CDF lot you got mixed up with are from?"

"Yes, as it happens, and we should avoid them. More guns than brains."

"You burned all your bridges, then? Would you not be welcome?"

"Quite the opposite. They'd have me back in a heartbeat."

"So what's the issue?"

"I just think that in a shitty situation like this, a person's sense of public duty will only last so long, know what I'm saying? If push comes to shove, they'd throw me under the bus or put a bullet in my head as fast as they would a Hater. Maybe even faster."

"Every man for himself, eh?"

"In my experience, yes."

"So why the crowds around there? Must be something worth having."

"Word gets around. I could think of better places to go begging, though."

Matt braces himself against the wind and crosses to the other side of the hospital roof to look out over No Man's Land and the wastelands beyond.

"What's going on out there?" Jason asks. There are definite signs of activity beyond the border and toward the outer edge of the dead zone. "More militia?"

"Not sure . . ." Matt replies, intrigued.

"Don't look like military to me. Where's the air cover for a start? I heard they never send people in on the ground without air cover."

He has a point.

"It's too far away for another attack on the border," Matt observes. "Some kind of ground offensive?"

Role reversal. Now it's Jason whose connecting the dots. "Don't think so. If it was a ground offensive they'd be pushing out from the city, wouldn't they?"

"Possibly."

"Whoever that is out there, they're coming this way."

"But they're not, are they?" Matt says. "Watch them. They get so close, then they stop."

"Weird."

Jason digs around in his bag and fishes out a pair of binoculars. "You didn't think to get those out earlier?" Matt asks.

"Wasn't sure I'd need them. Brought them along just in case."

Matt gives him a few seconds to focus and adjust, then asks the obvious question. "Well? What do you see?"

Jason's quiet. Too quiet. He scans the horizon from left to right and back again and the longer he's looking, the more Matt's concerned. He nudges Jason, who then hands the binoculars over.

Matt immediately understands Jason's reluctance to speak. There's no visible uniformity or order to the mass of vehicles he can see in the distance, nor to the many figures moving to and fro between them. What there is, however, is an undeniable shared purpose and an unquestionable intent.

"Haters," Matt says. "Fucking hundreds of them."

"Again, though, where's the air cover? Why aren't the military blowing the shit out of them?"

"Because from what I've seen of the military, I think it's less about civil defense now, more *self*-defense. They're less interested in protecting us, more concerned with looking after themselves."

"So all those Haters . . . why don't they just attack?"

"That's the million-dollar question, isn't it? Looks to me like they're strengthening their numbers. Building up an army big enough to try and take this place from under us."

"Then we have to get out of here."

"And go where? There's no way out and nowhere to go. Right now I think our only option is to keep doing what we're doing—"

"—and just wait for it all to blow over?" Jason interrupts.

"If you have a better idea then let me know, because I'm rapidly running out of options. Looks like we're under siege."

26

To stay locked away in the house and do nothing just isn't in Matt's nature, no matter how bleak things look. For the next four days he and Jason are looting from dusk till dawn to build up a decent stockpile of supplies. They target unremarkable-looking residential properties mostly, quickly developing a serviceable double-act routine: look for the houses where there are no obvious signs of life, or very obvious signs of death, then stake them out to be sure. Once they're as certain as they can be that no one's coming in or going out, they'll get closer. Once they're sure the houses are empty, they break in and strip whatever they can find.

There's slim pickings to be had. The effort involved does not directly translate into results. They're more than three months into the fighting. Even if there was food here once, it's almost certainly been used up, stolen, or gone bad by now.

They find plenty of bodies, though. In one house yesterday they were attacked by its sole remaining occupant who they'd presumed was dead. She'd crawled across the corpses of her housemates to get to them, disentangling herself from a mass of death. Events had clearly driven her out of her mind. She had all the ferocity of a Hater, but lacked the intent.

The military compound where Matt first encountered Franklin and Estelle is the last place he can think of trying. He'd previously made a conscious decision to stay away, but right now the military looks like their only remaining option. *No one else is going to risk stealing from the CDF.* He knows you'd have to either be desperate or a real fucking idiot to try it. Right now, he thinks he might be both.

death. Events had clearly driven her out of her mind. She had all

The compound has been overrun. This place had been a walled oasis of space in the midst of the otherwise endless congestion, but not today. The entrance gate lies buckled and smashed, brought down by a garbage truck which has been abandoned in the courtyard.

Jason hesitates when he sees the crowds. "Is there any point?"

"We're here now," Matt replies, already wading into the masses.

They go everywhere, checking the parts of the complex Matt knew and those he hadn't previously explored. "Waste of fucking time," Jason grumbles when they've completed almost a full circuit. "Doesn't look like your mates put up much of a fight."

"They weren't my mates," Matt quickly corrects him. "Think about what you're saying, though."

"What?"

"How many times have I told you to not just accept everything you're seeing? To think about *why* instead of just *what*?"

"You piss me off when you get pretentious like this."

"I'm being serious. Look around. What do you see?"

"Loads of people looking for stuff that isn't there."

"My point exactly. Where's the weaponry? The CDF people who were based here would have defended themselves. They were heavily armed, for Christ's sake. Where's the battle damage and the bodies?"

"So you're saying they abandoned this place?"

"Exactly. I reckon they packed up and shipped out while no one was looking."

He changes direction, heading back across the courtyard toward the stores building Estelle showed him first time he was here.

"What's this?" Jason asks as they enter the lockup.

"When I first came here this place was filled with supplies, now there's not a single scrap left. There was heavy duty, dual-controlled locks and everything. They must have airlifted everything out, either that or they'd been gradually emptying it over time."

"Great."

"There's no point wasting any more time here. If the CDF had left anything worth taking, someone else would have had it by now. Let's go home."

Back out on the street, Jason pulls Matt closer. "So who's in charge when the military disappear? The people? Militias?"

"You tell me. Scares me to think about it. It used to be whoever had the most cash or influence or fame . . . None of that counts for anything anymore. I guess it'll be the strongest who survive."

"Those who can hit hardest?"

"Probably."

"So the Haters, then? 'Cause that's what you're saying, isn't it? The strongest will survive, and that's them. Stuck in here like this, we're just sitting ducks."

27

"I'm scared, Matt."

"I know you are, love. I am, too. We all are."

They're lying in bed together, listening to the rain-soaked chaos consuming the streets outside. Another heavy downpour. Matt pities anyone who's out there tonight. He pictures people struggling to rescue the little they have left from raging torrents and waterfalls, storm drains failing to cope with the deluge. He imagines already overcrowded buildings becoming busier still as people look for shelter, rammed up against each other until they're unable to move.

"So what are we going to do?"

He doesn't immediately answer. His head's full of conflicting thoughts.

"That makes me feel even worse," she says.

"What does?"

"Your silence. You've always been so sensible, so grounded. My friends used to say you were boring and safe, but they didn't know you like I did. You're always weighing up the options and considering all the possible outcomes. I reckon that's how you managed to get back home when everyone else was panicking and fighting."

"So why do you feel worse now?"

"I know you better than anyone, and I know that when you're quiet like this, you're thinking. And the longer you're quiet, the more it makes me think you don't have an answer. Don't bullshit me, Matt, please. The time for that's long gone."

"Okay. I'm sorry."

"And don't apologize. You don't need to. Just answer me honestly. What are we going to do?"

"I don't know," he admits. She must have asked him that exact same question upward of a hundred times since he got home, but before today he's always had some kind of lifeline to throw to her.

But not tonight.

All their escape routes have been blocked off.

There's no way they can leave the city. The risks were already too great, and that was before he saw the Hater activity out in the wastelands from the hospital roof. The fact the population appears to have been largely abandoned by the CDF compounds the hopelessness of their position.

Hell, who's he kidding? It's getting too dangerous to even leave the house. From what he's seen he thinks the streets inside the barriers will become as wild as what's left of the world outside. He thinks back to when he and Jason looted the hospital ruin, and when Jason suggested they should stay there. Matt had argued that the building would inevitably become a tomb for them, but isn't that what the city itself has become for the six people in this house and hundreds of thousands of others? How long will they last here, struggling to eke out a meager existence on the derisory amount of food they've managed to forage over the last few days?

Since the first death on Skek all those months ago, Matt's tried to remain positive in the face of increasing uncertainty. As his colleagues were picked off one by one on the island, he was still able to cling on to *something*. The need to get back home to Jen kept him moving forward, and he allowed nothing else to get in his way. Even when he'd made it back to the mainland, when the stakes felt like they were increasing by the hour, almost by the minute, he was still intent on getting back to this house and Jen.

And for a time, even after he'd made it home, he remained focused. *Provide for Jen, protect Jen, make sure we're both okay . . .* Tonight, though, things feel very different. Tonight, for the first time, he can't see any way out. It feels like they're just waiting for the inevitable.

28

East Kent Road always used to be a desirable address: a quiet little road in a quiet part of town. But there's nothing quiet or desirable about this place today. The rain hasn't let up, and it's now so heavy that at times it's like a mist, making it impossible to see. The water puddles and pools in the gutters, forming huge lakes because there's so much detritus that the drains are blocked and there's nowhere for the standing water to go. Yesterday's streams have become raging rivers of foul-smelling water. "Just when you think this place can't get any worse," Mrs. Walker says to Jen, "it does."

Over the last couple of weeks, the number of people living in the streets here has grown exponentially. Outside the house, the floods have caused chaos.

"They're in the garden, Matt," Jen says, watching from behind the net curtains in the bedroom.

"And as long as they don't try and get in the house, it'll be okay. If we went out there and forced them to move on, more would only take their place."

"So what do we do?"

"I've got it covered. I took the shed apart last night. I'll use the planks to board up the doors if I have to and we'll move Mrs. Walker and the kids into the back of the house. Let them think there's no one here."

"What, apart from the bloke doing the hammering?"

"Give me a break. I'm trying my best here."

"I know, but what is this, Matt? Night of the bloody Living Dead? We'll all end up locked in the attic at this rate."

She has a point.

"Maybe we will. There are worse places, though, believe me. Look, when the rainwater subsides there will be more space outside again and they'll start to spread back out. It's only because the road and pavements are flooded that they've moved onto the gardens."

"I'm not convinced." Right on cue, someone starts hammering the door. "See," she says.

"Shit," Matt says. He wasn't expecting that. He moves toward the top of the stairs, but she grabs his arm and pulls him back.

"Don't. Just ignore it."

"I can't. I'll just go and see."

"Please, Matt . . . Like you said, let them think there's no one here."

He shakes her off. Heart thumping and feeling unprepared for the inevitable confrontation, he goes down and peers out through the spyhole.

Is this better or worse? He can't decide. He rests his head against the door, trying to process who he's just seen out there. More knocking. This time it doesn't stop.

"Well?" Jen demands from the top of the steps, frantic.

"It's okay. I know who it is. Stay here."

Before she can protest, Matt goes outside to speak to Franklin. He shuts the door behind him.

"How the hell did you find me?"

"It's taken a while," Franklin replies. Matt notices he's wearing civvies. Is he trying to hide the fact he's CDF, or is he now a deserter? "I've been looking for you for days."

"Why?"

"Anywhere we can talk?"

"You're not coming in, if that's what you're asking."

"Fine. We'll do it out here."

"I don't see we've got much to talk about."

"You'd be surprised."

"I doubt it."

"Look, mate, stop pissing me about. This is important."

"Why should I believe you? I was the bait on the end of your line, remember?"

"Listen, if you don't talk to me, you'll regret it."

"Is that a threat? I can look after myself."

"Yourself, maybe, but what about that girlfriend of yours I saw watching from the window just now? She didn't look too happy."

"Leave her out of this."

"With pleasure. Let's cut the crap, though. If you don't talk to me then you're both as good as dead."

"No thanks, Franklin. I'm through with you and your crazy friends."

Matt goes to shut the door but Franklin's boot is in the way. The soldier has a pistol aimed at Matt's gut, point-blank range, hidden from the crowds around by his long trench coat. "I'm not asking, I'm telling. Get your hunting gear on, mate, we're leaving."

He thought it might be better out here in the fresh air after the stale confines of their overcrowded house, but it fucking stinks out here. Stagnant water and sewage. But it's not the smell that's making Matt's guts churn, it's nerves. His pulse is racing, and its pace increases tenfold when they round the next corner. The pug-nosed military vehicle he remembers from the Hater hunts is here, tucked away in the shadows. Jayce, Franklin's ever-present driver, is leaning against it with arms crossed defiantly, watching them make their way through the heaving crowds.

"What the hell am I doing?" Matt says to no one in particular. Franklin, a step behind him, loaded pistol still pressed against his back, has his answer ready.

"You're doing exactly what you need to do. You're helping me, and you're doing something that's going to give you and your girl a fighting chance."

29

"Where are we going?" Matt's question goes unanswered. He asks again, frustrated by the lack of response. It's just him, Jayce, and Franklin in the military transport, and they've barely said a word to him. "We're pretty low on numbers if we're hunting," he says.

"Just shut up," Jayce tells him, her eyes fixed on what's left of the road ahead, wipers clattering back and forth across the glass. They followed their well-worn but otherwise little-known route out of the city to get here, but then drove in the opposite direction to usual. Matt's sitting behind her in the back of the vehicle, craning his neck to work out where they are. He can't see much through the grille-covered windows. "Keep your bloody head down," she curses. "Jesus Christ, are you trying to get yourself killed?"

Matt slides back into his seat. He's seen enough to know they're south of the city. Before the apocalypse he remembers there being an unusually sharp dividing line between the urban and suburban here, and it strikes him this is exactly the kind of place they don't want to be. "What are we doing out here?" he

ALL ROADS END HERE

hisses at Franklin, who's sitting alongside him, also keeping low. "There's nothing much 'round these parts, you know? You probably won't find Haters here, and there's fuck all around if you're thinking about looting."

"We're not looting."

"Then if we're not looting and we're not hunting, what are we doing?" Matt demands.

At least this time his question elicits something resembling a half-decent response. "Just do me a favor and shut the fuck up. It'll all make sense soon enough. You need to see this. Ask me all the questions you want later, but not here and not now. Understand?"

Jayce forces the trucklike vehicle up a steep hill, the engine struggling temporarily with the ascent, then takes a sharp left at the top, following a narrow track around into a country park. Now this place Matt definitely knows. It was a local beauty spot, though there's little beautiful about it today. Many of the tall pine trees he remembers have been destroyed by fire. The wreck of a downed plane has carved a deep, black furrow in the scenery. There are bodies—what's left of them—lying everywhere in various stages of decomposition. Some of the dead look relatively fresh but most are hideously withered and decayed. The fact that the death and devastation have extended out into isolated spots like this leaves Matt in absolutely no doubt as to the apparently endless reach of this infernal war.

Jayce revs the engine hard again and forces the vehicle off-road and up another steep rise. Matt remembers this, too. It's a lookout. A local landmark. There's an observation point up here with an uninterrupted three-sixty-degree view. She stops at the highest point then kills the engine and checks for movement.

"Get out," Franklin says when Jayce signals that it's safe.

"You're joking."

"I'm not. There's no one up here but us. Get out."

He's deadly serious, and he's also still armed. Matt does as he's told, instinctively eyeing up escape routes should this all go shit-shaped. The local geography will work to his benefit if they're attacked up here, he thinks. He'll use the natural downward slopes to build up speed and he'll run and keep running until he can't go any farther. Getting down from the top of the hill is easy. Where he goes after that, though, is anyone's guess. If he's forced to travel at the pace which got him back to the city in the first place, it could take him a week or more to get back home. Much as he doesn't like it, it's another reason for sticking with Franklin and Jayce for now.

The viewpoint is a waist-high, semicircular gray stone construction with several brass relief maps which correspond visually to the location of certain distant landmarks: more hills, a church, parts of the city. But Matt's not interested in the maps and what the world was, instead he's looking out over what it now is. The city and its traumatized population are behind them. Ahead of them the wilderness stretches out forever. Franklin nudges Matt and hands him a pair of binoculars. He almost doesn't want to take them because the less detail he sees, the better. He grudgingly holds the glasses up and soaks in the full extent of the devastation. "What do you see?" Franklin asks.

"A fucking ruin."

"Correct. Look harder."

Matt does as instructed. The view is immediately reminiscent of what he saw with Jason from the roof of the hospital. The longer he looks, the more movement he sees. "There's still plenty going on out there. Lots of activity."

"Correct again."

"It's all very one-sided. More Haters, but not a lot of CDF response."

"No response at all, actually. You know the city gates are finally closed now?"

"No more room at the inn?"

"There hasn't been a lot of room for a long time. The Hater attacks on the border have stopped, too. Had you noticed that?"

"I'd thought as much."

"Doesn't make sense, does it? The CDF stop defending the borders, and at the same time the Haters stop attacking."

Matt agrees. "So what's behind it?"

"Work it out for yourself. Go on, look closer at what's going on out there."

It's hard to make out any order in the distant chaos. There's constant fleeting, scurrying movement within the massed Hater ranks in places, but they're largely camped in one spot, sitting and waiting. There are likely tens of thousands of them out there. "They know where we are, and they know we're not going anywhere. I guess they're biding their time, waiting to strike. Either that or they're trying to starve us out."

"Maybe."

"I saw something similar on the other side of the city from the roof of the Royal Midlands a few days back."

"Yep, we're pretty much surrounded."

"Why aren't we carpet bombing them? They're easy targets in such large numbers."

"Word is the CDF has gone into lockdown at the airport. Every man for himself and all that shite. This is just one city, don't forget. There's a possibility we're caning them elsewhere."

"You think?"

"Not really."

Matt continues to study the distant Haters. "So what are they planning?"

"Come on, man," Jayce says, sounding exasperated. "Decode the behaviors. What would you do if you were in their shoes?"

"Their aim is only ever going to be to get rid of us, that much is a given," he begins, thinking out loud, "but they'll have their work cut out if they're planning an attack. It's shoddy and improvised, sure, but the camp's relatively well fortified. It'll take a certain amount of firepower to break through, and they just don't have that down there, from what I can see, just numbers. People power. *Hater* power. They'll have trouble getting into the camp, and it'll cost them big-time. Aggressive as they are, they'll still go down if they take a bullet. They don't know what defenses we've got."

"I agree," Franklin says.

"So is this a siege? That was my first thought. Like I said, are they trying to starve us out?" He thinks further about what he's just proposed, then talks himself out of it. "No, I don't think so. That doesn't fit. If that was the plan they'd be more visible. They'd want us to know they were there to send a message, let us know they're waiting. But they won't do that, because if they're too close, it could leave them prone to attack. And it would take a hell of a lot of effort for them to do that. Self-control's the thing they struggle with most. When they see us, when they know we're near, they generally have no option but to attack. So unless your friend Joseph has worked his brainwashing magic on all those nasty bastards out there, they must be planning something else. If it's not a direct attack and they're not trying to intimidate us into submission, then they're obviously trying to take a different tack."

"You're getting there," Jayce says. "Christ, this is like pulling teeth."

The penny drops.

"Wait. This isn't about what the Haters are doing at all, is it? They're surrounding us, and they're waiting. Things are already on a knife-edge in the camp. It's like a pressure cooker, and when it explodes . . ."

"Go on," Franklin urges.

"When it explodes as it inevitably will, the hundreds of thousands of people in the city will have no option but to get out if they want to stay alive, and getting out means they'll be forced out into the wastelands . . ."

"Which is exactly where the Haters are."

"Christ, that's it. They're waiting for the camp to fall. If it goes down they'll take us out in the thousands, those who aren't killed in the initial panic. They're not going to risk a full-on attack, they're waiting for us to go to them. We'll be even more vulnerable on the run. At least there are places to hide in the city."

"Exactly right. And it's not a question of *if* the camp falls, it's *when*."

"You've seen enough. We need to move," Jayce says, and neither man argues. They both take cover in the back of the military transport again. Matt's relieved to be out of sight.

Jayce drives at speed back down the track to the road, but instead of going back the way she came, she instead drives farther away from the camp. Matt senses the change of direction. "Wait . . . Where are you going? Thanks for the guided tour and all that, but we should be going the other way."

"Not yet," Franklin tells him. "We're not done."

Jayce accelerates again, heading deeper into Hater-held territory. Matt's quick to point out the imminent danger. "You do realize you're driving straight toward them, don't you?" He shuffles in his seat to get a better view of the world outside. They're motoring along a dual carriageway strewn with abandoned cars. There's a blockade up ahead, people swarming all around it. Haters, they must be. "What the fuck is she doing, Franklin?"

"Trust me."

"Trust you? Fuck, I can't think of anyone I trust less."

Franklin gets down on the floor of the vehicle and covers himself with a blanket, gesturing for Matt to get under with him.

"You've got about ten seconds," Jayce says from the front. "Don't make it your last ten seconds."

Matt risks one final look out. Jesus, they're in trouble now. The military truck is already attracting plenty of attention. *All* the attention, in fact. He's only looking for a half second, but it's long enough to see just about every visible Hater stop whatever they're doing, pick up arms, and get ready to face the oncoming vehicle.

"Last chance," Franklin says.

No chance, Matt thinks.

He gets down and tries to make himself as small as possible, finding his face uncomfortably close to Franklin's. As much as he doubts the other man's motives, he doesn't think he'd be stupid enough to risk everything so spectacularly.

Matt tenses up as he visualizes the pack of rabid Haters that will be stampeding toward them now, the scent of Unchanged blood driving them wild. He braces himself, and is surprised when the truck comes to a slow, controlled halt. This is audacious even by Franklin's standards. Matt listens for the sound of gunfire, because that's the only way he can see them getting out of this impossible situation.

But in the driving seat, Jayce doesn't panic. She doesn't pull a gun or knife, she simply winds down the window and acknowledges the nearest Hater.

"What the fuck is she doing?" Matt hisses to Franklin, but Franklin doesn't answer.

"Nice wheels," he hears a man say.

"Yeah, came across it a few days back," Jayce casually replies. "Thought it might be useful."

"Where you heading?"

"Looking for some folks who are camped just outside Droit-wich. Seen much activity that way?"

"Some decent numbers out toward Bromsgrove . . ."

The conversation sounds bizarrely relaxed. Must be a particularly dumb Hater, Matt thinks, because the only other explanation he can come up with seems impossible.

The truck starts to move again.

Matt stays where he is. Franklin lifts his head half a minute or so later then yanks the blanket off Matt, leaving him exposed. "Worked it out yet?"

"Jesus fucking Christ, you're both Haters?"

"Not me," Franklin says. "She is."

Jayce continues to watch Matt from the front. She can see the instinctive panic in his eyes. "Relax. You've spent hours with me. I'd have killed you by now if I was going to."

"Thanks, that's really reassuring. You could have told me," he says.

"We could have, but we didn't," Franklin says. "Wasn't worth the risk. Jayce is sound. She's on-side, and that's all you need to know. Now sit back down and strap yourself in, we've still got a lot to do."

Matt does as he's told, his mind racing. "So Joseph's bullshit really works?"

"Well the jury's still out on him," Jayce explains. "I worked with a chap called Simon. And don't go thinking it's all one-way traffic and we're all subscribing to the gospel according to Saint Joseph and seeing the error of our ways . . . some of us don't want this war and we've chosen to make a stand. I think the essence of what Joseph and the others are saying is right. Fighting's not the answer."

"Jesus, I've heard it all now."

"No, you've only heard half of it," Franklin says ominously.

They're driving for another half hour, maybe longer. Matt's lost all sense of direction now and has no idea where they are. He's forced to take cover with Franklin again several more times, but the roads are largely clear. He heard aircraft engine noise a while back and Franklin confirmed they'd skirted close to the CDF-controlled airport. Other than that, the only thing he knows with any certainty is that he's farther from Jen than he wants to be. Farther than he should be. The fact he has a Hater chaperone makes him feel secure and vulnerable in equal measure.

Without warning there's a sudden change in direction followed by a succession of several more sharp turns. The end of the line? "Stay low," Jayce warns. "Plenty of movement around here."

Matt figures they must have left the main road and are now in a housing estate or similar. He's about to ask when the transport is plunged into darkness. It then comes to an abrupt stop. Matt barely even breathes. He's ready for trouble, and though he can't understand why they'd go to such lengths to bring him out here and kill him, right now he wouldn't put it past either of them.

"Move," Franklin orders.

It's pitch black in here, wherever here is. Matt's tense, ready to make a quick getaway in case this is the trap he fears. Avoidance is preferable; fighting a last resort. At least the darkness will give him half a chance, he thinks, although a half might be generous. His usual tactic would be to take his chances and run, but out here—wherever here is—he's just as likely to run straight into a pack of Haters as anything. His options are reduced to zero when Franklin takes hold of his arm and pulls him out of the truck and into the darkness.

"If you wanted to get rid of me, why not just kick me out for the Haters?"

Franklin laughs. "Now don't start giving me ideas. I've been trying to get rid of you for ages, but you keep coming back. You're my good-luck charm, mate."

"Don't mock me."

"I'm not, I'm serious. By all accounts you should have been dead a hundred times over or more, but you always manage to find a way out."

The gloom begins to lift as Matt's eyes become accustomed to the lack of light here. "What is this place?" he asks as he's taken through a cavernous, warehouse-like building.

"Home," Franklin answers. "At least it will be."

"This was a printing house," Jayce explains. "Don't ask me anything more technical about it than that, because I can't tell you."

The floor space they're currently crossing is vast and is dotted with long-silenced machinery. Huge, dust-covered rolls of paper sit on colossal spools at the beginning of numerous snaking production lines, all frozen mid-job. Matt's taken aback by the sense of scale and the space. He can't remember having this much room to move freely since before he left home for Skek. For a while he's preoccupied, given an unexpected glance back into recent history. The printers must have been working on government contracts because the half-finished letters on the conveyor next to him are about benefits that'll now never be paid into people's bank accounts that'll never again be used. It's only after a few seconds that he finally reacts to what Franklin just said. "Wait. What did you mean, this is home?"

"Come with me," Franklin says, and together they head deeper into the building. Beyond the main shop floor there are a succession of offices, equally preserved and untouched, abandoned mid-shift and mid-meeting. Beyond them, a staircase leads down into a basement full of now redundant computer equipment. It feels like a tomb. "We're going to get all this cleared out eventually," he explains. "It'll give us more space."

"When we found this place it was pretty much untouched," Jayce says. "Why would anyone bother with a printing house?"

"So that's why we're based here," Franklin continues. "There are other places nearby which attract all the attention."

"Such as?" Matt asks, his mind racing.

"A couple of distribution centers. Amazon, supermarkets, places like that."

"Yeah, I can imagine there's not a lot of stuff left there."

"We've got a lot of it in here, to be honest," Jayce says, and she pauses to open another door which has been secured with a padlock and chain. This second room appears to be watertight, airtight . . . everything-tight. She holds the door open then hands Matt a flashlight and nods for him to go through.

"Fuck me."

He shines the light around a second, much larger underground space, and everywhere the light hits, he sees piles of supplies.

"This is where the UPS and power and all that was. Makes a perfect shelter," Jayce explains.

"Who for?" he asks, still trying to come to terms with the scale and richness of this place.

"Well that's the million-dollar question, isn't it?" Franklin says.

"I'm guessing you two have spaces reserved. So who else? Your boss Estelle? The camp commissioner . . . Jenna whatever-her-name-was?"

"Nothing to do with either of them. Jenna Holbrook's been dead for ages. She died a few weeks after the city-camp was established, but it was easier just to let people think she was still in charge."

"Who then? Why are you showing this to me? We're not exactly best buddies, Franklin. You left me for dead last time we worked together, so I'm hardly expecting my name to be on the guest list."

"This is how we see things panning out," Franklin explains, ignoring Matt's antagonistic tone. "As you know, the remaining population of the camp is cut off and can't go anywhere. The bulk of the military have either decamped to the airport, assumed control of the administration center, or have disappeared completely. We see the odd bit of aerial support these days, but nothing worth writing home about."

Matt takes over, because after what he's seen today he's already played this scenario out in his mind. "So the camp's going to reach tipping point sooner or later—probably sooner—and the place will implode. Anyone who manages to get out alive will be wiped out by those evil fuckers hovering on the outskirts. No offense," he hastily adds, nervously looking over at Jayce and hoping he hasn't pissed off the Hater in the room.

"None taken," she says, glaring at him. Matt realizes he needs to bite his lip, but the arrogance of the hordes of killers waiting out there to kill makes him . . . makes him hate them.

"So people like you and me," Franklin continues, "we're pretty much screwed whichever way you look at it."

Matt agrees. "I guess so. Even if you manage to evade the first wave of attacks, it's only going to be a matter of time before they get you."

"Exactly."

"And if you're outside the city in any kind of numbers, you're an easy target. You won't have a hope in hell."

"Again, you're right."

"But there's more to it than that," Jayce says. "We're just as bad. You can mock Joseph all you like, but him and Simon and Selena helped me to see past the killing and regain my focus. I'd already decided to try and pull back from the fighting, but the time I spent with them opened my eyes to the futility of it all. I've been thinking about what comes next."

Matt's worried. "Sounds ominous. Go on."

"I don't reckon the Hate will dry up once all you people are gone, I think it might change, but it'll just continue. It's the law of the jungle. We're already seeing stronger Haters dominating those who are less inclined to fight. There are some who can't do anything *but* fight. Brutes, they're calling them. Violence is all they know now, all they understand, and all they want. But a Hater who doesn't share the same desire to fight . . . now that's a problem. In some people's eyes they're almost as bad as you Unchanged."

"I doubt that."

"You'd be surprised."

"Nothing surprises me anymore," Matt says.

Back to Franklin. "So think about what Jayce is saying. What happens if the Haters think they've got rid of all of us? Will the killing just stop? I happen to think she's right. This is their way of life now. They won't just go back to their old jobs and routines, because they're gone. The old world's finished and there'll just be a vacuum left in its place. We're both of the opinion that they'll turn in on themselves. We think the other side will just splinter, then splinter again, then splinter again and again and so on until there's just the worst of them left alive. Or, better still, none left alive at all."

"Sounds feasible. So what's all this conjecture got to do with this place?"

"Because we think at the rate things are going there's a good chance they'll wipe themselves out. It might take six weeks, six months, or six years, but that's how we see it going down."

It all feels uncomfortably plausible to Matt. "So this place is your bunker, and you're planning on keeping your heads down and sitting it out?"

"Exactly right."

Jayce leads Matt even deeper into the large basement. It's filled with equipment. Piled high with food. "We've been planning this for some time."

Matt's finding it difficult to take it all in. "I can see that. Christ, there's more food here than there is left in the whole of the city."

"You're probably right."

And still there's more. In another section of the basement are rows of metal-framed camp beds as well as other supplies, clearly military in origin. Weapons. A full-on arms cache. Franklin explains. "There was an army barracks not far from here. Place was overrun pretty early on, but the focus back then was on people, not equipment. Looting this stuff after the event was as easy as nicking tins of food from supermarket shelves."

"So again, who's it all for?"

"Ordinary folk like you and me. People we have connections with. Decent people."

"According to who?"

"According to me and Jayce and a couple of others."

"How many?"

"Around fifty at the moment."

"All based around your convent?"

"Nope, elsewhere."

"So Estelle doesn't know about this?"

Franklin and Jayce look at each other. "Estelle's not in the picture anymore," Franklin admits.

"What happened to her?"

He shrugs. "Disappeared. Didn't show up one morning. Let's be honest, anything could have happened, and we're never going to find out. She probably saw sense and fucked off. Either that or someone did her in. She was very good at pissing people off."

"So is there anyone left in charge now?"

"Your guess is as good as mine. I'm sure we'll find out soon enough, though. Joseph's shenanigans are bound to attract attention."

Matt paces around the room. "So who exactly does know about this?"

"You, me, and Jayce, and the people we're taking."

"That's all?"

"Yep, that's all, and right now we intend on keeping it that way. The fewer people who are involved just now, the better."

"Not Joseph?"

"Nope. No one at the convent."

"So I'll ask you again, why are you showing me?"

"Needs must," Franklin says. "I already told you, there's no denying the fact you're good at what you do. You managed to survive on your own for a decent length of time, and I've seen you in action. Rather, I've seen how you avoid action. Like I said, I keep trying, but I just can't get rid of you." He pauses, leaving Matt to decide whether he's being sincere or sarcastic. "I know that you understand how the Haters think, so you know what you need to do to keep yourself out of trouble."

"Doesn't exactly feel that way at the moment."

"I'm sure it doesn't. Take it from me, though, compared to the other people who've come and gone since everything kicked off, you're damn good. Better than you probably think. You got caught out on your own during that last hunt, and not only did you make it back in one piece, you also managed to track us back to the convent and break in. You know what you're doing. Fact of the matter is, I want you to help us get our people out of the city. This job's too big for just me and Jayce."

"You want my help?"

"Yep, that's right."

"But there must be other people . . ."

"There was."

"So where are they?"

"You're the only one left. We've lost a lot of key folks recently . . . Graham, Chris Greatrex . . . all the original crew are dead."

Matt wanders around the stores, trying to take in the enormity of what he's hearing. "So do I get an invite if I agree to help?"

"Of course."

"I have to say, though, I don't think you've got a hope in hell of surviving out here."

"So what's your current survival plan?" Jayce asks him. "You must have one? Someone like you wouldn't not have a plan."

"Truth is, I don't. I thought I did. Right now I'm struggling to see a viable way out."

"So what have you got to lose by helping us?"

She has a point. "Nothing, I guess. Or everything. Depends how you look at it."

"Try looking at it positively," Franklin tells him. "So what do you think?"

"What about my girlfriend? What about Jen?"

"She can come, too. There's more than enough room down here. We need all the help we can get."

"There's a family living with us. A woman with a couple of kids and another guy on his own."

"You can bring all of them."

"Okay, so if I do decide to help, what plans have you made for getting your people out to this place?"

"This way," Franklin says, and he beckons for Matt to follow him back upstairs. He's led back across the work floor to the farthest corner of the building. It still feels strange to be walking freely in such an open space. Matt checks over his shoulder continually, but the only person there is Jayce.

There's a decent-sized truck parked in an internal loading bay. "I reckon we could get as many as a hundred folk in this thing," she says.

"Yeah, but can you drive it?"

"I parked it in here, didn't I? Took it from the distribution center next door."

It's clear this isn't some hastily thrown-together plan. The logistics are sound, but there are more than a few complications that Matt can think of. "Okay, let's back up a little. What do you think's going to happen when you rock up outside the city in this thing? Are you going to wait at some prearranged point for everyone to get on board like you're taking a frigging coach party to the beach?"

"That's where we want your help. Our people are already waiting at a rendezvous point. We'll get the lorry in and out quick. Literally a couple of minutes. We rock up, as you put it, we load up, and we fuck off."

"And when is this going to happen?"

"When it's time. Can't be any more specific than that. We need to judge it just right so that there's enough going on in town so that we can get away without attracting too much attention, but not so much grief that we're stopped from getting out. We're only going to get one shot at this."

"So are you in?" Jayce asks.

Matt's pacing. He nervously circles the truck, making them wait although he already knows what he wants to do. He doesn't think there's any alternative. He wants to keep Jen safe and, with the best will in the world, there's little chance of that happening in the city or anywhere out in the war-torn wilderness. He thinks this place might just be the salvation he's been too scared to start looking for.

"Fuck it, I'm in," he tells them.

30

A family meeting in the kitchen. Late. Dark. Mrs. Walker's kids are asleep in the room next door, but there'll be no sleeping in the rest of the house tonight. Matt's just given them a no-frills, spoiler-free version of Franklin's plan. He's told them about the safe zone he visited earlier today. They're conflicted; trapped between horror and hope.

"You promised me you wouldn't go out there again," Jen says.

"Yeah, and I also promised I'd keep you safe."

"And you expect us to buy into this bullshit?" Jason says. "An underground paradise."

"Believe me, it's no paradise, and I don't expect anything from any of you," Matt answers quickly. "I'm offering us all a potential way out. I think it's the best option for all of us. I also think it's probably the only option, if I'm honest."

Jen doesn't look convinced. She's sitting opposite, chewing her nails, just staring at him. "I can't do it."

"You can. You have to."

"I can't go out there."

"I won't let anything happen to you, love, you know that."

Mrs. Walker has her head in her hands, massaging her temples. She's been looking down at the table since this impromptu meeting began. She's exhausted. Face drawn. Graying hair scraped back. "You're seriously suggesting I take my children out into a war zone?"

"No, I'm suggesting we take them *through* a war zone to get to a place of safety. Look, I know how this sounds, but—"

"You're telling me you think being out there is safer than being in here?"

"Yes, and you're still working on the assumption that the city is safer than anywhere else."

"It is."

"At the moment, perhaps, but there's no guarantee it'll stay that way. Listen, we just need to—"

"You're seriously telling me I should trust you and take my children away from the safety of this house and take them who knows where to hide underground in a building for what could be months? Years even?"

"Like I said, I know how it sounds. Fact is, though, that's what's on offer. You come up with a viable alternative and I'm all ears."

"I don't think I can do it," Jen says again, her nervousness increasing.

"You *can*," he tells her, trying not to let his frustration show. "You have to. And yes, Mrs. Walker, the same goes for you and your kids. If we want to have any chance of staying alive, we need to leave. Wait long enough and this place will be as much a war zone as everywhere else."

"When do we go?" Jason asks.

"Don't know yet. We'll know when the time's right."

Mrs. Walker's still not buying it. "It's not that I don't believe you, Matthew, I just don't know if I believe you enough to be prepared to risk my children's lives."

"You'll be risking far more by staying put. At least this gives us a fighting chance."

"Why does it always have to be about fighting?"

"Figure of speech."

"Or a Freudian slip? You've not said anything to convince me. We're safe here, as far as I can see. Protected. I've seen you getting ready to board the doors and windows up and make the house more secure. Why should we give all of this up?"

Matt looks around the table at the faces staring back at him. "Okay, I'll level with you. There's something else you need to know. I didn't want to tell you because I didn't think there was any point. Maybe I thought that if I didn't tell you how bad things are, that you'd be able to make a decision without feeling pressured or coerced."

"Cut the crap, Matthew, and tell us everything," Mrs. Walker demands.

So he does.

"This camp's overfull, you know that much already. You also know that there's no more food. There's not a lot of water, either, apart from the standing rainwater, and I wouldn't recommend you drinking that. I haven't seen a working standpipe in days."

"Just tell us what we need to know," Jason says.

"It's still early in the season, and there's every chance the temperature will increase again. With the heat and humidity, there's probably going to be more chance of disease."

"Not if we stay here in isolation," Jen interrupts, clutching at straws.

"What you probably haven't realized because you've been locked away in here, is that the military support looking after us all in this camp has reduced massively. They've pretty much all gone. Given us up as a lost cause. We're being left to our own devices, and add the lack of food and water and potential hygiene issues into the mix, and it's a recipe for disaster."

"Yes, but when the soldiers get rid of the Haters, we'll be able to leave the city safely," Mrs. Walker argues. "We should just wait a while longer."

Matt tries not to lose his calm. "*If* they get rid of the Haters. We don't have any real idea what's going on out there. All we know is what we can see, because all communication channels are broken. We don't know what's happening in other parts of the country or other parts of the world and because we don't know, hunkering down somewhere safe is the best option for all of us right now. The place they took me to today is isolated and it has supplies. Enough for everyone."

Mrs. Walker's not listening. "I think we should stay here."

"Have you not heard a word I've said?"

"Yes, but I'm still not convinced."

"The Haters are closer than you think. They're massing outside the city in huge numbers, just waiting for the camp to be compromised. We saw them, didn't we, Jason?"

"Yeah . . . I mean, it looked like Haters, but—"

"Cut the crap. We were on the roof of the Royal Midlands Hospital and we saw Haters gathering out beyond No Man's Land. I saw it again today on the opposite side of town. More of them. Hundreds more. Thousands."

"And are they going to attack?" Jen asks, terror writ large across her face.

"They might, but not yet. They're waiting because they know at some point the shit's going to hit the fan in here. The camp will implode before it explodes, I think. Fact is, we're under siege, and as soon as we're compromised, they'll strike."

"So you're saying we're fucked whatever happens?" Jason says.

Now Jen's in tears. Mrs. Walker's struggling to keep herself together. Jason looks bizarrely angry, like it's all Matt's fault. Matt's exasperated. "You know as well as I do that this is our only option. I can get us out of here and past the Haters to the safe place. We might need to leave tomorrow, but it might not be for another month or more. All I want you to do is get ready to leave here the second I give you the word."

31

On Franklin's orders, Matt returns to the convent next morning to work. Franklin and Jayce want him close. He'd rather be just about anywhere else, but he knows that, for now at least, it has to be this way.

In the few days since he was last here, the place has changed dramatically. His natural assumption was that more CDF fighters would have wound up here, but that's not proved to be the case. The convent feels almost as deserted as the overrun CDF compound. The recent floodwaters have swept through the surrounding area leaving much of it clear and yet, unusually, no one's moved back to reclaim the space. It's almost like the population senses there's something not right about what goes on here, like they're keeping their distance for fear of contamination.

Volunteers and soldiers alike are thin on the ground and Matt's roped into helping Joseph. One of the Haters almost broke her bonds last night. She's tied to the bed again now, tranquilized with industrial-strength meds, but in the short time she was loose she made a real mess of her bedroom/cell. Joseph and Matt are working together to clean it, tiptoeing around her semiconscious body. "Her name's Diane," Joseph says, gesturing at the prisoner. "That's about all we know. She was brought in a couple of days ago. It's important to remember that many of these people are unwilling victims of this god-awful war, same as we are. Okay, so they're aggressive and capable of doing bloody terrible things, but I believe they must want the fighting over as much as we do."

"You still think that?"

"I do. I've studied their behavior, same as you. I couldn't do any of this if I didn't understand them."

"Yeah, but there's understanding and understanding, isn't there? I watched them and learned from them so I could avoid being killed, not because I want to know what makes them tick."

"It's the exact same thing. Believe me, Matthew, I know all too well what these people are capable of."

"And you're still here?"

"I don't have any choice. If you ask me, I think we've reached a pivotal moment in human history."

"Easy on the hyperbole."

"I'm serious. This is a conflict that'll define all of our futures. To me, this feels like the last world war. The final war, if you like. We can't not act."

The Hater on the bed stirs. Joseph is between Matt and the door, and though Matt instinctively tries to slip past him and get out, Joseph stops him. He smiles and puts a finger to his lips, then pushes Matt back deeper into the cell. "We need to be going the other way if she's about to explode," Matt warns.

"Calm down, man. Just observe, okay? Stay back and out of her line of sight and you'll be fine."

The woman on the bed stinks, and her stench is enough to make Matt gag. Her head's restrained so she can't easily look anywhere but up, and the tattered clothes she's wearing are soiled and sweat-stained. She strains and squirms, writhing in her

ALL ROADS END HERE

own filth. Hater or not, the conditions she's being held in are appalling. Inhuman. Matt thinks she'd be better off dead, but it doesn't appear to faze Joseph in the slightest. "Good morning to you, Diane," he says, his resonant voice filled with what Matt hopes is artificial warmth and familiarity. "How are you feeling today?"

He leans closer to the Hater. She's in some kind of stupor, driven out of her mind, Matt presumes, through a combination of being held captive, being pumped full of tranquilizers, and being subjected to Joseph's bullshit. It takes her several seconds to come around fully and to focus. When she realizes there's an Unchanged man standing in front of her, her reaction is violent in the extreme. She arcs her back wildly as if she's being electrocuted and screams with frustrated fury, the hatred clearly audible in spite of the gag in her mouth. She crashes back down onto the stained mattress then tries to lunge again. Matt sees that there are savage-looking welts and lesions on her ankles and wrists where she's repeatedly strained against them, desperate to escape and attack. Her right ankle looks particularly fierce. It's raw and infected, and he can smell the poison in her blood from where he's standing. Unable to reach her leg because of her binds, she instead constantly moves it. The nonstop rubbing is agitating the weeping wound.

The Hater is exhausted. She soon stops fighting and starts to drift in and out of consciousness, panting hard but doing little else, her leg jerking involuntarily, the mother of all sleep-twitches. Joseph waits for her to finish like she's giving a well-rehearsed performance for his benefit, then edges a little closer when it's safe. "We all done now, Diane? That leg giving you some trouble?" The Hater's eyes flicker again and she groans. "You want to scratch it? Want me to bathe it? It's looking pretty sore, if you ask me."

Both Matt and Joseph jump with shock when she lunges again. And then, again, Joseph waits for her to stop.

"Having all these tantrums and sweating like a pig . . . I'm starting to think that leg's never going to heal. I give you a few more days before the infection takes hold. Strikes me I'll come into this room one morning and find you dead. Pretty miserable way to see out your time, if you ask me."

He waits for a response which doesn't come.

"Maybe I could clean it up for you? Put a dressing on it to stop it getting worse? Imagine how much better you'd feel. No more pain. No more irritation."

She reacts by kicking out again, and Matt notices that she recoils whenever the open ankle wound touches anything.

"How long do we have to play this game for, Diane?" Joseph asks.

Nothing.

"Okay, you have it your way. We'll try again tomorrow. I'm in no rush. I've got all the time in the world."

He checks her binds are tight, exaggerating his movements to demonstrate his control, then goes to leave.

The Hater speaks. Is it a word or just a moan? It's hard to tell. Her leg is in spasm now. Joseph doesn't show any emotion. He stands completely still with his back to her, eye contact now made with Matt.

He waits longer. The seconds tick by. It's half a minute maximum, but it feels like forever.

Finally the Hater makes another noise, and this time it's clearly a choked word. Joseph closes his eyes and composes himself. Matt can tell from the self-satisfied expression on his face that this a breakthrough. He turns back to his prisoner and removes her gag. She swallows, mouth dry, then speaks again. "Please . . ." she croaks.

Joseph pours a little water over her wounded ankle, pats it down with a soft rag he takes from his pocket, then rubs antiseptic cream into the infected area. For the first time since he and Matt entered the cell, she keeps completely still and doesn't fight. He gives her a mouthful of water, then replaces her gag. "That'll do for now," he says, his tone borderline patronizing. "I'm very pleased with you. You're making real progress, Diane. I'll come back and see you again later."

Joseph ushers Matt out of the room. As the two of them leave, the Hater is overcome by her anger and frustration at being left again. She knows she's not going anywhere, that it won't make any difference, but she strains and thrashes and moans as much as she can in the confines of her binds. This time Joseph simply leaves the room and locks the door behind him.

"And that's it?" Matt says.

Joseph ushers him farther down the corridor before replying. "You might think I'm crazy, Matthew, but I happen to believe in what I'm doing here."

"I never said you were crazy. Misguided, maybe, suicidal . . . I think what you're doing's impressive to a degree, and it takes some balls to get so close to those animals, but I'm struggling to work out why you're bothering. Muzzling a handful of Haters is never going to change the world."

"Perhaps, but we have to start somewhere, don't we? As I see it, the biggest problem is the gulf that's suddenly opened up between us and them. Bridging that gap has to be the first step toward ending the fighting."

"I get that, but it's a hell of a gap that needs bridging. It's going to take more than you and me and a bunch of tame Haters."

"They're not tame. Don't ever make that mistake. Even those who've made the most progress here have the propensity to regress."

Matt stops walking. "You see, that's another issue I have. You use the word regress like they've gone backward. If you asked a Hater, I'm sure they'd tell you they'd advanced and we were the backward ones."

"I have talked to them, don't forget. This all boils down to perspective. I guess we're all looking down our noses at each other."

"Okay, but what good is any of this really going to do? No offense, but it sounds like whatever hoops you get them jumping through while they're chained up in here, they'll have forgotten about as soon as they leave."

"That might be so. Only time will tell."

"And do any of us have that time?"

"I get the impression you're just being difficult for the sake of it."

Joseph's clearly had enough of Matt's questions. He continues downstairs into the bowels of the convent, leaving Matt alone on the landing where he stops and listens to the echoes of the old, decrepit building around him. The muffled groans and stifled roars of imprisoned Haters. Whispered conversations between the few remaining CDF soldiers left guarding the place. Joseph's bizarrely cheerful whistling fading into the nothing. But the convent itself sounds weary today, as if it's struggling to stay standing under the weight of the madness inside and around it.

He looks out of the nearest window, down onto the courtyard below. Franklin and Jayce are out there talking. Is Jayce about to "regress," as Joseph put it? Matt doesn't know which of them he trusts least. Logic says it should be Jayce because of what she is, but how sure is he that Franklin's not a Hater, too? Or Joseph, maybe? Is this whole place just an elaborate ruse? He's been assuming all along that the Haters are in the minority here, but what if he's the one being played and he's actually the only remaining Unchanged? He consoles himself with the thought that as futile as Joseph's plan to retrain lone Haters sounds, a Hater plan to ensnare lone Unchanged would be even more pointless. Particularly here, where there are thousands and thousands of people like Matt literally just a stone's throw away.

He wanders down to the courtyard. Franklin's on him the moment he steps out into the open. "I've been looking for you."

"I was helping Joseph. Keeping him sweet like you told me to."

"Whatever. I'm not interested. What are you doing now?"

"Nothing. I don't know where he went."

"Good. You're coming with us."

32

They're walking this time, and though the area through which they're now moving is familiar, Matt's never been this far from the center of the city-camp on foot. The military transport they used last time, the battered Transit van, a stolen jeep . . . hell, even a pushbike would be preferable to being exposed and unprotected like this. It should help having Jayce with them, but somehow the presence of the Hater makes Matt feel worse. It was easier when he didn't know what she is. Since speaking to Joseph he's been watching her like a hawk. He followed her through the crowds, wondering if she was about to lose her grip and start lashing out. He thinks he would if he was in her position. He actually thinks he might.

KFC.

The front of the branch of Kentucky Fried Chicken they're now approaching has been hit by a pickup truck. The dust and rust indicates that the collision happened some time ago, yet the vehicle's never moved and remains sticking out of what's left of the restaurant's frontage. Colonel Sanders's stylized face looks down disapprovingly from a plastic sign which, although still in one piece, is hanging at a perilous angle, suspended by vein-like wires. "Is this safe?" Matt asks when he realizes they're going inside.

"Is anything safe these days?" Jayce says, answering without answering.

They enter through a broken window, their unannounced arrival causing a flurry of frantic rodent activity nearby. From the noise and chaotic scrabbling movement, Matt thinks they've disturbed a nest. He hates rats, but he has bigger things to worry about right now. "What the hell are we doing in here?" he asks, increasingly uneasy.

"Just passing through," Franklin tells him as they march through what's left of the seating area. There are plastic tables and chairs and the detritus of the last meals cooked and half-eaten here. They then continue down a short corridor and through a door marked "Staff Only." The PIN code entry pad which kept it secure has been prised off.

The deeper they go into the building, the worse the stench. Past the dried-up toilets, through the kitchen and stores full of rotten food and rancid fat, then out into a small enclosed yard out back with overflowing wheelie bins. "You never react, do you?" Jayce says unexpectedly. As keenly as Matt's been watching her, she's been watching him. He's several steps ahead, sandwiched between her and Franklin.

"What?"

"We could be taking you anywhere."

"If you'd wanted to kill me, you'd have done it by now," Matt answers, matter-of-fact. "Anyway, I'm busy soaking up the view."

Just ahead of him, Franklin grunts but doesn't look back. "So what do you see?"

"Fuck all, so I'm asking myself why we're here, not where are we. The front of KFC looked impassable from outside. I'd probably not even have tried to get in, and I'm assuming that's why you use it, to cover your tracks. And if we're thinking along the same wavelength, I think you're probably showing me a way of getting out into No Man's Land on foot without putting our heads above the parapet. Am I right?"

Neither Franklin nor Jayce answer, and that's all the confirmation he needs. There's a hole in a wire-mesh fence which leads to a well-worn path through a patch of dense, overgrown, rubbish-strewn vegetation which, in turn, finishes right on the border of the endless dereliction of No Man's Land, among the ruins of a collection of fancy-looking houses. Matt can tell they were decent because of the size of their footprints. There's a collapsed house with just the garage door left standing, and it's wider than the whole damn house he and Jen live in. How the other half lives, he thinks. *Lived.*

"So, if I've got this right, you're taking me to meet the group who are going to be moving into the des-res you showed me underneath the printing house yesterday. Am I correct?"

"Keep your damn voice down," Franklin mutters. Again, Matt takes that as confirmation that he's right.

In the midst of what must have been almost a hundred homes, a single structure stands relatively unscathed. It's a chapel. "What was this place?" Matt asks, looking around.

"Used to be a mental hospital, by all accounts," Franklin tells him. "They knocked it down and built these houses here a few years back, but never did anything with the chapel. It was a protected building. Would have cost a fortune to do anything with it. As it happens, the houses around it seem to have shielded it from the worst of the shelling."

"Divine intervention?" Matt asks, clearly taking the piss.

"No, just luck," Franklin replies without a trace of humor.

"That and the fact the church was built of bigger bricks than any-where else nearby."

The chapel door is boarded up, but the boards are easily moved. Light streams in through high, grille-covered windows, illumi-nating faded traces of the building's former glory. There was a fire here at some point, but the dereliction is such that it's im-possible to tell if it was a month ago or a decade. Jayce and Frank-lin walk through the debris, then disappear down a staircase behind an altar-less space. "What is it with you pair and under-ground hideouts?" Matt asks, but his pointless comment goes un-answered.

Belowground, there's nothing. Just a dark, musty-smelling space. The longer they're down here, the more Matt's eyes be-come accustomed to the lack of light. He sees faint traces of yel-low spilling across the ground, and soon he's able to make out the outline of a door.

Franklin goes first. He bangs his fist on the door. There's an overlong pause, then muffled scraping sounds as it opens. He waits a moment longer, then goes through. A second later and he's back, having prepared those on the other side for their ar-rival. Matt's ushered in, and all he can see is a mass of people crammed into a small cellar with a curved ceiling. All ages, all waiting, all eyes on him. "Bloody hell," he mutters under his breath. The room was previously filled with a low buzz of con-versation. Matt's only aware of this now because it's been abruptly silenced.

"Bloody hell indeed," a willowy man with a patchy beard says. He stoops as he approaches and extends his hand. "You come to join our little exodus?"

"No, this is the one I was telling you about, Darren," Frank-lin says, talking about Matt as if he isn't there. "He might not look much, but he's proved himself pretty good at staying alive and keeping out of trouble."

Matt disagrees. Keeping out of trouble? Christ, he feels like a trouble magnet right now.

"Good to meet you," Darren says. "How are things looking up top?"

"Shite," Matt answers, to the point.

"No change there, then."

"A lot more shite, actually," Jayce says. "His name's Matt, by the way."

"And how much have you told Matt?" Darren asks, looking directly at Franklin for an answer.

"Enough for now. We've shown him where we're going."

"You mean there's more you haven't told me?" Matt says, confused and concerned in equal measure. "So when were you going to let me in on the rest, Franklin? When we're out there with a thousand Haters on our back?"

"It's not like that . . ."

"Then what is it like? I think I deserve to know."

"We're giving you and yours a ticket out of here, don't push your luck."

Darren seems less antagonistic than either Franklin or Matt. "How much do you know?"

"What you're doing and where you're going," Matt replies.

"But not why?"

"That's pretty self-evident, isn't it? You want to stay alive."

"Yes, but there's more to it than that. This is more than just a mercy mission, Matt. This is bigger than you or me or any one individual in this room. This is about ensuring the survival of the human race."

Matt can't help but laugh at the unexpected grandiosity of

the man's statement. "Sorry. I thought this kind of bullshit was
that guy Joseph's bag."

Darren smiles briefly. "It's not bullshit. Think of it as us going into hibernation and not coming out again until it's safe. We
won't win against the Haters, that much is already clear, but in
time they'll burn themselves out. It's inevitable. And we're going to be ready to reclaim whatever's left."

"That's if there's anything left to reclaim."

"There will be. I'm certain of that."

Matt doesn't think he's ever been less certain of anything.

Darren continues. "The way I've started to think about it is to
talk about this group being a time capsule, buried in the ground
until the human race is ready to restart again. And yes, before
you say anything, I'm well aware of how pretentious that sounds.
I know it's going to be hard and I know it's going to take a hell
of a long time, but we have to believe it'll work. One day we'll
be able to walk out there in the open air without fear again and
feel the wind in our hair and the sun on our faces. It might be
months away, it might be years, but we have to believe it'll happen because if we don't, then what's the point of any of us trying
to stay alive at all?"

Darren's distracted by one of the other people down here. The
crowd have regained their collective confidence again and are
starting to go about their business, not that there's much business to be had. Franklin seizes the opportunity to corner Matt.
"Listen, before you say anything, I know what you're thinking.
For the record, you're right, Darren's full of crap. It suits us to
have him providing the focus down here and keeping this lot
calm and in check."

"Does he believe the shit he's spouting?"

"Completely. And it is shit, I'm under no illusions."

"So why are you involved?"

"Same as you, I reckon. Because right now this feels like my only chance of staying alive. Unlike you, I don't have anyone else left worth caring about. I'm a selfish fucker and I make no apology for it. I just don't want to die, that's what it boils down to."

Franklin suddenly seems freer with his words. More honest. Less aggressive.

"So does any of what you've seen change your mind?" Jayce asks Matt.

"Do they know what you are?"

"Nope. And keep your voice down because we want it to stay that way, right?"

"Sure. So what's your motive, if you don't mind me asking."

"You still think I'm going to screw you all over."

"I wouldn't put it past you."

"My stepbrother is down here, as it happens. My dad slept around, and Nathan was the result. He's eight years old and he's an absolute little shit, but right now he's all I've got left."

"Now you answer her question," Franklin says. "Does any of what you've heard change your mind?"

Matt shakes his head. "Not at all. Way I see it, my options are still exactly the same regardless of whether or not your man Darren is insane. I can get out of the city and take my chances in the wilderness and risk being hunted down by Haters, or I can sit tight at home and wait to be killed when the shit hits the fan in the camp. Or I can hide out in the middle of nowhere with all you folks and have a slight chance of keeping Jen safe and us not dying."

"Yep, that's about it."

"I'm not sold on the 'new start for humanity' bullshit, though. Not yet, anyway."

"Doesn't matter. Neither are we. It's not a deal-breaker."

"You just need to get ready and stay ready," Franklin tells him. "Prime your girl and whoever else you're bringing along, and keep working in the convent so we don't get that lot asking awkward questions. When the time's right we'll take one of their vehicles, bring it here and pick up a welcome party, then get them over to the base."

"Then you and me bring the truck back to the camp," Jayce continues. "We load up the rest of this lot, then get the fuck out of Dodge."

"We're only ever going to get one shot at this," Franklin tells him. He points at Jayce. "She'll drive, because having her behind the wheel is just about the only way we'll get through the Haters in one piece. You keep us moving and I'll keep us safe. Got it?"

"Got it."

33

"They brought this fella in a few days back, just before the heavens opened," Joseph says, peering into the cell through the half-open door.

"You're still bringing fresh Haters in, even now?"

"Fresh? Don't talk about them like they're dead meat, Matthew. They're people, just like us. Anyway, why wouldn't we be?"

"Forgive me, it's just that this place seems a lot quieter than when I first arrived."

"Things are changing by the day. It's a struggle to keep up sometimes. But you have to, you understand me? You have to stay ahead of the curve."

Matt feels uneasy this morning, here under false pretenses, but Joseph too seems different. He's not himself. Jittery. "Is everything all right?"

"Everything's fine," Joseph immediately replies, his voice unexpectedly brusque.

"I can finish up here if you want. If the Hater's still sedated then I could—"

"Don't be so damn naive. You really think you're qualified to be on your own with one of them yet? You think you have the ability to be able to reason with the unreasonable, to hold your nerve and put your neck on the chopping block like I do day after day after day?"

"Jesus, Joseph, I was only offering to help. I'm not the enemy here. I'll go find something else to do if it's that big a deal."

"You do that."

Matt turns his back but he's only gone a few steps before Joseph calls him back.

"Matthew, I'm sorry," he says.

"So are you going to tell me why you're acting so shitty this morning?"

Joseph waits. Thinks. Checks the landing is clear. "Can I trust you?"

"Of course you can," he answers without hesitation. Joseph shakes his head.

"I'm not sure."

"Put it this way, you can trust me as much as you can trust anyone these days. You can trust me because I keep coming back." Matt decides to engage full-on bullshit mode. "There's nothing for me here except a lot of risk and the chance of taking a little food and water back to my girl, but I want to learn more about what you're doing here. I'll be honest, I'm far from convinced of your reasons and your methods, but the one thing I'm sure of is that right now you're the only one still trying anything different. I've survived as long as I have by avoiding trouble. I think you're doing the same thing, just going about it in a different way."

Joseph chews over Matt's words, then makes his decision. "Come with me," he says.

He takes Matt to a vacant cell and shuts the door. Doing everything he can to remain outwardly calm, Matt's nervous as hell. He can't afford to get mixed up in any more trouble.

"There's something going on here."

Matt swallows hard. "What do you mean?"

Joseph answers in hushed tones. "I can't be sure, but I think some of the military have an ulterior motive for staying."

"What, other than staying alive?"

"It's more than that. I can't put my finger on it. It's since Estelle left. Look, just call it a hunch, a gut feeling. I don't have anything more to go on than that. Most of the CDF cleared out while they could. I don't know why the others have stayed behind."

"Who do you suspect?"

"I don't know for sure . . . Franklin, maybe. Some of the troops."

"Jayce?"

"Do you know about Jayce?"

"That she's a Hater? Yes."

"She's proof positive that what we're doing here works. No, she's completely on the level. I know that girl inside and out, better than she knows herself. She couldn't hide anything from me if she tried."

"So what do you think's going on?"

"I'm under no illusions as to how quickly this camp is disintegrating. This place remains relatively secure and not much overlooked. It's forgotten and tucked away, which I guess is the main reason I've been able to get on with my work here."

He pauses. "Go on," Matt urges.

"Franklin and the others . . . they had an opportunity to leave, and they didn't take it. They seem almost too keen to be left behind, does that make any sense?"

"Not really. You're going to have to give me more to go on than that."

"I think they have their eyes on this place. Get rid of me and get rid of the Haters, keep hold of the remaining stockpiles of supplies and weapons we have here, then wait for the rest of the camp to burn itself out."

Matt bites his lip. If only Joseph knew how close he was. "Why are you telling me?"

"Because you're an outsider. And because I know Franklin can't stand the sight of you. I had to speak to someone, and you're the safest bet."

"So what are you going to do about it?"

"What can I do? I've felt like this for a while now, but I can't risk what I'm doing being jeopardized. It's too important, you understand? The fact they abandoned their main base in the city and moved everything here was proof positive I'm right."

"I can see that now," Matt lies.

"Fortunately I do have some support in other quarters."

"You do?"

"Yes. There's no doubt the Civil Defense Force is becoming less effective by the day, but there are still remnants of an overall command structure in place. I have contacts, and they listen to me. I've already reported my concerns."

Again, Matt has to force himself not to show any emotion. "What was their response?"

"They're going to do everything in their power to enable my work here to continue."

"How?"

Joseph shrugs. "I'm waiting to hear. Until then, I'll keep doing what I'm doing, and hopefully their response will come in time. They know how important this is. I've got support at the highest level—the highest level that I know is still functional, anyway. You have to understand, what's happening here is too big for us to allow it to fail, Matthew. Everything and everyone else is expendable, you and me and the rest of this camp included."

34

Joseph's prayers are answered unexpectedly next afternoon. Matt's out in the courtyard with Jayce. They're cleaning soiled sheets in rainwater that's been collected in a water butt when the air is filled with noise. Though never quiet, the city-camp has a distinctive and relatively constant sound track which is easy to become accustomed to; the noise of the people, their movements and malaise, forms a steady, ever-present background drone. Matt's innate desire to stay alive means he's attuned to even the slightest change in frequency or pitch, reacting before most people have even looked up.

"Hear that?" he asks Jayce.

"I hear nothing."

At first it's just a subtle variation in the crowd noise, but it's moving, getting closer like a slowly approaching train, definitely heading in this direction. Matt pictures people parting like they did when he rode the garbage truck through town, diving out of the way. But there's barely been any traffic on the clogged-up roads around here over the last couple of weeks, so what the hell is it that's coming toward them?

The muted roar of engines grows over the hubbub, and now Jayce hears it clearly. The vehicles—because there's no question there's more than one—pull up outside the convent gates. Before anyone else can react, Joseph's already there. He slides the gate open and lets them in.

"Where's Franklin?" Matt asks Jayce.

"No idea. I'll find him. You stay here."

Here is the last place Matt wants to stay. "You think that's such a good idea?"

"Yes. Don't alert any suspicions. You said Joseph trusts you, so let him see that he's right. Stick with him. Let him think you're on-side and find out what the fuck this is about."

Matt would try and argue, but Jayce has already gone. He knows she's right, and he also knows that to disappear now would make him look as suspect as he suddenly feels.

Three vehicles enter the compound: two jeeps with a grubby but remarkably ordinary-looking sedan wedged between them. Times past, a Ford Mondeo like this would have been ten-a-penny—a nondescript sales rep's car you'd see in large numbers on virtually any UK road. Matt can't remember the last time he saw a car like this in use. It's been months.

Joseph has quickly closed the gates again and is now standing a short distance away from the Mondeo. Matt feels obliged to show his feigned support, and he moves to stand alongside the other man, shoulder to shoulder. "What is this?" he asks.

"Support and protection, I hope," Joseph replies.

There are three soldiers in each of the jeeps, and one driving the Mondeo. The Mondeo driver gets out and walks around to them. Joseph tries to introduce himself but he's trying to talk to the monkey, not the organ grinder, and his approach is rebuffed. The soldier opens up the back of the car, allowing an unimposing and diminutive figure to emerge out into the light. The respect being afforded to this little gentleman leaves Matt in no doubt whatsoever that he must be the main man. He straightens himself up, runs his fingers through his short, graying hair, then strides over to Joseph and Matt. He looks at both of them. "Which one of you is Joseph Mallon?"

"That's me," Joseph immediately answers, moving forward and offering his hand. His normally booming voice sounds disconcertingly unsure.

"Your message was passed to me, Joseph, thank you. You did absolutely the right thing. We can't let anything get in the way of what you're doing here."

"Thank you . . ."

"Oh, I'm sorry. I'm General Sahota."

"Pleased to meet you, General. *Very* pleased."

"Good. And who's this?"

"This is Matthew Dunne. He's been assisting me."

Sahota and Matt shake hands. "Good to meet you, General," Matt says, though right now this feels anything but good.

"Likewise," Sahota replies with a bank manager's grin writ large across his face. "Thank you for all the support you've been giving to Joseph. From what I hear he's a very modest man. I don't believe even he's fully aware of the potential impact his work will have. It could change the entire direction of this war."

"I've no doubt."

Sahota turns to address Joseph directly again. "How many subjects do you have here at the moment?"

"Four."

"And how many have passed through your doors in total?"

"Another seven."

"All successfully treated?"

"All but one."

"Yes, I did hear something about that. There will always be those who don't suit your approach."

"It's a huge disappointment when that happens."

"I'm sure it is. I know you'll have done your best, though."

It occurs to Matt that small talk is a dying art, because the three of them are now standing looking at each other, not knowing what to say. Sahota's guards constantly survey their new surroundings, automatic rifles held ready but pointing down. Several of the few remaining CDF soldiers already posted at the convent have appeared to check out the new arrivals. Matt senses a bragging contest brewing: *my gun's bigger than yours . . .*

"Well this is all very lovely," the general says. "I expect you need to get back to your work, Joseph."

"I should do, yes."

Sahota goes to walk toward the main convent building, then, almost as an afterthought, turns back to face Joseph and Matt again. "I'm going to be staying here for a while. A few days at least. I'll need a room."

"You can have Estelle's old office. Here, let me show you the way."

With that Joseph leads General Sahota into the building. His armed guards remain outside. Keen to put some distance between himself and all the weapons which are currently on display, Matt returns to the laundry work he was doing, scrubbing at a couple more soiled bedsheets before hanging them out to dry. He saves the water, ready for it to be used again tomorrow.

He's carrying the bucket over to one of the store buildings when Jayce jumps out at him from behind a wall. "Christ's sake, Jayce," he says, heart thumping. "You scared the shit out of me."

"Not interested. If you see Franklin, tell him to meet me by KFC."

"Tell him yourself."

"I can't. I'm leaving."

"What do you mean, you're leaving?"

"Stupid fucking question. What do you think I mean? I can't stay here."

"Why not?"

"That guy you were just talking to."

"General Sahota?"

"Whatever."

"What about him?"

"Do you know anything about him? Did Joseph say where he came from or what he's here for?

"No, nothing. He's CDF top brass, apparently. Why?"

"Because he's like me. He's a Hater."

35

Matt's only made it halfway home from the convent when he's jumped in the street. They must have been waiting. They must have seen him leave the convent before today and clocked the fact that he usually goes out carrying more than he took in. He curses his own stupidity, because no one has routines anymore except him. Why didn't he vary his route or do something else to be less predictable? The fuckers pin him down and rip his rucksack off his back before kicking him in the gut for good measure and leaving him lying in the stinking gutter in several inches of stagnant water. Bastards. He picks himself up and brushes himself down, more annoyed than hurt. He then checks the pockets of his trousers and the inside of his jacket where he's stored most of his stash. Thank Christ he had some degree of forethought in anticipation of such an attack. His muggers won't be best pleased when they realize his bag's a decoy, filled with useless crap. That's the problem with most people in this place, he reckons. They still don't understand that they need to think before they act. He knows that's true, because he can still see the little shits who did him over, and they've just been fleeced by a crowd of nasty-looking bastards who are even bigger and hungrier than them.

Jen's frantic when he gets home with a black eye and blood down his shirt, but that's the very least of Matt's concerns. It takes him a couple of minutes to realize his minor injuries are the lesser of her concerns, too. There's an awful atmosphere in the house, and it's deathly quiet, too. Something's very wrong here.

"What is it, love?"

She can't bring herself to answer. Jason appears in the kitchen doorway. Unusually, the door to the lounge is shut.

"We didn't know," Jason says. "Honest, we didn't hear a thing. Jen just went in to check everything was all right first thing and . . ."

Matt stops listening, because he thinks he already knows where this is going. As he moves closer to the lounge door, Jen backs farther away.

The smell inside the room is sweet and wrong. The temperature is lower than expected, the silence deafening. Mrs. Walker and her children are lying in bed together, one child either side of their mother, all three of them dead. There are empty medicine packets lying around. "Where the hell did she get all these pills from?" Matt asks, pointlessly shaking an empty plastic tub and equally pointlessly checking the label.

"We got it for her, remember?" Jason says. "She told us she needed it for the kid. All along she'd been planning a way out. Remember that *Titanic* movie when the mother puts the kids to bed while the ship's filling up with water because she knows they're all going to die and she decides she'll—"

Matt yells at him. "Fuck sake, Jason, shut up. I get it. I know what she's done and why she did it."

"At least they're free from all this now," Jason says, and Matt can't help but agree.

It might be a waste of time and of energy he doesn't have, but he does it just the same. This small plot of land is as irrelevant as any other part of the camp to the displaced Walker family, but it feels like the right thing to do in the circumstances. He wraps the bodies in their bedding, then buries them together in a single shallow grave in the back garden. It takes hours to dig the hole and fill it in again, and by the time Matt's finished he's physically and emotionally drained. Just a shell. He practically crawls upstairs to bed but no matter how tired he is, he knows he'll get little sleep tonight.

36

"Nothing's changed, right?" Franklin says, grabbing Matt as soon as he enters the convent.

"Good morning to you too, Franklin."

No time for niceties. "That prick has the place pretty much locked down. Shouldn't make too much of a difference now that Jayce has disappeared. She told you he's one of her kind, right?"

"Yeah, she told me."

"Like I said, it doesn't make any difference. We carry on as planned. What we're doing's not dependent on anything that happens here. We need access to a vehicle to get Darren and a couple of the others over to the shelter, then we need to get back with the truck. That's all."

"Sounds so easy when you put it like that."

"We both know it's not. We just need to keep our heads for a little while longer. It's getting close now."

"So when do you reckon?"

"A few days' time. If you haven't already got your folks moved nearer to the chapel, I'd suggest you get it done quick because when it does happen, it'll happen fast."

"So what are we supposed to do until then? Just carry on like nothing's wrong?"

"That's exactly what we do. Go find your mate and help him do whatever it is he's doing."

"My mate?"

"Yeah, Joseph. He's been asking for you."

The convent feels emptier than ever this morning. Matt rattles around the building trying to find Joseph while avoiding Sahota and his guards. Joseph is, as usual, on the upper floors, tending to his captive Haters. He spots Matt from the far end of the drafty landing and is on him immediately. "Glad you're here, Matthew," he says, booming voice filling the building. "Good timing. We have a busy morning ahead of us."

There's another person here. A soldier. One of Sahota's grunts, Matt recalls. He's a massive, mean-looking fucker with a buzz cut and a permanent scowl. He hands Matt a pillowcase. "What am I supposed to do with this?" Matt asks, but the guard doesn't answer.

Joseph enters the nearest room. Matt and the soldier are left out on the landing as Joseph crouches down and begins adjusting a captive Hater's restraints.

All Matt sees is a flash of movement from the bed, and the door's kicked shut. He and the soldier exchange glances and the soldier goes to enter, but it's blocked. They can hear voices and the sounds of Joseph grappling with the Hater inside, fighting for his life.

But they've got it all wrong. When the door opens again, no more than a minute later, it's Joseph in control. Against the odds he's got the better of the Hater, taking advantage of the evil fuck-

er's relative physical weakness and lethargy after the forced inactivity of his incarceration. The killer's on the ground, Joseph
standing over him. Joseph gestures at the soldier and Matt. The
soldier steps forward and picks the Hater up like he's made of
paper, then orders Matt to cover the prisoner's head. "Stay calm
and keep your temper in check and you'll be okay," Joseph tells
the captive Hater. "Fight back and you'll regret it."

The Hater's feet are shackled. With Matt on one side and the
guard on the other, he shuffles through the building with his feet
still chained together, and the farther away from his cell they
get, the more Matt sees his demeanor change. Full of aggression
when he tried to attack Joseph, he's now quiet and subdued . . .
broken? Is he crying? The unexpected vulnerability of the man
takes Matt by surprise. Maybe Joseph's right? Maybe there is
hope after all? The Hater whimpers—*he whimpers like a child!*—
when he trips up a low step. They enter the top-floor room Matt
visited when he first broke into the convent and which he's done
everything he can to avoid returning to since. There's not a lot
here: a bracket and chain on the wall, a bucket to shit in and a
bucket of water to wash with. Joseph motions for Matt to fetch
the chain and he wraps it around the Hater's waist, securing it
tight. "Stay and watch if you like," Joseph whispers. "Watch from
the doorway, though, so he can't see you. We don't want to an-
tagonize him more than we have to. I think you might find this
interesting. You'll be surprised how cooperative they can really
be when their neck's on the line."

Joseph whips the pillowcase off the Hater's head, then backs
away, regarding him with a curious mix of mistrust and pride.
He then leaves the room, returning moments later with food and
a pile of clothes which had been left out on the landing ready.
Matt remains out of sight, able to see the Hater but satisfied the
Hater can't see him.

"Move back," Joseph orders his prisoner. "Right up against the wall." When the Hater grudgingly does as he's told, Joseph puts down the things he's been carrying, then retreats a safe distance and sits down. "Help yourself."

To Matt's surprise, the Hater reacts. "What?"

"I said help yourself. The food tastes like shit today, but it's warm and it's better than nothing. And the clothes are from a dead man, I'm afraid. But hey, they don't stink of piss like yours do!"

The Hater edges forward, circling the food. He's clearly starving, and though he tries to stop himself, he drops to the ground and digs in hungrily. The food is demolished in seconds and is washed down with a bottle of dirty-looking water.

"Better?" Joseph asks him. Matt notices he's stretched out now, looking surprisingly relaxed. Is he as confident as he appears, or are these mind games, a performance designed to wrong-foot the Hater? "I'll get you some more later. There's soap and water for you to wash with over in one of those buckets over there. Scrub yourself down, Danny. Get rid of the stink and try and make yourself feel human again."

And to Matt's astonishment, this Danny creature does exactly that. With Joseph sitting just farther away than the full reach of the chain, the Hater washes himself, then dresses, then squats on the other bucket. While he's distracted, Joseph gestures for Matt to leave, and he does so without hesitation. He can't decide whether this is a groundbreaking treatment, a perverse form of torture, or ritual humiliation. Whatever the reason, Matt's seen enough.

He goes back downstairs and helps himself to a drink from the kitchen. He leans over the sink watching a dribble of water disappear, circling the plughole, trying to work out how he feels about what he's just witnessed upstairs. Is training one of those monsters to hold the Hate any different from teaching a parrot to talk? Do the Haters upstairs actually want to suppress their instinctive rage, or are they just mimicking Unchanged behavior? Is there even a difference?

"It's Matthew, isn't it?"

The voice catches Matt by surprise and makes his blood run cold. He knows exactly who it is, but he takes his time turning around.

Stay calm. He doesn't know you know, remember.

He looks for a way out of the conversation, but there's no obvious exit and no one else here. It's just Matt and Sahota.

"That's right, General," he replies, trying not to sound as unsure as he feels. "Am I supposed to call you General?"

"Call me what you like. I'm not one for formality."

I could think of a few more appropriate names for you, Matt thinks. "Joseph's busy upstairs. I should be getting back. He's on his own with one of the Haters."

"He knows what he's doing."

"He's expecting me. I just came down to get some water."

Matt's lying and he knows it's probably obvious. He just needs to stay calm and not draw attention to himself. And not get killed.

"I won't keep you, I'm sure you've got lots to do. A busy place, this is. An important place. What do you think about the work Joseph and the others are doing?"

"I think it's amazing. I've never seen anything like it." He answers honestly, but how far does he take this? Matt knows the Hater could kill him in a heartbeat, but he also knows Sahota's currently doing everything he can to hide his true allegiance. The fact the general obviously wishes to remain incognito gives Matt a crumb more confidence to speak up. "You have to question the overall effect of all this, though."

"What do you mean?"

In for a penny, in for a pound. If he talks candidly about his concerns, Matt thinks it might throw the Hater off the scent. "I've talked to Joseph about this. What good is what he's doing actually going to do? If he stops a hundred of them from killing, there's still another few million left out there ready to take their place."

"Fair point. I think you underestimate the impact one person can have, though."

"One Hater, or one of us?"

"Both. Either."

"I guess. I saw one of them let loose in the camp here once. He had a hell of an impact."

"I can imagine."

"So in answer to your question, I guess it's all about perspective. One Hater can have a huge effect on a crowd of people like us, but I just question what effect one pacifist Hater's going to have on the rest of their kind."

"Good answer. Maybe we'll find out one day, eh?"

"Maybe we will."

It's a relief when one of Sahota's guards appears and whispers in his ear. The general is needed elsewhere.

Alone in the kitchen again, Matt's legs turn to rubber and he leans heavily on the sink to keep himself upright. What the fuck is he doing? He's playing with fire here and he knows it, but staying close to Franklin and Jayce is the only chance he has of getting Jen away from this hellish place and keeping her alive. Christ, though, he knows he's risking absolutely everything. One wrong word to Sahota or one of his guards, one indiscretion, and it could all come crashing down around him.

Every second he spends here is a second too long.

37

Franklin barrels down the corridor looking for Matt, frantic. He finds him cleaning the cell where this morning's Hater had been held. "Follow him."

"Who?"

"Danny something-or-other. That stinking bastard Joseph kept in here. The one you took up to his bloody torture chamber earlier."

"You're fucking kidding me. You want me to follow him?"

"Do I look like I'm joking? Sahota's just let him loose. Get out there and track him."

"Track him where?"

"Stupid fucking question. Just go wherever he goes and try not to get yourself killed. We need to know what he's planning. We need to know exactly what's happening here."

"What about Joseph?"

"What about him? I'll cover for you. Jayce is waiting on the other side of the wall."

"Wait . . . am I missing a step here?"

"We all are. We've taken our eyes off the ball. We thought

once Joseph and the others had finished with them they were just being turfed out into the wastelands. Until Sahota turned up here we didn't know the Haters were involved with any of this, but they must be behind the whole damn program. They must have known what was going on here from early on and they've been pulling the strings, using Joseph to do their dirty work and teach more of them how to hold the Hate. Question is, why?"

Jayce jumps out at him from the shadows. "Jesus Christ, you nearly gave me a heart attack," he says, clutching his chest.

"You've spoken to Franklin?"

"Yeah."

"Good. Shut up and get moving. There's our man."

She drags Matt deeper into the shifting crowds. The Hater they're trailing is easy to spot, though Matt thinks it's only because he knows what he's looking for. The fucker has a rucksack full of supplies on his back and he moves with a casual arrogance, safe in the knowledge that if he needed to, he could kill just about anyone here. He marches with a purpose, and that too puts him at odds with the milling Unchanged masses.

"Where d'you reckon he's heading?" Matt asks.

"No idea. I'm just hoping he keeps his distance from the people in the chapel."

"You don't think he'd go there, do you?"

"We'd have to be really fucking unlucky for him to find it. There's only you, me, Franklin, and the folks already there who know where it is."

Matt keeps quiet. There's an addition to the list of people who know where the group are waiting for evacuation, and that's Jason. He took the decision to tell him last night. The order to leave could come at any moment. He had to tell Jason in case he's not around when it happens. He needs to be certain Jen gets on the truck out of the camp. Matt remembers their whispered conversation in the kitchen, after Jen had gone to bed in the early hours of this morning. "You memorize these directions and repeat them back to me every morning, got it?" he'd told Jason.

"Can't I just write them down? No one's going to know."

"No. We're not taking any chances. Memorize it. I'll need you to get Jen to safety when it all kicks off, and you're not going to fuck it up, understand?"

"I understand."

"Right, repeat it back to me."

"Follow the Elmswood Road into Highbridge, right on the outer edge of the camp. There's a KFC with a collapsed front-age, hit by a truck. It'll look like you can't get in, but you can. Go right through the building and out the back. There's a hole in the fence. Follow the path on the other side of the fence through the trees and out into No Man's Land. There's a church in the middle of a posh housing estate. It's the only building left standing. Get under cover and wait there for the truck."

He's confident Jason will remember. If not for Jen, then for himself. Matt's only known him for several weeks, but it's more than long enough to know that if there's a way out of this mad-ness, Jason will do everything he can to be first in line to take it. He'll remember the way to the rendezvous because *his* life de-pends on it, never mind anyone else's.

The Hater is heading toward the City Arena. As a food dis-tribution center it's been out of commission for some time now, but there are still scores of people here, camped out and waiting for food they're never going to get. Matt and Jayce pass the CDF-occupied school, and Matt's surprised by the amount of military hardware left here unattended. Many vehicles. "You think they'd take them," he says, thinking out loud.

"What?"

"All those trucks and jeeps. You think people would use them."

"Frightening, isn't it? These poor idiots still think they're safe here."

The Hater they're tracking appears distracted, his attention piqued by a fenced-off mound of bodies which have been casually cremated, presumably to slow the spread of disease. Matt too can't help but stare. It's sobering how badly things have deteriorated.

Up ahead there's a sudden burst of panic as the Hater collides with a refugee heading in the opposite direction. With lightning speed the Unchanged man is off his feet and on his back, the Hater reaching for a weapon, ready to finish him off. Jayce holds Matt back, and when she puts her hand across his chest Matt can't help wondering if she still feels the same urge to fight as the Hater they're watching. At the last possible moment the Hater remembers himself. He lets the other man go, brushes himself down, and carries on as if nothing's happened.

Jayce and Matt follow him across Millenium Square: a vast public space which is carpeted in shelters and people for the most part with wide, mud-caked plateaus where the rains have washed great swaths of the population away. Then he continues out toward the outermost edge of the camp. Wherever it is the Hater is heading, it's beyond the city's hastily redefined boundary. He's on his way back out into the wilderness.

Jayce and Matt skulk through the ruins in silence, keeping far enough back from the Hater to be sure he won't see them if he should stop and turn around. Fortunately he doesn't. He's clearly a man on a mission. They follow him through the dereliction until he reaches the remains of a concrete shopping plaza. He slips between two crumbling buildings. There's only one clear way through the rubble. "Wait here," Jayce tells Matt. "I'll check it out. There's less chance of him killing me."

Her words are of little comfort, but Matt does as instructed. He hides among the ransacked displays in an old hardware store and waits for her to return. He looks around for something with which he can arm himself. A garden shovel is the best he can find. It feels good to have something to hold, no matter how clumsy a weapon it might prove to be.

Standing here on the inner edge of the wilderness, Matt again questions his sanity. Frequently over the last few days he's felt as if he's losing touch with both sides in this most brutal of wars, leaving him standing exposed and alone in the center ground. Whose side is he on? More to the point, who's on his side? The lines between ally and enemy are becoming more blurred by the hour. Is Jayce coming back, or has she sold him out? Is she working with the Hater they're following? Will she return with an army in tow?

Thankfully not.

It's almost half an hour later when she comes back. He whistles to her as she creeps across the plaza looking for him, then gestures for her to join him in the shadows of the hardware store. She refuses, instead calling him out to her.

"Do you realize how dangerous it is for me out here?" Matt says.

"Yeah, I do as it happens," she immediately replies. "But you need to see this."

"If I get caught out here I'm a dead man."

She shrugs. "No worries. If they find us I'll just pretend I'm killing you, okay?"

He looks at her, unsure whether or not she's joking.

"This way," she says. "Move!"

Jayce ducks through a gaping hole in the outer wall of an otherwise relatively undamaged house. It looks like it was caused by a bizarrely precise missile strike, because although appearing outwardly structurally sound, the interior of the building is a ruin. Jayce climbs the badly damaged staircase and Matt follows, edging around the missing steps.

There's another hole in the bedroom ceiling, and a corresponding chasm in the roof through which sunlight pours. Using a chest of drawers, Jayce hauls herself up and into the attic. Matt follows, matching her athleticism, and they look out through the damaged roof together. Several doors farther down the road there's an ugly redbrick building. Even from this distance it's clear that it's a hive of Hater activity.

"So what do you reckon they're up to?" Jayce asks.

"Hardly an army, is it? Do you recognize any of them?"

"Apart from the bloke we just spent the last couple of hours trailing?"

"Yes, apart from him," he says, ignoring her sarcasm.

"Matter of fact, I do. Several of them have been through the convent."

"Our man down there, the guy we were following, I reckon he's a local. He seemed to find his way here pretty well, wherever here is."

"You think?"

"He didn't end up here by chance, did he? Someone told him where to go—presumably Sahota—and he did as he was told. Question is, why?"

"Any thoughts?"

Matt puts two and two together and comes up with an answer he's not sure he wanted to find. "You say you know some of

ALL ROADS END HERE

the Haters down there, so that makes me think this is the next step. I reckon Joseph and his mates must finish with them, then they're sent here."

"I didn't get an invite."

"Why not?"

"I was one of the program's first successes, though I still maintain it had more to do with me and less with Joseph and the others than they'll have you believe. I was determined to find a way to control what I was feeling for my stepbrother's sake, not for any other reason. It was early days when I ended up at the convent, less regimented, less military involvement."

"Did they hunt you out?"

"No, and that's the biggest difference as far as I can see. I was injured and I couldn't get away. After they'd finished with me I hung around to help Joseph out because I initially believed in what he was trying to do. The intention behind it, anyway."

"And you don't think any of these people have anything to do with Joseph?"

"Nope. I just think he's a means to an end now, Sahota's puppet. He supposedly sends them out into the wastelands when he's finished with them, off to spread the good word."

"But there's got to be more of a purpose to it than that, hasn't there?" Matt's struggling to join the dots. It's like doing a jigsaw puzzle without a picture: just a mass of random shapes which somehow have to be arranged to form a whole. "Hardly an army, though, is it? Even if there are other groups like this, they're still massively outnumbered. So what can they hope to achieve, other than causing absolute fucking chaos if they decide they preferred being Haters after all, and then—"

He stops abruptly.

"And then what?" Jayce pushes.

Matt's mind is racing again, working overtime to piece

together the things he's seen over the last couple of weeks and in the moments leading up to here. "Oh, fuck. That's it, isn't it? Those people down there, they're not the weapon, they're just the trigger. They can walk among us, and I reckon that's exactly what they're planning to do. They'll head back into town and start a chain reaction . . . waves of panic. It won't take a lot to make it happen. Once they start fighting, word will get around there are Haters in the camp, and the trouble will spread like a frigging bushfire. It'll get worse and worse, and what's left of the CDF who haven't already bailed are so stretched or so indifferent that they'll struggle to contain it . . . the people will panic and the city will fall."

"They'll be forced out into the open—"

"—straight into the arms of the thousands of Haters waiting out there for them. Exactly. It's beautiful in its simplicity, don't you think?" But Jayce doesn't reply because she's already on her way out of the ruined house. Matt lowers himself down from the attic after her. "Jayce, wait . . . hold up."

She stops just long enough to be sure he can hear her. "We need to get back to Franklin and let him know what we've seen. If we're going to get those people out of the city, then we have to do it now. This could all blow up at any second. We can't risk waiting."

38

The skies are heavy over the camp, and trying to get through the crowds is like wading through treacle; the harder you push and the faster you try to move, the more they suck you in and drag you down. It's humid on the streets, and hot as hell. After days of relative inertia, weeks even, Matt knows that the clock's now ticking at double speed. Franklin's plan starts today, and suddenly all the plotting, all the talking and preparation . . . it all feels hopelessly insubstantial. Matt had relative confidence in what they needed to do, until they actually needed to do it. Now it feels like a catalog of impossible tasks: get the van from the convent, get out to the base in the wastelands, get back with the truck, then get a chapel basement's worth of survivors loaded up and shipped out of the city-camp before it all goes to hell. But before any of that, Matt has an even more pressing task to complete. "I'll meet you back there," he says to Jayce and, before she can protest, he splits.

"Where the hell are you going?" she shouts after him, but he's not listening. None of this will be worth anything if he doesn't do this first.

Home.

He reaches the house breathless and lets himself in. Jason and Jen are in the kitchen, chatting like they don't have a damn care in the world. They look up when he bursts into the room, and they can see from the expression on his face that something's terribly wrong. "What is it, love?" Jen asks.

Matt looks directly at Jason. "It's today."

"What's today?" says Jen, sounding nervous.

"Time to leave," he answers. He turns to speak to Jason again. "You've got a couple of hours tops. Get your stuff together and get over to the place I told you about."

"What place?" Jen demands, increasingly agitated the more she's ignored. She positions herself between the two men. Matt senses her panic and pulls her close. She pushes him away slightly but he refuses to let go. He looks deep into her eyes, desperate to at least try and give her the impression he's not completely fucking terrified.

"I told you, love, there's somewhere safe we can go. Getting there isn't going to be easy, but it's our only option. Just do what Jason says and you'll be all right, okay?"

Numbed by the unexpected speed of events, Jen just nods. Mouth dry, she tries to speak but no words come out. Matt kisses her cheek and whispers into her ear.

"Get a few things together."

"Okay."

"You know I won't let anything happen to you, don't you?"

"I know."

"I'll always look after you, Jen, no matter what."

"I know," she says again.

"I walked half the length of the country to get back to you. I'm not going to let you go again now."

And before she can argue, before she can protest, before she can try and stop him, before she can do anything . . . he's gone.

39

"You took your time," Jayce says, unimpressed. "Do you not realize how fucking serious this is?"

"Of course I do. This isn't just about you and the people in the chapel, though. Had to make sure my lot are ready, too."

He brushes past her and enters the convent. Despite it being unusually late in the day, his arrival is met with very little interest. That's good. The last thing he needs right now is anyone sticking their nose in. Unfortunately Joseph Mallon seems intent on making everything Matt does his business. He spies him across the courtyard and calls out to him. "Evening, Matthew. What are you doing back here so late?"

Matt forces himself to engage in conversation while he looks around for Franklin. Franklin has the key to the van, the van is the key to Matt and Jen staying alive. "I thought there might be more I could do to help. I didn't do a full day. I had to go home for a while earlier."

"There's always more to do. I've got a whole list of things. You can start by helping me get a couple more rooms ready. It's been a good day. Several of our guests left while you were out."

Matt steels himself. He knows where they were going. He knows why. "Okay. Give me a minute. I just need to find Franklin first."

Matt enters the main building and starts searching the ground floor, going from room to room. There's a hand on his shoulder which grips tight and spins him around. Matt's filled with momentary panic which quickly subsides when he realizes it's just Joseph again. "Did you not hear me, Matthew? There's a hell of a lot to do upstairs."

"Sorry, I was miles away. I'll help you once I've found Franklin."

"Can't it wait? Sahota's men are out looking for more suitable Haters. We need to be ready by the time they get back."

"This is important."

Joseph just looks at him, and Matt wonders if he suspects something? "*This* is important. It's the whole reason we're here."

"I know. Have you seen him?"

"Who?"

"Franklin!"

"He's around the back, I think. I don't know why he didn't go out with the others. You can talk to him as soon as we've—"

"I need to see him *now*."

"You need to calm down, my friend."

Matt stops and checks himself. Forces himself to take a breath. "I know. I'm sorry."

"Want to talk about it?"

"About what?"

"About whatever it is that's vexing you."

"Vexing me? What, apart from the fact that the world's on its fucking knees out there?"

Joseph's demeanor changes. "Maybe you should take a break. Look, this work's not for everyone. I understand that. It's intense.

I can't let you work around the Haters in this kind of mood. They'll pick up on your unease and we'll be right back to square one."

"Back to square one? We never took one step away from first base, do you not see that? And as for your Hater pets, I want to be as far from those fucking freaks as it's possible to get. I quit."

Joseph looks like he's been punched. A couple of Sahota's guards are close, their interest renewed by the raised voices. Matt knows he needs to bite his lip before he says something he regrets.

"I'm going to get rid of this one," Franklin says. He appears from out of nowhere, grabs Matt by the scruff of his neck and pulls him toward the door. "I've had enough of him. He's a fucking liability."

"He came on your recommendation," Joseph says, seething.

"I know. My mistake. He's a loose cannon. I'll get shot of him." And before either Matt or Joseph can say anything, Franklin drags Matt away. When they reach a more secluded space he pins Matt against the wall. "What the hell are you doing? Are you out of your fucking mind? That prick's already suspicious enough without you giving him more ammunition."

"I was trying to look for you. He was getting in the way."

"He's always getting in the way. Why pick today to have a meltdown?"

"Have you spoken to Jayce?"

"No, I haven't left this place. Why?"

"Because it's time."

Franklin immediately relaxes his grip and drops his head. "Thought as much. We knew it was coming. What's the cause?"

"It's the Haters Joseph and the others have trained. We found them waiting on the outskirts of the camp. It's a bloody terrorist cell, Franklin. They're the trigger. We reckon they're going to head back into the center of the camp and cause absolute fucking carnage."

"Are they already on the move?"

"Not yet, but it's only a matter of time. The longer we leave it, the harder this is going to be."

"Where's Jayce?"

"Outside, waiting for the van. Do you have the keys?"

"Not on me. They're in the armory."

"This place has an armory?"

"Of sorts."

Matt follows Franklin back into the convent. The van has been left parked alongside a nearby outbuilding, appearing almost forgotten. It hasn't been driven for several days. What if it doesn't start? Matt thinks. What if their survival hinges on a dodgy starter motor or an empty fuel tank?

It's less an armory, more a pantry. An innocuous-looking room just off the kitchen. A plain-looking door that Matt's walked past a hundred times previous and never thought to look inside. Franklin struggles with the lock.

"Got a problem, Franklin?"

Both Franklin and Matt spin around, looking as guilty as they feel. It's Phil Henderson, one of the few remaining CDF soldiers from Estelle Bisseker's watch.

"No problem," Franklin answers quickly, mouth dry with nerves.

Henderson waits for a second, then nods casually. "Cool. I had trouble with that lock earlier. Need to get some WD40 on it. Catch you later, mate."

Franklin breathes an audible sigh of relief as he gets inside and grabs the keys to the Transit. "I can't be doing with all of this. It's making me paranoid."

"You're not wrong," Matt agrees. He looks past Franklin but

the cupboard's practically bare. Just a few clips, a stack of riot shields, and a disassembled rifle are all he can see.

"Can't wait to get out of this bloody place," Franklin mutters to himself.

With Henderson gone, back doing whatever the hell it is Henderson does, the convent feels empty again. Matt and Franklin move through the corridors toward the rear of the building, preferring the limited shelter of being indoors to being outside and exposed. "Is the tank full?" Matt randomly asks.

"What?"

"Where d'you get the fuel from? Most people can't put food in their mouths, yet you lot seem to manage to fill up your tanks regularly. Have you got enough to get us there?"

"What is this? You switching back into accountant mode again? Bit late to start getting risk averse, don't you think?"

"I'm nervous. It always happens when I'm nervous."

"We loot it, same as we loot everything. There's plenty left out there if you know where to look. Things haven't gone completely *Mad Max* just yet. Not far off, mind."

Matt thinks he detects the faintest trace of a supressed smile on Franklin's face. Is he getting through to him at last?

A door opens out onto the area where the van's parked.

"Act casual, like your life doesn't depend on it," Franklin tells him as they emerge back out into the open.

"Thanks, that helps."

"I'll drive until we're outside, then we get out and let Jayce take the hot seat. Got it?"

"Yep."

There are several soldiers out here, alternately busying themselves or just sitting around, waiting. They each appear wrapped up enough in their own little worlds to keep their noses out of Matt and Franklin's business.

"So how many are we taking out on the first trip?"

"Just a handful. Darren and a few others. Darren has it sorted, though. He knows who to take with him. Enough to get the place ready for the rest of us."

"But he doesn't know we're coming?"

"He's always ready. We all knew this was going to happen at some point."

"He's just not aware we've reached that point yet?"

"Exactly. I'm sure we'll make his day."

Franklin glances around the courtyard again, then opens the van and climbs up into the driver's seat. "Go man the gate," he orders Matt. "Once I've started the engine we'll need to move fast. Get ready, get it open, then follow me out. Try and shut it behind you if you can, give us a few extra seconds' head start."

It's only now it's sinking in that Franklin's about to desert the CDF and steal equipment from right under the nose of a Hater general. Matt walks casually around the perimeter wall. He considered skulking in the shadows, cloak-and-dagger, but until the engine's running all that will achieve is making him look as guilty as he feels. Franklin watches him like a hawk, one hand gripping the wheel, the other ready on the ignition.

Matt signals that he's in position and slides the gate across. Franklin turns the key and the Transit starts first time. Immediately there's movement all around the convent grounds: everyone's already on edge, and the combined noise of the gate being opened and the engine starting causes panic. Franklin ignores all of it and puts his foot down, sending the van careering across the gray courtyard.

Calm as anything, Sahota walks out of the nearest building and stands directly in the path of the van, blocking the way through. Franklin instinctively slams on the brakes, bringing the van to a juddering halt less than a meter short of Sahota. He's unflappable. The fucker doesn't even blink. He shouts to make himself heard over the rattling motor noise. "Mr. Franklin, where exactly are you planning to go with my vehicle?"

Franklin doesn't answer. Instead, he shoves the van into reverse and sends it juddering back. Into first gear again and he tries to drive around Sahota, but Sahota's having none of it. The diminutive Hater sidesteps into the way again, oblivious to any physical danger. He's reading Franklin like a book, anticipating his every move. It's as if he knows exactly what he will, and won't, do.

"I'll ask you once more," Sahota yells, his temper showing now, "where are you going with my van?"

Franklin knows he's going to have to take Sahota out and he backs up again. But before he's out of reverse, Sahota draws a pistol from a holster on his hip and fires a single shot with pinpoint accuracy. The windscreen cracks then shatters, and Franklin slumps over the wheel, dead instantly. His leaden feet slip off the pedals and the engine stalls. The silence in the grounds of the convent now is a thousand times louder than the chaos of seconds earlier.

Joseph's outside now. He looks from Sahota to Franklin, then back again. "What the hell? What have you done, General?"

"What I should have done when I first arrived here. Don't give me any reason to have to do the same to you."

Joseph backs away, struggling to compute. Sahota's face is hard to read. Detached. Cold and clinical. Filled with hate.

"Where's the other one?"

"Who?" Joseph stammers, terrified.

"Franklin's friend. *Your* friend."

"Who? Matthew?"

"That's right."

"I don't know . . . I haven't seen him . . ."

"Well he's the one who opened the gate. Wily little bastard must have made a run for it."

"Want me to find him, boss?" one of the nearby guards asks.

"No point. Not worth the energy. He won't be a problem."

Matt can hear every word of this conversation, because he's still in the convent grounds. They expected him to run, so he's done the opposite and has stayed close. He's crouching out of sight on the other side of the van now, watching Sahota's feet under the chassis. He waits until he's sure Sahota and the guard are looking in the opposite direction, then in one swift movement lifts himself up, opens the passenger door, then slides across the seat through the broken glass and shoves Franklin's corpse out of the driver's door. The dead man hits the ground like a sack of coal, and before Sahota, Joseph, or any of the soldiers can react, Matt restarts the engine and drives the van through the open gate and out into the camp.

Disoriented, he goes the wrong way and drives across a patch of boggy parkland, only the debris left by refugees and the speed he's traveling stopping his wheels from sinking into the mire. He keeps moving forward, sending the few refugees remaining around here scattering in all directions, refusing to slow down until he's on solid ground again.

Matt's sense of direction is all at sea. Thankfully, Jayce's isn't. She sprints after the van, homing in on its chaotic noise, gesturing wildly for Matt to stop. When he sees her he brakes and willingly gives up the driver's seat. In seconds she's in and they're gone.

Matt looks back at the convent, expecting to see CDF soldiers rushing through the open gate after them, but there's nothing. He sees the gate slide shut again.

"He doesn't care," Jayce says. "You nicked his van, but that's nothing in the scheme of things. Sahota's got bigger fish to fry than you. You're just one Unchanged nobody and he knows you can't stop him. You're no Hater. You're just another face in the crowd, and it won't be long before that crowd turns in on itself and starts ripping itself apart."

40

The summer heat is suffocating, even as the light begins to fade at the end of the day. The back of the van is packed with people now, all of them under cover except for Matt. Still doing everything he can to keep out of sight, he watches through the grille which separates Jayce in the front from everyone else, his eyes watering in the wind now the windscreen has been shot out. He's looking for Haters but, just as importantly, he's also watching the road, committing the route to the hideout to memory. "It's easiest to navigate by the landmarks that are missing now," Jayce told him as they left the chapel. "It's more about what's not here than what is." And she's right. Across the whole swath of No Man's Land, all taller buildings and any which were in any way distinctive have been pounded into oblivion. There was a business park here full of anonymous-looking redbrick buildings—all gone. A water tower dating back several hundred years—severed at half-height like a tree snapped in a storm. A black shell stands where a well-respected university used to be. A multiplex cinema reduced to a collection of roof-less, burned-out, amphitheater-like screens, open to the elements. It's devastatingly sad, Matt thinks. All the things that used to matter have been ground down to nothing. All that's left worth saving now is the people in this van and those still waiting to be picked up from the chapel.

Jayce throws the van around a sharp corner. Matt overbalances and thumps into the back of her seat. "The roads aren't what they used to be," she mumbles.

The ride's getting worse. Matt can see enough over her shoulder to realize her last comment was an understatement. "Fuck," he says, "where *is* the road?"

Jayce doesn't reduce her speed in the slightest. She weaves between two swollen piles of rubble which used to be houses and uses a parallel street to keep moving in the right direction. Matt looks down and sees that they're skirting perilously close to the edge of an enormous sinkhole.

"It was a missile strike, early days," she tells him. "I was close at the time. We were hunting out groups of stragglers."

Matt can't help himself. It's easy to forget what Jayce is. "What, like the group in this van?"

"Yes, if you want to be an asshole about it, exactly like the group in this van. Don't try and send me on a guilt trip because it won't work. You can't tell me you haven't done things you regret."

"Too many things . . ."

"Exactly. Shut up."

But Matt can't shut up. The higher the stakes, the more he talks. And right now the stakes are higher than they've ever been.

"Wait, which way are you going? This is a hell of a long way around."

"It's not just a case of putting the coordinates in your satnav anymore. You're right, as it happens, and I can think of several faster routes, but they all involve driving right through the middle of outposts. I don't have a particular problem with that, but I'm guessing you and everyone else will have, as will they."

"Point taken," he says, and he bites his lip again.

She pulls a folded-up map out of her jacket inner pocket and hands it to him through a gap in the grille. "I'm trying to keep us out of the red-hatched areas. That's where most of them are waiting."

Matt opens up the map and holds it up against the wall of the van. It's an old Ordnance Survey map of this entire area with the city front and center. It's hopelessly outdated, but the detail doesn't matter. Even in the shadows it's clear that large parts of the area around the refugee camp have been crudely outlined and shaded in to show where a strong Hater presence has been observed. It strikes him there's more red ink than anything else.

"We're using the main arterial out of town as a bearing," Jayce tells him. "There are gangs blocking the motorways, tightening their chokehold on the city. The back streets are the safest option for now. Our place is just off the M42, a few miles farther on from the airport. We'll have to drive close to a couple of decent-sized encampments to get there."

Matt doesn't reply. Instead he finds himself watching Jayce with renewed caution. Until now it had been relatively easy to forget she was a Hater, but the reality of their situation is hitting home. He's completely at her mercy. They all are. She could be taking them anywhere.

There are Haters everywhere—even in the spaces that looked clear on the map. It's like they're being drawn here by a call to arms only they can detect, as if it's the very smell of the desperate

Unchanged masses in the camp which is bringing them to this place; an invisible, instinctive, unstoppable compulsion. They're circling their prey, waiting with an audacious arrogance for the Unchanged camp to self-destruct. From where he's sitting, Matt can see glimpses of the outside world reflected in a side-view mirror, and the constant movement he sees is unnerving in the extreme. This precarious journey is like a tightrope walk across the deepest chasm, and the thought of making this same drive twice more tonight feels like an impossible undertaking.

"Get down," Jayce shouts, and the borderline panic in her voice is clear. Almost as one the Unchanged refugees in the back of the van flatten themselves down and freeze, covered with blankets, duvets, and sheets, knowing that to give even the slightest indication they're there might be enough to bring the wrath of an army of Haters bearing down on them.

Matt buries himself alongside the others, his face pushed hard against the soles of someone else's boots. It's pitch black under here. Muted sounds. Hard to know what's happening. The van slows to a gentle, controlled halt. He'd braced himself for an emergency stop, and he can't decide if this is reassuring or more concerning? Someone stirs on the ground next to him and he thumps them hard. "Shut up. Not a damn sound. Don't fucking move!"

Inside the van now there's a deathly, fragile quiet. The only noise comes from the idling engine and then the door as Jayce gets out. There's movement alongside the van. Footsteps. Voices. Matt screws his eyes shut and waits, knowing that anything could be happening out there. There could be a huge mass of Haters gathered around the van, there could be just one. That's all it would take—if a single Hater gets even the faintest sniff of him and the others, it'll all be over. There's no chance of running this time, no hope of escape. And it's not just him who's at risk now . . . it's everyone in the van here with him, and all those waiting in the chapel, too. And Jen and Jason. The pressure is immense and intense, and there's not a fucking thing he can do but wait.

Matt takes an unexpected kick to his face, a boot catching his cheekbone with a painful crack. He bites his lip to stop himself yelling out. The man he's lying alongside is reacting to the pressure. Is he on the verge of cracking completely? Matt has to do something—not least because he knows that no one else will— and he grabs the man's belt and drags him closer. The man fights back, kicking out at Matt and writhing furiously, but all that does is make Matt hold him even tighter. He wrestles a hand free and clamps it down over the man's mouth, hissing in his ear, "Stop fighting or you'll get us all killed."

Outside there are voices now. Several of them, clearly distinguishable. Jayce is talking to at least two others. Matt strains to hear what's happening, but the panicking survivor he's holding on to is still making too much noise and Matt can only make out intermittent snatches of the conversation outside.

"So you bailing out?" a Hater man is saying to Jayce.

"No."

"You're driving away from the city, though."

"I've been on a supply run. I've heard it's all starting to kick off in there."

"Yeah, we heard the same. Won't be long before it all comes to a head."

The refugee Matt's got hold of hears this too and reacts badly. He knows as well as Matt just how close to danger they are, but this is new territory for him and he bucks and kicks and shakes himself free from Matt's grip. He stands up, and though the Haters outside don't immediately hear him, Matt knows it's only a matter of time before they do. Exposed and visible now, he clambers over the other Unchanged refugees who are still under cover as he tries to get to the back of the van. Darren—leader-elect of this bunch—starts to move. Matt stops him. "Don't. I'll sort it."

Outside, Jayce realizes something's not right. "You got any food you want to trade?" she asks, voice deliberately loud enough to disguise the noises coming from the van.

"Thought you said you'd been collecting supplies?" one of the Haters says.

"Yeah . . . bedding, firewood, and stuff. Didn't find much in the way of food. I'm starving."

"Ain't got a lot myself," the man she's talking to says. "There's a Tesco about a mile back, though. It's been pretty well done over but you might find something there."

"Show me?"

Matt knows she's trying to distract the others, doing what she can to draw them away. He crawls over to the panicking man who's now trying to get the back door open. "For fuck's sake, you're going to get us all killed."

"We're all dead anyway," the man spits back at him, feeling for the lock.

Going against Matt's orders, Darren is uncovered. "Come on, Jake," he says. Matt spins around.

"I told you, keep your fucking head down," he hisses. "Stay out of it."

"Jake's a good man," Darren says. "Come on, Jake, don't fuck things up now."

But Jake's not listening to anyone. He finds the latch and clicks the door open slightly, letting in a sliver of fading evening light. He hesitates, but Matt doesn't. He knows what he has to do and he shoves his fellow refugee out of the van.

Jake lands on his backside in the dirt, stunned. The door's only open for a couple of seconds before Matt pulls it shut again, praying no one out there has seen or heard him. He holds the door tight, hanging on to the handle to make sure it can't be opened from outside.

The lone refugee picks himself up from the road. It takes him a second to fully realize what's happened and to appreciate how much danger he's now in. He staggers away from the van disoriented, stumbling farther into the open, then starts hammering on the metal door to be let back inside. There's a campfire nearby. A Hater who looks more like a college lecturer than a killer is the first to look up and see him. "Jesus. What the hell's this?"

Jayce knows she has no choice but to react. "Unchanged!" she screams, and she throws herself at Jake with all the venom and anger she can muster, tackling him to the ground and dragging him away from the van. She knows she has to throw the others off her scent, so slams him into the dirt again then snatches a shiv from her belt and hammers it into his heart. The blood which pumps and flows over her hands is warm and comforting. She feels no guilt or remorse. No nerves. No right or wrong. Just hate.

Killing this dumb Unchanged bastard feels good—too good— and it's all Jayce can do to swallow down the fire now burning in her belly and suppress it like she's been forced to for weeks on end. For a few long, uncertain, unsteady, and indecisive seconds, the rush is such that she considers throwing the back of the van open and letting the other Haters have their fill.

But she doesn't.

She pushes the stunted blade deeper into the man's flesh again and twists it, then lets him go. She wipes her hands and staggers back from his corpse.

"Where the hell did he come from?" a woman asks, looking down at the blood-soaked body with disdain.

"Little bastard must have been hanging off the back of the

van," Jayce answers quickly. "He's dead now, though. That's all that matters."

"Couple of days and there won't be any of them left alive," the woman says. She looks around, perhaps hoping she'll see others like the dead man, then gives a disinterested shrug and returns to the campfire.

Jayce prolongs the illusion, watching the van from the corner of her eye should any of her other passengers decide on making a similarly misguided suicidal bid for freedom. She talks to the other Haters and lets them show her where to find food. She joins in with the talk of killing and of winning the war, of the battles which have been fought and those which are still to come. She feels alone. A traitor to both sides. Stuck in the middle, straddling the divide. Neither one thing nor the other.

A while longer and she's done enough to demonstrate her allegiance. The last thing these fighters suspect is that she has another seven Unchanged in the back of her van. She gets back behind the wheel, briefly catching a glimpse of Matt's pallid face in the rearview. "Least you know you can trust me now," she tells him.

Darren glares at Matt. "We can trust you more than we can trust him, Jayce."

"I did what I had to do," Matt replies without hesitation. "Jayce and I both did. I'll do it again if I have to."

"Maybe I'll throw you out first . . ."

"Cut the fucking posturing, Darren," Jayce yells from the front, slamming her fist against the wheel to silence the argument before it gets out of control. "You listen to me and you listen to Matt if you want to stay alive. He knows how to survive out here, you don't. You need him a lot more than he needs you."

41

There's no celebration when they near the hideout, just subdued relief. It's maybe ten miles from the city, fifteen at most, but it's taken the best part of an hour and a half to get here, each mile a slow slog. Once Jayce gives the word, the refugees in the back finally risk lifting their heads and looking out into the open; their first glimpse of the fucked-up ruin of a world where they're destined to spend what's left of their lives. The low light seems apt for people who are to spend their foreseeable futures underground, getting accustomed to living mole-like.

"Back down. Stay under cover," Jayce barks aggressively as she wrenches the steering wheel of the van around, making a sudden change of direction. Then she stops. "Trouble ahead."

"What kind of trouble?" Matt asks, knowing he can't risk looking himself.

"My kind."

"Haters?"

"Yep."

"Many?"

"Enough. I'll draw them away. Give it a couple of minutes until it's clear, then get this lot to safety."

Not waiting for acknowledgment, she just scoops up a rifle and a couple of grenades, then gets out of her seat and runs.

Someone behind Matt goes to move. "Wait. Stay still," he orders. "No one goes anywhere until I say."

He waits a moment longer, listening intently, then slowly lifts his head until his eyes are just above the bottom edge of the window. Where the hell are they? He naively expected them to have stopped right outside the printing house, and though he thinks they can't be far, safety still feels an immeasurable distance away. There's not any of the immediate chaos he was expecting to see outside, but there's no question the danger's close. He can see Jayce in the distance, a couple more Haters chasing after her. Even in the half-light she cuts a distinctive-looking figure: hair whipping in the wind behind her as she sprints away, disappearing around a bend in the road.

"This it?" Darren asks.

"Almost," Matt replies, and he crawls over the others on his hands and knees to look out the other side of the van. This is slightly more promising. It's the back of a warehouselike building: a long, corrugated metal wall which seems to go on forever in either direction. He's confident they've reached the industrial estate, at least.

There's a door in the wall they're facing. It's open, but Matt has no idea what they'll find on the other side. He massages his temples and thinks, considering his limited options. His train of thought is derailed almost immediately by a loud detonation in the near distance. He looks back and sees a burst of orange flame bright against the graying sky, belching black smoke billowing up over the tree line.

"That's either Jayce attacking someone or someone attacking Jayce," Matt tells the others. "Whatever it is, it's our cue to move."

He climbs out the back of the van and ushers the group out. He starts herding them toward the door in the anonymous-looking building they're parked up alongside. "Is this the place?" a terrified-looking woman protests, not going in until she's sure. Matt pushes her through.

"Just get under cover, for fuck's sake. We can't risk being out here."

The seven of them bunch up in a tangled mass as they run through the innards of a long-empty building. Some kind of production line, maybe a workshop, its stillness is sarcophagus-like. The refugees weave through the frozen chaos of the shop floor, untouched since the moment the Hate first showed its face here. There are several corpses, badly decayed. The remnants of one of the workers turning on their colleagues mid-shift, no doubt.

"Wait here until I tell you to move," Matt orders when they reach the other side of the building. "Keep out of sight."

He goes back outside and, to his relief, no one follows. There's another building dead ahead, with an enclosed, straight-up metal fire escape ladder bolted to one side. He checks there's no movement around then runs for all he's worth, feeling like he's permanently caught in a sniper's sights out here. When he reaches the bottom of the ladder he scales it as fast as his tired, nerve-heavy limbs will allow. He's soon up on the roof on his hands and knees, panting for air and crawling through puddles on the asphalt, cold and wet and uncomfortable but momentarily safe. He stays low and keeps moving until he's looking over the opposite edge, and though the encroaching darkness keeps the detail hidden, at last he's able to orient himself to his surroundings. Directly ahead is the massive distribution center Jayce talked

about, and in its shadow is the printing house, dwarfed by its su-
persize neighbor. Most importantly, he can't see any movement.
No other vehicles, no sign of other Haters. The only noises come
from the activity around the area where Jayce detonated her grenade and, beyond that, the airport in the distance. It's easy to
pick out from up here—a flood of illumination in an unnaturally
lightless world. Planes and helicopters climb into the darkening
sky. All taking off, Matt observes, none of them landing.

Back down to the others. He moves so fast that he almost loses
his footing at the top of the fire escape ladder. *Slow down*, he
warns himself. *Don't make any mistakes now. No second chances. You
can't afford to fuck this up.*

When he gets back to the others, they're not where he left
them. On Darren's word they slowly reemerge from hastily found
hiding places in the shadows. "It's not far," Matt tells them,
breathless. "Couple of hundred meters at most. You follow me
and once we're out there you don't stop moving. Whatever happens, whatever you see, you don't stop. Got it?"

Terrified expressions. Numb realization that there's no choice.
They look to Darren, who nods agreement.

Matt knows the longer they wait, the worse it'll get. He leads
them back out and points to a narrow gap between two buildings opposite. "Down there," he says, and Darren takes the lead
and starts to run. Matt brings up the rear. A strangled scream
from somewhere in the near distance followed by a round of automatic gunfire make a woman whose name Matt doesn't know
freeze dead in her tracks. He runs into her but doesn't stop, half-
shoving, half-carrying her forward. She reacts badly to his
manhandling and lashes out at him. He takes the beating, soaks
up every punch and kick, still keeping her moving because he
knows that at any moment they might be seen. "If they catch us
we're dead, understand?" he hisses at her between attacks. She

either can't hear him or doesn't want to listen and she continues to fight. It's all he can do to wrap his arms around her and drag her into the alleyway. He pins her up against the nearest wall. "Do you want to die today?" Now she's listening. She shakes her head, eyes wide with terror. "Nor me, so stop fucking about and do as I say. We're almost there. Don't fuck up now." She stops attacking, and Matt thinks he's got through. The immediate shock of being exposed out in Hater-controlled territory is beginning to fade, and the reality of their situation is starting to sink in. "This isn't impossible. We can do this."

When the woman's sufficiently calm, Matt pushes his way along the line. Darren's up front, but he's as clueless as the rest of them. "Which way?" he asks.

"Blue-walled building over there. See it?"

"I see it."

"Good. Keep everyone together and follow me, okay?"

"Okay."

This last dash is all that separates this group from relative safety. If they can do it, then it makes him think he and Jayce might actually be able to bring Jen and the truckful of refugees back here later. And a life spent underground with the woman he loves in squalid, cramped confines is a better option than anything else right now.

Do it.

He runs for the printing house building. His focus is getting inside, but he's distracted by the things he senses on the periphery. Jayce has done a good job of keeping the Haters at bay until now, but whatever's been holding their attention elsewhere is clearly less effective than it was. He can see flashes of movement through the gaps between other buildings, figures edging back toward the industrial estate. It's a relief when he reaches the door which he, Franklin, and Jayce used previously and it's still open.

Thankfully this place feels as cold and unused as when he was last here. His eyes adjust quickly to the gloom, only marginally darker inside than out now, and he's able to make out the shape of the truck where they left it by the loading bay doors. Everything appears untouched.

The others push their way inside, racing with each other to be the first through the door. There's a piercing scream from the woman Matt had trouble with a moment earlier, and he spins around to see she's stuck in the doorway with a Hater kid hanging on to her back, spiderlike. The child is clawing at her face, ripping at her skin. Darren's there first, and though he's not had anywhere near as much experience of being this close to the enemy as Matt, he does what he can to separate the woman and the kid. He's shocked by the child's relative strength and fury—daunted, even—and he's initially brushed aside. He comes back again and this time manages to force an arm between the woman and her attacker. With a grunt and a sudden burst of strength he peels the child off her and leaves the despicable little fucker writhing furious on the ground at his feet. He can't see if it's a girl or a boy through the blood and dirt and fury. He plants a boot on its chest to stop it getting up, then pulls a pistol out from inside his jacket.

"Wait, don't!" Matt screams at him but it's too late. Darren shoots the child at point-blank range. Darren stands over what's left of the corpse, panting hard, more satisfied than he should be. Matt glares at him. "Are you out of your fucking mind?"

He pushes Darren indoors, then goes back out for the dead kid. "What are you doing? Leave that thing out there," the sobbing, pain-in-the-ass woman screams at him, blocking his way back inside. He barges past her.

"Don't you get it? Your friend here has just let every one of them for miles around know there's fighting going on in this place, and if they know there's fighting then they know there are going to be people like us here."

"Yes, but—"

"Leaving a Hater kid that's been shot in the face on the doorstep will give them a pretty good idea where we're hiding, don't you reckon?" Matt dumps the body out of sight, then ushers the group of refugees toward the steps leading down into the darkness underground. There are protests and more questions but he's having none of it. "If you want to stay alive, just fucking move!"

He feels his way through the bowels of the printing house. They inch slowly through the unfamiliar shadows of the computer server room, then stop, backed up against each other, heel to toe.

"What now?" someone asks.

"The door's padlocked," Darren answers.

"And who's got the key?"

"Jayce," Matt tells them.

"And what if she doesn't come back?"

"Then you'd better hope she does. Otherwise we're all dead."

42

It's been several hours. There have been Haters moving in and around the building above them, Matt's sure of it, but he thinks they've come and gone. He says nothing to the others, because to do so would mean he'd have to deal with even more unnecessary panic and noise, and right now that's something he could well do without. As it is he's already wondering what hope there is for these people. The whispered conversations he's been a party to have been pitiful. "If we're underground, what about sanitation?" His answer to that: You get used to the smell of shit. "How long will we be down here? When will I get to see the sun again?" His response: Think yourself lucky that there's still a chance you might actually see the sun again, no matter how long you have to wait. There's plenty of people who'd give anything to trade places.

But for now the people down below are playing ball and are deathly silent because someone—*something*—is turfing through the offices at the other end of the staircase they descended to get down here. One careless noise and all their planning and effort will have been for nothing. And if things go wrong at this stage, he knows Jen's already slim chances of getting out of the city will be slashed to zero.

The noise upstairs is increasing. Christ, it sounds like a frigging stampede, like there's a whole pack of Haters riding roughshod over what's left of the printing house. What if they take the truck? Matt thinks. What if they slash its tires or cut the brakes? Absolutely everything feels like it's balanced on the most precarious of knife-edges.

It's getting louder. Thumping footsteps everywhere. Muffled cries and shouted orders. Distant rumblings. Gunshots and detonations. The occasional belly-shaking roar of helicopters and jets racing away from the airport.

"You still got that pistol?" Matt whispers to Darren.

"Yep."

"Many bullets?"

"Not as many as I need. It's academic, anyway. I'd never have enough."

There's another crash from the shop floor above which silences him. He pulls the rest of the group closer. "If they get down here, just attack. Kick, punch, scratch, bite . . . whatever you need to do. Darren, only use the gun if you don't have any other choice."

More movement. Top of the steps. In the offices now.

"Are we going to make it?" Darren asks. Matt refuses to answer because he thinks if he doesn't admit that they're fucked, maybe there's the slightest chance they'll survive.

They're on the other side of the door, about to break through. Matt braces himself. Until now he's stayed alive by distancing himself from trouble and letting someone else take the heat, but how can he run when they're at a dead end with nowhere left to go?

"Ready?" he says to Darren, but before Darren can answer the door at the top of the steps flies open.

"Don't attack!"

Matt falls back against the wall with relief. It's Jayce. "Thank Christ," he says as she feels her way down. "Thought you were never coming back."

Jayce gestures for Matt shut the door behind her. Once they're sealed in, she produces a flashlight from inside her jacket and switches it on, filling the small space with light and taking the faintest edge off the refugees' collective fear. She fishes in her pockets for a set of keys and, with a little effort, manages to open the padlocks which are keeping the second door secured. She throws it open, and a blast of stale air hits the gathered Unchanged like the seal has been broken on some long-forgotten tomb.

All nerves and complaints are immediately silenced when the new arrivals finally get inside their bunker. Jayce issues a couple of them with lamps. Matt goes to follow but she stops him, putting an arm across his chest. "Not you, sunshine. We've still got work to do."

Jayce removes the clamps and gets behind the wheel of the truck. It's pitch black outside now but the dark is a help, not a hindrance. Jayce flashes a light in the window: Matt's signal to move. He gets up from where he's been crouching behind a spool of paper the height of a car, then races across to the loading bay door which he opens with a manual hoist, Jayce having already prepped it.

Jayce starts the engine as soon as Matt's on board and revs it hard. He gets down into the front passenger seat footwell and covers himself with a long coat, safe from prying Hater eyes. He wedges himself into position with his head against the door as the truck swerves out of the printing house and onto the road. He folds back a corner of the coat and watches Jayce. Her eyes are fixed dead ahead. She seems preoccupied. Distant. "You okay?"

"I'm fine. Shut up and let me concentrate."

There are flashes of light which illuminate her face for split seconds at a time. Matt knows that trying to plow through the chaos of this industrial estate and the battle-scarred world beyond in an unfamiliar vehicle of this size is harder than it looks. They're unmarked and unknown: a target for everyone and no one.

Jayce grips the wheel tight. A jet takes off from the airport then races across the sky, directly crossing her line of vision. Matt can't see it, but there's no mistaking the noise. For a few seconds the deafening din consumes everything. When it's faded away sufficiently, Jayce speaks. "There's something you need to know."

Matt feels his gut constricting with nerves. "What?"

"Things are bad. Far worse than they were."

"But we've only been out here a few hours."

"It's a domino effect. Everything's falling apart. I think whatever that cell we saw earlier were being primed to do, chances are they're going to be executing their orders now if they haven't already. We'll be okay getting back into the city, I think, but getting out again is going to be a nightmare."

"It always was. We knew this was going to happen."

"Yes, but the plan was always to get in and out before the camp completely collapsed."

Another whoosh of noise seems to take Jayce's breath away. It sounds impossibly close. She follows the arc of a missile, then turns away at the moment of detonation. "There are thousands of fighters surrounding the city now and more keep coming. They're more coordinated than we thought. They've got a chokehold on all the main approaches and they're tightening their grip. I knew there was some level of organization, but nothing on this scale."

"In and out. We can do this, Jayce."

43

After all the waiting and inactivity of the preceding weeks and months, the chaos-strewn roads out here are now alive with enemy traffic. The balance has shifted. A little coordination was all that it took: once the first of the Hater forces began to advance and tighten their grip, the rest followed. A chain reaction has spread through the thousands upon thousands of them gathered in their unruly ranks. None needed any encouragement; they are desperate to kill and have been left waiting interminably in the wilderness for this final battle to begin in earnest. The Hater-instigated trouble in the city has acted like the starting gun setting off the deadliest of races, and now the Unchanged exodus has begun. It is unstoppable, and the wave of hate surrounding the city is impenetrable. This battle is all or nothing. There is no turning back for either side.

From his supine position on the floor of the truck, Matt can't see any of what's happening, but he can hear it and feel it and somehow that makes it a thousand times worse. The cumbersome vehicle swerves and weaves continually, rocking and shaking with nearby detonations and impacts as the ferocity of the fighting increases. Jayce brakes hard and swerves around the back of a wreck, then accelerates again. She wrenches the steering wheel, turning the truck with such force that, for Matt down at her feet, it feels like the vehicle's up on two wheels and is about to tip over. "Jesus Christ," he shouts involuntarily, but Jayce doesn't take her eyes off what's left of the road, barely even reacts.

"You could always walk, see how long you last," she grunts at him.

"I thought you said we'd be all right heading into town."

"Yeah, I thought we would."

"So who's firing at who?"

"Everyone's shooting at everyone else as far as I can see. I'm trying not to think about it. The military are firing at us because we're driving in with the attack, but if this lot get a sniff of you being out here, we'll be in their sights, too. We can't win."

She's right. Matt realizes how much he relied on the inefficient yet frequently effective military support provided by the CDF and militia squads when he was out in the field previously. "So what you're saying is everyone's trying to kill us?"

"It's not just us. Right now I think everyone wants to kill everyone else. Shoot first, worry about who you've killed later."

Matt can't stand not being able to see. He figures that as they're moving at breakneck speed along such an unpredictable route, if he keeps his head covered he can probably risk sitting up. The motion sickness and nerves are combining to deadly effect down on the floor. "Got to get up. Can't hack it down here."

"Are you out of your fucking mind?"

"Probably. Anyway, like you said, if we're under attack from both sides at once, I don't think it matters who sees us."

"Who sees *you*," she reminds him, but he already knows that. He's seen the way the Haters react—how they *don't* react—when they make eye contact with Jayce and he knows exactly how they'll react when they see him. Killing him will become their only focus. It wouldn't matter if there were ten thousand Unchanged a mile down the road, Matt knows they'd all be forgotten in a heartbeat if just one poor Unchanged bastard was left standing front and center in full view. And right now, that poor bastard is him.

He hauls himself up into the seat next to Jayce and sits with his mouth hanging open, barely able to take in the scale of what's unfolding up ahead of them. The city-camp is a mass of light and activity in the near distance, isolated and exposed deep in the blackness of everything else. Fires are raging. Helicopters, drones, and jets continue to crisscross through the skies overhead. Right now, with everyone and everything being steadily sucked toward it, he thinks it looks like a collapsing black hole. The city's destruction is of such strength that it's even sucking in the light, nothing being allowed to escape. He looks left and right at scenes reminiscent of an old war movie: a massive forward attack from the Hater ranks. "It's like the end of days," he says, and Jayce doesn't disagree.

"They can't suppress it," she says. "They've waited long enough. Now they know the city's in free fall, they're going in for the kill."

Until tonight the city-camp's position gave the impression it was strong and defendable. Now its isolation leaves it looking desperately vulnerable; the last human outpost in an increasingly inhuman world. For the moment, Jayce and Matt have a modicum of protection by virtue of the fact they're moving in the same direction as the Hater traffic. The journey back the other way will be a different matter altogether.

"Think the CDF will be able to hold them back?" Matt asks, though he already knows the answer.

Jayce's response is brief and to the point.

"No fucking chance."

Up ahead there's a huge concentration of Hater fighters. It's a blockade. In the time since they were last here, the fighters have used vehicle wrecks to sever this route in and out of the city. Now, with the way through narrowed and the flow of traffic controlled, a bottleneck has formed. The closer they get, the more Matt's able to make out. It isn't just the road that's blocked, the Hater barricade stretches out in either direction. It's not a substantial-looking defense by any means, but it doesn't need to be. The odd wreck here, a pile of rubble there . . . just enough to mean there are no longer any clear routes in and out of the city, just enough to slow down the fleeing refugees. "They're cutting the camp off from everything else."

"There isn't anything else," Jayce reminds him. "Now get out of sight before someone sees you."

He does as ordered. They're still a hundred meters or so back, but it's close enough and he slides down into the footwell and covers himself up.

The truck slows to a crawl, and Matt instinctively tightens into a smaller and smaller ball. Vehicles are queuing to get through, hordes of fighters salivating at the prospect of bringing down the Unchanged enclave. There's an air of euphoria and expectation, and absolutely no fear. It's infectious. Jayce, surrounded by them . . . *one of them* . . . does everything she can to hide her reasons for being here. She knows they'd kill her as quick as they'd kill an Unchanged if they knew.

But Christ, it's hard for her to not be overcome by the collective fury on display here, the unquestionable hate. She feels it deep down in her gut. She can hide it, she can suppress it, she can do everything she can to try and deny it, but the fact is her instinctive bloodlust still remains, buried under layers. It's a fundamental part of her being that'll never fade. It's at her core. As natural as breathing. *But I can hold my breath, and I can hold the Hate,* she tells herself, desperate to cling on.

There are cheers and shouts, thunderous roars of adrenaline-fueled excitement as each vehicle crosses the line and races toward the collapsing city. The truck barely squeezes through the narrow gap. Haters hammer on the sides of the vehicle as it passes through, the noise reaching a deafening crescendo.

Then it stops. Nothing but engine noise again.

"You can get up," Jayce tells him. "We're through."

Matt braces himself against the unsteady movement of the truck and picks himself back up. He sits down, head still covered, and glances over at Jayce. "You okay?"

"Fine," she replies, monosyllabic.

"I was starting to think we wouldn't get through."

"You're not out of the woods yet."

He catches her eye. There's something about the way she regards him that's changed, something slight and almost indistinguishable. There's a coldness to her, a newfound focus, and it catches him off guard.

The endless ruination of No Man's Land perpetuates the illusion of this being some medieval battle being fought with modern-day machines. Here amidst the mountains and valleys made of rubble, the ruins of the past, the definition and delineation of the roads has all but disappeared. The low light completes the deception. Each individual vehicle has to hunt for a way through, others following close behind when one manages to find a clear path. Occasionally an Unchanged military strike takes out one of the attackers. A well-aimed warhead slams into the front of a battered sedan that's currently alongside the truck, and Matt watches in the side mirror as the flaming wreck rolls over and over and over behind them, disappearing into the dark.

In the chaos Matt's become completely disoriented. "You know where we are?" Jayce swerves the truck to avoid a ruin, again making it feel like it's about to overbalance. The other traffic around them has thinned out the deeper they've made it into No Man's Land. The truck is one of the few vehicles to have made it this far and the darkness is beginning to feel impenetrable. The moon occasionally peeks out from behind the clouds when it dares, and its stark light helps Matt pick out the shapes of things; no details, just the faintest of outlines. He's totally lost in this apparently endless devastation. "Do you know where we are?" he shouts at her again. "For fuck's sake, Jayce, answer me."

"Yes, I know where we are," she replies. Her voice is monotone and flat, her eyes fixed forward. Another jet races out across the city and flies overhead, raining oblivion down on the Hater hordes still massing on the border behind them. Jayce watches the carnage in her mirrors, scores of people like her wiped out by an indiscriminate, white-hot wave of fire.

Another sharp turn and now, to Matt's relief, there's finally some familiarity to their surroundings. The edges of half-ruined buildings he recognizes start to come into focus, and once he's recognized one place other landmarks begin to become clear. Way over to their distant left is the eerily comforting glow of the still burning landfill site he remembers. They've almost made it.

Jayce brakes hard. Almost tips the truck up onto its nose.

"What?" Matt asks, frantic.

She flicks the headlights onto full-beam and illuminates a mass of people up ahead, coming toward them. Scurrying, insectlike movement everywhere he looks. Some cover their eyes at the sudden brightness, but most just keep moving. They quickly reach and pass the truck, moving around either side of it like it's a rock in the middle of a stream.

"The ship's sinking," Jayce announces ominously. "Your people here are the rats, getting out while they still can. Stupid fuckers don't have a hope in hell. They're heading straight to their deaths."

But Matt's not looking at any of the terrified faces in the surging crowds. Instead, he's now looking directly at Jayce and is unable to turn away. That unnerving edge he thought he detected a moment ago, that uncertainty . . . he now senses it coming off her like a stench. The Hate.

"Don't do this, Jayce," he says. "Please, try and fight it."

She grips the wheel and screws her eyes shut, dropping her head. "I can't . . ."

"You *can*. Think about your brother. Think about everyone you're helping here. Think about Franklin and the others . . ."

She breathes in deep, and Matt has no idea what she's about to do. If she loses control now he'll not get anywhere near the people waiting in the chapel. He feels for the door handle beside him, not wanting her to see, not wanting her to react . . .

Jayce sits up straight again and lets out a cry that's a half-pitiful, half-terrifying scream of stifled pain. She lashes out, slamming her fists against the steering wheel and door, then shunts the truck forward again, pushing through the crowds until their numbers begin to thin slightly and she's able to pick up a little more speed. The refugees are out here in massive numbers and yet he knows these are a mere fraction of those still to come.

These are the trickles of panic which precede the flood.

44

The chapel.

Matt's reassured when a burst of light from an exploding munition illuminates the scene like a camera flash. Save for some minor damage to the roof at one end, the imposing building appears to still be standing defiant while all the newer buildings which have been built around it have crumbled.

There are people everywhere here, swarming through this space on their way out of the city. Their constant movements mask their true numbers, making it look like there are more of them than there actually are. "Are any of these ours?" Matt asks, aware that Jayce can only see as much—or as little—as him.

"No, the door's still boarded up. Franklin told the group to stay in the basement whatever. Even if we never made it back, it's safer down there." She stops the truck in a pocket of space right in front of the chapel, then reverses back up to the door. "Get moving. I'll stay here, you get them loaded up."

Matt does as he's told without hesitation. He jumps down from the cab and is immediately aware of a constant noise all around, an eerie, suffocating din. It's the death throes of the camp. Until now the truck insulated them from the very worst of it, but all he can now hear is a succession of awful, horrific sounds which seem almost to be vying with each other for his attention. Screams of pain and fear. Savage attacks, some taking place in the distance and others close at hand. Uncontrolled panic. Anger, desperation, and confusion everywhere.

He forces himself to block it all out.

His only focus is the people in the chapel cellar and Jen.

He weaves through the throng to get to the chapel door and squeezes through the gap Jayce has left, knowing he has to move fast now because the second this crowd realizes the truck is heading back out of the city, every last fucker will be trying to hitch a lift. There's a very real danger they'll be overwhelmed, the truck filling so fast that there won't be room for those who've been waiting underground for this moment for weeks on end. For now there are as many trying to get away from the truck as there are trying to move toward it.

It's pitch black in the chapel but Matt remembers the way through. A voice calls out to him from the gloom. "Matt!" It's Jason.

Thank fuck.

The relief he feels is overwhelming. "Get in the truck. Make sure you both get in the fucking truck."

"Wait, Matt, I need you to—"

Matt screams back into the blackness. "No time. Get in the fucking truck! Now!"

Matt could disappear back out to the wastelands now he knows she's here, but he has a job to do first. He feels his way through to the steps behind where the altar used to be, climbs down and lets the refugees out. He's aware of muted panic in the cellar when the door first opens. Dull light spills out like a puddle.

Inside a wave of people shuffle farther back instead of moving forward.

"The truck's out front. If you want to stay alive I suggest you get on it now. The city's going down in flames."

They move like a sticky mass: once the first few start to shift, the rest follow, bound together almost as one, their speed increasing as they head up the steps and over to the chapel door. Jayce has reversed farther back so the truck's almost up against the brickwork, preventing those outside from getting in. Matt can see Jason helping people up into the back.

Outside, other desperate people are starting to realize what's happening. Many of those who've found themselves here by chance are beginning to sense a possible way out and are banging on the sides of the truck. The last of the group are helped up. As soon as he's sure they're all on board, Matt shouts to whoever can hear him. "Close the door. Close the fucking door!"

A man he doesn't recognize stretches up and grabs the roller-shutter, then pulls it down and seals them in.

No time to waste. The noise outside continues to increase, and Matt knows he has to get out to Jayce to let her know they're clear to leave. He drops to the ground and crawls under the truck on his belly, figuring this is the only way through. He scrambles back onto his feet and brutally shoves away a would-be escapee who's about to try and steal his seat in the front. Grabbing hands pull him back into the crowd and he kicks out at them as he climbs into the cab, barely managing to pull himself up into his seat.

"Go!" Matt shouts at Jayce. "Now! Fucking move!"

But Jayce doesn't react. There are masses of people crowded around the front of the truck now. She stares unblinking into a sea of desperate Unchanged faces looking back at her, pleading for help, *demanding* help. More of them try to pull Matt out of the cab and he grabs on to anything he can.

"Jayce, we need to go now," he says again, clinging on to the edge of his seat for dear life, and the lightning flash of a nearby detonation seems to snap her out of her dangerous malaise. "What the hell's wrong with you?"

When she turns and looks at Matt, the answer to his question is immediately clear. "I'm sorry," she mumbles, and before he can fully comprehend the enormity of what she's saying, she launches an attack.

All the programming. All the work. All the dedication. All the control and the long-fought suppression of instinct . . . all undone. All gone. All forgotten.

As Jayce lunges toward him, Matt reacts with equal speed. She goes for his face, he dives for her feet and, in the process, he frees himself from the grasp of the crowd outside. Jayce freezes at the sight of another baying mass of Unchanged faces beneath her. Matt takes advantage of her momentary distraction to squeeze through the narrowest of gaps between the seat and the gears and handbrake, then drags himself up onto the driver's seat on the other side of Jayce. No time to think, he shoves her in the small of her back and she half-falls, half-leaps out into the cold night air, fists flying.

Matt reaches across and snatches at the passenger door handle, pulling it shut, locking it, and doing everything he can to block out the panic that's rapidly consuming the ever-growing crowd now that they realize there's a Hater in their midst. Matt's on autopilot, his survival instinct kicking in, knowing that everything that still matters to him is in the back of this truck, and knowing also that the lives of every last one of these people are his responsibility alone to protect. Adrenaline and fear stop him freezing up.

The noise inside the truck is deafening: is it the people in the back trying to get out, or those outside trying to get in? He glances in the side mirrors and sees that it's the latter. The truck's surrounded, and more people are converging on it by the second. They're streaming through the devastation from all directions, attracted by the headlights and noise. Others do everything they can to get away from Jayce, who's blood-soaked and killing freely now, and as she moves deeper into the mob, more people do everything they can to escape her reach. A slender strip of space opens up in front of the truck. Matt puts his foot down on the accelerator and stalls.

Fuck. Calm down. Don't panic.

Hands shaking, he turns the key and starts the engine again, and this time he coaxes the heavy vehicle forward inch by inch, little baby steps, trying to nudge his way through the tightly packed masses. But they're so dense now that they refuse to part and he wonders if this is how it's going to end: stranded here in this truck and killed not by Haters, but by the population of the dying city preventing him from getting away.

He knows he has only one option left.

He revs hard and the truck lurches forward like a battering ram. One man is dragged beneath its wheels and Matt feels the crack and crunch as he drives over him, bumping up as the huge tires crush the poor bastard's rib cage. The masses begin to part because it's that or be mowed down, and with each passing meter the way through becomes clearer.

He knows he has to stay focused. He's almost done it. One last trip through the madness beyond the edge of the city and they'll be at the printing house.

45

Time is evaporating. It's the early hours of the morning, and Matt knows there's no going back now. This was inevitable. It was never a question of *if* the camp was going to fall, the population was always just waiting for *when*.

The torrent of people trying to escape the city has quickly become a deluge, an unstoppable flood. It's a struggle to make out the road ahead now because there are so many of them out here, all dragging themselves toward an unavoidable head-on collision with the massed enemy ranks now moving through No Man's Land toward them. Matt knows the same fate awaits this truck. His only option will be to try and punch his way through: this was only ever going to be a one-way trip and it doesn't matter what state they're in when they get there, just as long as they get there. Right now it feels like an impossible task. He thinks they might have stood half a chance with Jayce behind the wheel, but the odds of them getting through have been slashed now she's gone.

Another bottleneck of people and possessions blocks the way through. Matt's trying to work out how to get past yet another plug of refugees when the decision's taken out of his hands. A missile strikes, leveling the area up ahead and killing more civilians than Haters. Was it a mistake or planned? Did a Hater pull the trigger? He knows there's every chance the truck he's driving will be the next target because his is one of the only vehicles moving in this direction. Matt's plan was always to blend in with his surroundings and go unnoticed, but it's out of his hands now. Might as well have painted a target on the roof of the truck.

Stay focused. Keep driving.

He retraces the route he's traveled out of town as a passenger numerous times before. His knowledge of the area coupled with the size of the truck allows him to overtake the bulk of the refugees on the roads and finally pick up a decent head of speed. But the faster he drives away from the camp, the quicker he'll reach the predatory Haters who've been waiting impatiently for this night. There's no way around them, because they've got the entire camp surrounded with scores of vicious, kill-hungry bastards whose only purpose now is to destroy the remaining Unchanged.

An advancing line of Haters are coming down the rubble-strewn road Matt's now hurtling along. The headlamps of the truck pick them out intermittently, their confident aggression making them easily distinguishable from the people fleeing the camp. The Haters are wild, feral creatures now, barely recognizable as human. Individually they're no match for the power of the truck, but they fight on regardless. Although only fleeting, he makes eye contact with numerous enemy fighters who immediately recognize that he's not like them. They hurl things at the truck. Some hurl themselves at it and bounce off, landing in crumpled heaps of broken bones at the roadside, still trying to get up and fight despite horrific injuries, never giving up. Tonight, even after all he's already seen of the enemy, their tenacious savagery is completely fucking terrifying.

Matt's increasingly unsure about the route he's taking, because if this is the same road he traveled down with Jayce just a short while earlier, it looks very different now. He keeps the dying city behind him, his only point of reference in the darkness. The truck's lights illuminate more and more Haters up ahead and all around. Their numbers are rapidly increasing and as the gaps between them disappear, he realizes he's almost reached the blockade.

Can't stop.

Can't slow down.

Can't fight.

Can't turn back.

The engine's already straining, but Matt ignores its tired protests and accelerates harder, wringing the last few revs from it and virtually standing upright on the accelerator to keep up the speed. Because he has no choice, because he knows he has absolutely no other option to get his precious cargo away from here and to safety, he simply locks his arms and braces for impact.

The truck plows into the crowd.

Haters hit the front of the vehicle like flies. Another chunk of rubble smashes into the windscreen and cracks the glass directly across Matt's line of vision, limiting his view still further. But he doesn't brake, doesn't change direction, doesn't slow down even a fraction, because he knows there is absolutely no other way. It's like driving through a brick wall. Bodies fly in all directions. Other vehicles and obstructions are crushed and battered and dragged along. One of the truck's rear tires bursts, and the loss of control is an unexpected benefit as the back of the vehicle slides out in a lazy arc, wiping up many more fighters. Just about managing to keep control, Matt refuses to stop, slow, or stall, because he knows that the second he does, it's over.

Why aren't they following?

There are some Haters in pursuit, but nowhere near as many as he expected. He can see them heading in different directions; scores of them continuing to advance on the city, others rebuilding the blockade, many more swarming toward another unseen distraction way over to his left.

The damaged truck is struggling with the increasing gradient of the road. It's a steep hill Matt doesn't remember from before. And the reason he doesn't remember, he realizes, is because he's on the wrong fucking road. He panics and looks for a place to turn or tries to picture the junction he missed, but he knows that none of it matters. Getting away from this war zone is all that's important. He glances down at the fuel gauge. Half a tank left. That's enough to put some considerable distance between him and what's left of the city, assuming the engine keeps going and the rest of the tires hold. For a moment the prospect of driving all night gives him some hope, but it's fleeting. He knows that no matter how far he goes in whatever direction, when they eventually stop there will be Haters waiting.

The truck's speed slows perilously as it crawls toward the crest of the hill. Matt works his way down through the gears and coaxes it gently along, knowing they'll likely hit a downward slope soon enough. When they do, Matt barely notices. Something else has caught his attention now. It's the airport, properly visible for the first time. He can see it way over to his right. That means that even though he's not following his intended course, he's still heading in roughly the right direction.

The airport is a hive of floodlit activity tonight. It's like a beacon, bright against the suffocating gloom of everything else like a remote offshoot of the collapsing city-camp. Before now Matt's only ever been aware of the activity in the skies around it, but his unexpectedly elevated position now gives him an unparalleled view. As he picks up speed along a relatively clear downward stretch of road, he looks across and sees troops being loaded into helicopters and planes which take off as quickly as they're able, protected by a handful of other aircraft which circle overhead, firing on the thousands of swarming Haters who have the place surrounded. Matt knows what he's witnessing here. There's no question—it's a parallel of what's happening in the main camp. This is the balance of power finally being tipped. These are the climactic stages of a frantic CDF evacuation.

The air cover is disappearing, and with it the gun power. Sensing victory, the surrounding enemy fighters bring down a section of the fence and pour in through the gap. A Chinook manages to take off, able to climb vertically at speed before the sprinting fighters can get anywhere near, but a heavy transport plane doesn't even make it to the end of the runway before it's overcome. The sheer number of Haters now running down the tarmac strip toward it forces its pilot to take evasive action and abort their takeoff. The enemy are immediately all over the stranded plane like venomous ants over sickly sweet food.

All that firepower and all those troops, and they can't deal with a mass of relatively uncoordinated fighters like this? Matt can't believe what he's seeing. Surely the CDF, no matter how ill-disciplined or untrained a fighting force it's become, can do better? Are they just giving up and rolling over, or is this a planned evacuation? Are they getting what's left of the military machine out of harm's way?

The truck starts making a hell of a noise, refocusing Matt's thoughts. The ride's become increasingly unsteady. Now that they're in clear space, he risks slowing down slightly and trying to fully get his bearings to work out which way next. Trouble is the roads are indistinguishable from everything else tonight.

Another attack comes from either side at once, two cars driven by Haters coming at him from out of nowhere at breakneck speed, moving far faster than the slothful truck. Matt steers hard to the right, forcing one of them off the road, but he's blindsided by the other vehicle, which clips the front of his cab and is caught under the bumper and dragged along. The car that's been snagged throws up a shower of sparks for a few seconds longer before hitting another previously unseen wreck on the road and being smashed away. Matt glances back and sees there's a convoy of Haters racing after him now, coming down the hill behind him at a furious speed.

They must be close to the industrial estate and the printing house. Matt scans the landscape, searching desperately for something he recognizes in the little he can see, but everything looks the same out here now: ruined, bleak, endless. Over another sudden climb, though, and more of what's left of the world is finally revealed. Way over to his right he sees a vast column of advancing Haters, their movements lit up by the lights of their vehicles and the weapons they're firing toward the city. They must be marching along the motorway, and that gives him some hope because it's proof positive he's not a million miles away from where he needs to be. And yet, at the same time, with so many Haters following and gaining fast, he knows he can't risk reaching the printing house, either. The truck is unquestionably conspicuous tonight: a lone vehicle heading in the opposite direction to everything else. Matt knows he's leading the Hater hordes back to base with him.

Another helicopter just about manages to take off from the airport to the east but, like Matt's truck, it's going nowhere fast. There are Haters hanging off its skids. The desperate pilot is doing everything he can to keep flying, but his vehicle is hopelessly overloaded and unable to climb. It brushes the control tower, scraping away some of the fighters clinging on, then banks hard right like a drunk, listing over to one side. It's on an inevitable fast descent and Matt knows its current trajectory will bring it dangerously close to the road along which he's driving. He accelerates again, dividing his attention between the chopper and the road and the pack of Haters all over the back end of the truck, and manages to pick up just enough speed to squeeze through before the helicopter comes down. There's only a couple of meters of air between the roof of the truck and the helicopter's landing skids. The skill of the pilot is undoubted because he manages to land on the road and not crash, but it would have been better for all on board if they'd hit the deck hard. The soldiers are stranded and quickly surrounded. The truck is all but forgotten as the downed aircraft becomes the focus of enemy ire. The troops unload, all guns blazing, but there are always more Haters than bullets.

One more Hater vehicle is still in pursuit. It overtakes, and continues a couple of hundred meters farther down the road before the driver executes a textbook handbrake turn, then revs the engine and launches back toward the truck. The two vehicles race toward each other. It's a question of nerves. Who'll crack first? Even from here Matt can see the hate in the other driver's eyes.

Whatever they're expecting you to do, do the opposite.

At the last possible moment Matt slams on the brakes and wrenches the wheel hard right, filling the width of the road with the truck. The Hater driver takes evasive action a fraction of a second too late, and is unable to stop the front of his car hitting the back of the truck and glancing off. Dropping into reverse, Matt forces the car off the side of the road.

A break in the clouds.

A moment of relative stillness.

Nothing else on the road.

Matt thinks they might be through the worst of it.

They're almost home.

46

The fighting here is over. The industrial estate is eerily quiet; a stark contrast with everywhere else. The distant sounds of battle can be heard coming from all directions as the city-camp is torn apart from the inside out and the airport is overrun. The chaos elsewhere is like a magnet for thousands upon thousands of Haters for miles around, and a single truck limping through the darkness is easily overlooked.

Matt's barely able to keep the tired vehicle moving now. It feels like the engine's constantly on the verge of giving up for good, but he manages to keep it going as he weaves through the estate. The sun is threatening to rise, giving away their location to anyone left watching, and even though they've made it this far, the pressure Matt feels is undiminished. He knows a wrong turn might still prove to be their undoing.

There are bodies here, but no signs of life. A macabre maze. More death and destruction than he remembers. Could it be that the refugees he and Jayce delivered here earlier have already been found out?

It's getting harder and harder to the turn the wheel. The truck won't go much farther, but it doesn't have much farther to go because Matt can see the printing house dead ahead, protected by what's left of the immense distribution center next door. The neighboring building has been partially destroyed. Much of the roof is just a mass of tangled steel and ruptured metal, an open wound.

He lets the truck pick up a little speed as it rolls down a gently sloped road, then loses control completely when he tries to turn into the printing house loading bay, the steering wheel now useless in his hands. The front of the truck thuds into the side of the still-open door, and their journey comes to an abrupt, unceremonious halt.

Doesn't matter. Made it.

With the engine now dead, the world becomes silent. Muffled noises soon come from the crowd of refugees in the back who have no idea where they are. They don't yet know if they've made it. For all they know they could be deep in Hater territory and surrounded by killers when they're finally unloaded.

Matt should be cautious—he usually instinctively is—but all thoughts of his own safety are forgotten and he races around to the back of the truck and throws the roller shutter up, desperate to see Jen again and to hold her and to tell her that everything's going to be okay. They've done it. He can't believe they've done it.

He's sure there are more people coming out than went in. The stream of frightened, shell-shocked refugees doesn't seem to ever end. He helps some of them down, others just jump and push past him, and all the time he's looking for her. Darren and others from the advance party emerge from the basement and start to usher the rest of the group down toward the shelter, keen to get back under cover fast, and most are equally keen to follow.

Finally, there's a face he recognizes. It's Jason. He's almost the last one out. He jumps down and stands facing Matt, shifting from foot to foot, eyes wide and terrified.

"She's not here."

It's a simple enough statement, but Matt has to ask him to repeat. "What?"

"She's not here, Matt. I tried to tell you back at the church but you wouldn't let me speak and—"

"What?" he asks again, understanding now, but not wanting to believe what he's hearing.

"I couldn't get her to leave the house. She wouldn't take a step out the front door without you. I swear I tried. I begged her. I practically dragged her but she wouldn't move. I said I'd go and find you and bring you back to get her and—"

Matt takes a swing at Jason, who manages to duck out of the way. Darren grabs Matt's arm and pulls him deeper into the printing house. "Not now. We need to get these people under cover."

Matt rips his arm away and goes for Jason again. "You bastard. You fucking bastard . . ."

He has Jason by the throat now, up against the side of a dust-covered printing machine. Jason's in tears, completely broken, barely able to speak. "I swear, Matt . . . I tried . . . she said she wouldn't go anywhere without you."

Darren pulls Matt away again, separating the two men. "I'm getting this lot downstairs and closing the door. I don't know what the hell's going on, but if you don't—"

"Close your fucking door," Matt screams at him, filling the cavernous room with his voice. He pushes Darren away, then starts to run back toward the truck.

"Where are you going?" Darren shouts after him. "Matt, come back." But Matt's not listening, and Darren knows there's no point trying to stop him. "You go back out there and you're as good as dead," he warns.

"Without Jen I might as well be."

47

The truck's a write-off. Only one option left. He goes back out to find the van they used to bring the first group here earlier. There's no consideration of the enormity of what he's about to do, no thought for his own safety, no recognition of the impossibility of making it back into the city in one piece then out again.

But he has to try.

He pictures Jen in their house in the middle of the collapsing chaos, terrified and alone, and the pain he feels is unbearable.

The industrial estate is deserted and the van's where he left it earlier, in exactly the same state with its doors hanging open and the keys in the ignition. It starts first time and he shunts it around then drives as hard as he's able. It feels like a performance motor in comparison to the truck. Matt's dead inside, but the wind rushing in through the broken windscreen reminds him he's still alive. Just.

The area around the estate is ominously quiet. Virtually dead. But that's of little comfort because where he's heading is where every Hater for miles around will almost certainly be. They will have continued to converge on the city in their tens of thousands, pushing for the total elimination of the Unchanged. And by the time he's reached the open road with an uninterrupted view all the way back toward the camp, it's clear that's exactly what's happening.

From out here he can almost see into the heart of the city. He's lost all track of time, but it must be close to dawn because the first few tendrils of gray morning light are now snaking across the ruined landscape, enabling him to see the true scale of the myriad battles which have unfolded over the last few hours; the incalculable magnitude of the ongoing bloodbath he's about to drive headlong into.

The world below is a mass of confused movement. For so long the wastelands have been desolate and quiet, but now they're alive with activity. There are an impossible number of Haters choking the life out of what's left of the city. Some are still in vehicles, but many more are on foot, surging forward as a ragtag and uncoordinated, yet devastatingly effective, army. And just as Franklin and Jayce foresaw, the people are evacuating the camp in equally huge numbers.

They're like lambs to the slaughter.

The last of the city-based CDF forces take the lead in long convoys of vehicles and people racing away along all the passable routes out of town, and where the two sides opposing meet, there is absolute carnage.

Yet Matt takes some slight comfort from what he's seeing, because the majority of the fighting right now appears to be taking place in and around No Man's Land. He knows that'll change once the Haters have established full control out here—which they inevitably will—but for now he thinks this gives him the slightest chance of getting back to the house, getting Jen, and getting out again before all is lost. It is only a slight chance, he knows that much, but this morning that's all he's got left to cling on to.

But hold on . . . This isn't right . . . This isn't what he was expecting to see. Some of the Haters are retreating, too. It's not important. It doesn't change anything. The only thing that matters is getting back into the camp and—

Wait. What's that?

There's a single speck racing at an immeasurable speed across the rapidly lightening blue-black sky overhead. It doesn't look like a plane and it can't have come from the abandoned airport . . . he watches it flying toward the city with a mix of unease and awe. He's not seen anything moving so high and so fast since long before the war began. It even outruns the jets.

He realizes what it is just microseconds before it happens.

Matt brakes hard and brings the van to a barely controlled stop. The front swings out wildly and is hit by another vehicle going the other way. He's thrown backward then forward in his seat and his head cracks against the wheel, but the pain is an irrelevance now because he knows what's coming.

He drops to the ground and covers his head as the world around him is filled with an unbearable white light. He screws his eyes shut and covers his head, but even that doesn't block out the brightness. It only lasts for a fraction of a second, but it seems to take forever to fade. And all that Matt can think in that split second of white-hot heat and absolute madness, is that Jen is gone.

The blast wave hits next, immediately followed by a ferocious dry-hot, hurricane-strength wind. There's a gut-churning feeling of weightlessness as the van is picked up and thrown through the air, and though Matt braces himself for impact, he loses consciousness and doesn't feel the return to earth.

48

He vomits. Throat dry. Raw. Nerves, it must be. Too soon for radiation, but that'll get him soon.

Survival instinct.

It still drives him, still keeps him moving, even though everything that mattered is now lost. The van's on its side. He picks himself up and crawls out through the hole where the windscreen used to be.

Hands and knees through the gravel and dust.

He waits. Listens. Slowly gets up.

Absolute fucking silence.

Am I already dead?

The sky is the color of bile. The city is gone, just black ash remaining. A mushroom cloud climbs up forever from its ruin, hanging over everything like a malevolent demon, the fucked-up king of all it surveys. A warm wind nudges Matt into action and he starts to move. If he doesn't he knows he'll die. He thinks he probably will anyway. The Haters will get him even if the radiation doesn't.

Keeping the cloud behind him, he works his way back through

a world which has changed again beyond all recognition. Legs numb with shock, heart heavy with grief, he half-runs and half-walks. Has to move fast, but at the same time he doesn't want to breathe in hard for fear of sucking in more and more of the toxic shit that'll soon be filling the air.

Nothing is as it was. All structure and form have disappeared. The world, already scarred by months of fighting, has now been seared and scraped clean. He pauses at the top of another hill, and it's as if he hasn't moved any farther from the mushroom cloud. It's still on his shoulder, towering directly overhead. Looming. Poisonous. Full of hate.

It takes him more than an hour to retrace his steps, and in all that time he sees no one else alive.

The distribution center has collapsed, and the printing house has been partially crushed beneath it. Already weakened by the crashed truck, half of the building has fallen in on itself. The walls which separate the offices from the rest of the site have gone down like dominoes, and Matt has to dig his way through to find the door down. He hammers against the entrance door, exhausted and broken, calling for help with a weak, rasping voice which sounds like no one he recognizes. When they hear him and it opens, he virtually falls inside.

They ask him what happened and, when he tells them, the little hope that's left in the survivors' enclosed world disappears for good.

They know they'll never leave here.